The Book of Prophecy

Steven J. Guscott

kristell-ink.com

Paperback ISBN 978-1-909845-45-9
Epub ISBN 978-1-909845-47-3
Kindle ISBN 978-1-909845-46-6

Cover art and design by Ken Dawson
Typesetting and e-book design by Book Polishers

Kristell Ink

An Imprint of Grimbold Books

4 Woodhall Drive
Banbury
Oxfordshire
OX16 9TY
United Kingdom

www.kristell-ink.com

To Starbuck: For Giving My Dreams Life

"Muad'Dib could indeed see the Future, but you must understand the limits of this power. Think of sight. You have eyes, yet cannot see without light. If you are on the floor of a valley, you cannot see beyond your valley. Just so, Muad'Dib could not always choose to look across the mysterious terrain. He tells us that a single obscure decision of prophecy, perhaps the choice of one word over another, could change the entire aspect of the future. He tells us 'The vision of time is broad, but when you pass through it, time becomes a narrow door.' And always, he fought the temptation to choose a clear, safe course, warning 'That path leads ever down into stagnation.' "

From Arrakis Awakening by the Princess Irulan,
Dune, Frank Herbert

Fuel

Chapter 1
Wolf and Man

10/6/695

The snarls of the wolf were drowned by Branon's command.

"Protect your brothers Dragatu! Remember your promises!"

Dragatu's attack stopped dead. The danger they faced was too great not to obey. If he followed his fighter's instinct and attacked this monstrous wolf he was going to get them all killed. Instead, he froze, suddenly realising what his father was doing. Branon, who was on the far side of the wolf, released an arrow.

Snarling with the sudden sharp pain, the beast whirled around, ready to punish the culprit. The distraction had worked, saving Dragatu and his two brothers, but all they could do now was watch as their father turned and ran into the trees. As Branon ran, he gave one final glance towards his sons before he was enveloped by the darkness of night. The enraged wolf bounded clumsily after him, hindered slightly by the wound. Suddenly everything was quiet and still in the forest.

Dragatu snapped into action.

"Let's go!" he cried, sheathing his knives and gripping the bear skin pack on his back.

Unilus was first to respond. He took Phoenon by the arm and dragged him into a run. Dragatu took the rear. They were running blind. From the dull outline of the western hills to their right, and the stars twinkling through the trees, he knew they were heading in a southerly direction. There was no time to focus on the best path out of the bowl-like valley though. He kept them at a fast pace: the trees becoming a never-ending dark green and brown blur. Phoenon sobbed, but Dragatu knew if they stopped to console each other they risked their lives. Abruptly the triplets emerged from the tree line.

"Argh!" Dragatu exclaimed. "We've come too far west. This isn't the way we came in."

He took a moment to catch his breath. His brothers said nothing, just staring at him, waiting to be told what they should do next. Dragatu wiped the sweat from his forehead. Looking up at the stars he forced himself to stay calm as he re-plotted their course.

"This way," he called.

He led them in a straight line south along the flat of the valley floor, making sure they didn't stray west up the gradient towards the hills, or east towards the vast open flat of the floor that had no trees to give them cover. It wasn't long before the steady gradient of the western hillfoots steepened dramatically, creating a grey wall. Dragatu glanced at it as he ran and caught sight of a small canyon.

"That should give us cover," he said, pointing.

"That's the wrong way?" Unilus protested.

"Yes, but it'll give us some cover. Then we can continue south over the hills. We'll wait there for Father, then go back home across the desert."

Unilus didn't argue anymore. They entered the small canyon, walking quickly and cautiously, following it to its end. They crept from the shadows to discover what they had been searching for; what had led them to this dreadful place.

"Water." They gasped in unison.

Dragatu stepped forward slowly, all previous haste vanishing as he saw this hidden lake. He crouched at the edge of the solid ground and put his hand into the water. It was cold, but he didn't mind, they had found it. They had found what the Nation needed so desperately. The weak reflection of his black hair, square jaw and broad shoulders rippled beneath him, reminding him of his father. The sight quickly dispelled the trance that had come upon him, bringing his awareness back to focus on the threat they still faced. He stood up, shook his head to focus, and strained to see how far back the lake extended. The starlight didn't help much, but it was clear that water stretched out in all directions. It was what they needed, but nothing could be done now. He scanned the area for a way out. There was none. The walls were too steep to climb and he turned back around. The only option was to lead them back the way they had come.

Unilus had already noticed this and as Dragatu turned to face them he said,

"Come on Phoenon. We have to go back."

Phoenon sobbed again, turned around and breathed deeply in preparation for the inevitable running that lay ahead.

They hastened back through the passage, Dragatu taking the forward position this time, ready to protect his brothers if they should meet anything on the other side. Emerging from the darkness of the canyon, they slowed to a walk.

"We must go on south, and leave the valley," Dragatu announced. "If we can make it over the hills we will be safe. Father may have killed the wolf. He could be waiting for us."

"I told you that was the wrong way," Unilus said.

"This is no time to argue, and don't be such a child."

"Technically I am a child," Unilus said flatly.

"We're thirteen, and can no longer act like children if we want to survive this. Now get moving, we can't waste any more time."

Unilus didn't say anything else and they started running again.

They ran on, and just as they felt they were safe a familiar sound froze them to the spot.

"Arrraaaoooooooooo!"

It was the same deep howl they had heard at the far north of the bowl of hills, hours before, and it was close.

"Father . . ." murmured Unilus.

Dragatu focused: looking around to assess his surroundings.

"What shall we do?" Phoenon said, panicking.

"Quiet. Let me think," Dragatu said harshly.

"The trees," Unilus whispered, pointing up.

"Go then!" Dragatu hissed. "Be as quiet as you can!"

He pulled himself up his tree with great agility and gave a last command:

"Do not move, or even speak until you hear my voice again."

They climbed as high as they could, and waited, barely daring to breathe. Mere seconds had passed when suddenly they could hear the ominous panting of the wolf. Dragatu slowly moved his head, squinting down through the canopy of leaves to look at the predator. Its white fur was matted with even more blood than before. It was the size of a bull, with the piercing eyes of a merciless hunter; the mouth, filled with razor sharp teeth dripped with blood. The blood of their father. A single tear ran down Dragatu's cheek.

The wolf prowled and sniffed at the ground, circling the area. Twice it let out a loud howl of frustration. Suddenly it stopped, and then sprang to Dragatu's tree. It reared up, scratching at the bark and tearing flakes from it. Dragatu closed his eyes in despair. What could he do to escape?

Two things happened in quick succession; the wind changed, and then there was a loud *thud* in the darkness. The wolf darted off in the direction of the noise and Dragatu sighed with relief.

"What now?" Unilus called.

They had two options, stay and wait to see if the wolf returned, or get down immediately and run as fast as they could, hoping the wolf didn't pick up their scent before they could be free of the valley.

"Down," Dragatu called.

He reached the bottom first, followed by Unilus, and they both helped Phoenon down from his tree.

"Now – run!" Dragatu said as loud as he dared.

They set off, barely noticing the ground of the southern hill becoming slowly steeper. All their senses were alert for danger, all silently praying that the wolf was not following. They ran on and on until eventually Dragatu gained the courage to look back down the slope. He saw no sign of the wolf amongst the trees, but didn't allow their pace to slacken, calling out instead.

"Keep going, don't stop! Just keep going!"

Up and up the hill they ran, and after what felt like an eternity they emerged above the treeline, close to the top. Again Dragatu looked back the way they had come. Seeing only trees and no monstrous predator he slowed the pace to a walk, stopped, and bent over, trying to catch his breath. His brothers followed his lead, but collapsed onto the floor, laying on their backs and struggling to breathe.

"Has . . . has it gone?" Phoenon managed to ask.

"I believe so," Dragatu said, listening and surveying the surroundings, but once again seeing no sign of the wolf.

"It would have got us by now . . . if it was still following," Unilus concluded.

Phoenon and Unilus sat up, recovering slightly and beginning to feel the cold of the ground.

"We must keep going to be sure," Dragatu said. "We can rest once we get down the other side. It's still not safe here."

Phoenon and Unilus grudgingly nodded knowing he was right. They staggered to their feet, legs aching, and chests burning with every breath. They continued on, until finally they reached the top and Dragatu let them rest for a brief moment.

"It's beautiful," Phoenon said, looking north beyond all the hills that rolled towards the snow covered mountains barely visible in the distance. The rising sun was hidden behind them, but the light it gave was enough to show the greens of the valley and the browns of the closest hilltops. They formed a large circle in front of them, part of which they were currently standing on.

"Let's keep going," Dragatu said heavily, turning and looking south towards the Great Desert. "Once we've rested at the foot of the hill, and restocked our water at the spring, we'll have an even harder journey to get back home."

They trudged down the hillside, briefly surrounded by trees once more, until finally they came to the flatlands of grass. It would be the last greenery they saw for two weeks.

"We can rest now," Dragatu said when they reached the spring. "Refill your canteens and have some food. Then you can sleep."

"We're going to need to share our food and water. I don't have my pack anymore," Unilus said hesitantly.

"Where is it?" Dragatu asked sternly.

"I threw it away as a distraction when the wolf was trying to get you."

Dragatu looked down, his anger dying. "Thank you, you saved us. However, this makes the journey home more difficult. We're going to have to be very careful with how much we eat and drink. Let's hope we find the same small springs, and can catch some desert animals when we cross. Although I don't fancy any more lizard." He smiled weakly. "We can worry about it later. Get some sleep."

"What about you?" Phoenon asked.

"I'll keep watch in case the wolf comes down here. I don't think it will, I think it'll return to its territory when it can't find us."

Once they had eaten and drank, Phoenon and Unilus lay down and Dragatu sat on a boulder next to the spring. He listened to their sobs, but it wasn't long before exhaustion took them and they fell asleep. Dragatu sat still on the boulder, beginning to re-live the horror of what had just happened. He wrapped his arms around his chest, bowed his head and tried to come to terms with the death of his father, crying silently into his arms. He remembered Branon's last words and thought about his unique burden: the burden of the Book of Prophecy.

Chapter 2
Secrets and Promises

One month earlier . . .

9/5/695

Shouts and grunts, followed by laughter and chuckles could be heard from the courtyard of the only three-storey house in the wealthy southern part of the Nation. The house was the familiar square design of brick that belonged to the rich, but its extra level made it stand out amongst the normal two-storey houses that had been built nearly a century earlier.

The streets and better houses were designed by those who had stored wealth and decided to extend their growing Nation. Each street had been made wide enough for two carts to pass side by side, and each had a row of houses down either side. The courtyards to the rear of the houses were shared by another row of houses, their backs facing the courtyard and fronts leading onto another street. These changes had been the first signs of a class divide, bringing very subtle divisions amongst this innocent and mostly united people.

"Ha! I win again!" came the shout from Dragatu. "You should really stick to your inventions and animals," he said, boasting as he held Unilus in a chokehold.

Their playful wrestling match had come to a familiar stalemate, lasting a few minutes. However, Dragatu finally shifted his weight, moved his arm over Unilus' corn yellow shoulder-length hair, and down past his face, linking his own hand to his wrist and applied pressure. Unilus squirmed with his whole body, grabbing with his strong but toned arms, trying to get a hold of Dragatu and force him off. The intense struggle continued under the warmth of the high sun. Locked by Dragatu's ox-like strength and muscular bulk Unilus was like a fly trying to escape a spider's web. Finally, he accepted defeated and tapped out.

"Well done!" Branon shouted leaning against the stone wall that ran down the side of the courtyard of their deep-red brick house.

Dragatu made his quick boast, released Unilus and they both stood up. They breathed heavily and bowed their heads, acknowledging their father's praise.

"I'm so blessed to have such strong sons who are still so young," Branon continued.

"Thank you, Father. We learned from the best," replied Dragatu, looking up at his father, who stroked his short black beard out of habit. The beard was the only thing, apart from the effects of age, which separated Dragatu and Branon in their facial appearance. Dragatu had inherited his father's strong square jaw, high brow and jet black hair, and people always commented on how similar they looked.

Branon's habitual movement was followed by a sly grin and playful retort. "And who was that then, eh? I'll not have another man teach my sons to fight!"

There was a brief silence and Dragatu struggled not to roll his eyes.

Branon suddenly let out a bark-like laugh in feigned surprise, "Oh, you meant me?"

Dragatu couldn't help but sigh and Unilus wasn't exactly sure what was so funny, but smiled and nodded, humouring his father.

"Okay, I'm sorry, that was a bad joke," Branon admitted through deep chuckles. "Unilus I guess you'd prefer something that's a bit more sensible than my silly jokes?"

Unilus hesitated, unsure how to reply, but finally nodded.

"Well, how about you go inside and get Phoenon for me? I've something I want to discuss with the three of you."

Unilus nodded once in obedience, turned around and walked with his head held high and back straight as he always did. With Unilus gone, Dragatu took the chance to discuss his wrestling.

"Do you think Unilus will ever beat me?"

"Probably not son, you're very strong and very skilled," Branon replied.

"So you agree that I'm the best?"

There was a brief pause.

"Yes," Branon said hesitantly, "you are the best at wrestling, but remember that everyone is good at something. Your brothers have amazing strengths that make them special. It's not always the strongest that succeeds. It's often the wise, or even the compassionate."

"But if you're strong then you can beat them in a fight?" Dragatu protested.

Branon frowned, and opened his mouth to speak, but as he did Unilus and Phoenon appeared from the open backdoor of the house. "We'll talk about this some other time," he replied quietly.

The other two boys strolled over, Phoenon smiling widely at his father, and they both stood beside Dragatu.

"Thank you Unilus." Branon smiled and turned to Phoenon. "Are you having a good day, son?" His voice was gentler for his more sensitive son.

"Yes, Father," he replied bouncing on his toes. "I was just helping Mother prepare some snacks for Dragatu and Unilus."

"That's very kind of you. What do you say, Unilus? Dragatu?"

"Thanks," they replied in unison. Phoenon's round baby-like face beamed with the joy he felt from knowing he had helped someone else.

"I've some exciting news for you," Branon declared as he crouched down and placed a hand on the dry, dark brown soil. "Sit down my sons," he continued soberly. "And listen well. When I was your age this ground was green with fresh grass, but now it is hard and it is difficult to maintain. Do you understand why this has happened?" he asked.

Unilus answered first. "Because the number of people has grown so dramatically, and we don't have enough water to sustain everyone anymore."

"Correct," Branon replied and continued, trying to paint a picture to lessen the shock of what he had planned. "We know from the records people have left, and from the Book of Law, that our ancestors have been here for six-hundred and ninety-five years. We've always had what we needed and never had a reason to search beyond the land we already know." He stopped for a moment and stared at the soil as he crumbled it between his fingers. "In more recent times some people have taken it upon themselves to explore. This is out of desperation. We really need to find a new water source that would be big enough to help us, but no one has been successful."

He stopped talking. As he crouched he began to draw on the surface of the dry dirt with his finger, drawing a circle to show the population of people, and continued to draw a small rudimentary map. Once it was finished he spoke again.

"Those who went east, past the ore pits, only found canyons and mountains. We know that to the south is the salty sea, and the forests that are close to our people in the west appear to go on forever, and only very small lakes have been found." He started to make a lot of little dots to the north of his map, pressing hard with his fingernail. "The one place that hasn't been explored is what lies beyond the Great Desert to the north."

The boys took a sharp intake of breath, pre-empting their father and guessing what he was suggesting.

"I wish to explore what lies beyond the desert," Branon declared, confirming their thoughts. "I believe there must be land beyond the desert. We know of the lions that sometimes appear and try to take our livestock, surely they must come from somewhere? If we explore I'm sure we'll find where they come from and there might be water that can be transported here. This will restore health to those who are suffering and stop this problem before it gets any worse." The passion in his voice and love for the people was obvious and there was a long pause as the reality of what their father suggested sunk in. It was Phoenon who spoke first:

"Isn't it too dangerous?"

"It could be dangerous, but I believe we can do this and find the water that will save many lives," Branon repeated re-assuring his son with a smile.

"We?" Unilus asked noticing Branon had used this term a few times.

"Yes. I want the four of us to go together. It'll be a great adventure. Your mother took some convincing, but she's finally agreed to let you come with me. Would you like that?"

"Yes!" Dragatu exclaimed without any hesitation. Branon smiled at the enthusiasm and looked at Unilus and Phoenon.

"I will," Unilus said after a few moments of thinking. "It will be a good chance to see what exists beyond the desert, and maybe there'll be some new wildlife to study."

Branon's eyes fell lovingly on Phoenon.

"Are you really sure it won't be too dangerous?" Phoenon asked softly, repeating his worries.

"This is so exciting Phoenon, don't be such a coward," Dragatu said cutting in.

Branon turned his head patiently towards Dragatu. "Please don't talk to your brother that way," he scolded, giving Dragatu a look worse than any shout of anger. Dragatu looked down at the floor apologetically.

"Yes, it will probably be dangerous," Branon said comfortingly turning back to Phoenon and placing a hand on his shoulder. "But if we can find a way to help our people it's worth the risk. If we can find a new water source and find a way to get it across the desert, we'll help generations of people." He looked at all three of them now. "I want my son's there beside me if I find it. It'll be your legacy as much as mine." He squeezed Phoenon's shoulder gently. "However, if you don't want to come I'll not force you, but if you do, I promise I'll look after you and so will your brothers. No harm will befall us, I promise."

There was a pause and finally Phoenon spoke up. "I'll go for you Father, and for the people. I trust you."

"Thanks son." Branon smiled, hugging Phoenon tightly. "So it's settled. We'll leave in a couple of days. Start preparing your packs with things you'll need, and please spend as much time with your mother as you can. She is worried for us and will miss us terribly. Reassure her that you're confident about this trip and calm her fears with your love. I must go and start preparing a few things and barter for some goods. We'll need some good hunting knives for you, and a new bow for me. I'll see you later."

12/5/695

Dragatu stood facing the mirror at the far corner his bedroom and sighed with frustration. Turning to the doorway, he made his protest once more.

"Must I wear these trousers Mother? Can't I wear my normal ones?"

"It's going to be very hot as you cross the desert, and your leather ones will make you sweat and waste your body's water. So once again the answer is no," Healana repeated for the fourth time in two days.

He looked back to the mirror annoyed, whilst at the same time running his hands over the new hunting belt and admiring the custom made knife holsters on either side. He tried another angle.

"Can I take them with me in my pack? There could be anything beyond the desert. I'd rather have them than these stupid cotton things if I need to hunt," he pleaded.

Healana finally gave in. "Fine. But I'll speak to your father and he'll make sure you don't put them on until you find whatever's across the desert. You don't want to make your exploring any harder than it already is."

A half smile appeared on Dragatu's face. "Thanks," he said, turning to his bed that lay parallel to the far wall of the room. Folding them, he added the trousers to his bearskin pack and took a last glance at the mirror before he swung the pack over his shoulder. He walked between the two other beds that were on either side of the room and followed his mother down the stairs to where his brothers and father were waiting.

"Is everything okay?" Branon asked as Healana and Dragatu stepped from the front door into the shadows cast by the houses in the fragile light of dawn.

"Yes. It's fine," Healana said, smiling softly. "Just please make sure he only wears the cotton trousers while crossing the desert. He wants to wear the leather ones, but they'll not be good in the heat."

"No they certainly won't," Branon agreed, and as Dragatu walked over to stand beside his father, Branon winked at him whispering, "but maybe on the odd night they'll be okay." Branon quickly spoke louder to cover what he said, "Let's do a last check of our packs before we go." He stepped back toward the house and stood beside Healana, turning to face his sons. "Does your pack have dried food, a large blanket, spare clothes, and a full container of water?"

The triplets nodded.

"Good. I've everything else so we can start our adventure." He smiled, rubbing his hands together with anticipation. He waited for a moment as Healana closed the door of the house and as she came to his side he took her hand.

As they walked down the street the light began to turn the greys into dull reds of the brick houses, bark-like browns of the hardened mud street, and the glossy light greens from patches of grass that was well nurtured by those who lived there. Dragatu took a few brisk steps to be at the front, and the two pairs followed behind him.

It wasn't long before the excitement could be sensed as people watched, or spoke to them, wishing them luck and good blessings. News of the adventure had spread quickly, as it always did, and many people had gathered specifically to say their farewells, others did so in passing on their way to work, or to trade.

"See you again soon!" Dragatu's friends called from their windows and doorways as he passed the houses of those he knew from the surrounding streets. He waved back, but walked on swiftly, hoping they didn't notice the cotton trousers he was wearing.

They pressed on north through the streets and it wasn't too long before the extravagance of the houses decreased: passing wooden, clay and even some of the rare mud houses of the very poor. It was now Phoenon's turn to say goodbye to his friends. The people he knew hugged him goodbye, thanked them all for what they were doing, and quickly made their way to work.

By high sun, they reached the farms and it was time to say goodbye to Healana. Phoenon was the first.

"I'll miss you every day," he said crying and hugging her tightly. When he let her go Unilus took his turn and said, "If I find a new species of flower, I will name it after you," and turned away as she smiled nodding her head, knowing he didn't like to hug.

"I'll help look after them," Dragatu said casually, stepping passed Unilus and hugging her, whispering, "I will miss you Mother," so no one else would hear.

Branon was the last to say goodbye.

"Everything will be fine. We'll be back before you notice we've left." He chuckled in his usual way.

She smiled weakly at his attempts to reassure her and they embraced. He let her go and tears fell from her eyes as Branon turned to lead their son's towards the Great Desert. Healana stood watching as they passed the large reservoir, turned north-east away from it, walked by the farmhouses, through the livestock and crop fields, finally becoming dots on the horizon, and then they were gone.

The four family members walked on and the grass of the fields turned to dry mud, like their courtyard, and by late afternoon it became sand. When Phoenon saw it he asked hopefully, "Is it time to rest?"

"Not yet." Branon smiled. "It'll be best if we keep going long into the night and sleep in the shadows of dunes by day."

Phoenon sighed in disappointment.

"Take a sip of your water to refresh yourself," Branon continued, "but remember to use it sparingly. Adjusting to this pattern will be hard at first, but once we do, it will make the journey easier. This is the start of a wonderful adventure so let's enjoy it!"

Now that they had come to unfamiliar territory Branon led the way and they walked onto the sand trudging onward, adjusting to the almost fluid foundation beneath their feet. Night came and still they pressed on, making light conversation when they needed to break the silence.

"This feels like it is going on forever," Dragatu complained for the hundredth time.

"I know," Branon said sympathetically, "how about some songs to lighten the mood?"

"I guess that will help," Dragatu replied.

Branon suddenly broke into song, making them all laugh. Phoenon and Dragatu joined in while Unilus hummed along. The rest of the night's walk passed in song, and finally, to everyone's relief, Branon stopped walking.

"I think this will be a good place to stop," he said. "This dune is high and its position will give us shade until late afternoon."

The moment he had said, "Stop." The boys flung down their packs and lay down, stretching their aching muscles. However, it wasn't long before they felt the cold of the night and took out their blankets ready to sleep. Branon took out the main sheet of the tent from his pack and put some poles together, creating a makeshift roof to cover his sons.

"I'm going to go hunt for some desert animals. We'll need to make sure we have plenty of food and tomorrow we can dig for some more water. I'll be back soon, sleep well."

"Night," Dragatu and Unilus said half-heartedly, already drifting to sleep. Phoenon said nothing, breathing heavily. Branon smiled affectionately at Phoenon, took his bow and climbed up the dune to scout the area.

♦ 🔥 ♦

It was late afternoon and the sun crossed over to their side of the dune, the intensity of the light waking the three boys.

"Who wants some fresh meat?" Branon asked seeing them stir as he sat next to a small fire.

"What is that?" Dragatu asked being the first to get up and walk over to look at what was cooking.

"Lizard," Branon said with a grin on his face, acting as though the obscurity of the food somehow made it good.

"Lizard?" Dragatu repeated hesitantly.

"It's not really what we're used to, but try it with some of the dried rew berries. They'll turn your lips red, but they add to the taste."

As they began to eat they knew the reasons for eating it with the berries. It wasn't a pleasant taste at all, but they knew it was better than nothing. After they had finished their 'breakfast', they packed up and continued on their way, heading north.

This pattern continued: stopping only to eat, sleep, and dig deep for water. It was the most difficult thing any of them had experienced, but they kept their spirits as high as they could by singing songs, telling stories, chasing lizards and shooting their father's bow at the wild birds that sometimes flew overhead, making a race out of collecting the arrows.

One evening, a week into their journey, Dragatu was talking to Branon while Phoenon and Unilus were sleeping. They were discussing how incredible it would be to find a new water source, and how he was looking forward to hunting new animals, when all of a sudden Branon changed the subject.

"Dragatu?" Dragatu stopped talking, and waited. "I've something important I want to speak to you about." His tone was unusually serious. "You know what the Book of Law says?" he asked.

"Of course. You know I've read it," Dragatu said, a bit confused by the change in tone and topic.

"What does it teach us Dragatu?" he asked testing his son.

Dragatu paused, trying to remember, he had only read it once and hadn't paid too much attention. He managed to remember the fundamental part of it, because everyone knew this, and he spoke confidently so his father wouldn't be disappointed.

"It contains the laws and teachings that we must obey to please the Creator. Then if we obey what it says we will return to live with the Creator when the Creator comes to judge the living and the dead."

'Why is he asking this?' Dragatu thought.

"Good." His father nodded with a knowing smile. "And where did it come from?"

Dragatu couldn't guess where his father was going with these questions, or what purpose they served, but answered obediently.

"The Creator gave it to our first parents nearly seven hundred years ago."

"Good," Branon repeated. "I have some important secrets that very few people know, but I feel it is right to tell them to you at this time."

Dragatu's confusion suddenly turned to excitement.

'Secrets?' he thought. 'I like the sound of that.'

"You are strong and have a lot of confidence," Branon continued. "We have discussed this recently, but I wanted to tell you that you must use this strength to truly help your brothers and our people. You must think about their needs above your own. Do you think you can do that?"

Dragatu didn't quite understand the question. "I think so," he replied.

"All I ask is that you think about it and try to do it."

"I will try," Dragatu replied with more confidence.

"Thank you. So here is the secret." He took a deep breath. "There's another book that the Creator left for our people. It's called the Book of Prophecy."

Dragatu repeated the words in a whisper, "The Book of Prophecy . . ."

Branon gave a weak smile at Dragatu's intrigue.

"It was given to our first parents after they received the Book of Law. Once they read and learned what the Book of Law said they read the Book of Prophecy. They were told to hand it down to the first child who married in their family, each generation having to follow this pattern. The Creator commanded them to protect it and keep it secret. Only those who inherited it through marriage could read it, and when their children turned eighteen they could be told about it too." He paused briefly, letting Dragatu digest what was said, and then continued. "There was a warning. If they didn't keep their promise of secrecy, a curse would come upon those who failed to protect it and upon the unworthy that knew about it. The Creator also left a blessing with the book, declaring that when the time was right the book would be made known to all the people."

Dragatu was shocked and overwhelmed.

What did the book contain? Why was it kept secret? Why was he being told if he wasn't eighteen yet?

This last question came out first. Looking him in the eyes with love, and a hint of caution in his voice, Branon answered it.

"Because I see greatness in you and I need you to know that I trust you, but also because of your leadership and your confidence. I look to you to be an example to your brothers. I need you to be an example of goodness and strength. The three of you may have been born together, but you're all so different. I need you to protect them and help them learn to be confident like you are, but you must learn from them too. They have strengths that can help teach you to be an even greater man than you would be by yourself. Can you promise me that you will always look after them and try to learn from them?"

"Of course Father," was the best Dragatu could muster after the shock of the revelation. He had barely taken in what had been said, but finally his shock turned to enthusiasm.

"When can I read it?" he blurted out.

"You can't yet son," Branon said frowning. "Remember that it goes to the first to marry and maybe one day that'll be you, but if it's not, you must not read it. You must protect it so that it stays a secret. I have told you about it so you can be ready to either read it, or learn to accept that you may never read it, but must protect it. Protecting it is the most important thing. This is what the Creator wants from us. Protecting it is the first commandment and reading it is only a luxury some are privileged to experience, but one day all will get to read it. Do you promise to always protect it?"

Dragatu found this hard to accept. The name alone gave it an air of importance and made him want to read it. 'The Book of Prophecy! The Book of Prophecy!' he repeated in his mind, feeling the mystery of this book, but finally he had to say something.

"I promise," he said, trying to hide his frustration and intrigue, but decided to push for more information. "So what exactly is in it?"

Branon laughed. "If I told you that you might as well read it, and then I would break my promise. What you can already guess from the title is that it contains parts of the future. This is a huge responsibility to have and a great gift from the Creator." He bowed his head and sighed to himself.

"Wow . . ." Dragatu gasped, not having had time to realise 'Prophecy' meant it contained the future, and not seeing his father's gesture said, "The future . . . I wish I could read it."

Branon looked up sharply. "Always remember your promise Dragatu. I have told you before your time because I trust you and need you to prepare yourself for the future. Put it out of your mind for now. We will talk about it some other time, but only when we are alone. Your brothers will find out when they are eighteen. Do you understand?"

"Yes, Father," Dragatu said, wondering what was meant by, ". . . need you to prepare yourself for the future."

'Does he know about my future?' Dragatu wondered but was interrupted.

"There's one more thing. I want you to have this," Branon reached behind him and pulled out a book from his pack. "It's a journal that I want you to keep," he said, handing it over. "I think it would be good for you to write down your successes and achievements."

"Thanks," Dragatu said weakly as he took it. He hated writing, but accepted the gift from his father and exaggerated his gratitude.

"Thank you for this gift."

'I probably won't use it,' he thought to himself as he put it into his bag.

"Now let's get some sleep." Branon smiled. "Tomorrow is another day."

With that, he lay down on his blanket, which rippled as his weight shifted the sand beneath it. Dragatu did the same, but found it hard to sleep. He couldn't stop thinking about what he had just been told. However, after a long time of fighting his thoughts sleep claimed him.

The journey continued the same as it had before, except Dragatu really wanted to talk more about this Book of Prophecy. Yet after a few questions to Branon he realised he wasn't going to get any answer except for, "It's your job to protect it and keep it secret. You must keep this promise. We can talk about it more when we get home."

He gave up his efforts and focused on the adventure that lay ahead, after all: 'It was only a book,' he told himself.

δ 🔥 δ

A few more days passed and the pains of the adventure were taking a toll.

"How long must we go on like this?" Phoenon asked, completely exhausted and noticeably thinner.

"I'm not sure," Branon replied his optimism and desire for adventure nearly spent. "Let's give it another day or two and if we haven't found anything we can turn back."

They all agreed this was best. The idea of turning back sickened Branon, he couldn't believe this journey hadn't given him what he wanted, but this struggle couldn't go on forever. That night they lay down to sleep, wondering if tomorrow they would turn back, and a part of them really hoped they would if only to have some goal because heading north had given them no sign that this desert ever ended.

🔥

"I can see hills!" Unilus shouted flatly as he stood on the ridge of a high dune, scouting the area before they decided what to do.

The others were lying on the sand, having just woken, but at his call they leapt to their feet, sand flying behind them as they ran to him. Unilus pointed from the ridge that was surrounded by sand in all directions except one, and they stared in wonder at the hills that lay far in the distance.

"I can see green!" Phoenon called out, and they all saw it.

They shouted for joy, hugging each other without reserve, Branon crying a couple of tears, relieved that they had found something at last.

"Come on, let's go," Branon said nearly falling down the dune side as he ran towards their packs, the boys followed him with similar enthusiasm. They ate and packed in haste, and under the setting sun they began walking briskly towards the hills, excited to see what adventures lay ahead.

Chapter 3
Welcome Home

Present Day . . .

11/6/695

"Remember your promises!"

They were his father's last words, and since escaping the wolf it was all Dragatu could think about. A new sense of responsibility for his brothers, and promises to protect the Book of Prophecy, weighed heavily on him as he sat watch. The hours passed in fits of numbness and confusion. Among the chaos, he pulled on the threads of determination to honour his father and wove them into focus. *Focus.* Their father had told him to focus on survival. With this thought the Book of Prophecy was pushed to a part of his mind that wouldn't be visited for some time. It served no purpose to the goal.

Unilus woke at high sun, and saw Dragatu perched on the stone. Rummaging in Phoenon's pack, he found some of the rew berries and dried meat. He walked over to the spring, sitting on the ground, with his back against the big stone. No words were spoken as he handed Dragatu some of the food.

After they had eaten, Unilus decided to break the silence.

"At least we found the water. One day it might supply the whole Nation with the water we need. I imagine a great aqueduct and channel system could transport it across the desert." There was a rare excitement in his voice.

Dragatu wanted to shout at him. 'At least we found the water!' he bellowed in his mind, his hands tensing into tight balls as they rested on the top of the stone. The night had been so long and this was the last thing he needed. Breathing deeply he controlled himself and realised he didn't have the energy to argue. He knew deep down Unilus was only trying to deal with the loss in his own way, his own scholarly and bookish way.

"Can you keep watch?" Dragatu asked through clenched teeth. "I need to get some sleep."

"Okay," Unilus replied as he noticed a flower by the spring and shuffled towards it.

"Thanks," Dragatu said. "Wake me early evening."

Unilus nodded, still looking at the flower. Dragatu stood up slowly, grabbed his pack, walked about ten metres, unravelled his blanket, took off his knife belt and lay down, falling asleep almost straight away.

♦ ♨ ♦

He was running faster than he had ever run before, fear pushing him forward. The wolf was still chasing him and he couldn't outrun it. The darkness hid any sign of escape and the beast was right behind him. At any moment, Dragatu expected to feel sharp teeth or claws tear into his back. Suddenly, he heard Unilus calling him, "Dragatu, Dragatu." He couldn't see him, where was he? Where was his brother? Breath. Moist. Cloying. The wolf. He could feel the hot breath of the wolf on his neck.

A hand grabbed his shoulder and shook him hard. His eyes snapped open, one hand shot to the wrist at his shoulder, holding it tightly, and the other went for the knife belt close to his waist. As quickly as he did, he stopped, struggling to control the instinctive reaction within him.

"You're having a dream," Unilus said as he crouched over him.

"Okay," Dragatu said breathing heavily, blinking fast and letting Unilus' wrist go. "Okay."

Unilus backed away, and Dragatu sat up quickly, twisting his neck to the right then to the left, trying to loosen some of the tensions in his body and mind. He noticed Phoenon was awake and sitting on the stone, staring at the water in the spring.

"Wow, my muscles ache," Dragatu said, trying to break the awkwardness of the situation they were in, knowing any conversation was going to be tough.

"Mine too." Phoenon sniffed as he turned to face Dragatu. Dragatu saw the tear stains on his brother's face and nearly began to cry, but stopped himself.

"Stretching will help," Dragatu said comfortingly. "Drinking a lot of water will also be helpful. Have as much as you can while we're here at the spring."

"What do we do now then?" Unilus interrupted, as he started packing up the things he and Phoenon had been sharing.

"We go home," Dragatu said flatly. "What happens after that doesn't matter. Our only focus has to be getting home to Mother."

Phoenon sobbed at the mention of Healana and Dragatu understood: his own pain at missing her stabbing at his heart, but the determination to honour Branon held the emotions back.

"The sooner we get going, the sooner we'll see her again. We can rest for a few more hours, but then we must start the journey back."

Phoenon and Unilus sighed: the memories of the long journey weighing heavily on their minds.

The sun had set and the long row of hills loomed over the three boys like a giant vertical shadow. The two hours that had passed were spent dozing or offering words of comfort and support. Eventually, it was time to leave and they turned their backs to the darkness of the hills.

Each day was a struggle. Dragatu did his best to push his brothers on, but Phoenon often lagged behind, stumbling and gasping, despite their weeks of trekking his lack of fitness was glaringly obvious. When they reached the familiar water holes they had dug before, Dragatu and Unilus always took pity on him, allowing him to drink first.

13/6/695

"Get it!" Phoenon called out as he ran across the carpet of sand, herding the lizard towards Dragatu, who dived forward, plunging his knife towards it with deadly accuracy.

"Yes!" Phoenon called out as the knife stopped it dead, sand spraying into Dragatu's face from the impact. Dragatu spat and stood up, wiping his face. Unilus walked over and stood over the dead animal.

"It's such a shame we have to kill them," he said.

"It's a shame we have to eat them," Dragatu replied, and Phoenon let out a giggle. The sound hadn't been heard for what felt like forever and was like beautiful music, both Unilus and Dragatu smiled.

"We have to eat," Dragatu continued. "If we had father's bow we could use the lizard as bait for birds, but we don't, so lizard will have to do."

The mention of their father evaporated all positive feelings and they went quiet. Dragatu stooped down heavily, pulled his knife out the lizard and picked the lifeless creature up by the legs. They walked back to their dune and silently made a fire from the sticks they had gathered at the spring, using the leaves of small delda plants to add some flavour and sustenance to the meat.

23/6/695

The days blurred into each other as they walked, fixed in the seemingly never-ending routine of walking, resting, eating, sleeping, eating, resting, and walking. It was in the cold early hours of the morning when they stumbled across solid ground, exhaustion stopping them from running with excitement at seeing familiar buildings. They passed cattle and horses, finally reaching the first farmhouse. It felt like a mirage as they took each heavy step towards the long and wide wooden building that had grey cloud-like smoke rising from a small chimney. They continued: each step bringing them closer to safety, watching helplessly as the farmer moved buckets full of feed to the rear of the house. It wasn't until Dragatu was close enough to call out that the farmer noticed them, the three beaten, broken and scorched brothers who could barely stand. He dropped the bucket at the sight of them and called to his wife, who rushed out, and the couple took the brothers into the house.

As the boys ate, they relayed their tale, Dragatu taking the lead, Unilus commenting from time to time, and Phoenon saying nothing, wiping his tears away when it was too much.

"You boys have been through the worst," the farmer said quietly, the compassion in his voice thick. "We must get you to your mother," he continued.

"They're in no state to be walking all the way to the south, just *look* at them," his wife scolded. "They look like they would faint before they got past the fields."

"Okay *dear*," he said hotly. "But these boys need their mother. I'll send one of the workers to get her."

Dragatu went to object, wanting to press on, but when he looked at Unilus and Phoenon he could tell they were in no state to continue.

"My brothers will need some sleep," he said as he sat at the wooden table in the farmhouse's open kitchen and dining room. "Is it okay for them to use a bed? Or even a sofa if you have one?"

"Of course dear," said the rosy-cheeked lady with a smile. "This way."

Dragatu nodded to Unilus and Phoenon to follow her.

"Are you not going to get some sleep?" Phoenon asked as he stood up.

"I'll wait until we're home. I'll wake you when Mother gets here."

"Thank you," Phoenon said, trying his best to convey his gratitude in the two simple words.

Dragatu felt the extra emphasis to the words, but couldn't let any emotion stir within him, they were not home yet, and until they were he hadn't completed his goal.

As Unilus and Phoenon followed the farmer's wife through a door at the far corner of the room, Dragatu got up and sat on a wooden bench that was along the far wall. He shut his eyes, trying to hint politely to the woman that he didn't want to talk. She returned and to his relief didn't disturb him. With his eyes shut he nearly drifted off several times, but fought it, and just as he was about to lose the battle Healana burst into the room.

"Where are they?" she cried hysterically. She saw Dragatu and swallowed hard at the sight of her weathered and worn son. "What has happened? Where's your father?" she managed to utter, her voice breaking with emotion.

The farmer stood behind her and spoke to Dragatu over her shoulder.

"I didn't tell her. I thought it would be best if you told her."

'Coward,' Dragatu thought and took a deep breath to control his own emotions.

"He's dead," was the only reply he could manage.

Her face dropped and tears welled in her eyes. "How?" was the weak and tortured reply.

"Come sit down," the farmer's wife said taking Healana by the arm, nodding to her husband that he should go back to work. She put Healana in a chair at the table and Dragatu forced himself out of the bench and back to the table to sit opposite his mother.

His focus only wavered a few times as he gave her the story of how they had travelled along the east side of the valley, to the north end, and still hadn't found the water. That after five days of being there they were walking back along the west side when they heard the loudest wolf howl they had ever heard. He faltered as he struggled to keep his emotions at bay, letting just one tear escape as he recounted everything that Branon had done to save them.

She wept through the whole story and ached for the loss of her husband and for what her children had suffered. With comforting gestures, the farmer's wife helped Healana compose herself enough that she could speak.

"How are your brothers?" she asked as she wiped her tears with a cloth.

"Not good," he replied honestly. "Unilus is Unilus, and will deal with it in his own way, but Phoenon needs you more than he ever has."

She nodded with understanding, and saw something new in Dragatu, something that scared her. He had grown up dramatically and she hoped it wasn't permanent. He was still so young. Knowing she could do nothing about this here and now, she spoke to the farmer's wife.

"Can you take me to them?"

"Of course. This way m'dear."

Healana entered the room and Dragatu stood in the doorway, the farmer's wife finally leaving them alone.

"It's a shame to wake them," Healana whispered. "This must be the only solace they have had."

"Don't be so sure their sleep is peaceful," he replied, remembering his own nightmares.

She turned her head towards him inquisitively, then realised what he meant. Turning back she gently called Unilus and Phoenon's names, waking them. Phoenon opened his eyes first, saw her, and instantly threw himself into her arms and began to cry.

"It will be okay," she said softly, trying to console him. Unilus got up and sat on his bed.

A few emotional moments went by.

"We should go home," Dragatu said, wanting to complete his goal by reaching the safety of their house. Only then could he relax, only then could he let out the pain that threatened to strangle him.

"Yes. You're right," Healana replied, letting Phoenon out of her arms and walking over to Unilus. She looked into his eyes and took his head in her hands, kissing him on the forehead. Finally, she moved to the doorway and hugged Dragatu, whispering in his ear, "Thank you."

They took some food and fresh water from the farmhouse, Healana thanking the farmer and his wife sincerely before they started to make their way home in ragged silence. The only conversation came from Phoenon as he tried to lift the mood, but even declaring Branon was a hero for saving them, and leading them to find the water, wasn't enough to console any of them, it was too soon.

To the relief of the broken family they eventually arrived at the only place they felt they could possibly be safe while they healed. They were home. Having rested already, Unilus and Phoenon stayed with their mother, but Dragatu was exhausted, and Healana saw it.

"You've done your father and me proud," she said as he stood in the hallway, caught between staying with her and going up the stairs to his room. "Go rest now my son," she said to his relief.

He was too tired to respond and climbed the stairs slowly, one step at a time. Once in his room he unbuckled his belt, which fell to the floor with a clang, and he collapsed onto the bed, not even pulling the covers over him, and fell asleep. Yet once again the wolf was there, attacking them over and over again.

Chapter 4
Evidence

24/6/695

The haze of dusk cut through a gap in the curtains, piercing the dullness of the room and making a long line of light on the closed door opposite. Dragatu lay on his bed staring intently at the strip of light warming the wood of the door, sweat beads appearing on his face. He had been awake for five minutes and his first and only movement had been to grudgingly untangle the blanket from underneath him and hide under it, leaving only his face free from its comfort. This done, he cracked with the recollection of all that had happened, each crease on his face suddenly tensing and his jaw locking tightly.

'I don't want to feel this,' he told himself over and over. 'I must be strong!' But the one thought he battled most broke through, and all his efforts crumbled a pain-filled sob escaping his lips. 'My father is dead!' The memory of the wolf's blooded teeth flashed before him. Closing his eyes tightly, he pulled the blanket over his face, trying to escape. But the memory remained and all he could do was cry, sob and choke as the cruel embrace of his loss forced itself upon him.

25/6/695

There was nothing now, nothing left to give and he lay still, his breathing slow and barely noticeable. Time escaped him and as he huddled under the blanket some awareness finally returned. Dusk had long since passed and it had to be sometime in the night, all was dark and he could hear his brothers breathing heavily. When they came in he couldn't recall and gave it no more thought. Laying still he finally repeated the painful thought without breaking down, 'My father is dead!' He took a long slow breath and exhaled even slower.

'How could this have happened? How could such a large wolf exist? Could I have done more? What do I do now?'

The final memories of his time with his father flashed into his mind: the discussion about the Book of Prophecy, being given the journal, the wolf attack, and once again those last words. Those words suddenly became an explosive fire in Dragatu's heart and mind. 'I will remember my promises,' he repeated over and over. The controlled purpose gave him a bittersweet comfort and his mind relaxed slightly letting exhaustion take over, and before he could think about anything else, he fell asleep.

25/6/695

Dragatu crept past his sleeping brothers, out the room, down the hall passing the library, and crept down the stairs, turning left at the bottom towards the back of the house and entered the kitchen. It was quiet in the house. The eerie stillness prickled at the back of his neck. Dawn approached.

With a full plate before him, he nearly smothered himself in the bread, inhaling for as long as he could. It was soft on his nose and cheeks, and as he pulled it away he let a weak smile appear on his face, 'What a beautiful smell.' His stomach gurgled as if calling out for it and he obeyed happily. Feasting on the bread, some meat, milk and fruit, he finally felt satisfied and sat on a stool, resting his head on the square island table in the centre of the kitchen.

Eventually, he got off the stool, finally deciding what he was going to do. He retraced his steps to his room and silently emptied the contents of his pack onto his bed, taking the journal in his hand. Leaving the room once more he walked towards the stairs, but this time entered the door on his right. It was a room he rarely visited, but one his father and mother loved, and he wanted to feel close to his father, and this was the place he chose. Row upon row of scrolls nestled on the shelves that covered the walls, and a couple housed the rare leather bound books. The contents of the scrolls varied dramatically; some were histories of Dragatu's ancestors and family friends, some were housing plans and contracts of trade, and some were stories and fables.

Each generation a couple of really good storytellers were able to circulate their work due to the freedom of their circumstances. The stories always started as scrolls, but those who could afford it turned really good ones into leather bound books. As with Dragatu's journal, some of the richer people were able to keep their records in leather bound books, and those in this library were a mixture of stories and journals.

The first thing Dragatu noticed was the unique smell, the only way he could describe it was 'old', but this time the smell took new meaning. It brought him comfort, and memories of Branon reading stories to him and his brothers filled his mind. A tear ran down his face, but he brushed it away and sat in one of the comfy chairs near the only window. He opened the front cover of the journal for the first time, and to his surprise there were words already written. He read quickly:

Dear Dragatu,

I have given you this journal so you can record your thoughts, feelings and the events of your life. Records are so important and you will do amazing things. Having a record will allow you and the future generations to remember them, so please keep this journal, even if it is just small entries. I love you and look forward to sharing each experience of your life with you.

More tears fell, and he shut the book. He wiped the tears away. He needed a distraction, looking around he focused on the few shelves with the leather books to his left. He looked back down to the journal and guessed that one day this journal would be added to it.

Taking a deep breath, he opened it once more. 'Where to start?' he thought as he leant over to the table on his right. He took a quill and decided to start with his name, and slowly began to write on the next page. After introducing himself and explaining the reasons for writing the journal, he wrote the promises he had made to Branon and listed them, giving a brief thought on how he was going to keep them.

My Promises

Keep a secret and protect the secret:

How? Not sure. Should I speak to Mother? Not sure what to do about this. Think about later.

Be a Leader:

I already am with my friends. Find ways to do this more.

Prepare for the future:

Not sure what was meant. Think about later.

Help People:

Be more generous? Means being good. The Book of Law teaches people how to be good so I need to read it again. This would make father very proud.

After he had finished, he looked to the wall opposite him and scanned the shelves absently. It wasn't long before his gaze rested on a copy of the Book of Law that was out of place amongst the scrolls. The Book of Law was the only bound book the majority of people in the Nation owned, either possessing copies that had been made generations back and handed down, or trading until they could afford to have one bound for their family.

Seeing the book he wondered why it wasn't with the others and closed his journal, put it on the table and started to rise. As he did he heard a floorboard creak and let himself fall softly back into the chair, staring towards the half opened door, listening intently. A figure walked passed.

'Blonde hair . . . Unilus.'

Dragatu stayed as quiet as he could, he didn't want to talk now. To his relief Unilus went down the stairs.

'I'll look at the Book of Law some other time, when I have more privacy.'

Taking the journal he walked back to his room and decided to get a few more hours sleep, and face his family later.

26/6/695

Dragatu had spent this day, and the previous, taking it upon himself to make sure they had everything they needed. 'It's too much and too soon to ask Mother to take charge,' he thought, recalling his attempt to speak to her.

"Are you all right?" he had called through the closed door of her room late the previous afternoon. They hadn't seen her all day and Dragatu decided to check if she was okay. There was no response and he knocked louder. There was still no response and he heard a muffled sob. His hand went down to the handle to speak to her, but he heard the sound of footsteps on the stairs behind him. It was Phoenon.

"Is she okay?" he asked, his voice breaking slightly.

"I don't know," Dragatu replied.

"It has only been a day for her," Phoenon said, his face tensing as he held back his own emotions.

"I guess," Dragatu replied, knowing Phoenon's empathetic insight was right. "We'll leave her for now then. Let's go prepare some food in case she does come out."

Phoenon nodded once and gave a strained smile, turning back around, they both walked down the wooden stairs, Phoenon running his hand along the banister as he went.

27/6/695

Another whole day passed without her appearing, and it was a few hours after Unilus had returned from the farms that the ghostly figure of their mother appeared: her face was pale, shadows darkened her eyes, her hair was matted and tangled, and her eyes were more red than white. She simply walked into the kitchen looking lost.

"Mother?" Unilus asked looking up from the book he had been reading on the island table.

The two other boys looked up.

Dragatu managed to hold back his shock at seeing his mother so different from how he had always known her, but Phoenon let out a slight gasp and darted off his stall, hugging her tightly. She seemed to come around with the physical contact and managed to speak, but stumbled.

"I'm . . . sorry. It's going to . . . take some time . . ."

Phoenon let her go. "It's okay," he said. "We have everything under control. Have some food."

He took her hand and led her to his stall. He removed the cloth that had been placed on top of a plate of food and gently placed it in front of her. She nibbled at some of the bread and Unilus poured her a cup of water, which she drained quickly.

"Thank you," she said, her voice quivering a little. "We have to be there for each other in this difficult time, and together we will get through this . . . one day at a time."

"As Phoenon said, we have everything under control," Dragatu said, smiling softly to her.

She smiled back. "Your father would be so proud of you all being so strong and brave. I am proud of you. Tomorrow we will begin trying to get back to normal." As she said this she stood, refilled the cup, took the rest of the food and left the kitchen.

The boys sat there unable to say anything as they heard her walk up the stairs, the footsteps finally fading to nothing.

"She'll be fine." Dragatu said seeing the look of concern in Phoenon's face.

"Of course she will," Unilus said, looking back at his book.

"I know," Phoenon replied giving a brave smile. "Has anyone else come by yet?" he asked, changing the subject.

As always word had spread like wild fire through the surrounding areas, and their return and tragedy would be common knowledge from north to south and east to west before long. People had already come by to offer their condolences, but Dragatu had always politely told them everything was fine and they just needed some space.

"There hasn't been anyone for an hour now," Dragatu said. "I think they are getting the hint."

"They are just worried," Phoenon replied.

"Do you want to have to speak to every person who comes by?" Dragatu said hotly.

"Well not everyone," Phoenon admitted.

"Well then be grateful I told them to leave us alone. If anyone else comes you can answer it I'm just going to ignore them until mother is better." With that said he then let his frustration get the better of him. "I need some space. I'm going to the library and I don't want to be disturbed."

"Okay," was Phoenon's timid reply. Unilus just gave a quick nod and wave of his hand.

6/7/695

The following day had seen a complete change in Healana, and to the relief of the boys she was more focused on making sure they were united as a family, supporting her sons as they had supported her.

The days continued to pass and Healana began to welcome visitors into the home and kept a brave face. It wasn't until those visitors had left that she would return to her room to be alone. If the boys were in their room, and quiet, they could hear her sobbing. They soon realised much of her apparent recovery was a mask, but they did their best to give her space and tried to get life back to normal, which was hard as the boys had a lot of free time, through Branon's family being rich and well-connected. Connections that dated back to the time the brick houses were built. Dragatu's great grandfather had sold his first house and land to build his own larger brick house. Yet unlike others, who kept some land to maintain their wealth, he sold everything, making contracts with those he sold the land to that a small percentage of the commodities produced were forever tithed to his family.

Dragatu spent his free time at the ore pits with his friends, enjoying a couple of days of games and digging for clay and gems, and telling stories around their campfire. It had been a fun and tiring few days, and when they decided it was time to go home, Dragatu felt the pang of pain once more. For those precious two days he had been free of the memory of the wolf, of his father and the loss he had suffered.

"That's your pile there." Corich pointed, wondering why Dragatu hadn't moved to pack his clay like everyone else.

The twelve boys had started wrapping the clay blocks up in cheap cloth, and a few of them turned to look at Corich and Dragatu.

"I know," Dragatu said rubbing his chin. "I just think we should leave the clay for those who live here. They need it more than we do."

"Don't worry about them," Corich said, confusion crossing his face. "They didn't work for it, we did. Let's take it home and we can trade it for something at the market. We can use it to barter for some new flint and good kindling, mine's getting blunt."

"I'd rather give mine to someone here, I don't need it. I think we should all give ours away, none of us really need it," Dragatu replied thinking of his father and the words from his lessons.

"What's brought this on?" Corich asked taking a step back and resting his hands on his hips. "You've always taken it in the past!"

"I just think the Creator would be happy if we left it for those who have less than we do."

Hearing the discussion all the boys had turned to watch.

"When did you start caring about the Creator?" Corich questioned shaking his head and snorting.

"Since I started reading the Book of Law," Dragatu mumbled, before coughing and adding, "I believe what it says about doing good for others."

Corich rolled his eyes, dropped his hands from his hips, looked away to the side and then back to Dragatu. "Dragatu," he pleaded. "Don't let that book hold you back. We worked for this clay, therefore, it's ours. If there's such a thing as a Creator I don't think you giving clay away is going to make any difference."

"Don't you believe in a Creator?" Dragatu asked surprised.

All of the boys had left their clay now and stood nodding or shaking their heads in a semi-circle around Dragatu and Colrich as the debate continued.

"Well, my father says there can't be such a thing as a Creator," Corich replied. "He says the only proof we have is one book, written by some 'all powerful Creator' whom we haven't heard from since. He says as long as we make sure we have as much as we want we'll be happy."

A few of the boys shook their heads, but most of them nodded in agreement, nudging each other and whispering.

With Corich's statement Dragatu thought about his own father and how Branon had believed in the Creator. With a sharp stab, he realised that he believed too. He wanted to stand up for this, for the Creator. How could he argue, though? There was no proof. Then his mind suddenly flashed like lighting to the Book of Prophecy. Opening his mouth, Dragatu went to speak, and then closed it quickly, remembering his promise to his father.

Corich saw the hesitation. "Look, if you want to leave yours here then I'm not going to stop you, heck I wouldn't be able to even if I wanted to," he said with a smile. "But you shouldn't miss out on the benefits of your work for some mystical Creator who never helped us, so why should we help others?"

Dragatu was struggling to know what to say. His father believed, he believed, and he thought everyone believed in some way. He wanted to make a point that showed giving was better than keeping, but it was all so new to him and he didn't have any response to give. He thought of the Book of Prophecy again, really wanting to use it as something to counter Corich's points, but realised that even if he did break his promise: there was no proof. There was nothing he could do so he stood his ground as best he could.

"I will leave mine here and I think anyone that wants to should do the same."

A few of the boys nodded and said they would, the rest were quiet. Dragatu noticed the hesitation in some of the boys.

"Look, I don't want to turn this into a preaching argument about belief and faith, so look at it this way, think about how great it will be to help someone else, not just ourselves. We don't need it, someone else might. Why be greedy when we can give?" Dragatu didn't know where the words came from, but as he spoke, they felt right.

"Fine. Fine," Corich said, raising his arms. "You all do want you want, but don't moan at me once I've got my new flint and can start fires faster than you." He laughed.

The laughter evaporated some of the tension and Dragatu bowed his head quickly, smiling at the comment, then jokingly gave his reply.

"Yeah, but you'll never beat me at wrestling." He laughed, the other boys joining in and nodding in agreement.

"Probably not," Corich admitted shrugging. "But I always give a good fight, don't I?" He turned towards the clay, Dragatu stepping to his side, the other boys breaking into two's and three.

"Always full points for effort," Dragatu continued. "And maybe one day you'll keep me down," he said.

"I doubt it." Corich snorted, crouching at the pile of clay and adding three blocks to his pack. "So you're just leaving yours here?" he added, looking to Dragatu's blocks enviously.

"I guess I can't just leave them lying here," Dragatu admitted. "There are plenty of houses around. I'll just give them to one of the families who live here."

Corich gave a half shake of his head and changed the subject.

"So I was thinking we should have a good wash before we leave? You stink worse than a Yuhe-Beetle!"

"I think we both do!" Dragatu laughed. "Race ya!" he suddenly shouted, and the two of them raced to a well two hundred metres away, the other boys trailing behind.

After they had soaked, they sat or lay in the sun to dry off. Dragatu sat alone and thought about the debate with Corich. He went over and over it, thinking about the questions Corich had brought up, and his mind returned to the Book of Prophecy.

'Maybe the Book of Prophecy could show that the Creator cared for us more?' he thought. 'The Book of Prophecy would show the Creator had given us more than one book. If only I could see that book for myself, then I would have proof.'

After some more debating, he made his choice.

'There's no harm in just seeing the book.'

Chapter 5
The Book of Prophecy

_11/7/695_

Once home Dragatu spent a whole day trying to decide if looking at the Book of Prophecy was actually the right thing to do. Doubts crept in and he had carefully written out the debate, filling five pages of his journal with his concerns. To his surprise, it had become a valued cathartic resource and a place where he poured out his thoughts, doubts and dreams. Finally, he had written a conclusion, clinging to this justification: _At the very least I should see it, even if it's only so I can know it exists._

For several days, Dragatu waited for the right moment to talk to his mother. Finally, it presented itself. He opened the door to the library and smiled to his mother as she sat reading with her back to the window, basking in the light that shone through, her long blonde hair glowing as the sunlight kissed it.

"Can I join you?" he asked.

Healana looked up, the soft beauty of her face having returned over the weeks that had passed.

"Of course, Dragatu. How are you today?"

"I'm fine," he said casually, shrugging his shoulders.

He walked over to a shelf and took a book Branon had once read to him when he was younger, sat in a chair, and began to flick through the pages. Healana watched him curiously for a second then continued reading her book. Minutes passed and Dragatu chose to break the silence, closing the book.

"What is the most important book?" he said straightening in his chair.

She looked up again, her face contorted in confusion. Closing the book she drummed her fingers on the cover as she thought.

"Well, the most important book to me is one your father gave me before we got married. It's a book we both loved and he had a copy specially written and bound for me." She took a deep breath, attempting to keep her emotions at bay.

"Wouldn't the Book of Prophecy be the most important?" Dragatu said boldly.

Healana's face dropped. After a moment of confusion, she composed herself.

"How do you know about the Book of Prophecy, Dragatu?"

He confessed that Branon had told him and that he had promised to protect it. While he told her, Healana struggled to understand why Branon hadn't mentioned he was going to do this and she tried to trust his choice.

"I'm glad you have been told Dragatu," she said when he had finished, trying to hide her confusion with encouragement. "It's a lot of responsibility and having someone to share it with is a comfort."

Dragatu smiled inside. His plan was working.

"What does it look like?" he asked.

She paused to think about the question. "I guess there's no harm in knowing that. It's ordinary enough and bound in simple brown leather. What makes it unique in looks is that it has three straps as the cover. There's one that you would expect, holding the cover together and wrapped around the middle, but there's also one at the top and one at bottom that overlap to completely cover the book in the leather and fasten back into each other. It's very old, but the writing is beautiful and clear. On the inside page is simply written, 'The Book of Prophecy.' Maybe, if you marry first, you'll see it for yourself one day."

"I would like that. Have any of the prophecies come true?" he asked, his curiosity getting the better of him.

"I have seen some come true," she said, her head dropping and arms folding.

Dragatu noticed that she was uncomfortable and decided to press for the last bit of information he wanted.

"I hope you don't mind me asking this, but where is it kept?" She looked up quickly, but before she could say anything he quickly added. "If I am to protect it I feel I should know where it is."

She hesitated, looking at him inquisitively. Then she smiled.

"It's kept in my room, in the small storage room to the side. It lays in a chest at the back of the room." Her tone then became more serious, the lines on her forehead creasing. "Now that you know this you must take your promise very seriously. You must not read it, but always protect it."

"I will protect it," he said, as though to himself. Then he smiled at her gently. "Thank you for answering my questions."

"I trust you Dragatu, so if I can, I will answer them," she replied.

A pang of guilt came over him, but he pushed it aside, happy his plan had worked.

"Enough talk of serious things," she continued, smiling back and brushing her hair with her hand. "Life seems to be so serious recently. How are your friends? Have you still been winning when you wrestle?"

Having no more questions, Dragatu was happy to be drawn into the change of topic and telling his mother about the fun he had with his friends.

19/7/695

The house was quiet. It had taken another week, but it was finally guaranteed to be empty for most of the day. Dragatu found himself outside his mother's room, feeling like a thousand birds fluttered inside his chest.

Taking a deep breath he cautiously opened the door. It squeaked loudly and he winced at the noise. Pausing, he held his breath. The moment passed and he let out a small laugh. No one was around to hear. Everything seemed quieter than it usually did and it was making him paranoid. Laughing at himself again, he pushed hard on the door and stepped forward into the room. He scanned it once and seeing the storage room walked over to it and entered. There at the back was an old chest just as his mother had said.

Reaching it he crouched, put his hand on the lid and went to pull it up slowly. It didn't move. He tried again, and in his excitement he hadn't noticed the lock holding the lid down. Frustration circulated Dragatu's body and he stood up, about to pace the floor, but he controlled himself. He stood still, breathed deeply and tried to think. 'I need the key,' he thought, and looked around the small room, but there was nothing.

'What now? The key has to be somewhere.'

He looked at the lock that had a big keyhole. He scanned the room again, still no sign. Leaving the room, he walked into the main bedroom and circled on the spot, scanning for the large key. Still nothing. His frustration grew, but he didn't want to give up already. He stopped circling, trying to think again.

'Could Mother be carrying it?' He shook his head. 'No, it would be too heavy to carry around all the time, and I would have noticed it.'

"Where is it then?" he said out loud.

He walked around the room looking everywhere. Suddenly he noticed a Book of Law on the table next to his mother's bed. There was something about it that didn't look right. He walked over to it, noticing how old it looked. It looked older than any Book of Law he had seen and he put his hand gently on the cover, seeing the words written there.

'The Book of Law: A Key to Salvation.'

'A Key to Salvation,' he repeated. He had never heard or seen that before. Opening the cover, he laughed with surprise. There in front of him was a key shaped hole in the pages, and it contained a very old key, almost the size of a whole page. The frustration quickly turned back to excitement. He took the key out of the book and walked briskly back to the chest, put the key in, turned it, and opened the lid.

Peering inside, all he could see were random items. There were old clothes, a lot of books and some jewellery too. He took out a few of the books, mentally logging where they had been, and opened them up. To his disappointment, none of them matched his mother's description. Every time he opened one he saw it was a journal of someone long since dead.

After removing all the journals, he finally found what he had longed to see. There at the bottom was a big, book-shaped object wrapped in black cloth. He took it out carefully and delicately removed the cloth. It was an old book, the faded leather cover, dust, and crinkled pages giving away its ancient origin. He placed it gently on the floor. This was it, this had to be the Book of Prophecy. He sat down and stared at it. A thought crept into his mind.

'It matches the description, but how do I know for certain?' He dwelt on the thought, and struggled to make up his mind. 'I can either accept this, or put it back. Or maybe I can just open the front page and see the words Mother said were written there.'

He slowly unclipped the first of the three bindings. It wrapped horizontally over the spine, over the front cover and connected again to the back cover. With this removed he open the other two bindings that went from the top and bottom of the book, clipping over each other. When these were free and folded back he gently opened the cover. The hairs on his neck tingled and he read the words out loud.

"The Book of Prophecy."

'This is it.' He smiled. 'This proves that the Creator didn't give us just one book. This book has the future in it and Mother said she had seen some prophecies come true.' These thoughts whirled in his mind like a vortex and it spiraled into dangerous territory.

'I wonder what prophecies came true? Surely if they have already come true it wouldn't do any harm to look, they have already happened after all. It would be okay to do that, and then I would know without any doubt this book does contain the future. Then I could put it back and protect it as I promised.'

His heart was pounding as he slid his fingers down the pages. He stopped his hand and opened the book at random, reading the line of words on the chosen page.

"When the three are divided and two remain, the third will be the bringer of misery and pain."

He read it again, his face screwing up. It made no sense and he felt a pang of disappointment in his chest. He read it a third time but still couldn't understand it. Out of frustration he turned to the next page and read. The new page made no more sense than the last. He closed the book hard out of frustration, dust rising from the pages. All he could do was sit there, thinking about what to do.

'Is the Book of Prophecy a lie? Is the Book of Law a lie? Is the Creator a lie?'

The words of Corich circled his mind and he started to wonder if he had been right and the Creator was a lie. Then he shook his head. 'No! I believe in the Creator, I will not dishonour you Father.' He buried his head in his hands. 'Although I have already . . . I'm sorry. I should never have read this stupid book. I believe in the Creator. Corich is wrong. The Book of Prophecy must be wrong! Nothing it said made sense! But how could it be wrong? What is it?'

Lost in his doubts, he pulled his head out of his hands and looked up towards the ceiling. "What is the Book of Prophecy?" he said through clenched teeth. He then let his head drop and breathed heavily, still trying to understand the existence of the Book of Prophecy.

'It must have been made to make our family feel special. It's incredibly old so any one could have written it. Someone has tricked us and written things that don't make sense so we would think them mysterious. But then Mother had said some of the prophecies came true?'

"Arrrrrrgh," he growled as his head began to hurt from all the confusion.

'It must have been coincidence,' he concluded. 'I don't know how she understood anything that was written in this book.

Maybe she interpreted it the way she wanted to? It is nothing like the Book of Law. This 'Book of Prophecy' is a waste of time. No wonder we are told not to tell anyone about it, we would get laughed at if people read the nonsense I did.'

There was a long pause. Finally, he let out a long breath and smiled weakly to himself. His mind was settled. After a recap of his conclusions, he became aware of his surroundings. He quickly re-clipped the book, folded the cloth back over it, and put it back, placing all the other books on top of it. With everything back in place, he closed the lid, locked the chest, put the key back and checked everything was the way it had been when he entered, and left.

He stayed at the top of the stairs for a few moments, listening, but heard nothing. Running down the stairs, he went straight to his room, grabbed his journal and went to the library, closing the door behind him. He began writing about how everything he had done had been pointless and the Book of Prophecy would not be proof the Creator was real. He wrote the prophecy and that it was nonsense. Concluding that he would have to ignore Corich, or anyone else who said they didn't believe in the Creator. He was determined he would still honour his father and keep his other promises though. Finishing the entry, Dragatu put the journal in his room and went to get some food from the kitchen.

Halfway through his meal Unilus entered holding a potted plant that had white petals.

"What's that you have there?" Dragatu asked curiously.

"It's a plant that only seems to grow near one tree. It's very peculiar but fascinating." Dragatu smiled inside at the rarity of this enthusiasm from Unilus, who continued, "The tree the plant grows around has no other trees near it and I go there to think. I've been thinking about something I would like to try to do, but I don't know how to do it yet. I think it could help our whole Nation, but it's going to be some time before I can tell anyone what it is."

"Okay, well, I hope you figure it out," Dragatu said turning back to his food.

"Thanks," Unilus said looking at the plant, walking to the far side of the kitchen, watering it, and going back out the way he had come in.

Dragatu shrugged as Unilus left, and ate the rest of his food. Once he'd finished he went out the front door into the bright daylight to see some friends. The Book of Prophecy already starting to fade from his thoughts.

Chapter 6
Protect the Pride

Life continued and time passed as it always did. It had been a month since Dragatu and his brothers celebrated their fourteenth birthday. The day had been dulled, and at times painful without Branon, but the family continued to stay strong. Memories of their loss would never fully heal, and it wasn't long before Dragatu had new wounds added to the old.

The sun reflected off the reservoir as Dragatu pulled his arm back and with great power launched the stone forward into the air. There was a long pause as all eight boys watched the stone fly, hands shading their eyes as they looked skyward.

"Looks like you win again," one of his friends called as the stone dropped from its arched trajectory and plopped with a splash. Dragatu felt a hard slap on his back.

"Incredible," muttered Corich, shaking his head in disbelief. "Don't you get tired of winning every time?"

Dragatu laughed. "It comes with a price Corich. You know I've worked hard to be this strong."

"Yes, yes you have," Corich agreed, and hesitated before continuing. "But we've all worked hard to be strong. You just seem to have so much more strength than the rest of us."

Dragatu smiled, enjoying the recognition. "You know I want to be the strongest I can be. I probably just put in more effort," he said, trying to brush it off, but added, "One day it will serve a bigger purpose than just winning our games."

"You and your desire to make the Creator happy, I'll never understand it." Corich smiled, shaking his head.

"Yet we're still friends," Dragatu said with a grin.

The other boys continued their games and a procession of plops and golden splashes decorated the backdrop as Dragatu and Corich kept talking.

"Of course we're still friends," Corich said. "Who else is going to challenge you when you go on one of your little missions to help dig in the ore pits, or help the farmers build barns, or lifting hay bales for them?"

"And yet you still come along and help?"

"You know I didn't want to at first, but I was going to be left behind if I didn't come along. I see now it can be fun, and it's good to do something that's productive. But don't go thinking it's to help the Creator, if anything it's to help you."

"To help me?" Dragatu asked giving him a look of jovial disbelief.

"You're my friend, but it's more than that. You know we all follow your lead Dragatu, and sometimes it's just the way it is. You want to do something and we follow. Just don't go leading us into anything stupid, okay?"

Dragatu hadn't been sure what to say. The words made him think of Branon and how he was slowly becoming the leader his father wanted him to be.

"That's why I have you," Dragatu replied after a brief pause. "To keep me from doing anything stupid," he added, and they both laughed.

A sudden call broke the laughter and they turned around.

"Lions . . . at the . . . farms!" A young boy of about seven years old panted. "Do you know . . . anyone who can help?" he pleaded, brushing his fringe of raggedy brown hair away from his eyes as he gasped for air.

There was a pause and Dragatu looked at Corich, then his friends, and then back at Corich.

"Oh no," Corich said. "I know that look. Don't forget what we just talked about. This must be my time to stop you from doing something stupid."

"Oh, come on. We can do this," Dragatu said confidently. "We've taken bears when hunting in the forests together. Why should lions be any different? It'll be a great challenge."

"A challenge?" Corich choked, "That's an understatement. It's lions, Dragatu. You don't even know how many?"

"How many are there?" Dragatu asked turning quickly to the boy.

"Three, I think? That's what I was told."

"We can take three. There's eight of us," Dragatu said, turning back to Corich with a confident smile.

"They could kill any one of us though," Corich protested. "Don't think me a coward, but this is too risky. We can get more people."

"There won't be enough time," Dragatu protested, "They might kill the livestock or the workers who can't defend themselves the way we can. Who else is going to help them before it's too late? I know we can do this," he said raising his voice. "Of course there's a risk, but there could be deaths if we don't act now. We're used to hunting and killing animals, we'll be okay. Think of the stories we'll have to tell when we have killed the lions."

Corich sighed. "Okay, okay. I'll follow your lead." He smiled, confidence building from Dragatu's assurance.

Dragatu smiled and nodded his head. Turning to the other six boys, he said, "Who's up for a real test of strength?"

The others had been watching the discussion unfold and Reon, Tero, Linur and Ternon looked at each other, smiling and nodding their heads. Benue and Yelhen didn't look so convinced and whispered to each other unhappily.

"We'll be heroes," Dragatu said, perceiving their doubts, "The eight of us can deal with it. We can't do it without you." The other boys made similar pleas and Yelhen and Benue succumbed to the pressure. Smiling with excitement, Dragatu turned back to the boy.

"Lead the way."

They followed him, jogging fast, but not so fast they exhausted themselves.

Slowing to a quick walk, the boys removed the restricting shirts and tightened their hunting belts. Reaching the farms they could see people in farmhouses pointing across the livestock field towards the cornfields. There, slowly creeping towards the animals, were three golden dots.

Dragatu scanned the scene and spoke quickly.

"They're not lions, they're lionesses. I want three of you on my left, and four on my right. They'll be cautious of the danger, but we'll show them that there's something worse than danger approaching." He reached for his two hunting knives, pulling them from their holsters, and walked towards the golden predators.

The boys gathered either side of Dragatu, stretching, jumping and loosening their muscles in preparation. At about one hundred metres from the lionesses, Dragatu spoke.

"Remember to use strength, power and control."

The lionesses were completely visible now and moving cautiously towards them, crouching low as they stalked, ready to pounce or charge, each muscle moving under the sand coloured fur, teeth bared, a starved and concentrated look in their dark black eyes: hunger.

"Those on my left, take that one. Those on my right, take that one," Dragatu said pointing with his knives in his hands. "I'll take the one in the middle. They'll be fast, so don't take pointless risks."

Corich gave a quick questioning look of concern. Dragatu gave a half smile and a confident nod. "Focus," he whispered, and Corich snapped his head back towards his target, gripping his knife tighter.

The heat of the sun beat down and sweat beaded down their faces as they concentrated. Two lionesses slowly flanked them, coming closer and closer. Dragatu could see the flecks of brown and red in the fur, mud and blood. As the beasts crawled along the ground there was a cautious intelligence in the movements. These strange eight figures were not their usual prey.

"Now!" Dragatu roared.

The two groups separated from Dragatu, swinging out like fists punching simultaneously.

Dragatu ran forward. The lioness matched his pace, a primal intensity in both their speed. Mid run, Dragatu stooped a little. Putting his arms behind him, he quickly swung them forward, rising from his stoop, as if he was going to jump at the lion. It took the bait. The lion pounced high, her huge paws ready, claws extended and reaching for him. Dragatu let his legs go from underneath him and fell on his back, skidding, gripping the knives tight and pushing down with his arms to absorb the impact. The lion went straight over him and, as fast as he could, Dragatu turned on to his front, pushed himself up with his knuckles and sprinted forward. Just as the lion turned, Dragatu managed to throw himself onto its back, thrusting his knives into her neck, one on either side, and with controlled movements he sliced. Blood splattered everywhere, cutting the lioness's growl short, and it collapsed to the floor.

Dragatu fell from the lioness and rolled along the floor, dust and dirt clinging to the sweat on his skin. He got up quickly, adrenaline shooting through him. He had no time to celebrate. Looking to one group, he watched them stab their lioness over and over again, until it fell to the ground. A pang of guilt hit him in the chest as he saw only three of his friends still standing. He quickly scanned for Corich, and sighed with relief as he saw him at the side of the group. Yelhen, however, lay in front of the dead lioness with a wild and savage bite on his neck and scratches over his arms and back. Dragatu hung his head for a split second and tried to block the guilt, 'he knew the risks.' It was only a half-truth and he felt shame for the callous remark.

Hearing the other group shouting he quickly turned towards them, blocking out the pain. They were struggling. Benue lay on the ground, unmoving, another friend dead. The pain and guilt became a cold agony. He was frozen momentarily in a paralyzing shock. The other two boys were withdrawing slowly as the lioness crept forward towards them. A desire to save them snapped Dragatu out of his initial shock and horror.

"Hey!" Dragatu shouted at Corich and his group. "There's no time to stop. Our friends need us." He pointed in the direction of the other group.

The call brought their attention back to the scene, and, backing away from their dead friend Yelhen, they turned and ran towards the last lioness, expelling cries of rage and anger. The boys came together in a group, surrounding her, like a predator to the prey. She panicked and tried to lash out at the boys, but they dodged and jumped to avoid the strikes. The lioness was tiring, her swipes slower, clumsier now, and those behind her sensed her weakness and swarmed like leafcutter ants. When the stabbing ended the lioness couldn't use her back legs and those at the front advanced, coming together to silence her growls.

Losing control, they ferociously stabbed the lion. Crimson strokes filled Dragatu's vision. The lioness was still. They stopped, dropping their knives. Suddenly a roar echoed from the crop field, filling the air and space around them. The boys looked at each other with apprehension and fear, but Dragatu felt a flame of excitement: the leader of the pride was coming. The corn parted as if bowing and the lion emerged a full mane decorating him like a crown of power.

"What do we do?" Reon said stumbling as he picked his knife off the ground.

"We kill it," Dragatu said flatly. "We still have to protect the livestock and farmers, and"—his voice dropped to a whisper—"and get revenge for those we have lost." His guilt turned on the lion; he was going to punish it for the loss of his friends. "Stay focused," he said loudly, looking around at the five boys, "If we work together none of us will get hurt." 'I hope!'

The lion was steadily advancing, its head held high and Dragatu felt a sense of awe for this creature, but it soon passed as he recalled Benue and Yelhen.

"We'll work in twos. Corich and I will take the front," Dragatu said.

"We will?" Corich exclaimed.

"We'll be fine," Dragatu replied. "Reon, Tero you take the left. Linur, Ternon you take the right. Attack it directly from the sides and we'll provide the distraction. If you can get underneath and stab at its chest then do it, but get out as quickly as you can," he said, wiping his mouth with his forearm.

The lion was twenty metres away when it stopped, standing noble and defiant as a mountain.

"Go," Dragatu said to the two pairs. They began sidestepping away from Dragatu, not taking their eyes off the lion, and barely daring to blink. Still the lion stood there, but now its head moved slowly from side to side as it kept track of the attackers.

"Let's do this," Dragatu said as he began to walk forward, each step confident and sure.

Corich took a deep breath and followed, staying level with Dragatu.

Ten metres separated Dragatu, Corich and the lion and Dragatu gave a slight nod while looking the lion right in the eyes. The lion took in a sharp breath then let out another long roar that made them pause for a moment. Dragatu advanced causing Corich to quicken his step to keep up. Suddenly, the battle commenced.

"Now," Dragatu cried and the pairs sprinted towards the lion's sides.

At the same time, the lion charged forward as if the shout had been its signal to act. Before the boys reached the lion it leapt towards Dragatu and Corich. They dived to the sides, separating and landing heavily, both rolling and scrabbling to get to their feet. The lion whipped around to its right and pounced as Corich rose. Another roar.

"Nooo!" Dragatu screamed as the lion's full body wrapped around Corich, the sounds of crunching and snapping a staccato in the air. The lion's head dipped. Shock and horror froze Dragatu to the spot, but then rage and bloodlust took over. Charging at the lion, he didn't even notice the other four boys also sprinting to Corich's aid. He took both knives in his hands, blades facing down and jumped, plunging them into the back of the lion as it shook its head, its paws still wrapped around Corich. The pride leader yelped and growled with pain and twisted, releasing Corich, but throwing Dragatu off to the side.

Dragatu landed awkwardly, his left arm hit the ground first, and then the full weight of his body following. He felt and heard a snap, and even the adrenaline pumping through his veins couldn't mask all the pain. He spun several times and growled like an animal. As he stopped he used his good arm to push himself to his feet, he suddenly felt the arms and hands of his friends as they helped him up. The lion spun to face them and blood dripped down its sides and from its mouth.

"Give me your knife!" Dragatu shouted. Tero handed him a still dripping knife, too shocked to argue. Dragatu then ran forward, his friends caught off guard by his lack of reservation.

In those few moments, Dragatu continued forward, his broken and dislocated arm hanging loose, his other hand gripping the knife tightly. The lion pounced before the others could do anything to help. Dragatu saw the attack, stopped dead and deliberately fell backwards. The jaws of the lion opened, and he looked into the black tunnel of death that came towards him. He plunged the knife deep into the tunnel, the glinting point aimed at the roof. Dragatu withdrew his hand quickly, the tunnel closing mercilessly on the knife. The jaw closed down on the blade and it pushed deep through the vulnerable flesh and straight into the lion's brain. With the killing blow, it collapsed into a heap on Dragatu's legs and chest. Blood poured from its teeth and the point of the knife could be seen like a silver horn.

Everything went still. Dragatu stared at the lion's face. It almost touched his own. The smell of rotting flesh and blood enveloped him. Sour yet sweet, 'Corich's blood.' He breathed heavily, pain lacing his senses, but its full impact dulled by shock. His friends tugged and pulled him out from under the lion. They helped him to his feet, but he could barely stand and everything became a blur.

"Are you all right?" Linur and Ternon asked.

Dragatu didn't respond. He still couldn't focus properly.

"Your arm looks a mess," Reon gasped.

The mention of his arm jolted Dragatu's senses forward, quashing the shock, and an eruption of agony fired along his arm and shoulder. He went to cradle it then stopped, moaning loudly with agony.

"Are you all right?" Linur asked again as the boys stood around Dragatu.

He was aware now and the memory of Corich played in his mind and he turned.

"Corich . . ." he uttered pleadingly as the guilt and pain swelled inside him, hoping it wasn't true. "Nooo . . ." he moaned bitterly as he saw the torn figure of his lifeless friend. He staggered forward and the others watched feeling a similar pain, but void of the guilt that continued to grow in Dragatu.

"Noooo!!" he suddenly bellowed, falling to his knees at Corich's side, staring at him for a few moments then his head fell, uncontrollable tears staining the ground pink, and tinged with the blood of the beasts.

"We need to get your arm looked at," Linur said gently after a few moments, standing behind Dragatu.

Dragatu didn't say anything. He continued to mourn and try to understand his part in it all. After a few more moments, Linur signalled to the others, and murmured that they should get Dragatu to the nearest farmhouse and see to their own wounds.

They took Dragatu under his good arm and lifted him to his feet. He was reluctant at first, muttering, "It's my fault, he said not to go . . . my fault."

He took one last look at Corich as his friends gently guided him away, and together they staggered to the nearest farmhouse.

The people from the farmhouse met them halfway, and took over guiding Dragatu's disoriented and broken body into the house. The farmer looked at the arm while his wife poured them water.

"It's a nasty one. Seen a couple like it in my time," he uttered. "Going to have to put it back in place quickly, set it nice and straight. It's going to hurt a lot."

Dragatu had gained some composure. "Good," he mumbled through clenched teeth. The farmer mistook it for a grunt to go ahead and took his arm.

"On the count of three, one . . . two . . ."

"Arrrrrrrrrrrgh!" Dragatu roared: his friends holding him in his chair as he writhed in pain. After his scream of agony he hung his head and sobbed a couple of times, sniffed to catch his breath, and focused on: inhale, exhale, inhale, exhale. He raised his head and nodded his friends could let him go.

"Not too much I can do about the break. I'll put it in a sling, but it will need a proper healer to look at it and strap it up. It's a small price to pay for what you did here son. I can't thank you and your friends enough. I'll be forever in your debt," he said humbly, taking some material and making a sling for Dragatu.

"Just make sure my friends are okay," Dragatu said looking to the four boys who stood around him.

"Of course," the farmer replied, and once Dragatu's arm was in the sling he signalled to the farm workers, who'd stood in the background, to take each boy and make sure they had no critical wounds and to get them food and drink. As everyone rushed around Dragatu slowly went to stand.

"No. No. You need to rest," the farmer said, placing a hand on his shoulder. "Just sit there. Everything will be taken care of. We're making stretchers for your friend's who are . . . well . . ." There was an awkward pause as the farmer tried to be sensitive. He brushed past the painful word, ". . . and we'll take them to their parents when you feel okay to tell us where they live."

"I'll tell you now," Dragatu said, ignoring the farmer and standing. He gave the location of Yelhen, Benue and Corich's family. The farmer wrote them down and went outside to give it to the other workers. Dragatu slowly made his way out of the farmhouse, his body aching and his arm tingling and throbbing with pain, but it was nothing compared to the fire inside. The farmer saw him and went to protest again, but as their gazes connected, he saw the direction Dragatu was heading and the look of determination in his eyes so let him be. Dragatu walked passed the bodies of Yelhen and Benue, who had been carried close to the farmhouse and covered in a homespun sheet, and as he did the pain in his chest weighed heavy within him. All he could do was repeat a pleading apology in his mind, 'I'm sorry, I'm so sorry.' His face tensed under the stress as he looked at them. Passing them, he came to Corich who had been placed on a stretcher and was about to be moved.

"Give me a moment," Dragatu managed to say as his lip quivered and eyes filled up once more. The workers stepped back several metres and turned around awkwardly, not knowing what to do.

"I'm so sorry." Dragatu wept as he fell to his knees, putting his good hand over his face to try and hide himself. Pride, shame, fear, loss, were all mingling into one. "I thought I was doing the right thing . . . we were helping people . . . and I . . . I thought we would be okay." He sniffed. "I didn't really think any of us would die. We were helping people . . . we were doing good! How can doing good lead to so much pain and death? Should I have listened to you? I should have listened to you and you'd still be alive . . ." He sobbed now. "But then more people could have died? We've prevented that . . . haven't we?" he pleaded, almost hoping an answer would come from somewhere. "How do I know I made the right choice?" he said angrily, and a thought entered his mind.

'Those that sacrifice for others receive the greater reward.'

It was something he had read recently in the Book of Law, and the simple phrase gave him a slight ray of hope. "I know you didn't believe, Corich, but your sacrifice can't have been in vain. You're a hero and I'll tell people that Corich, I will write it in my journal so you're never forgotten." The words gave Dragatu more hope and purpose. "I'm just so sorry . . ." he muttered under his breath. "I don't know if I made the right choice, but I hope I did. I just wanted to help and make my father and the Creator proud of me. I'll try harder to make sure I know the right choice, Corich. Your death hasn't been in vain,"—there was a long pause—"but I'll miss you," he said finally and sobbed bitterly.

A minute passed, and after a few deep breaths he managed to stand, silently letting the tears run down his face. Turning he coughed and the workers took the signal, lifted Corich with respect and tenderness, and followed Dragatu back to the farmhouse.

ᛉ 🔥 ᛉ

The three boys lay on the stretchers, being carried to their homes for burial. A long procession of people following them. News of what had occurred spread fast and people couldn't believe what these young boys had done for the farmers and workers.

Dragatu noticed the pointing and whisperings as he walked. They praised his killing of the pride leader and a small part of him enjoyed the recognition, but it was smothered by the loss of his friends. All he could see in his mind's eye was their deaths and he tried to tell people that his friends were the true heroes. Finally, it got too much, his guilt still lingering heavily on his conscience, and he slipped down a side street to be alone.

Keeping to the quiet and dark streets he made his way home. As he entered his house silence welcomed him, and he was glad. He knew his mother and brothers would be trying to find him in the procession, but he just wanted to be alone for a little while longer. Seeking comfort he took his journal in his good arm and went to the library to record what had happened. He needed to make sure Corich's death and heroism was recorded.

At times, his emotions were too much and he stopped writing to weep, or continued the battle in his mind as to whether he had made the right choice. The same consoling thoughts of sacrifice and honour helped him through his moral struggle. And then there was the slowly growing realization of what was actually achieved. He had killed a pride leader and they had saved many people's lives and livelihoods by risking themselves.

After sitting in the library for some time, the pain of his arm gnawed and grew until it could no longer be ignored, it needed a healer's attention, and he put his journal back in his room. As he walked down the stairs the front door flung open.

"We've been looking for you," Healana said, a worried look turning to anger then turning to relief. She walked briskly to him, went to hug him and stopped, unsure what to do on seeing his arm, and leant forward instead, kissing him on the forehead.

"I heard what happened," she said concerned, and then anger rising in her voice. "What were you thinking?"

"It's what Father would have done. I wanted to help the people."

Healana buried her anger and she choked, holding back her emotion.

"Are you okay?" she said finally.

"My arm is broken and I need it set," he said.

Healana took a deep breath, "Okay, let's go."

The healer strapped up Dragatu's arm and prescribed rest for two months, which Dragatu knew was going to be almost impossible. Once they returned home he was exhausted and after rejecting requests from Phoenon to tell the story he went to bed.

2/3/696

The burials took place at family plots that were located at points throughout the Nation. Feasts were held in honour of the dead and Dragatu managed to face the families of Yelhen, Benue and Corich. Questions were asked that evening, and Dragatu's first reaction was always to turn the focus on his friend's sacrifice for the people and their heroism, and that people were saved because they stopped the lions. This gave comfort to the families, and the more Dragatu said it, the more he felt his choice had been the right one.

Days and weeks went by and Dragatu struggled to be patient, and what made it harder was the new thirst that had arisen within him, a thirst for greater challenges. In his hours of resting and being alone, or being out with his friends, but unable to join in with the games, he had a lot of time to think.

'If I could kill a pack leader, what else am I capable of?'

'No sport here will be satisfying now,' he thought as he sat in the library one day. 'But the hills have tougher game.' Nerves and excitement grew at the thought. 'When my arm is better I'll go and hunt, and see the water source again.' He was quickly caught up in his youthful confidence.

"Maybe I'll see the wolf and kill it," he whispered.

Chapter 7
The Consolation

13/3/697

Due to outbursts of impatience and frustration the strap on Dragatu's arm had been painfully replaced several times. He tried his best to rest and distract himself by thinking, planning and writing about the adventure to the hills he wanted to undertake. As time rolled by he found himself unable to let his arm hold him back any longer, and impatiently, and before the healer had given permission, he removed the strap. He tested the arm, clenching his hand and twisting his arm. The pain was still there, but it was minimal and as he continued to exercise, it ebbed away. It was time to talk to his mother.

Despite Branon and his sons having found the water source, no one had gone back to the hills revisit it. Those that had the resources, time and money to see if the water could be transported were from renowned families of the Nation. A small group had been prepared to travel, however, they had been persuaded by others not to go. "It was too dangerous," was the common plea: everyone knew about what had happened to Branon. The poorer would gladly have gone, their need outweighing their fear, but they were restricted by their circumstances and poverty. Dragatu had watched the attempt to go with interest and exasperation. He wanted to help, but didn't know how. If he could go there and hunt more challenging beasts, he could also think about the water source and how to get the water to the Nation.

Approaching his mother, he told her of his plan and his desire to return to the place of their nightmares. His request nearly broke her heart. Finally, and reluctantly, Healana accepted his promises and reassurance that he would be cautious. She tried to convince him to take seasoned hunters, but he refused, saying he would not put anyone else at risk, the loss of his friends still fresh in his mind.

His first visit was an anxious time for all. After more than a month, he returned and told stories of his journey to all his friends and anyone that would listen. With every step that had brought him closer to the hills his confidence had faded, and to his relief he hadn't seen the wolf, having stayed far away from the northern part where they had first heard it. The water source had been where he pitched his tent, and when he wasn't hunting he tried to think of a way to transport the water back home, but he couldn't. Eventually, he had to put it to the back of his mind and hoped that one day an idea would come to him.

And so the cycle continued. A year went by and Dragatu repeated his trip several times, enjoying the difficulties of hunting wilder animals like the jaguar, leopards, and aggressive species of bear, as well as the ordinary yet still ferocious wolves. When he was home, he often reminded those in his neighbourhood and surrounding areas of the water source, hoping someone would think of how to use it to help the people, but no one did.

At the same time, Dragatu continued to strengthen his body, becoming broader and solid as a rock. He kept his hair short and didn't shave the light growth on his face, loving the reminder that he looked like Branon, but hating the fact that every time his mother looked at him there was pain in her eyes. That couldn't be helped, though, and to him it was a thing of pride, helping him to remember who he was and the promises he had made. Unilus grew taller than his brothers, he was thin like a sunflower, and he let his straight blonde hair grow long. But where he was slim, Phoenon was plump and small, regaining his lost weight and more.

One day, as Dragatu sat in the courtyard salting meat from a deer he had killed in the forests in the west, Unilus came to speak to him.

"Are you going to the hills soon?" he asked.

Dragatu looked up. "Maybe, in a month or so," he replied casually. "I think I'm going to spend some time by the ore pits first."

Unilus, never the one for subtleties, made his intentions clear.

"I have been working on a project for a long time, and I would like to take a trip to the north to look at the water source again. Can you take me?"

"No," Dragatu said, shaking his head. 'It's too dangerous for you,' he thought, concerned by Unilus' lack of hunting skills and what would happen if they were attacked by wild animals. "I doubt Mother would let you," he continued. "She still hates that I go."

"The project is really important Dragatu," Unilus continued, ignoring Dragatu's rejection. "The population continues to grow, and yet the water falls less and less. We need both sources of water to support all the people. My project is extreme, and people probably won't believe it at first, but I have designed a way to move the water across the desert. I cannot be sure if it's possible until I have looked at it again. It is very important," he pleaded.

Dragatu was intrigued. 'Could this be the idea I've been waiting for? If Unilus has a project that could get the water then maybe a trip to the hills would be worth it. Maybe Father's death won't be in vain.'

"Okay," he said, letting his curiosity and desire to honour Branon persuade him. "We'll take a trip there, but you must do everything I say. Mother would never forgive me if I let anything happen to you." He rubbed his chin. "Assuming she lets you that is. But we'll try."

"I will do anything you need me to. When can we leave?"

Dragatu looked at him surprised. It was unlike Unilus to be impatient. 'He must really think he can do this.'

"Erm, three days at the earliest," Dragatu said, running it through his mind and changing his plans. "We'll need to get organised first thing tomorrow. We'll speak to Mother first, and if it goes well I'll get a list of things you'll need."

Unilus nodded and walked towards the house, halfway, he stopped and turned, "Thanks Dragatu," he said casually, and then left.

Dragatu smiled to himself as he looked down to the meat, turning it over. If Unilus actually had a way to get the water to the people, then he really wanted to help. The Creator would be so pleased if they could do this. His father would have been proud too.

14/3/697

Once again Dragatu needed to do everything he could to convince and reassure Healana that Unilus' going was a good thing. It wasn't until Unilus explained his plan, to try and help the people and honour Branon that she was finally convinced to let him go.

1/4/697

Dragatu knew the best course to take, and as such the journey was easier than Unilus remembered. Conversation revolved around the project and as they walked Dragatu listened intently as Unilus spoke animatedly about his designs.

"The project begins by building a large screw like mechanism that sits inside a cylinder. It will be built with one end in the water on a steep incline and it will have a wind catcher built high over it. The wind catcher will be connected to it and turn the screw and water will work its way up the cylinder." As he spoke he moved his hands and arms, and twirled his fingers, explaining his ideas through actions. "The wood will be treated by illona sap so it is waterproof and doesn't rot," he added. "At the other end of the cylinder, which will be high in the air, there will be a wooden channel on a very gentle decline. This will cling to the side of the valley until the decline eventually meets the floor at the south end. A pool will be made to gather the water and this will be before the hills become too steep.

Coming out of the pool there will be more cylinders with the screw mechanism inside. These will be powered by smaller wind catchers that will also turn the screws. There will be a lot of these pools and cylinders, each going up the side of the hill to take the water to the top.

After this, there will be a large pool made at the top, and channels zigzagging down the southern side of the hill to yet another pool at the bottom on the desert side. More channels will be built on top of two upside down 'v' legs, which will go over the pool and have holes in the parts above the pool to drop some water into it. Lastly, these aqueduct channels will continue across the desert, reaching the Nation to replenish the reservoir."

With the description over Dragatu realised two things, firstly, Unilus was far more intelligent than he had realised, secondly, that he hadn't only underestimated his brother, but he had underestimated how big this project was going to be. The people had attempted nothing like this and he wondered how they were going to get so many to help, and he confronted Unilus about this.

Unilus nodded he understood, then spoke. "It's the one thing I don't really know how to calculate. People are so unpredictable. No two people are alike. I'm struggling to think of how many people it is going to take. This may come as a surprise to you, but I'm not the best with people."

"No surprise at all," Dragatu said in a lighthearted tone, stifling a laugh as his brother regarded him with light curiosity.

When the moment passed Unilus continued.

"I need you for more than just this trip Dragatu," he confessed. "You know people, and when you do things, your friends follow, you know how to lead. I think you can work out how many people it would take . . ." he paused.

"What is it?" Dragatu asked.

". . . and I think you could lead all the people in this project."

Dragatu took a few moments to digest what Unilus had said. He liked the thought of leading the people, but would the people want to help them? They were only fifteen years old. "There's a lot to think about Unilus," he said. "What you have planned is incredible. I believe you if you think we can do this, but people might not listen to us."

"People will listen to you Dragatu. People know our family, and they know what you are capable of. It was you who got us safely home when we lost father. It was you who killed the pride leader, and you do so much for the people every day. You are well known, we all are. You know Phoenon spends his time amongst the poorer people and they love him for his kindness towards them. I'm known amongst the farmers for helping their animals and helping them with their farming. Even if they haven't met us most of the people know who we are, and they knew of our father and all he did to try and help people. They will listen to you and if we show them my plan they will see it's possible."

Dragatu was impressed by Unilus' confidence and determination. "You really believe we can do this, don't you?"

Unilus' voice shrank to a whisper. "I have to. Father died because we went to find the water. If we don't find a way to get the water it's dishonouring him."

"I understand," Dragatu said, seeing a side to Unilus he hadn't seen before. "Okay, we'll try, but there's a lot we're going to have to work out before we tell people about this. How are we going to pay people for the time and energy they're going to have to give up? This project will take months. How are we going to compensate them?" He scratched his head as he talked. "I could probably get some of my friends and ask people who live around us to volunteer, but that wouldn't be nearly enough. We would have to have help from the poorer people, but they would need a lot of food and supplies before we even go to work."

"I don't know the answer," Unilus admitted. "But we will figure it out. We have to," he said desperately. "It's another reason I want your help. If anyone can figure this out and get people to help, you can."

"Thanks," Dragatu said, blushing a little. "I'll give it some more thought. We'll do this for the people, and for Father, and for the Creator."

Unilus smiled, grateful for Dragatu's help and understanding.

2/4/697

The next day they reached the water source and sat at the mouth of the canyon, staring westward out across the water. There was nothing else there except for a few small plants and weeds growing on the ground, which stretched from the entrance of the canyon for about a hundred metres. It was like an untouched secret that no other animal or creature knew about. In the tranquillity, Unilus studied one of the small plants and Dragatu continued to sit and look out thoughtfully across the water, towards the far end, guessing it was about a kilometre away. Circling along the wall to his right, where rain would run down to replenish the lake, he followed the line that marked where the sides began to incline back, the rock below it plunging vertically into the water. Having surveyed the whole wall he chatted casually to Unilus.

They spoke quietly, reminiscing how different it felt, even though nothing had changed in the canyon. It was strange for Dragatu to be sitting in a place so synonymous with pain and his father's death, and yet feeling so peaceful and calm. Eventually, Unilus took out some parchment and made more drawings and calculations while Dragatu left, scouting the area and hunting for food.

Once they were both happy with the plans Unilus had made on the parchment they spent a few days relaxing, enjoying the open space on the valley floor, and taking advantage of the break away from the Nation. They knew it couldn't last, and the novelty wore off quickly leaving them wanting to go home to see their friends and family, and most importantly to organise the project.

On the journey back, Unilus told Dragatu how the project should be constructed. "I think it will be done in three stages: first, the large cylinder, screw, wind catcher and channels, then the smaller cylinder, screws, wind catchers, the pool on top of the hill, and channels, and lastly the building of the channels across the desert."

"That does break it up nicely," Dragatu replied. "But none of this will happen unless we have people to work on this project. I've an idea of how many people we'll need, but the question of pay still remains," he said kicking at the sand. "I've been going over and over how this project will take a lot of energy out of the people that do it. Then on top of that we have to compensate them for leaving behind their families and the work they would usually do to support themselves. The amount of water alone will be incredible. Food and transporting everything across the desert should be manageable, but the water is the issue, as it always is . . ." he sighed, stopped walking and began to think, suddenly exclaiming:

"I have it!" he laughed, "The water . . . it's so simple. We can pay them in water!" he said holding out his hands. "The project will provide water to all the people so we can pay the poorer workers in water. We can make sure they take an advance from the reservoir a couple of weeks before the project starts. They will be healthier and can use left over water to trade for things they need to prepare for the journey. Then when we return they can be given priority in water and be paid with it. It will give them an advantage over others who didn't come and this will motivate many to come and help us." He laughed confidently. "It's a good idea, isn't it?"

Unilus gave it a few moments thought. "It seems that your idea could work," he said, a smile spreading slowly across his face. "Well done Dragatu."

Dragatu continued to laugh, relieved he'd figured out the problem.

During the rest of the journey they went over the fine details of the construction: how the people would be gathered, and how the labour force would be organised. Dragatu decided if he was going to do this he would have to oversee the entire work force, with Unilus making sure the technical plans were done to his specifications. Dragatu also wanted to organise a group of people to oversee the workers with him and they would report back as to how the work was going. It was adapted from what larger hunting parties would do. Often the hunters would take it in turn to be 'Hunora' and their job would be to watch for wild animals while the others slept, or scout ahead during the day to look for tracks. This would be adapted, and its original purpose continued, but the Hunora would also make sure everyone worked hard. Unilus agreed that having this new type of Hunora would be beneficial, and good for making sure everyone worked hard: those from richer suburbs would have to sweat right alongside those from the poorer areas. If they were to all benefit, then they would all have to work.

When they returned home they put aside the concerns about their age and began telling people about the project. Word spread quickly that Unilus had designed the project and full plans were written up for all the people to see. Excitement thrummed through the Nation. The thought of free-given water stirred up enthusiasm in all, but especially the poor. There were some doubts about the dangers of the desert and hills, but fears were calmed by the fact such a large group of people would be travelling together.

22/4/697

Over the week that followed, Dragatu instructed those he selected to be Hunora. They were mostly his friends and those whom he knew from the surrounding area to take up their role and make sure water and food were distributed abundantly and fairly. Unilus and Phoenon went amongst the poorer people, and with the compensation of water, promise of food while they worked, and two weeks worth of pre-work supplies, they beat the estimated target of a thousand workers by five hundred.

It had moved faster than they had expected and the goal was to leave in two weeks, knowing the sooner this project was done, the sooner lives would be benefited and saved.

8/5/697

Unilus walked into the bedroom. "I have something to show you," he said to Dragatu, and without waiting for an answer he turned and walked out. Dragatu followed curiously. They walked side by side through the streets and finally reached the fields, approaching a large tree near to the southwest of the reservoir. It stood alone and Dragatu recognised the white flowers around it. Unilus had shown him one once and he smiled to himself as he remembered. As they got closer Dragatu saw something very strange.

"What's that?" he asked.

"A scale model," was the short reply.

Dragatu noticed Unilus' nerves were making him even more awkward than usual. They reached the model and Dragatu was amazed at the detail of the hills and the small replica of the project. It was about waist height and made out of wood, baked clay, straw, and mud. Unilus didn't say anything and drew out a skin for drinking water. He looked at it, then at Dragatu, and offered it to him.

"Can you add the water to the water source, and we'll see if it works?"

Dragatu could still sense Unilus' nerves, but took the skin, unstopped it and poured the water into the replica of the lake. The water filled it and Unilus blew on the wood and straw replica wind catcher. The water went up and began trickling along the small wooden channels. They both blew the smaller wind catchers and the water made its way up the hill to the pool. Once at the top the water trickled down to the pool at the bottom and as that pool began to fill Dragatu spoke in a relieved and awed voice.

"It works."

"Of course it does," Unilus replied, a controlled but smug smile forming on his face.

Dragatu gave a little laugh.

"So everything is ready to go?" Dragatu asked.

"It's only a replica and doesn't mean too much, but yes," Unilus affirmed.

"Excellent. We will make Father proud."

Unilus nodded.

"We'll set off tomorrow as planned?"

Again Unilus nodded.

"Well done, brother. I'll see you later," Dragatu said, aware that Unilus didn't want to talk. He walked off to finish packing, leaving Unilus, who was still staring at the model. After a couple of steps, Dragatu heard Unilus whisper.

"Thank the Creator. It works. "

9/5/697

The host had gathered at the edge of the Nation and Dragatu scanned the crowds of people. He felt a lump form in his throat. His mother's eyes locked onto his own and she smiled. He recalled their stubborn argument just a few hours before. He had wanted her to stay and be safe, but she had declared firmly that she would be accompanying her sons on this momentous occasion. It was then he truly recognised the strength in his mother and it was humbling. He had lost his father, but she had lost her best friend, her lover and her husband. As the recollection faded, he nodded to her gently and broke eye contact.

Reon handed him a list of all those coming, there were almost two thousand people ready to make the long and dangerous journey across the desert. Dragatu was apprehensive about the optimism that was buzzing through the people. He knew it wouldn't take long for the people to see that this wasn't going to be an easy stroll across a child's sandpit. He wished they would be more realistic, and told the Hunora to be cautious of the morale dipping very quickly about two or three days into the hard journey. Telling them to motivate people with thoughts of how the project would help them and benefit future generations.

Dragatu continued to watch the people as they waited to begin the journey. He recognised farmer Heth, who had set his shoulder, brushing his old shire horse Gynopa. Dragatu twisted and flexed his left arm with the memory and frowned at the horse. The animals and supply carts would slow them down as they crossed the desert. They were a necessity, especially with all the precious barrels of water they had needed to take, but a hindrance to their pace.

At just past high sun, Dragatu gave the order for those at the front to start moving north and to keep the people moving forward in one group. The Hunora took up their positions, spread out along the group, and Dragatu waited until the last person passed him. He smiled inside, knowing that he was helping lead the people, and continued to achieve many of the goals in his journal.

Gradually, he made his way to the front, stopping as he went to talk to his friends and the people who excitedly bombarded questions at him. It took several hours, but eventually he reached Unilus, Phoenon and Healana. They walked as one, unified by their courage and desire to honour the man they had lost.

Chapter 8
Blood Brothers

29/5/697

Dragatu was right. The journey was long and hard. They travelled by night and rested in ventilated tents, pitched in the shadows of dunes during the day. Exhaustion soon became the norm, and even when they rested properly in the day the brief exposure to the sun scorched their skin. The night was only slightly kinder and the dry wind often whipped around them harshly and it took more than words to enthuse the people. Dragatu often found himself carrying supplies, chatting with the women and brushing down the horses at night – anything to help and keep himself in good favour. And when the heat of the desert took its toll, he would stop the convoy and bury his frustration deep, holding water skins to the mouths of those that had succumbed, reviving them and allowing them rest.

Eventually, they camped at the foot of the hills for a day and night, and as the second evening approached they scaled the hills and arrived at the small canyon. Darting his gaze around those closest to him, he saw the tiredness, desperation and the longing, cloud their once-excited faces.

"It's time to show you the water source!" Dragatu bellowed as loud as he could.

He stood at the entrance of the canyon, the people spread out amongst the trees, many of those near the back hidden. He could see worn smiles ripple throughout the group, the anticipation of seeing the water swelling inside them.

"Come forward, a few at a time and we'll show you the reasons we have suffered so greatly these last couple of weeks."

He beckoned first to Healana, Unilus and Phoenon. And as his mother emerged from the canyon and saw the shimmering water, she began to cry. Phoenon held her hand, squeezing it gently. After a few moments of staring at the pool she wiped away the tears and through watery eyes looked at her sons.

"I am so proud of you," she said smiling and sniffing. "Despite your differences you do so much to help people, and there is not a mother more proud of her sons than I. I know if your father were here he would be so proud. Thank you for all you have done, and all you continue to do."

She wiped away a few more tears, let go of Phoenon's hand and followed the canyon back to the people. The three boys followed and they began the long process of showing the water to all. The journey had nearly broken the people's hope and resilience, they needed to be uplifted, and the brothers knew seeing the water would do this.

Once everyone had seen the water source and settled in groups, Dragatu hunted, returning with a stag that he gave to his friends to prepare for cooking. He then walked a distance from the camp, up one of the sides of the hills. Sitting down he could see all the little orange dots of fires and could hear distant songs and shouts of laughter. An hour passed, and he enjoyed the stillness and watched the fires dim as people prepared themselves to sleep.

Snap! A twig behind him broke, and he spun round, reaching for one of his knives.

"It's us," a voice whispered, and Dragatu relaxed as his brothers sat either side of him in silence. There was no need for words. It was enough that they unified their thoughts of their father, that they had conquered so many of their fears by just being there and that they were about to help the people the way their father would have wanted.

10/6/697

The following days were spent clearing the area and cutting the trees down to be used for the project. Water skins and containers were filled and distributed amongst the people, and hunters were sent to make sure a good supply of food was established. Groups of carpenters, tree cutters, manual labourers and hunters, were led by Dragatu and the Hunora, and this helped the project stay organised and productive. The first part of the project was well under way by the tenth day of the month and the large cylinder, the structure that would hold it at the correct angle, the screw, and the large wind catcher had been made, but they still needed to be put together and built in the proper place.

21/6/697

After another ten days, stage one was complete. It was time to put together the screw mechanisms and wind catchers. Complicated and precise, their construction took all of Unilus' time and concentration, leaving Dragatu frustrated, impatient and irritable because he didn't have much to do.

"Dragatu. Can I speak with you quickly?" Reon asked, a look of apprehension on his face as Dragatu glowered at him.

"What's wrong?"

"Well . . ." he paused as he took a breath. "Some of the other Hunora have been taking more water for themselves, and not giving the right amount to the workers."

"Who?" Dragatu demanded, confused and angry that people would be so selfish.

Reon named them quickly, and Dragatu asked him to gather all the Hunora together. Walking to his brothers, Dragatu spoke.

"There's something I have to deal with. Tell all the workers they can have a day off and we will begin work again either tomorrow or the next day."

"What's wrong?" Phoenon asked.

"Nothing I can't handle," Dragatu said sharply.

Phoenon's face dropped.

"Sorry," Dragatu said, feeling a pang of guilt. He stepped forward and put a hand on Phoenon's shoulder. "It's something I need to deal with. Just take advantage of the free time, okay," he said, forcing a smile.

Phoenon gave a weak smile back and nodded.

"I'll see you when I get back," Dragatu said, walking briskly to meet the Hunora, readying himself to deal with these people who thought they could cheat both the people and him.

"Fellow Hunora. Thank you for meeting me here," Dragatu began.

"We're going on a scouting trip. We will be heading north to hunt and relax. The work load has been demanding and we need some time to enjoy ourselves." It was a half-lie. There were cheers from the group and nods of gratitude. "Go get your packs and hunting gear, and bring your water. We leave in an hour from this spot."

Everyone dispersed and Dragatu went over the plan he had formulated. He was ready to expose those who were stealing water. His plan would prove the truth of the accusations and he was ready to do whatever he could to make sure it didn't happen again.

As they travelled, some hunted, some rested and others chattered and laughed. They had reached a small lake and this was what Dragatu had been waiting for.

"Everyone gather round," he called out beckoning them forward.

Several minutes passed, and finally they were all in front of him by the lake. Dragatu got straight to the point.

"I need you all to empty your water into the lake."

There was a lot of murmuring and the relaxed atmosphere suddenly became very tense. A few of the people protested more than most and Dragatu kept a close eye on them, his desire to call their bluff appearing to have worked.

"Empty your containers and skins one by one into the lake," Dragatu repeated, this time with more authority in his voice. Some people began to do as he had ordered, and then one by one they all emptied their water into the lake. Dragatu walked up the line and most people emptied about the same amount into the lake, but eventually he came to the accused. They emptied a significantly larger volume of water and there were gasps and shouts of disapproval from those around them. Dragatu sighed heavily. He had hoped the accusations had been false, but they weren't and he had to make the hard choice of following his plan.

"As you can see, we have been betrayed by our brothers," Dragatu shouted. "The reason I brought you all here was to bring to light those who took more than they are supposed to. The water is precious. There has to be consequences for their disregard of the rules and for taking more for themselves and not thinking about others." His voice got louder and louder and his arms shook, anger rising at the betrayal as he spoke. "I told you all we would be like a family, and you shouldn't hurt your own family. The Book of Law says not to steal, and if you had stolen while at home you would have to pay back double what you had stolen, or work off the equivalent. We are not going to do that here, as I do not want to bring the shame of what you've done to everyone's knowledge, but the seriousness of your greed, selfishness and betrayal must not go unpunished. Do you agree?" he asked, looking around at the other Hunora.

There was a pause and then a few people called out, "Yes!" and as their shouts died out the rest began to nod and call out, "They should be punished."

Dragatu was thankful that the people saw that this was wrong and the culprits should be punished.

"Good. I feel they should be punished and I'm going to punish them. I'm responsible for you all and if people shame themselves then they shame me. Therefore, I must deal with this as I see fit. You all pledged yourself to me, and now you will face the consequence of stealing from the workers who need the water just as much as you do." He took a deep breath. "Your punishment will be to face me in a fight."

There was a ripple of whispers, and a few looks of uncertainty from the Hunora, but Dragatu called out over them.

"If those who had stolen water had been allowed to continue people could have been hurt and suffered by not having enough water. Therefore, it's only right they be hurt. You will think twice before doing it again," he said looking at those who had stolen the water.

There was a deep bellowing laugh from the biggest of the men. Dragatu snapped his head to look at him. Dragatu noticed he had a look about him that was so reminiscent of Branon: tall and broad, and older than most there, but with the hardness and muscle tone that only came from years of hard work.

"That's a joke!" the man spat venomously. "We followed you here because it would help the people, and we're happy to work, but we'll take what we want if and when we want it. It's our right as Hunora. We have more back in our Nation so we should have more here. We are not going to be told what to do by some boy," he said, looking around for support. Getting none, he continued, "I know you claim to have done a lot, and you are stronger than probably all boys your age, but we are men here and can do what we want."

The man's defiance and dismissal of what he had done transformed Dragatu's anger into something close to rage. He clenched his fists tightly, the nails digging into the palms. Struggling to hold back his anger he called out to those around him.

"Those who want justice for these crimes circle them so they cannot escape."

On seeing the tensed muscles in Dragatu's face and how his arms shook the Hunora hesitated. However, Linur, Reon and Dragatu's other close friends stepped forward feeling similar anger towards the men and the rest of the group finally followed to create a two-row circle.

"Either you fight me or you fight all of us," Dragatu said through gritted teeth as he stood at one end of the circle. "The choice is yours." He then pointed to one of the accused, and the Hunora who were in the circle pushed him from the periphery into the centre. 'Weakness and cowardice,' thought Dragatu, his eyes trained on the men, his breathing level and regulated.

The man who had called out before shook his head and muttered, "This is ridiculous," and went to walk through the circle. The people there locked together, blocking the way. "Let me pass," he growled. They shook their heads. "Fine, but don't be angry with me when I beat this boy," he said, turning and folding his arms to watch the first fight begin.

It was the first of seven and Dragatu worked his way through six of them solidly and without competition. Each fight was fair, but Dragatu's experience, strength and anger, as well as his agility of youth, meant he won, punishing each person with measured blows and ensuring he avoided leaving any permanent damage. The Hunora got caught in the thrill of the fight and cheered as Dragatu won. They took the defeated men to the side one by one, and then let them recover until all the fights were over.

The last fight was with the man who had been the most vocal. Dragatu was tired and bruised, but he had been saving his anger for this man. The fight began and the man took a few heavy swings at Dragatu. He dodged those, however, the last powerful jab caught Dragatu directly on the nose. It broke. He felt his control slip. He took several steps back, taking a few moments to recover as the man smirked at him. The smirk was the last straw, something in Dragatu's mind snapped. He spat the warm salty blood at the floor and stood as tall as he could. There was a moment between them where time seemed to stop, and the smirk vanished. Suddenly Dragatu broke the stillness and unleashed all the rage that had been building. He ran at the man and began punching and didn't stop. A haze of red blurred his vision. The first few swings were blocked, but the constant and relentless attacks broke through the man's defenses. Within seconds, Dragatu was on top of the man, beating him as if he were a pillow.

At first the Hunora had continued to cheer, but as they watched Dragatu beat this man over and over a silence of shock crept over them. Eventually, a few of the men shouted for Dragatu to stop, but he showed no sign of letting the man go.

Linur and several others then ran forward, pulling Dragatu off the man. Linur stood in front of him as the others held him.

"Dragatu!" he shouted, "That's enough." The rage slowly faded, and breathing heavily he calmed down. They cautiously let him go. The man lay on his back, bleeding, moaning and gasping for air.

"See to his injuries." Dragatu panted, coming out of his rage.

A few Hunora scuttled over and gave the man some water and sat him up.

"Set camp here for the night," Dragatu said to the thin air, unable to focus fully.

A few of those around him heard and spread the word.

"What was that about?" Linur said handing him a cloth for his nose, when the two stood alone.

Dragatu wiped the dried blood away. "They needed to be punished," he said, then took a swig of water and spat it out with the last of the blood from his mouth.

"I know and you did that," Linur replied. "But you didn't look like you were going to stop with that last man. Why didn't you stop?"

Dragatu couldn't think straight. "I don't know? He needed punishing more. He didn't feel any remorse for what he had done wrong and . . . well . . . I lost it . . . I'm sorry," he stammered.

"It was scary Dragatu," Linur said.

Dragatu hung his head, trying to know what to say. "It's done now," he said weakly. "Just make sure they're okay."

"I will. What about you, are you okay?" Linur asked.

"I'll be fine," Dragatu said giving him a grateful smile. "I just need some time to recover. I'll be back soon."

"Okay, I'll keep watch over the Hunora."

"Thank you Linur," Dragatu said putting down the cloth. He staggered slowly around the lake, through some of the trees, and when he knew the Hunora wouldn't be able to see him he took off his clothes, becoming more aware of the aches and bruises as he did. He walked forward, stepped into the lake and crouched, submerging fully. The cold water shocked his body, and his nose felt like several hornets had stung it at the same time. The pain made his eyes water, but he ignored it as best he could. He let all his breath out. When he could hold it no longer he re-emerged, gasping for air. Gathering his senses he walked out of the lake slowly, as though he was exploring the land for the first time.

'It feels good to be clean again,' he thought. 'Like the wrongs I was responsible for have been washed away.'

Dragatu put his clothes back on and walked back to the camp, letting the air dry him slowly and ignoring the cold he felt from the night wind. As he entered the camp Linur walked up to him.

"Better?" he asked.

"Much," Dragatu said.

"What should we do now?" he asked, looking towards those who had been punished, who were being watched by other Hunora. Dragatu sighed, but said nothing and walked over to them, Linur following close behind.

"I'm willing to let what has just happened go and never speak of it again if you are," Dragatu said. "We'll all keep what you did a secret if you promise not to do it again. That way your families will not know the shame you brought upon yourselves, and that way no one needs to know you were punished by a 'boy.'" Dragatu glanced to the man he had fought last, and winced slightly, the man's face was swollen and almost unrecognisable.

With this the other six men got slowly to their feet, still sore from their beatings. They apologised and agreed they wouldn't do it again, but the severely beaten man sat and said nothing.

"You are free to go," Dragatu said to the others. "You are our brothers and will not be treated any different from anyone else. You have apologised and accepted that what you did was wrong."

The men walked off, heads lowered. Once they left the last man struggled to his feet and stood looking down at Dragatu. Dragatu kept eye contact and tried to extinguish the tension as best he could.

"We don't need to be enemies. You shouldn't have done what you did, but you fought well. Do you understand why I did what I did?"

There was a tense moment of silence as they kept eye contact. Then the man hung his head and spoke as best he could through the pain in his face.

"I understand more than you realise." He sighed heavily.

Dragatu went to speak, but the man looked up again and cut the words short.

"The Hunora follow you like you were a father, yet in age you are a boy?" disbelief laced the words. "Today I have seen why, and that I mis-judged you. You are a man in spirit, though not in years. I took the water and coaxed others to do the same because I didn't think anyone would stop us. I've looked for someone to be a leader for a long time. I know I could never be, but I've never found anyone I could put my faith in, as so many people are too weak." He caressed his face, wincing with some of the pain, and then continued. "That's all changed. I may be a stubborn man at times, but I can admit when I'm wrong. I was wrong about you. If you accept my apology I would like to promise my friendship and commitment to you in the future."

The reaction was not what Dragatu had expected and there was something about this man's words that reminded Dragatu of himself. The man just needed direction. His own had come from his father and the Book of Law, and this was a chance to honour both.

"Nothing would make me happier," Dragatu said extending his arm.

The man took it and they gripped each other's arm tightly, sealing a new bond of respect, and tentative friendship.

"What's your name?" Dragatu asked.

"Honrus."

"Thank you Honrus. Do you want to get some food and sit with me at my fire? I would like to know more about you."

"Only for a little while. I'll need to rest a lot to heal these injuries, and by the look of you, you should rest as well."

They gave smirks of laughter as they walked to Dragatu's pack, and talked about their histories. Some of the Hunora watched in confusion as the two sat together, but others smiled with understanding, knowing the mutual respect that can form between those who have overcome their differences through blood and pain.

Dragatu listened and learned that Honrus was forty-one years old and a wealthy blacksmith. He had few friends, was a widower and had no children, but he was happy enough keeping busy with his work, and going to the ore pits. After talking longer than they had anticipated, Honrus finally had to submit to his pains and excused himself from Dragatu.

Dragatu watched Honrus walk away and thought, 'Who would have thought a few hours ago that this man would become my friend?' Shaking his head in amused disbelief, he lay down and pulled his blanket over him. All regret of his loss of control, and any doubts about his strict punishments, being swallowed up by the positives that had come from it.

22/6/697

The sun's approach had turned the sky a grey-blue and the Hunora were stirring from their rest, recalling the drama from the day before. Dragatu spoke to his friends and asked them to gather everyone together so he could address them.

"Everything that took place yesterday should be forgotten as if it never happened. I've spoken with those who betrayed us, and they have promised never to do it again. In turn, we'll not bring shame to them and their families by telling the people what they did. As a result of this, we must also keep the punishments a secret. Tell anyone that asks that they happened while we were wrestling and that we got carried away, this will cover up the injuries. Does everyone agree to this?"

Dragatu looked around and saw most of the Hunora nod, but some showed no sign of agreement or disapproval, their faces were unreadable.

"Thank you for your continued support. We shall go back to the workers and we can continue helping the people work the way they should, and to support them in this."

They set off and arrived back at the camp about half way between high sun and dusk.

"What happened to you?" Healana asked as he walked back to the spot where his family camped.

"Just a few bruises from wrestling. Nothing to worry about."

She frowned. "I know when you're lying Dragatu. What happened?"

"Please just leave it," he replied.

She frowned but didn't say anything.

"Sorry." Dragatu sighed. "I just need you to trust me. I've done what I had to do to put everything right."

"If there was something wrong you should really have spoken with Unilus and Phoenon."

"Why should I have spoken with them?" Dragatu asked his forehead creasing with confusion.

"You've done what you felt was right, but sometimes it's good to get other opinions. Your brothers might have been able to help in a way you hadn't considered."

"I didn't need them for this. I'm strong enough to do it by myself," he replied.

"You know I don't mean to say you aren't strong enough, no one doubts that, least of all me, but they have different strengths that might help."

A memory flicked before Dragatu's mind, brought to the surface by his mother's words, but before it could take root Healana continued, compassion swelling in her voice.

"All I ask is you try to include your brothers more."

"Fine. I'll try," he said grudgingly as he put down his pack, casually said goodbye, and went off to find Reon, Linur and the rest of his friends.

5/7/697

A few more days of rest were granted and then the project continued. The cylinders for the smaller screw mechanisms, the screws, and the brackets to hold them in place were made and meticulously put together, while Unilus kept watch over the whole process. The manufacturing of the wind catchers was constructed in the same way and a medium sized pool had been dug at the top of the last hill nearest to the desert.

The first test of the project took place. Cogs joining the large wind catcher and the cylinder with the screw inside were connected, but both could be removed with ease. The height of the wind catcher allowed it to catch good winds and as the winds blew it turned the cogs, and in turn, the screw. The water was taken from the lake by the rotation of the screw and flowed up to the channels. Dragatu followed it as it moved around the valley, meandering through the wooden channels. There were people every fifty metres to keep a close eye on it, in case anything went wrong. An archer was on standby with a flaming arrow, ready to fire it into the sky should a problem arise. Eventually, the water reached the top of the hill and two fire arrows were shot into the air to signal that it had worked. Cheers echoed as the confirmation signals flew through the air and made their descent towards the ground. Finally, the pool was filled and one arrow was shot to signal that the water flow should be stopped and the main cog of the large catcher was disconnected.

It was becoming dark as Healana, Phoenon, Unilus and Dragatu entered the camp. There were shouts of celebration and congratulations to the brothers. People rushed up to Unilus and thanked him for all he had done, shaking his hand and patting him on the back. Dragatu watched, struggling internally.

'I was the one that had made this work,' he thought. 'Unilus had only come up with the idea. I was the one who had to organise the people, I had to oversee everyone and I had to punish those who stole water. And now they are thanking Unilus. Why are they thanking him more?' he wondered. 'I guess it doesn't matter,' he finally thought, struggling to shrug it off. 'It works and people will be so happy when it's finished. We've done something that will help everyone and I know Father would have seen how important I am in this project and I know the Creator knows.'

With this thought, he let the people continue to thank Unilus. After a while he left and went to find Honrus. They sat and ate, laughing and talking about how they had reached a great point in their people's history.

3/8/697

Construction had become routine and second nature for the workers and with everyone applying themselves the work progressed efficiently.

At last, the Nation was in sight and people came to greet the workers with food and supplies, and to see their loved ones once more. It was a glorious occasion. Everyone found satisfaction and relief in what they had accomplished. At this point, the workers needed to be encouraged by the Hunora who were working alongside them; the sight of the Nation and thoughts of an end to this project tempted them to slacken their pace. However, the work continued with only a slight delay and the last channel was connected to the reservoir in front of a massive audience of workers and people. Cheers and claps roared as it was finished and it was time for Dragatu to return with Unilus to let the water flow freely.

"Can I come?" asked Phoenon, as they talked as a family about the imminent journey.

"No," Dragatu replied straight away, almost laughing at the request, "It'll be a boring trip that Unilus and I have to make. There's no need for you to come."

"But I want to come. Please Mother? I'll be safe with Dragatu."

The plea to Healana annoyed Dragatu, but he was sure she would say no, so wasn't worried.

"I think it would be good if you went too," Healana said, to his surprise.

Dragatu was about to argue when his mother said something that stopped him.

"I trust you Dragatu."

The words, and how they were said, cut him to the core. "As you wish," he said, not wanting to let her down. He turned to

Phoenon. "You must be careful at all times and do as I say. Do you understand?"

"Of course," Phoenon said, a massive smile spreading across his face.

The project had built their confidence and they felt the dangers in the hills were past, but there were always going to be small doubts, and Dragatu knew the responsibility he had by taking both Unilus and Phoenon to the hills by themselves.

18/8/697

Phoenon's light-hearted nature was contagious and made their journey almost enjoyable. They reached the water project and attached the main cog and lowered the screw device, locking it in place. As they walked down the hill towards the desert side Phoenon spoke to them.

"You know what would make journeying here and back easier?"

Unilus and Dragatu looked at him inquisitively, waiting for the reply.

"Well, I don't see why we can't put little holes in all the channels across the desert. The water would drip on the sand in the areas here, and at the Nation. Surely the grass would eventually spread and join to make a green path that was easy to walk on?"

Both Dragatu and Unilus were stunned. Then Dragatu spoke.

"Theoretically, that sounds good, but it would waste the water, and the people need every drop they can get."

Unilus stopped walking, thinking very hard. Dragatu could see he was going to side with Phoenon, and let out a sigh of frustration. He was about to try and back up his argument further, when Unilus spoke.

"It is a good idea. There are greater consequences to this than what Phoenon's said. If it can make the area fertile then there can be more farmland for future generations. It would also give more access to the north and for people to explore those areas. It's a good idea. We should make a tiny hole every fifty metres."

Dragatu wanted to argue that this was a waste, but he did see the logic, it would make his journeys to the north easier. So he decided to let his argument go and agreed to help put holes in the channels. Every fifty metres they climbed up the big wooden legs of the channels and made the hole, letting water drip through, and hoping in time it would have the effect they had discussed.

2/9/697

The work had finally come to a close, and the three brothers couldn't help grinning as they walked through the streets. People came to greet them and offered their thanks, and as before, praised Unilus the most. Dragatu's jealousy crept back into his heart and he tried to fight it, but finally it was too much and he told his brothers he was going to go and see his friends, and left.

He couldn't understand why they thanked Unilus more. He mulled over how they should have shown him more appreciation. After walking the long way to Reon's, he realised he didn't even want to speak to any of his friends anymore and found a quiet space to sit, and updated his journal.

Journal Entry 2/9/697

> I know I shouldn't be jealous. But I've worked so hard and done so much. Surely it's not too much to ask for the gratitude I deserve? Especially when they are giving it to Unilus. My friends know how hard I've worked and they show their thanks, but why don't the other people? I guess I'll have to work harder to show them my strength and then they'll thank me more, the way Honrus does and the way my father would have.

He closed the journal and sat thinking for a while before he rose and made his way home.

🧪

In the weeks that followed it became clear the water project had the positive effect that was desired. There was a change in the health of the Nation almost straight away. The poorer people had been prioritised, but eventually water became abundant amongst all the people. Crops grew better, grass was greener, the gap between rich and poor decreased, and the people as a whole were a lot happier.

The summer ended with almost all the people healthier and happier, autumn and winter went by like a dream, and as always spring arrived as the bearer of new things, but also brought back the old.

Chapter 9
First and Second Meetings

17/2/698

Dragatu checked the water source and all was working well. With this task accomplished, he walked out of the canyon and turned north, rubbing his arms to fight off the spring morning chill.

'This is it,' he thought, 'time to go further than I ever have.' A slight twitch in his hand betrayed his nerves. He slung his bow over his shoulder and kept his two knives loose on his belt, and walked cautiously northward. Another birthday had come and gone and once again he craved the thrill that came from accomplishing his goals. All his experiences had forced him to grow up a lot in the last couple of years, and what was once a naïve youthful dream of revenge and glory, quashed by fear, had become his only desire. The only challenge that would satisfy him now was to kill the wolf. When he returned, having slaughtered the beast, no one would ever doubt his strength or resolve to honour his father, and maybe the nightmares would stop, too. Dragatu continued to walk, automatically scanning the area as he went, his hand still twitching nervously as memories of the wolf haunted him.

'That's unusual,' he thought, suddenly stopping and focusing on a tree. 'That can't have been one of mine. I've not been this far before.' He walked over to the tree and ran his fingers over the arrow cut in the wood, fresh sap bleeding down the bark. His mouth tightened into a frown and his brow creased.

'It's fresh. Whose is it?' he wondered.

His eyes left the mark on the tree, but his fingers still touched and rubbed the groove. He scanned from the direction the arrow must have come from to the direction it was going.

'Footprints!'

As he saw them his hand dropped from the arrow mark in the tree and he walked towards a light imprint of a human foot. A light breeze caused the foliage to rustle. He crouched and lightly touched the prints, studying them. They were fresh too. Close to them were the tracks of a stag, and a big one at that.

'Could someone else be hunting here? But no one else hunts here.'

Dragatu shook his head and studied the prints again. Running his fingers along the indentations a thought formed.

"A woman." He gasped aloud. He ran his hand over the stubble on his face. 'Up here? I must be wrong.'

Pushing aside his desire to hunt the wolf, he decided to track this mysterious hunter. He followed the trail, seeing a few more arrow marks nicked in the bark of trees as he went. After half an hour, he came to an unexpected clearing. There, in the middle, was the owner of the prints. Dragatu stared in disbelief. Crouched over a large stag was a thin, but athletic girl, with long blonde hair tied back into a ponytail. She was pulling an arrow out of the stag as Dragatu stepped forward. A twig snapped under his foot.

Hearing the sound, the girl moved with lightning quick agility, doing two things simultaneously. She finished pulling out the arrow with one hand, and with the other, grabbed the bow that lay at her side. She spun a half rotation, joining the two parts together, and stopped, ready to fire at the source of the noise. Her face screwed up, then went flat and motionless, her bow still ready and pointing at Dragatu. Five long seconds passed, in which they tried to read each other and finally Dragatu raised his hands and took another step forward.

"Are you going to shoot me?" he said bluntly. 'Surely she wouldn't.'

She lowered the bow slightly and Dragatu continued to step forward, his head held high, but his confusion and shock got the better of him, and he blurted out.

"What are you doing here?"

She looked at him, then at the stag, and in a tone that showed she thought it was a stupid question replied with, "Hunting."

For the first time in his life, Dragatu felt very small. "Sorry . . . of course you are." After the initial stumble, he continued. "You hunt well. It must have been hard to stalk that stag without it running off."

As he said this she lowered the bow completely. Dragatu was now half way to her, but decided not to get any closer. The bow was still strung and he didn't fancy his chances.

"It was easy enough," she replied.

The arrow marks he had seen told him otherwise, but this wasn't the time to be questioning her.

"It's for my food supplies. I'm hoping to hunt something bigger, if I can find it."

Dragatu let a small smile appear on his face, she certainly came across as courageous, and he liked it.

"What's your name?" he asked.

"I'm Freta," she said formally, and casually turned to the stag, pulled some rope from her pack, and tied the hind legs together before dragging it to a tree. Dragatu stood there watching. He felt a bit awkward and unsure of what to do with himself. Throwing the rope over a branch Freta hoisted the deer up, letting it dangle in the air. Drawing her knife she cut the stag's throat.

As he watched Dragatu was fascinated by her strength and skill. Once the stag's throat was cut he managed to gain some courage, and despite her complete disregard for his presence, he introduced himself.

"I'm Dragatu, by the way."

She looked at him, her eyes dropping to his feet and working their way to his head and then back down again. Dragatu was unsure if he was being sized up for a fight, it was certainly how

102

it felt. Nothing was said and she went back to the stag. Once more Dragatu felt awkward. It was time to get back to his own hunting, and thoughts of the wolf spurred him to leave. He turned to go, but Freta spoke.

"Where are you from?"

Dragatu paused mid turn and hesitantly turned back to face her.

"The Nation to the south of here, across the desert."

She laughed.

"What's so funny?" he asked hotly, his patience wearing thin.

Her laughter faded, but some still fed through into her words. "It was your answer. Of course you're from the Nation. Have you ever met anyone who wasn't from there? We have always been in one group, and if there were people anywhere else I'm sure we would know about it."

Her words were so patronizing that Dragatu really started to dislike her. There were only a few things that kept him there, his pride, his respect for her hunting prowess, and maybe her good looks.

She repeated her question slowly as though he was simple.

"Where about . . . in the Nation . . . are you from?"

"The rich part," he said, hoping to garner some admiration.

She frowned at this response and turned her nose up.

"What was that for?"

"All the people in the rich area think too highly of themselves," she replied. "You have it easy while so many have to work hard all day, like my father."

"Things have got better since the water project was built. It was some of the rich people who helped that come about, wasn't it?" he challenged.

"I guess," she said dismissively. "But that was only a few of those who live in that area, and it was only because of a boy called Unilus and his brothers, that it all came about."

Dragatu bit his tongue from blurting out it was him who had made the project work, instead he managed to turn his frustration into a sort of condescending laugh.

"Why are you laughing?" she asked.

"I know the brothers you just mentioned."

"I hope they had a good influence on you," she said, looking him up and down again with a raised eyebrow.

"They have certainly influenced me. I can promise you that." He smirked.

"And why is that?"

Dragatu laughed inside at his little game. "I'm one of the brothers," he replied simply.

"That's where I know you from!" she exclaimed. "I thought I recognised the description of you, you're Unilus' brother." Suddenly her demeanor changed, and she relaxed and appeared almost vulnerable.

"I'm sorry Dragatu," she said smiling for the first time. "If I have been rude then please forgive me. I get very defensive around strangers and especially if they come from the rich area. I've watched my father work hard all his life at the ore pits. I wish sometimes he could get a break. I wish we didn't have to work so hard." She let go of the stag and walked over to her pack, continuing to talk: "I see many of the people in your area not having to work every day to simply stay alive, and I get angry and jealous. I know I shouldn't." She got a cloth from her pack and wiped the blade, pausing as she did. Dragatu continued to wait and listen, a bit stunned by the change in behavior and the way she spoke so freely now. "This is why I'm here hunting," she continued as she put the cloth beside her pack and checked her arrows and bow, "so I can bring good food for my father. The food we have in the ore pits isn't the best, however, the meat here is fresh, tender, succulent and because of this we can trade it for the things we need."

Dragatu couldn't help but put aside his defensiveness.

"I'm sorry you've had a difficult life," he began. "I've spent a lot of time at the ore pits, and try to help out a lot because I see the conditions are tough." He paused then asked, "I go there a lot. I'm surprised I haven't seen you?" He knew someone like her would have caught his eye.

"I live on the far east side of the pits," she replied.

"Ah, that's why," Dragatu said. "I'm usually on the west side close to the Nation. I'm sorry I've never ventured further east."

"We make do so don't worry about it," she said becoming slightly defensive again.

Dragatu decided this was probably a good time to say goodbye. "Well, I'm going to continue my hunting. I'm sure I will see you some other time." He was thinking about visiting her at the ore pits when he got back.

"Oh, okay," Freta said, her face dropping a little. "Goodbye," she added, and she began walking back to the stag.

Dragatu turned and took two steps forward, when a noise made him stop abruptly. His feet locked to the floor. The sound was deeper than he remembered, but it was the same loud howl that haunted him.

"Was that a wolf?" Freta asked looking to him with a mixture of curiosity and fear at the unnaturally loud and rumbling howl.

The question brought him out of his memories. Suddenly all his senses were alert. He was back in control. He tried to focus on the direction of the sound as it faded, scanning the perimeter, thinking fast.

'It must have caught the scent of the stag,' he thought, his wariness turning to excitement. 'This is it!'

"It is a wolf isn't it? Why is it that one second you look petrified, and now you're happy?" Freta frowned.

"There's no time to explain. You need to get out of the valley," Dragatu said, his words almost too fast to understand.

"I'm not going anywhere," she said. "Whatever that was I wouldn't go hunting for it alone, if that's what you are thinking?"

Dragatu let out an exasperated sigh; they were wasting valuable seconds. "I have to hunt and kill the wolf. It killed my father. I can't have you around distracting me or getting in the way."

"The two of us could kill it together?" she suggested, a hint of excitement in her own voice.

'If she knew how dangerous this wolf was she wouldn't be so keen,' he thought, remembering his father. "No!" he suddenly shouted. "I go alone." And with that he began to run north-west in the direction of the howl. After a short distance he realised she was running behind him, bow over her shoulder, arrows in a quiver and knife on her belt.

"You don't want to do this! Go south!" he shouted, still running.

She didn't reply, but kept running behind him. His hand twitched again, but this time with anger and he flexed both his hands, 'She's going to get in the way.' But he couldn't do anything and ignored her, focusing on his hearing and hoping to hear another howl. No howl came and they continued to run, but finally, in frustration, he lost his temper. When he turned around he was ready to explode, but then he saw the determination on her face.

"You're not going to leave me are you?" he asked, his anger deflating.

Freta shook her head defiantly.

"Fine," he said, giving in.

Freta stayed a pace behind him and they continued to run through the trees. Suddenly they halted as they came to some tracks. They were massive and Freta gasped at the sight of them.

"See?" Dragatu said. "You should have gone home."

"Is it really wise for just the two of us to hunt it?" Freta replied. "We could come back with more hunters and kill it."

"No," Dragatu said loudly, rejecting such an idea with all his heart and mind. "This is the first time I've heard it since the night it killed my father. I can't risk letting it get away. I have to kill it. If you're afraid then go home as I told you to. I can't protect you."

"I'm not leaving you to get yourself killed," she replied. "With two of us we will have a better chance."

Letting out a growl of frustration he continued running, following the tracks. It wasn't long before they realised they were slowly circling back and then there was the familiar howl from the direction they had come.

'Clever beast,' Dragatu thought, and his mind raced trying to think the best way to continue this hunt.

"Okay, maybe two people will be good," he began, looking at Freta. "If you run north-east, then cut south to meet me back at the clearing where we left the stag. I'll go south-east and then cut north. I think the wolf has taken advantage of the free meal. We should be able to attack the wolf from both sides."

She nodded, checked her hunting gear quickly, and then ran.

'It worked. By the time she gets to the wolf, it'll already be dead.'

When she was out of sight he ran in a direct line towards the clearing.

Chapter 10
Made of New Scars

Dragatu pushed himself to his limit to beat her. He had to protect her. The wolf wouldn't hurt anyone ever again. His heart pounded as he heard the sound of tearing flesh and gnashing teeth. He slowed to a light jog and crept through the trees, sidestepping behind one for cover, then peering out to look at the monster. It was even bigger than he remembered. Scars covered its body and as Dragatu recognised the one on its face, a sly smile spread across his own.

'I will kill this wolf for you, Father.'

Withdrawing back behind the tree, he readied himself, taking a deep breath. He peered out again and waited a few seconds. The wolf raised its head, licking the blood off its muzzle. Dragatu was about to attack when suddenly every muscle on the wolf's body contracted. It sniffed inquisitively and snapped its head to look in Dragatu's direction, howling loudly. Dragatu resisted the urge to cover his ears and quickly shot back behind the tree.

'The wind has changed,' he thought angrily. 'Once it had helped me, and now it curses me.'

The only choice he had was the same tactic as before. Dragatu scrabbled like a squirrel, and didn't stop until he was far up the tree. The wolf bounded forward, reached the bottom, and began sniffing and snarling around it. Dragatu stayed as quiet as he could. The wolf stopped suddenly and turned back. Dragatu looked in the direction it moved, and there stood Freta.

'How did she get here so fast?' he wondered. 'She must have known I was trying to get rid of her. She should have gone home!'

The wolf stalked towards her, walking one curious, but confident step at a time, sniffing and snarling at the air as it moved. Freta drew an arrow and in a blink had notched and fired it. It grazed the wolf's shoulder, leaving a shallow wound. Dragatu was impressed at her speed and skill. The wolf, however, didn't even flinch. It kept true to its path and walked menacingly and mechanically towards her.

'Should I let it kill her?' Dragatu thought for a split second. 'No of course I can't,' he answered, ashamed, and shook his head. He shot down the tree like a meteor hurtling to earth, and with the noise the wolf turned back around. At the sight of Dragatu it snarled, then looked backwards and forwards between Freta and Dragatu. Freta took advantage of the distraction, drew another arrow and released it. It hit the wolf and it half howled, half yelped. It chose its victim . . . Freta. She threw her bow aside and unlatched the quiver from her back. Drawing her hunting knife she took a wide base stance. Dragatu sprinted towards them, but before he got there the wolf leapt at Freta. She crouched and sidestepped swiftly, dodging a bite that was aimed for her throat. Dragatu reached the wolf. It had turned in the direction Freta had sidestepped, but she tripped. Dragatu attacked the exposed side, plunging his knife into the warm fur and flesh, feeling the blood run down his hand. The wolf yelped again and backed away from Dragatu, giving him enough time to dash to Freta, who was sitting on the floor.

"Are you okay?" he asked, keeping his eyes on the wolf and holding out a hand she pulled herself up.

"I'm fine," she said quickly, holding her knife ready.

Dragatu drew his second knife, still holding the first blade that dripped blood on the floor. The wolf stood still, snarling and growling, and neither side moved toward the other.

"Do as I do," Dragatu whispered, breaking the stalemate.

He began walking towards the wolf, making himself as big as he could, and the wolf glanced back and forth between them.

"Start circling left," he commanded.

She obeyed and he circled right. It was the same plan he had used with the lions. A stab of guilt pierced him as he remembered Corich and the others. 'That won't happen again,' he told himself, and hoped with all his heart it didn't and refocused.

The wolf began slowly backing away as they circled. Cautiously they moved closer, coming from both sides, watching for any quick movement from the wolf. It suddenly changed its tactic and bounded at Dragatu, moving with desperate haste. Dragatu stopped and stood his ground, trying to be as solid as stone. As it came upon him the jaws snapped violently. Dragatu quickly adapted: becoming more fluid with his movements, dodging the attacks, if only just. The wolf stopped its gnashing and leapt, a paw hit Dragatu's face, its claws sharp and gouging.

Freta tried attacking from the rear, but the wolf pushed forward as Dragatu jumped and dodged backwards, and she couldn't do any serious damage. Suddenly Dragatu lost his balance and the wolf bounded and reared up once more, again a clawed pad close to Dragatu who ducked just in time, but as he came up the other paw swiped down at his face. Three rigid claws tore the flesh on the left side, the middle gash slicing from above his eyebrow, missing his eye and continuing down his cheek. He staggered backwards, his hand automatically reaching for the wound, but he stopped it. Blood began to run and he swayed a little. Snarling with frustration, he focused ready for the next attack.

The connecting blow had slowed the wolf down and Freta seized the moment. She moved from the back to the front and thrust her knife into the side of the wolf's neck and twisted. The strike stopped a deathly attack on Dragatu, but with a mixture of rage and instinct the wolf threw all its strength sideways towards her. The blow knocked her clear off her feet and she flew back several metres, landing with a loud 'thud!'

Dragatu saw her lying there, she didn't move. In the corner of his eye he saw the wolf slowly turn back towards him, panting and gasping for air. He took his eyes off Freta, and focused. Instinctively, he wiped the blood, rage building as pain lanced through him.

Taking a few steps forward he faked to move to his right, the wolf took the bait and turned, Freta's knife now exposed in the side of the beast. Dragatu ran the last few steps, jumped up, placed his foot on the embedded knife to get more height, and mounted himself on the wolf's back, wrapping his legs around it as best he could. He began stabbing ferociously, over and over, and the wolf tried in vain to buck him off. With this new attack, it lost its remaining strength. It's legs gave way, collapsing like felled trees. Dragatu half-jumped, half-fell, and caught his balance as he landed. Once still, he watched the wolf lay there. Its breathing slow and laboured.

He staggered to the front and stared into its eyes. It snarled with what little energy it had left. Dragatu stood watching it defiantly. The last snarl turned to a pup-like whimper, and for a brief moment Dragatu almost felt sorry for it, but all sympathy was quelled with the maelstrom that rose inside. Hate, blood lust, satisfaction and thoughts of finality consuming him. Ignoring the whimpers, he wiped his blade clean and walked forward, keeping eye contact. The wolf was silent now, but its eyes watched Dragatu. The top of the wolf's head was almost at Dragatu's waist and his next movement was one continuous motion of opposites. He rose to his full height, the blade moving up with him, raised high above his head, and then he came down with his full strength,

'CRACK!'

The knife pierced and split the skull. After holding it there for a few seconds, Dragatu yanked the blade out, took a step back, dropped it and fell to his knees. The wolf was dead. It was done. It was over. The hunt was finished. He was victorious and he did something he hadn't done for some time, he wept. He wept for his father, for closure, and for his victory.

A noise interrupted this rare release of emotion. Wiping away the tears, he looked over to where Freta lay. She was stirring and began to groan. Wiping his face again, Dragatu got up from his knees and ran over to her.

"Are you okay?" he asked.

Sitting up slowly, she went to speak but coughed, covering her mouth with her hands. As she removed them she saw blood and leaned a little to the side and spat. She ran her tongue along the inside of her mouth and felt a stinging cut.

"Not great," she winced. "I see the wolf's dead," she added with a weak smile, struggling to breathe with all the pain she felt.

"Yes, I . . . err . . . we killed it," he replied.

"It didn't die without leaving us with some bad wounds," she said. "Your face looks awful."

Dragatu put his hand to it, feeling mostly viscous blood and hot swollen skin.

"Is it really bad?" he asked.

"It will need a good clean . . ." she coughed, wincing and holding her ribs. Taking a slow breath she continued. "We can stitch it up, which will hurt, but it will heal leaving a noticeable scar."

"Wonderful," he said sarcastically. "You need a hand up?" he said, offering both of his. Taking them Freta stood up very slowly.

"Thanks," she said weakly.

"What hurts the most?" Dragatu asked.

"It's my ribs. I think the blow has bruised or cracked them."

She lifted her top and Dragatu winced at the swollen skin, it looked like it had been painted with the purple-black ontaberry.

"Yep, badly bruised, if not worse," Freta concluded, continuing to wince, "It's going to take some time to heal . . . and getting home is going to be a very long journey."

Dragatu decided to distract her from the pain. "You fought well. I've rarely seen that sort of bravery from anyone, even seasoned hunters."

"You sound surprised," she said, laughing a little, but stopping herself with a grimace.

112

"I am surprised. I haven't met anyone like you. Well, any girl like you," he said.

"Well, now you have, so count yourself lucky because, without me, you would have died," she said, the corner of her mouth rising.

Dragatu went to argue, still believing he could have done it by himself, but he saw the smile.

"I guess," he said. "Your blow to its neck did allow me to get up on its back."

"All part of the hunt," she said confidently, "You have to win, so the risk is worth it, and it paid off, didn't it? Anyway, we better get our packs and use some water to clean your face."

Dragatu agreed, but had one final thing to do before they left the wolf. He walked over to it and opened its jaws, taking his knife he cut out the two canine teeth as evidence and as a memento. Standing up he bowed his head in a final farewell, a mix of emotions pulsing through him. Turning his back to the wolf, he went to his pack and wrapped the teeth in a clean piece of cloth, putting them at the bottom of the pack.

They found a small stream and drank what they needed, carefully washing their wounds with the remainder. Dragatu's face took the longest and Freta helped clear away the blood and mud, then stitched it up as best she could, applying a thick green paste of crushed gealor herbs to help fight infection. When it was finished they sat under a tree to rest.

"We're going to have to clean that a lot and apply the gealor paste three times a day," she said as they sat.

"Three times? But it smells so bad."

"Well, it's better than it becoming infected. Not much I can do if that happens. The smell of your corpse would be a lot worse," she said, half joking, half serious.

"Good point. Anyway, I'm a quick healer so we won't have to apply it for long. The scar's going to be big, isn't it? I can feel the wound now, running from the top of my head, right over my eye to my jaw." He traced the marks with his finger, making sure he didn't touch them.

"Yep. They're going to be pretty noticeable. It reminds me of the scar the wolf had," she reflected.

"It's a fair trade to have the wolf dead," he replied simply. "Having one similar will remind me of what we did, and what my father did. I'll wear the scar with pride."

With this statement, he decided to tell her what had happened that night with the wolf when he was thirteen. He was surprised how easy it was to talk to her about it.

"I think you should get some sleep," Dragatu said, when he had finished the story, noticing how tired Freta looked. Agreeing, she took out a pelt from her pack and wrapped herself in it.

Dragatu listened to her heavy breathing for a short time. However, his face stung and throbbed too much, so he repeated the fight with the wolf over and over again to distract himself. It worked for a while, but the pain was too much, so he closed his eyes and breathed deeply trying to grow accustomed to it. As he did he couldn't help thinking of his father, his family, the goals in his journal, and, with pleasant surprise, of Freta. Lost in his pain and his thoughts, night finally came, and an hour after nightfall Freta woke.

"You should get some rest now," she said as she sat up and clutched her ribs, her face tensing.

He wanted to argue, but accepted it was the best thing and let himself sleep. When he woke the first thing he noticed was that his face stung even more than before and he let out a small groan. He slowly moved his face muscles and felt the scabs crack and strain. The pain was intense and he could feel some blood run from the wounds. He sat up and let the air dry the small beads of blood. As he did he noticed the smell of food and realised how hungry he was.

"Sorry. I didn't mean to wake you," Freta said when she saw him looking in her direction.

"You didn't wake me. I'm so hungry I think I could sense there was some food." He laughed.

He crawled over and sat next to her by the fire, waiting for the meat and roots she had collected to cook. They ate in silence, enjoying every bite of their meal even though it hurt their wounds. When they finished they talked about their lives and found they were similar in many ways, including the loss of a parent: Freta's mother had died from a persistent influenza two years before. It was late when Freta finally said she should get some more rest and Dragatu said he would keep watch.

18/2/698

Dragatu opened his eyes and groaned as the sunlight dazzled him, blinking fast his eyes finally adjusted to the light and he looked around to make sure everything was okay. Freta still slept and he watched her for a few minutes, thinking about her uniqueness and sharp tongue, her humour and seriousness, her aloofness and her care of him. Realising he should return the favour he started the fire and cooked breakfast, selecting some joben nuts and picking some red rew berries. When it was ready he woke her gently.

"We should start making our way back," she said as they ate.

"I agree."

They then began the long journey home. After a few days, Dragatu found time in the evening to write in his journal. He gave a detailed record of meeting Freta and killing the wolf, taking satisfaction in each word and tear that flowed.

11/3/698

The journey was slow and painful, but they rested and ate as needed. Wounds healed, and it slowly became easier to cross the desert. To pass the time they invented little games, both of them enjoying the competition that came from trying to better the other.

"I would like to get home as quick as possible so I can see my father," Freta said one day. "I'll need to head east soon. I guess we'll have to say goodbye, but I hope we can meet again. You know I live by the ore pits, so come visit sometime."

"I don't think I can leave you until you get home," Dragatu said. "With all the trouble I've seen you get yourself into I can't be sure you won't attract more danger." He smiled.

"I think I can handle myself." She grinned back. "And I think you're the one who attracts trouble."

Dragatu's face dropped a bit, it wasn't the answer he had hoped for. Freta noticed it and smiled inside, continuing, "Well . . . if you feel you have to get me home safe then I guess you can come with me, if you wish?"

Dragatu gave a split second smile, "Well, I wouldn't want you to think me rude by not making sure you arrived home safely."

They both laughed lightly. As they journeyed east towards the ore pits they rationed their water and food meticulously.

23/3/698

"What have you done to my daughter?"

The angry man shouting at Dragatu had a greying beard, broad chest and stomach that bulged with un-toned muscle. His arms were even bigger than Dragatu's, and he was taller, too. Dragatu hesitated as the anger from Freta's father poured over him. For Freta's sake, he controlled his own defensive nature. Her father had seen the faded yellow bruises on her arms, and a few on her face, and he had exploded.

Standing outside the dome clay house Dragatu was trying to decide what to say back. Suddenly her father surged forward like a statue of stone come alive, and grabbed Dragatu by the throat with one large calloused hand. Out of respect for the older man Dragatu didn't fight back and simply pulled on Jolonus' wrist with both his hands so he could breathe.

Freta screamed.

"Let him go! What are you doing?"

Dragatu was released and rubbed his throat. He went to speak, but Freta's father cut him off.

"What happened to you?" The anger was clear in his voice.

As quickly as she could Freta explained the story, Dragatu nodding to confirm her words. When she got to the wolf and how Dragatu had told her to go home, but she hadn't, her father despaired and threw his hands in the air.

"Why do you feel it necessary to put yourself in such danger? Do you have no concern for my feelings? How do you think I would feel if I lost you, as well?"

"I couldn't leave him to get killed," she replied sharply.

Dragatu sniffed with disapproval but said nothing. She continued the story. By the time she finished, her father had calmed a little and spoke to Dragatu.

"Thank you for making sure Freta got home safe. However, you cannot come back here and you certainly can't see her again. It's already hard enough looking after her without someone like you, who seems to go looking for danger, encouraging her."

"You can't be serious?" Dragatu protested and at the same time Freta said. "Oh, don't be silly Father. He's proved himself responsible by helping me get home safely."

"Yes, but he went looking for the wolf," her father replied. "He should have taken you south and ran away knowing what it was. I cannot trust him and that is final."

Dragatu's anger was about to explode, but Freta saw it and put a hand on his chest.

"It's okay Dragatu, do as he says. I will see you soon," she added in a whisper. She quickly withdrew her hand and stood behind her father.

"Fine!" Dragatu said, looking her father straight in the eyes. Raising his head, he looked behind at Freta, gave her a half smile and began the walk home, passing the other clay houses that covered the area like large, upside down bowls with holes for windows.

As he walked he touched his scar every so often, as much out of habit, as to see how much it had healed. It had sealed over and the scabs were starting to peel, revealing fresh pink skin. Thoughts of Freta consumed him and he hoped she would keep her promise. To his dismay, however, he realised she didn't even know where he lived and his heart sank. He would have to find a way to see her without Jolonus finding out, but he didn't know how. As he got closer to his home people stared and pointed at the scar-lines on his face. Some came and asked him what had happened, but he gently dismissed their concern and intrigue, they would find out soon enough.

Eventually, he arrived home and opened the door. Healana was walking from the living room to the kitchen at the same time and turned to look as the door opened. When she saw him she burst into tears. He had been gone longer than normal and Dragatu was about to speak, but she stepped forward and hugged him tightly, tears dampening his shoulder.

"Where have you been? What happened to you?" she sobbed looking at the scar.

"The wolf is dead," he said simply.

She looked at him with surprise, anger and relief on her face.

"Why? Why would you risk yourself like that?" she stuttered and chastised.

"I did it for you and for our family," he said. "I did it to get revenge for having Father taken from us."

"Oh, Dragatu," she said with love and pain. "You didn't have to do that. You should not have risked yourself like that."

Dragatu was confused, 'Why isn't she overjoyed with what I've done?'

"I did it to get peace," he said, trying to get her to understand. "And it proves that I'm strong. I did it to make you proud."

"Son," she began, but then she stopped. Taking a few moments to wipe her tears, she continued, changing what she was going to say. "I'm just glad you're back. You don't need to prove yourself. You've already done this so many times, and I hope you know I am so proud of you."

"Thanks," he replied. "I have to be strong, though. It's what Father would have wanted. How else can I gain people's respect?"

"They already respect you. The water project proved that. Out of all the people here you were the one who led them. You led the Hunora. You're doing so much for someone so young. Please don't be so hard on yourself."

"Well, now they will never doubt it," he said. Crouching, he reached inside his pack and took out the canine teeth, showing them to her. "And here's the proof if anyone doubts it."

She gasped as she looked at the large teeth. Dragatu gave them to her and she handled them with trepidation. Knowing what they had done she quickly gave them back to him and began to cry. Dragatu didn't know what to say and crouched to put them back in his pack. As he stood up, Healana tried to control her breathing and hugged him again, whispering, "I love you Son."

"I love you too, Mother," he said as she let him go, and feeling tired he turned and walked up the stairs to his room. After emptying his pack, he took his journal and wrote his latest update in the library.

7/4/698

Finally, Dragatu's wounds healed fully and an angry three-lined scar graced the right side of his face. He spent the following two weeks telling the story to Honrus, Reon, Linur, his other friends, and all the people who came to hear it. They asked about Freta and he told them he was sure he would see her again, he just didn't know how. The story about his killing of the wolf spread to most of the Nation and he turned one of the wolf's teeth into a necklace, a worthy trophy of his victory. He kept the other in his room.

8/4/698

Dragatu's desire to see Freta had reached boiling point and he couldn't wait any longer. He decided to go to the ore pits, but didn't dare venture too close to where she lived. This way he could pretend he was there to dig, but surreptitiously look for her. Hopefully, he would find her without her father knowing and together they could make plans to see each other secretly. At the ore pit, he began digging and kept a look out for her, but he noticed people tutting in his direction and frowning as they passed him.

"Why are you tutting at me?" Dragatu asked them in annoyance.

"We know you shouldn't be here," one person replied. "Trying to see Freta, are you?" another called.

Dragatu was shocked that they knew why he was there. 'How could they know?' he wondered.

One man saw his confusion and took pity on him. "Jolonus is well known around here. He asked us to keep an eye out for you and to remind you not to go visiting Freta. I suggest you either leave, or don't go further east. People will not be happy to see you if you do."

Dragatu was disappointed, getting angry at the stupidity of it. All he wanted to do was spend time with his friend. 'Why were they being so unreasonable?'

After another day of being there, he decided to give up. Trudging home he tried to formulate a new plan and thought about sending one of his friends, or even Phoenon, to get a message to Freta, but he needn't have worried, Freta kept her promise.

Chapter 11
Measuring Up To Expectation

14/4/698

Rata-tat-tat went the door. Healana came from the library to greet the visitor.

"Hello," she said, unable to contain her surprise. A knowing smile crept across her face as she recognised the blonde ponytail and athletic figure. "Freta, isn't it?"

"Yes . . . I'm Freta," she replied with equal surprise.

"Dragatu has mentioned you," Healana said.

"Is he in?"

"I'll check. You can wait in the library if you want?"

Freta beamed at the mention of the library.

"I take it you like stories, scrolls and books?" Healana asked as she stepped to the side and ushered Freta into the house.

"Yes. My mother taught me to read and we have a few scrolls, and I've borrowed books from people who have them, but I don't have any of my own."

"Well, feel free to borrow some of ours, if you want."

"Really?" Freta exclaimed excitedly. "That's very kind of you, thank you."

They reached the library and Freta gasped at all the scrolls, and especially at the books on the far right of the room.

"I'll be right back," Healana said smiling at Freta's open mouth and wide-eyed expression as she went to find Dragatu.

Freta went straight to the books and managed to find one of her favourite stories. Dragatu arrived as she'd started to read.

"Hi," he began, his hand twitching a little as he tried to mask how happy he was to see her.

"I told you I would see you again," she said smiling proudly.

"I take it your Father doesn't know you're here?"

"Nope, he thinks I'm going hunting in the forests."

"So you lied to him then?" Dragatu said, not worrying so much about the lie, but what Freta's father would do if he found out where she was.

"Well, no actually, I didn't lie," Freta replied. "I'm going to go to the forests, and you're going to come too." She grinned.

"What makes you think I'm coming too?" he said casually, still trying to mask his enthusiasm.

"I know you came to see me at the ore pits," Freta said.

Dragatu's hand twitched, and his brow creased.

"One of the people told Father," Freta explained, "So I know you wanted to see me," she said playfully. "Let me tell you, he wasn't happy."

"I just wanted to make sure you were okay," he replied as coolly as he could.

"Well, as you can see, I'm better." She patted her ribs hard like a drum. "So, are you going to come?"

Dragatu rubbed the stubble on his chin. "I suppose it will be fun to go hunting, and the company wouldn't be *too* bad." He smiled.

"The company will be great, and don't you forget it."

"I'll get my hunting gear," Dragatu replied chuckling.

"Do you think your mother would mind if I borrowed this?" she said, glancing at the book.

"I'm sure it would be fine." He smiled. Then noticed the book's cover, and his face dropped, he hated romance stories.

"Thanks," she said looking at the book and smiling, oblivious to his look of disgust.

Once Dragatu was ready they said goodbye to Healana and set off in the direction of the forests, trying to avoid being noticed by people, in case any of them knew her father. It was unlikely, but they tried to be cautious. The conversation flowed as it had before, and Dragatu asked about her friends.

"I don't really have many," she said with difficulty. "I go hunting a lot, and have to work with my father when I'm not hunting. I don't really have much time to make friends. I used to have loads, but as we grew older it was clear I didn't fit in. I think it's because I can be a bit forward and I didn't like the same things. In the end, I just stopped spending time with them."

"I think I know what you mean," Dragatu said. "I'm lucky with the people I know in my neighbourhood and I have a lot of friends, but they do just follow my lead a lot. I sometimes wish I could find someone that didn't act that way, someone that was more like me. You know what I mean?"

"Yeah, I do." She smiled at him softly. "Have you ever had a girlfriend Dragatu?" she asked, catching him by surprise.

"Err no . . . no I haven't." He paused, taking a breath and decided to be honest. "I guess I've just not found anyone I wanted to have as a girlfriend," he said, feeling a bit embarrassed. "Have you ever had a boyfriend?"

She hesitated and looked at the floor, then took a deep breath. "Yes, one, but I'd rather not talk about it, if that's okay?"

Dragatu wondered why she had asked him, and why suddenly she didn't want to talk about it. He could see the pain in her face, and hear it in her words, so decided it was best to change the subject.

"So what do you think your father will do to us if he finds out we're spending time together?"

"Us?" she laughed, obviously grateful for the change. "It's you who should worry, he still sees me as his little girl."

"Oh great. Thanks for that." He laughed as confidently as he could, but the thought of facing Jolonus worried him a little.

The rest of the walk was spent talking or walking peacefully, the silence easy and comfortable. When they reached the forests they organised their gear for hunting.

"I think I've a way to solve our problem with my father," Freta said, stringing her bow.

"Really? That's a relief, because I'm struggling for ideas," Dragatu admitted. "What's your plan?"

Freta continued to kneel for a few more seconds while she finished stringing her bow, then began to explain as she put it to the side and stood up. "I think I've come up with a way that you can gain his respect. Gaining his respect will make him see you're a good person and someone who looks out for other people. My father has very negative feelings towards the richer people you see, which was how I felt when we first met, but his feelings are worse. He says the rich people are lazy." Dragatu's face tightened, but he refrained from retorting. "I know it's not what the Book of Law teaches, but he finds it difficult not to be angry. If you prove him wrong he'll have to accept you're as good as I know you are. Then he'll respect you and let us see each other . . . I hope."

"How do I prove it to him?" he asked. "You know I already do a lot. How's that not proof enough?"

She paused and shrugged her shoulders. "I don't know yet," she said gingerly. "He also thinks people in the rich areas do things to make themselves feel better for having more than others. He says they do it so they can push aside the guilt they have for not helping those who are poorer to be equals." Dragatu snorted at the accusation, but once again let her continue. "I guess you could show him it's not true," she said, as she formed a more solid plan. "You could go to the ore pits, close to where I live, and mine a lot, then do as you have in the western parts and give it to the people. If you kept doing it he'd hear about it. He'll see that you don't care for it and that you're simply there to help people. If you stay for a long time he'll see how hard working and generous you are."

"How long do you think it would take?" Dragatu asked.

She hesitated. "I'm not sure."

Dragatu sighed but made up his mind. "It sounds like this could work. I'll stay there as long as it takes. If it works we'll get to be friends and see each other whenever we want. The work will be worth it."

She smiled and he smiled back, but suddenly she turned and crouched back to her pack that lay by her bow, hiding her blush. Once it passed she picked up the bow and quiver ready for their hunting.

"Well, I guess we can sort out our plan after hunting," she said and Dragatu agreed as he bent and lifted his pack.

In between hunts, they played games. It was a fun few days, but eventually they had enough meat, so reluctantly made their way home, discussing the ore-mining plan on the way.

Once they reached Dragatu's house they said goodbye to each other. Freta wished him success at the ore pits, knowing it would be too risky for her to visit him. He was annoyed to see her go but focused on the task ahead, hoping when it was over he would be able to see her without worrying about Jolonus' disapproval and threats.

21/4/698

Chink, chink, chink. Thud, thud, thud.

Dragatu woke to the repetitive sounds. He saw that even though it was early the miners had already begun their day's work. Once he had eaten breakfast he took out his spade and pickaxe and began digging. Only a short time passed before someone came up to him.

"What are you doing here?" the man asked.

"I've come to mine," Dragatu replied. "I want to give what I find to you and the people here in your neighbourhood. I'll probably be here for some time. My name's Dragatu," he said, waiting for a polite reply and to learn this man's name, but neither came.

"Typical." The man sneered instead. "You do realise you can't mine here?" He saw the confusion on Dragatu's face so impatiently explained. "This is someone else's place to mine."

More people had appeared now and were watching the situation develop.

"I can dig where I want," Dragatu said defensively.

'Such arrogance and ignorance,' the man thought. Then replied in a condescending manner, "You'll have to go north and find a new place to dig. This area belongs to someone else," he repeated.

Dragatu was confused. "I've never been told this before. I always dig where I want."

The man laughed and shook his head. Dragatu was losing his patience. He knew Jolonus would hear about this, however, so he held back his frustration.

The man stopped laughing. "I'm sure people have let you do what you wanted in the past because you were with your friends. No one wants to create trouble, but as you're by yourself it's time you knew the truth. You'll have to find your own place to dig."

"Someone should have told me this from the start," Dragatu protested. "I don't see what the problem is anyway. I've always given most of what I find to other people. You should be glad I come here."

The man laughed again, and a few of the onlookers laughed, as well. Dragatu had almost reached his limit. "Why do you laugh at someone who tries to help you?" he almost shouted.

"Help us!" the man sneered. "Don't lie to yourself. You only come here to make yourself feel better."

The words reminded Dragatu of what Freta had said about Jolonus feeling this way. He saw now that it was more common than he had thought. Struggling, he realised he had to be careful about what he did next, or Freta's plan could be ruined.

"If you want to help go home and stop patronizing us," the man continued.

With great effort, Dragatu swallowed his pride and said, "I will go north then."

The people were surprised to see him go, but after the initial shock they mocked him with sarcastic, "good lucks", and smirks. Dragatu didn't understand why they behaved that way, but when he got further north he understood. The soil there was dry and hard. There wasn't a person for about a mile in all directions and he knew this was going to be harder than he'd originally thought. Digging and mining was going to take three times as much effort here as it would have been back where he had come from.

Sighing, he set up camp and decided there was no time like the present. He set out three separate square areas that would be his digging pits, and he began to remove the top layers of dry earth. He hoped if he dug down he would find clay, and that there were some big rocks around that he could break with his pickaxe and perhaps find some precious stones. He wasn't optimistic about his plans, but he had to try.

27/4/698

The first pit was dug about a metre down and Dragatu ached from the effort it took. He hoped that another metre would produce some moist soil. Once he found some clay he would spend a day carrying it to the people in the sacks he had brought and they would have to accept they were wrong about him. However, his plans were shattered, after digging for another two days he only found moist soil in the pit and no clay, whatsoever. He took advantage of the moisture though, and dug a little deeper, making a small well.

Another three days of backbreaking work had passed before Dragatu decided it was time for a rest. He walked to the wells and enjoyed the quality and quantity of water. As he walked passed the people they laughed, jeered and pointed at him. He was covered in mud and dirt, but Dragatu ignored them and went right up to a well, drew a bucketful and tipped it over himself. As well as to clean and refresh himself he did it as an act of defiance, and an attempt to remind them that the abundance of water here was actually a consequence of his and Unilus' work on the project. He drenched himself a couple of times and once he felt refreshed he held his head high and walked back to his camp. They didn't snigger at him this time, and they began to wonder why he was going back when he could easily go home.

As the camp came into sight Dragatu saw someone sitting there. As he neared he saw it was Freta, and dropped his head, grinning with gratitude for the pleasant surprise. When he was close enough he called out to her.

"I thought you were staying away while I was here?"

"Well, that was so people didn't see me. When I heard you had gone up here by yourself I decided it wouldn't be a risk. So here I am."

"Always the rule breaker." Dragatu chuckled.

"Hardly," she replied. "How's the work going?"

"Easy." He smiled.

"It looks it." She laughed.

"I've shown the people that I'm not leaving and am not going to quit. Now I just need to find something to take to them."

"I'm sure you'll find something soon. I would help but if I get dirty father will suspect something, I'm sure he knows you're here by now."

"Well, if he knows I'm here working hard then that's a good start . . . I hope . . . and eventually we'll show him I'm not the bad person he thinks I am."

The conversation continued, and when it was time for Freta to leave Dragatu asked her to come back in a few days.

5/5/698

Freta did visit a couple of times and it helped Dragatu to stay motivated. He finished the second pit and to his relief there was some clay at the bottom. He took it to the wells as he had planned, and left it there for anyone who wanted it. No one mocked him. He could sense that they were finally seeing there was more to him than they had originally thought, and he smiled to himself when he left.

After this he rested for a day, but then started work on the big rocks, chipping away at them with his pickaxe. To his surprise and joy he found little red stones at the bottom of these rocks, and once they were polished they looked beautiful. He decided to keep breaking the rocks, hoping to find more. The stones were curious. Green inuade and blue huetire gems were known, and there were also the deep yellow rocks that served as ornaments, but these vibrant red stones were new. Dragatu knew the rich people would love them and he began to wonder if these stones were the key to gaining Jolonus' respect.

He continued to collect them and decided to give them to the people he had met when he had first arrived. They could then give them to all the people in the ore pits and they could use them to trade with the rich people for things they needed or wanted. In time, Jolonus would hear about it and see he was willing to give up such a thing to help people. Dragatu decided to keep the largest stone and give it to Jolonus as a gift, to show him he valued the opportunity to see Freta that much. 'Surely then he will accept me and let us see each other?'

With this thought, Dragatu filled his pack with the red stones. The day before he was going to give them away Freta came to visit. She agreed his plan was the best thing to do and was hypnotised by how beautiful the stones were. She held one up to the sun and it glimmered in the light like a glass rosa petal. It was tempting to tell Dragatu to keep them all, but she accepted this wouldn't be right so kept her thoughts to herself. They agreed on the plan and began fantasizing about all the different adventures they could go on once it had worked. By which time night approached and she had to leave.

6/5/698

"And what is that?"

Dragatu sat with his back to the well, throwing a pebble-sized red stone up and down in the air, looking very smug with himself.

The people hadn't noticed at first, trying to ignore him, but as they saw the sun reflecting off the strange stone and came to investigate. They walked closer, pretending they weren't trying to see it, but they couldn't help being mesmerised by its deep, majestic colour. Finally, a man came forward to ask about the stone. Dragatu ignored him at first, so the man repeated himself.

"What is that you have there?"

Dragatu took his time but then looked up at him. "What? This?" he said, as if it were merely a common stone. He held it up to the sun, between his finger and thumb, and it shined in all its glory. "Oh, it's just something I found when mining rocks." He couldn't help playing a little game. "You want to see it?" he asked, becoming more serious.

The man nodded with covetous eyes.

Dragatu said nothing and casually threw it from where he sat, throwing it under arm in a high arch. The man caught it and studied it, letting out sounds of amazement and awe as he rotated it on his palm and then held it up to the light. As he did, Dragatu took the opportunity to implement the pivotal point in the plan.

"There are quite a lot more," he said.

The man looked down at him, eyes wide as Dragatu opened his pack, showing all the stones he had found. The man's jaw dropped, and people walking by gasped, jealousy clear in the eyes and faces of all those who saw.

Coming to his senses the man reluctantly went to give the stone back to Dragatu.

"I don't need it," Dragatu said holding up his hand as the man went to toss it back to him, "You can keep it."

The man was shocked. He didn't know what to say and stood there with his arm half stretched out mid-throw.

Dragatu repeated himself.

"Take it. I want you to have it," he said firmly.

"Why are you giving it to me?" the man asked as his surprise faded.

"I have my reasons," he said. "You see all these stones," he continued, looking at the bag. "I want you to give one to everyone who lives here. The stones can be used for trade and to help the people here. If anyone asks where they came from I want you to say it came from a new piece of land that I own. Lastly, I have a request. You are not to give one to Jolonus, who lives east of here, about a mile or two away. Do you know who I mean?"

The man nodded.

"Good. Do you promise to do as I've asked?"

The man nodded again, shock returning, as Dragatu had just given away a fortune to complete strangers, moreover to people who had shown him no kindness.

"Yes . . . Yes, I promise I will," the man managed to stutter.

"Thank you," Dragatu replied as he stood up with the bag, gave it to the man, and simply walked away. He saw the people run to the man to get the full story of what had happened, and he heard the shouts of amazement and gratitude. At that moment, Dragatu knew the plan was one step closer to working.

Chapter 12
Someone

_10/5/698_

Four days went by. Dragatu was about to give up, find Freta, and learn what was going on when finally he saw Jolonus stomp towards him like an angry child.

"What's your game lad?" he said sternly, cheeks red and breathing heavily.

"No game sir," Dragatu said as he sat on the dry mud piled up as a makeshift chair.

"Yes there is," Jolonus insisted. "Why does everyone get one of those stones you found except me? Is this some sort of petty punishment for not letting you see Freta? Or did you think you could bribe me to let you see her?"

"I just wanted to talk to you. I guessed you would come and talk if I did what I did, and I guessed right. It seemed the only way to get your attention. I knew you wouldn't talk to me if I came to see you. You would think I was coming to see Freta."

Jolonus took a few moments before replying,

"Well. Talk."

Dragatu quickly recited the speech he had prepared in the days he waited.

"What's the most important thing to you sir?" he began.

"Freta," Jolonus said.

"And what comes next?"

"Doing what the Book of Law says."

'Good,' Dragatu thought. Freta had said that the only book her father had read was the Book of Law and it was what her mother had used to teach her to read.

"What does the Book of Law say about helping people?" Dragatu continued.

"We are always to help others if and when we can," Jolonus replied. "Where are you going with this lad?"

Dragatu bowed his head looking at the floor, and then continued.

"I need your help."

"What could I possibly do to help you?" Jolonus said the hotness fading slightly.

Dragatu paused for effect. "I want to be able to see your daughter and be her friend. I'll do anything to make this happen, and prove to you that I'm a good person. I've spent the last few weeks here all for this purpose. I've dug more than any person would, on ground that is three times harder to dig on, all so I could give what I've found to the people. I've done this so you would hear about it and see I'm willing to work hard to do good for people. It was difficult to mine here. I could have given up, but I didn't. I'm not the self-centred person you assumed and I want to gain your respect so you'll let Freta and I have a friendship." When he finished he was breathless.

"Haaah! Haaah! Haaaaaah!" Freta's father laughed deeply, his hand on his hips.

Dragatu flexed both his hands in frustration but waited.

"You did all this to prove to me you were good?" Jolonus said as his laughter faded.

"Yes sir," Dragatu replied, his frustration fading. "And so I could gain your respect. I hoped you would let me see your daughter. She makes me happy and I know I make her happy."

Jolonus didn't say anything for a few moments, his face unreadable, but finally a light smile appeared on his face.

"I must confess she has been happier since coming back from the hills with you." His face suddenly screwed up a little, becoming stern again. "You're still seeing each other, aren't you?"

Dragatu winced hesitantly wondering if he should lie.

"Come on boy, spit it out."

"Yes . . . we've seen each other since you told us not to," Dragatu confessed.

"That girl," Jolonus muttered under his breath, dropping his hands from his side. "She never was one for doing what she was told," he said louder, a wide smile suddenly creeping across his face. "Because of what you've done, and all the energy you've put into trying to prove yourself, as well as giving away such a large amount of wealth, I'll let you and Freta see each other. Not that I've been able to stop you," he said, giving Dragatu a disapproving look.

"Sorry," Dragatu said guiltily, but couldn't help giving a small smile as he hung his head.

"If you do anything to hurt her I will personally see to it that your life won't be worth living. Do I make myself clear?" Jolonus said.

The smile faded and Dragatu looked up. "Yes sir. Thank you sir. I've something to give you," he added and pulled out the biggest red stone.

It was the size of Dragatu's fist, and he offered it to Jolonus, who took a step back shaking his head.

"So, all along you were going to bribe me?" his said loudly, his cheeks going red with anger.

"No, No!" Dragatu said quickly, panicking, "That was never my intention. I was going to give this to you no matter what the outcome. I promise with the highest oath of honesty that I'm telling the truth," he said desperately.

Jolonus looked Dragatu up and down, trying to assess the statement.

"You would have given me the stone, no matter what I had said. Even if I had told you still couldn't see Freta?" A hint of disbelief darkened his voice.

Dragatu nodded looking him in the eye.

"Well, I certainly misjudged you," he replied eventually. "It appears you're a boy, no, a man of much honour." He held out his hand. Dragatu stood up and gave him the stone and Jolonus continued. "I hope you know I only acted the way I did because I love Freta and am so protective of her."

"I understand. She's a great girl," Dragatu replied.

Jolonus smiled, nodding. He offered the stone back to Dragatu, who refused.

"I insist you take it back," Jolonus said, "I don't need it and would feel better if, for all your work, you got something as payment."

Dragatu could see he wasn't going to convince him to take it. "Thank you, sir."

Jolonus just nodded, turned and walked away. As he did, Freta appeared from behind a rock, ran up to him, hugged him, and whispered lovingly in his ear.

"Thank you, Father."

He chuckled and laughed at his daughter.

"There's just no winning with you, is there?"

"Nope." She laughed.

He sighed. "Go on then, you two have fun." He watched Freta walk over to Dragatu, and as he walked he laughed to himself, knowing that for all their efforts to be 'friends', there was more to this, and his desire for Dragatu to prove himself trustworthy and loyal had been satisfied.

"Now that was easy." Freta laughed after she hugged him.

Dragatu laughed and shook his head, "For you maybe."

He watched fondly as Freta walked around the camp tidying, he was so glad to have her as a friend. As he did he felt something he had never felt before, but quickly ignored it, it scared him. He re-focused on filling the pit, not giving it a second thought.

Once they had finished they decided to go to Dragatu's house, as Freta wanted to meet his family. Dragatu protested at first, worrying his brothers might seem odd to her, but she insisted.

"I'm so glad you're home," Healana said when she saw them in the kitchen. She thought about hugging him, but with Freta there she just smiled, knowing he would feel embarrassed. Instead, she asked what they had been doing. Freta told her the story of Jolonus' disapproval and their plan to gain his respect and acceptance. Once the story was over Healana could see the way Dragatu looked at Freta and was full of joy. At long last, Dragatu had found someone he considered a true friend, and more importantly, someone he was allowing to see behind the walls he normally put up. Leaving the kitchen Dragatu gave Freta a full tour of the house and they ended it in the library.

"I'll remember to bring the book I borrowed next time I come," Freta said.

"It's okay. I think it'll be fine if you keep it. Call it a gift," Dragatu replied.

"I'll bring it back."

"Honestly it is fine. Keep it."

She grinned and hugged him. "Thank you," she whispered.

As she hugged him the new feelings returned and they were stronger. Trying to ignore them again, he stammered, "Would . . . you like to stay for dinner?"

"I would like that." Freta smiled as she stepped back from her hug. "But afterwards I'll have to go home. I don't want Father thinking I've abandoned him."

During dinner Dragatu noticed Phoenon smiling knowingly at him, and wondered why he was doing this. Dinner ended and Freta thanked them. As she left Dragatu walked her to the door, and offered to walk her home.

"I'll be fine," she said. "It'll be good to have some time to myself. You understand?"

Even though Dragatu wanted to go with her, he did understand and accepted her wishes and nodded.

"Goodbye, Dragatu." She smiled softly.

"See you soon," he replied.

As she walked away Dragatu watched her, picturing her smile in his mind, and for the third time that day the new feelings fluttered deep inside. It made him feel happy, but also incredible vulnerable and the latter was hard to digest. Once she had turned behind a house, and was out of sight, he realised what these feelings were, they complicated everything. Closing the door, he went up to his room and lay on his bed to think.

He thought about how she hadn't wanted to talk about her previous relationship.

'Maybe she doesn't want a relationship at the moment? Would she even feel the same way? What if I told her and she didn't want to be friends with me anymore?'

He felt powerless. There were so many outcomes that were unknown, and for one of those rare moments in his life he didn't know what to do. His mind swallowed itself in all these thoughts. Dragatu was stuck. What should he do and what would be the right choice? He kept debating if he should tell her, but all the doubt in his mind stopped him from making a choice. It was as though every time he made a choice doubt came and made him second guess himself, almost like doubt was an expert hunter waiting until he made a choice, and then pounced at his mind to force him to change that choice. After an hour of lying on his bed in this way, Unilus and Phoenon entered.

"Are you okay Dragatu?" Phoenon asked after a few minutes, noticing he was in a somber mood.

Dragatu thought for a second. Although he hated it, he decided this was something they actually might be able to help him with.

"It's no big deal, but I suppose you could help," he said casually, trying not to show how much he actually needed them, "I'm just thinking about Freta. I think she only sees me as a friend, but today I realised I see her as more than that." It was hard to say, but once he had he was surprised to feel less burdened.

Phoenon grinned and let out a quick laugh. Even Unilus smiled.

Dragatu hadn't expected these reactions and sat up, swung his legs to sit on the edge of the bed, and glared at them.

"What's so funny?" he demanded.

Phoenon struggled to contain his laughter. "You only just figured out today that you like her that way?"

"Well . . . yeah," Dragatu said, slightly angry, but mostly confused by Phoenon's words.

"We knew from the moment we saw you two together." Phoenon grinned. "Isn't that right Unilus?"

Unilus nodded. Dragatu sighed with despair. It was bad enough that Phoenon could tell, but if Unilus could tell then it was likely Freta knew too. Dragatu hung his heads into his hands groaning. Then a thought occurred to him and he looked up.

"How'd you know before I did?"

"I guess I'm just good at observing how people feel," Phoenon said. "It was your body language and the way you were relaxed around her. You smiled more than I think I've seen you smile in your whole life. It was just obvious," he said.

"Fine," Dragatu said, not really sure what Phoenon meant and too much was going on in his mind to ask about it. Then he had what he thought was a genius idea.

"So . . . can you tell if she likes me in return?"

There was a pause of hesitation from Phoenon.

Dragatu became impatient, "Well?"

"She's more complicated to read because I've only known her for a little while and I don't know her usual behaviour," Phoenon said. "But from what I could see there's a strong chance she feels the same way."

Dragatu finally smiled, but Phoenon hadn't been sure . . . was taking a risk on his brother's words a wise choice? He continued his questions.

"Do you think she knows I like her?"

"Probably not," Phoenon answered. "If she does like you in the same way then she's probably asking herself all the same questions you are, and not seeing beyond her own feelings."

"How do you know these kinds of things?" Dragatu asked.

"I don't know, I just seem to understand people," Phoenon replied again.

There was silence for almost a minute as Dragatu reflected on Phoenon's words. Unilus lay on his bed, drawing as he listened. When no more questions came, Phoenon shrugged his shoulders and lay back on his own, smiling as he shut his eyes. Dragatu continued to sit on the edge of his bed thinking. Were Phoenon's perceptions right? Was it worth taking the risk and telling her how he felt? He needed more time to think about it.

Suddenly, Unilus put down his drawing pad and spoke up. "There's only one obvious conclusion."

Dragatu looked at him expectantly.

"If she's a true friend, and only wants to be friends, then she will understand your feelings and respect them. You will have to control how you feel, but then you will stay friends. If she's not a friend worth having, then she will probably let the friendship go, and you will be better off, because a true friend wouldn't do that. However, if she does like you . . . and I can't understand why." He smiled, and Dragatu rolled his eyes. "Then it will all be fine and you will both be happy."

Dragatu thought about the words.

"He's right you know," Phoenon interrupted opening his eyes.

"I know," Dragatu said in a defeated tone, "so I have to tell her how I feel?"

"Yes," was the synchronised reply from his brothers.

"But how?" Dragatu groaned. "She's smart and funny. She'll not like it if I fumble some pathetic confession of my feelings, making me look like an idiot. I don't know how to do this," he said defeated, giving up any barriers against being helped.

"You know her best Dragatu," Phoenon said encouragingly. "What do you think will impress her most?"

Dragatu's forehead screwed up and he began to think.

"She likes hunting and games . . . and books and reading . . ." His face dropped and he hung his head in dismay, his hands over the back of his head and his elbows on his knees.

"What's wrong?" Phoenon asked.

Dragatu dropped his hands and lifted his head.

"She likes romantic stories," he said despairingly, "I have no chance. I know nothing about romance. What can I do that's romantic? This is a disaster." For the first time in his life, he contemplated giving up on something. It was too much effort. "Maybe I should just give up now."

"Is that really what you want?" Phoenon asked knowingly.

Dragatu thought for a second. "No, I guess not," he said, sighing. "If nothing else I will try."

"That's more like the Dragatu we know," Phoenon said, and Unilus nodded. "So what do you think you could do that's romantic?" Phoenon asked.

"I don't know? She likes reading romantic stuff, so maybe I could write something. That would be impressive, but I wouldn't have a clue where to begin."

"We can help you with this," Phoenon said excitedly. "We could help you put together something beautiful that expresses how you feel? That would be romantic. Unilus is excellent at writing. If you told us what you wanted to say we could work together and put it on parchment, in a way that would impress her."

Dragatu thought to himself about the offer, and couldn't believe this was happening.

"Okay. We can work together."

"Brilliant," Phoenon said with a big smile as he got off his bed and walked over to Dragatu. "Unilus get parchment. It's time to write . . . with all our romantic might." He sniggered.

Dragatu shook his head in disbelief as Unilus brought the parchment, and they worked long into the night.

♦ ♨ ♦

Finally, it was finished. Phoenon read out their combined effort. As the last word left his mouth both he and Unilus smiled and looked at Dragatu.

"It's perfect, isn't it?" Dragatu said amazed.

Unilus and Phoenon nodded.

"If she isn't impressed by that then she hasn't got a heart." Phoenon laughed.

Dragatu smiled. "Thank you both for your help," he said humbly.

Unilus bowed his head with a smile and a broad grin lit up Phoenon's face.

"But if you tell anyone else about this you can bet I will string you up by your feet and beat you to a pulp," Dragatu said sternly.

Phoenon's grin burst into laughter, and Unilus joined him a moment after. Dragatu shook his head, ignored them, and set the parchment on the table. It was late and he got into bed. As he pulled the blanket over him, listening to the laughter fade, he smiled.

11/5/698

The next day Dragatu waited until late afternoon to see Freta, taking the parchment with him in his pack. He wanted to take her to where he had found the red stones, and at night-time, when the stars were out - she loved the stars.

Later that night they arrived together at the ore pit. The sky was like a pitch-black blanket with an innumerable number of pin holes scattered randomly across it. The torch he had carried and the fire for their food were the only other lights for miles. Dragatu's heart hammered, his nerves dancing.

"Dragatu, are you okay?" Freta asked as Dragatu stared into the fire and threw a couple of stones into it.

He took a deep breath and turned to her. "There's something I have to tell you, but I don't know how you will react. Firstly, I have a couple of gifts for you."

She was silent as he moved.

Dragatu pulled the sheet of parchment out of his bag and put it on the ground beside him. He pulled out the other wolf tooth that had been strung onto a necklace like his.

"I want you to have this," he said, offering her the necklace. "I want it to always remind you of when we first met, and what an incredible thing we did together."

"Thank you." She smiled, taking it from him, putting it around her neck and pulling the knots to tighten it.

Dragatu watched her: gaining some confidence. It was going well so far, but the biggest risk was about to come and he took another deep breath.

"I've also written something for you, I hope you like it. Is it okay if I read it to you?"

He picked up the parchment and looked at her. She nodded and smiled. With her acceptance he read the words of his heart:

"Perception has often been the fuel to change a person's existence. The opening of the eyes to something never seen before, and then seeing something you always knew was possible, but never considered. It was revealed to me in a single instant, and I was blinded by a revelation that turns a seed unknown into a rosa fully understood.

"But what to do with that rosa?

"Give it to you with the chance of reciprocation? Or hide it under glass from fear of rejection? How did the seed turn into this rosa? What circumstance led to this moment?

"It was a humble parting and regular event. Yet that parting smile, the feelings I felt as you left me standing there. I have never seen you so radiant, so unique, and so perfect.

"At that moment, I realised I would do anything to make you as happy as I had known you were when you were with me.

"The perception had changed. I saw all the time we spent together, and all I had ever done since we met was for you. I had done it as more than a friend.

"To see all this in a single moment cannot be described. I came to realise a simple truth. You are the only exception, the only star at night, and that this fact remains when all dies, I care for you more than I care for anything else.

"Yet what to do with this enlightenment? What to tell you? What to say? I had never known such fear, I who had faced beasts three times my size, and been victorious.

"I know I have discovered in you a treasure far beyond riches or power. I have become the richest man with fewest possessions, but my conscious has made a coward of me. Is the risk too high?

"I never want to lose your friendship, and I fear what I feel could be a rift between us.

"Would you return my feelings?

"The hope in me cannot understand why you wouldn't feel the same way. I am a man of strength, of power and of honour. I would dedicate every breath to seeing you smile and laugh.

"How could you not want this?

"You who are different to most, surely you would understand? But I see you have previously been burned. I hate the thought that you have been hurt so much. How I wish I could take that pain away from you.

"I have done my best to relieve any pain by making you smile and laugh. But even if you've felt pain from someone who wasn't right for you, I can still see your strength and capability to love. Please don't close your heart because of any bad experiences. Just learn to position your heart towards someone who will always be there for you.

"Someone who understands your feelings.

"Someone who has and who will be there for you as long as you need him.

"Someone who loves your secret desire to be comforted, even though you are so strong and hide this vulnerable side.

"Someone who loves your desire to achieve and be successful, and would encourage you to be the best at everything you do.

"Someone who would dance with you forever, holding you close to shelter you from any storm.

"Someone who comprehends your space and time, someone who would acknowledge and appreciate when you needed your own, but would let you have his when you needed it.

"I could be that someone. But if not, I hope one day you will find him."

Dragatu finished and nervously folded the parchment, waiting for her to say something as he looked up at her.

She was silent for a few seconds and stared at the ground. Then slowly she looked up. She spoke so softly he nearly didn't hear the words.

"That was beautiful Dragatu. I feel the same way."

He smiled with relief and joy, and she smiled back. Dragatu held out his hand and she took it. He stood up, and once more she followed his lead. He took a step towards her and again she mirrored his actions. Their reflection met, and they kissed gently underneath the starlit sky.

Oxygen

Chapter 13
The Gift of Power

15/2/700

Over the next two years, Freta and Dragatu saw each other whenever they could. Freta didn't need to hunt as much as Dragatu shared his family's abundance, and with the free time they helped people whenever they could by spending copious amounts of time digging at the ore pits. They also went to the hills every three months, enjoying hunting and checking the water source for repairs.

Another love story took place in these two years and it came as a surprise to everyone. Unilus returned home one day and told them he was engaged and to be married. The family met Tursea, a farmer's daughter, and everyone commented on how similar they were in both looks and personality. The wedding date had not been set, as they had to wait until they were both eighteen: the age of adults. This had only just occurred for the triplets, but Tursea was still not of age.

On their eighteenth birthday the boys were fully accepted as men and, as was tradition, they celebrated with a large feast, and received many gifts. Honrus made Dragatu large, elaborate hunting knives.

The day after the feast Healana gathered her three sons together. She revealed the existence of the Book of Prophecy to

Unilus and Phoenon, and reminded Dragatu, who had all but forgotten. She explained that as Unilus was engaged he would inherit it after he was married and would be the one allowed to read it. Dragatu casually brushed this off, remembering how he had read it when he shouldn't have, but not recollecting what it said. He promised once more to protect it, but gave it no more thought. His only concern was for the Book of Law and trying to help the people. It was the part of his promises to his father he had focused on, as the Book of Prophecy had made no sense and seemed a fool's errand.

☘ 🔥 ☘

The sun was high and only faint shadows of the channels carrying the water were cast as Dragatu walked to the hills alone. It was strange not having Freta with him, but Jolonus was ill and she had stayed to take care of him. About half way to the hills, he suddenly heard a soft but commanding female voice. It felt like water, gentle and strong, as it whispered to him.

"Dragatu . . ."

He looked around, unsure of the direction it came from. There was no one there. Shaking his head, he kept walking. After a few paces, he heard it again but this time it was louder.

"Dragatu . . ."

The voice sounded familiar. He turned on the spot, and for a third time the voice called to him.

"Dragatu . . ."

"Who's there?" Dragatu called out. He started to wonder if the heat was affecting him.

Suddenly there was a blinding flash of light. As his eyes refocused he was startled and took several steps back. There in front of him was the tallest man he had ever seen, well over two metres tall. He had wavy golden hair that was mostly covered by something Dragatu had never seen before. This strange hat-like object looked like it was made from some kind of metal. The only things not covered were the man's eyes, parts of his cheeks and his chin. Dragatu guessed it was some sort of protective or decorative device. The colour of the metal was similar to the deep-yellow rocks that could be found at the ore pits. It shone and glistened in the sunlight, but it was the eyes that drew Dragatu's attention, the irises were not blue, or green, or brown. They were a mixture of red, green, orange and blue, the separate colours dancing around each other like smoke.

Once Dragatu drew his own eyes away he surveyed the rest of the man, and saw that he wore more strange apparel like the hat. He had a metal shirt that covered the front and back, and it was cut off at the shoulders. Other items he wore consisted of metal sleeves over his forearms, a metal skirt that went to his knees, some metal on his shins, and more over sandals that covered the whole foot. What caught Dragatu's eye most about the man's clothing was what lay at the man's hip. It was like a hunting knife, but far longer, almost as long as the man's arm. It was made out of the same deep-yellow metal and had seven stones in the blade. The stones were all different colours and the closest to the point was red followed by green, orange, blue, purple, yellow and lastly white at the hilt. Dragatu began to wonder what this longer hunting knife was for, and what kind of animal it would be used to kill, but before Dragatu could think anymore the man spoke.

"Greetings Dragatu."

"Who . . . Who are you?"

"I am a Messenger sent from the Creator."

Dragatu dropped to his knees in reverence, but as he knelt the man spoke again.

"Rise and defend yourself!"

The words startled Dragatu. He looked up and saw the man taking large steps towards him, grabbing the hilt of his weapon, drawing it, and holding it in front of him. Dragatu couldn't make sense of it, but instinct took over and rising he drew his hunting knives, readying himself. The man reached him, swinging the weapon at Dragatu's head. Dragatu ducked and stepped to the side. The giant man's side was now open. Dragatu went to attack, but the man was too quick, and the metal on his arms protected him from the blow. Dragatu jumped back as another attack came. This time it was close and he was baffled by the whole experience. 'Why am I being attacked?' The thought vanished. He didn't have time to think, he had to fight. He needed to use his own speed, and not just strength to win this fight.

He began circling, his attacker following the movement, his weapon stretched toward Dragatu like a long pointing golden finger. Dragatu took several steps forward, but had to dodge an attack. He blocked the second, using both of his knives. It nearly knocked him off his feet, but he managed to hold his ground. He saw an opening as the man drew his weapon back and went to attack the man's neck. However, the man was still too fast. Dragatu watched out of the corner of his eye, bracing himself for the killing blow, his own arm still moving towards the man's neck. Suddenly he felt himself 'thud' on the floor. He opened his eyes to find himself lying on his back several metres away from the man.

"Enough!" the Messenger bellowed. Dragatu lay there looking up.

Out of nowhere he heard the female voice again.

"I know this is confusing, but all I can say is remember choice."

'Choice,' Dragatu repeated, no less confused. He looked around, but there was no woman there, just the man.

"You are indeed a skilled fighter, Dragatu," the Messenger said, cutting through his thoughts. "Your skill, determination and courage are commendable. These are qualities that could make you a great leader."

Dragatu staggered to his feet and stared. So many questions circled his mind. Almost as if his thoughts had been read, the man continued.

"You must have many questions. Firstly, I am a Messenger from the Creator. I am here because you have been chosen, Dragatu. You have been a great helper of the people. Your work in providing leadership for the water project was highly commendable. From a young age, you have desired to help people and worked hard to achieve your goals. You have a lot of potential and could achieve a lot of good for the people.

However, I must warn you, Dragatu. Sometimes your desire to help has the wrong intentions behind them. You must learn to help others for that purpose alone. Think about this, but remember that your efforts have been good.

With that said it is time to reveal why I have been sent. I am here to give you a gift . . . a gift that you can use to help the people. With it, you can guide them to make better choices and be an example of all that is good.

Before I offer you this gift I need to remind you of what is written in the Book of Law: this ground you walk on was created by the Creator. It is a spherical body, much like a round stone with moss growing on it. It is much more, but this will help you understand. In many ways, you and the people are the moss. It is known as a planet or world. It has been created for you to live on. It contains life and houses life. I want you to think of the night sky Dragatu. Think of the stars. Out there are worlds similar to yours and many very different from yours. There are many creations, but above all humans are the most important to the Creator.

I am going to show you many of these creations that exist on worlds like yours. Some of these Worlds have humans on them, but some do not. Many of the creations you will see couldn't be imagined unless shown to you. Each has many unique qualities and it's up to you to see those qualities. You will then be able to pick the creation you think has qualities that will help you help the people on your world. Are you ready to accept this great gift and honour?"

Dragatu had stood there staring. Slowly accepting what was happening, but it was overwhelming. Finally, he took hold of his thoughts, 'I'll be able to help the people more than I could before.' "I accept this great gift," he said reverently, but with a hint of excitement.

The man nodded and walked forward, bending down to touch Dragatu on the forehead, his hand sideways, then brought it down to cover Dragatu's eyes. There was another sudden flash of light. The flash of light faded and Dragatu saw the night sky and stars all around him, as if he was floating amongst them.

Looking around he tried to find his legs and arms, but there was nothing, as though all that existed was his ability to see. Suddenly a small round object approached. As it did it grew larger and larger until it almost took up his whole vision and then it stopped. He knew it was a world like the Messenger had spoken of. From the bottom, it began to peel and unfold as one piece, like a fruit skin, or ball wrapped in a cloth, and it spread out like the top of a circular table. As it did Dragatu began to move and looked at it from a bird's eye view. Then suddenly he rushed down towards it, approaching as if he was going to crash into the surface, but stopped just above it, turning to view it as if he was standing on the surface. He then found he could move by himself, moving as if he could fly at any speed he wanted.

Whipping and weaving amongst the surface of the world he saw that it was damper and wetter than his own, and there were a lot of forests covering the land. He saw humans and many creatures he didn't recognise. A huge creature caught his attention. It was bigger than a house and it had five long snake-like necks attached to a big body that had four legs. On the end of each neck there was a narrow horse-like head that was a blue-green colour, just like the rest of the body. It had a tail that was long, and this creature was a great threat to the people. Dragatu saw that it took a lot to defend themselves and this was because the creature could spit a poison substance from its heads, and it burned the skin of the humans. They had learned to defend themselves well though and learned to use juices of strange plants to cover arrows and poison these creatures. The creature's skin was also waterproof and the people wore the skins as protection in the very wet climate.

Once the curiosity had passed he continued moving rapidly through the world's surface, but nothing else caught his attention. As he thought about wanting to see the next world this one began to pull away from him. He lost the ability to control his movement and viewed it from a bird's eye view again, not able to tell if he moved away from the world, or the world moved away from him. The surface then folded back to create a sphere and it moved away, getting smaller and smaller. Dragatu waited amongst the stars and black space and another sphere approached with the same process occurring as before, and then repeated over and over with each world.

Just then, he saw a creature that grabbed his attention more than the others. It was on a very dry world. There were areas of plants and forests, but they were few. This world didn't have any humans on it but had ferocious beasts, like giant lizards. Some were bigger than many houses and some were on two legs and ran fast, and then others had long necks and large bodies with four legs.

The creature that caught Dragatu's attention was the main predator on this world and it had wings like a bat and four legs. It also had a long tail and a long neck. The head was crowned with horns, and it had fangs that were sharper than knives. What really caught his attention was that it could breathe fire. The first time he saw this he was filled with awe, and then he saw it do it again, and this creature captivated him. It had such strength and power, and in his awe he put it straight to the top of his list, thinking of ways the creatures abilities could help the people.

The worlds continued to flash before him. Millions upon millions populated some and some were covered with incredible buildings that reached to the heavens. Others had small populations with very few buildings, the people living in tents as Dragatu's people once had. And others even had humans that flew around the skies in metal creations and some even used these to fly amongst the stars.

It was almost more than Dragatu's mind could take. Finally, no more worlds appeared and the stars went out and all was black. He was unsure of how much time had passed and in the darkness all that existed was thought, and he tried to understand all he had seen. Some worlds he had forgotten already, and after some more immeasurable time others vanished from his recollection. With this process, his mind began to feel normal and less overwhelmed. Most of what he could remember was the creature he had chosen and only a few of the planets he had seen. Suddenly he felt something on his face and light crept into his eyes. His world slowly came back into focus as the Messenger withdrew his hand. Dragatu fell to the floor as he felt his body again and he breathed deeply, propped up on all fours. The Messenger spoke as Dragatu slowly staggered to his feet.

"Now that you have seen these things it is time for you to decide. Pick the creation whose characteristics you think will best serve others. These characteristics will be given to you and you can use them in the way you think is best. Which one do you choose Dragatu?"

Dragatu had chosen and didn't need any time to debate his choice.

"The creature that was strong and could breathe fire is the one I choose. I believe the strength it would give me would allow me to be a better leader, and I would be able to use it to help the people. If I were stronger I would be able to work hard every day to help more people. Also, the Book of Law says that fire allowed the first people to be happy. It gave them light in darkness, warmth, protection from animals, the ability to cook food, make tools, pans, metals and many other things. If I could make fire in some way like that creature did I would use it to give light, protection and make things for the people."

"That creature is known as the dragon," the Messenger said, and held his hands out flat. A miniature dragon suddenly appeared on them. "Is this what you choose?"

"Yes," Dragatu said smiling with excitement.

"This shall be your gift then. It will give you great physical strength and you will be able to create fire with your thoughts."

Dragatu's repeated the last part in amazement in his mind, 'create fire with my thoughts!'

"This is a great and powerful gift," the gleaming, armoured Messenger continued. "You will be able to focus on any object you can see, and as long as the material can burn, and you have enough strength, then it will. This gift will require different levels of energy from you depending on the material you are trying to burn, and you will have to eat and drink a lot because you will use up energy to perform your fire gift. The gift is like your muscles, the more you use it the easier it will be to use. At first it will make you very tired, but in time, and with use, it will become easier. The material you burn must also be in sight and it will only work within a twenty-metre radius from where you stand. Do you still desire this gift?"

"I do," Dragatu replied.

The Messenger stepped forward, putting his hands on the sides of Dragatu's head. Dragatu felt a burning sensation spread all over his body. It started at his heart and spread throughout his whole body. He felt like he was on fire, yet it didn't hurt. It was more like being consumed by positive energy. Finally, his vision went black, and as his awareness returned he found himself lying on the floor.

The Messenger knelt beside him and helped him up. Dragatu noticed the Messenger didn't look as big as he had. He then looked at the floor and saw that it was further away. He was taller. He looked at his feet, legs, torso, hands and arms and saw he was larger and more muscular than he had been.

"You have noticed one of the changes. There is another change, but you will notice this in time. There are a few other consequences we must discuss. The first is that when you have children your first child will inherit the gift when you die. This will only happen when they are eighteen or over. Secondly, your name is now a title, which will belong to you and those who inherit your gift. Each person who has the gift will be known as the Dragatu.

Lastly, you will not be able to speak of the things that I have shown you. You can tell people you have a gift from the Creator, and that it will be passed on to your children, but that is all. If you try to say more your tongue will not let you. The only people you can talk openly with Dragatu, are your two brothers. You may also write in your journal that I have visited you, and that this gift came from the dragon, that it will be passed on, and how it feels, but not anything more of what you have seen. Do you understand?"

There was a pause. Dragatu had been caught up in all the wonder and failed to register much of what had been said. His thoughts consumed by this gift.

"I understand," he said quickly, registering the question, but not much else.

"Good. Remember that everything you do is a choice Dragatu. Choose well."

As the final words ran through Dragatu's mind there was a last flash of blinding light. When his sight returned the Messenger was gone, and he was alone. He stood still for a few moments, thinking about it all, and wondered how much time had passed for it was still daylight. Putting his hand up to shade his eyes, he looked to the sun. It was still in the same spot it had been when the Messenger had appeared. He wondered how that could be, and shook his head, guessing he would never be able to understand. Dropping one hand, he looked down at the ground and crouched, balancing himself as he adjusted to his increased size. He decided to let himself fall backwards, and sat on the harder but still sandy ground, deciding to write in his journal, he needed more time to digest this.

After writing all he could about the encounter in which he noted the weaknesses of the gift, that it took energy, and that he needed to see the object to burn it, plus it had a limited range, he sat thinking, a lot of the last parts of the Messenger's speech rising to the surface.

'Why is okay for me to tell my brothers about what I've seen and no one else?' he wondered. 'It will be good to have someone to talk to, but why them? Why not Freta? There's so much I don't understand.' He sat thinking but couldn't find an answer. 'I guess it doesn't matter. I have the gift and will be able to lead the way Father always knew I would. I will be able to do more to help others. I wonder how this fire gift works. The Messenger didn't explain that fully. He said with my thoughts, so I guess I have to concentrate on what I want to heat or burn.' He looked around, but there was nothing except his equipment, and he needed that. 'I'll have to wait until I reach the hills and find some wood.'

Other thoughts then popped into his mind.

'Whose was the woman's voice? Was that the Creator? Is the Creator a Woman? The Book of Law just says we were made in the Creator's image. How does she have the power to create worlds? Whoever she was, why hadn't she said more? I don't understand. What had the voice said? 'Remember choice.' Why do I need to think about this?' He continued to think, struggling to find answers. After a lot of speculation he shook his head frantically, 'This is pointless. I don't know why more wasn't explained, but there's no point in wasting time when I can go use my gift.' He went to say something as a conclusion to his thoughts, but found he couldn't speak. Confused he suddenly remembered what the messenger had said. Instead, he repeated in his mind what he had wanted to say out loud, 'If that woman's voice was yours Creator, thank you for the gift.'

He then stood quickly, excitement taking over as he thought about using the fire gift. He put the journal back in his pack, slung it over his shoulder and began to walk as fast as he could. It took a while to get used to the larger stride, and his new size and strength, and as he journeyed he burst into laughter from time to time, unable to contain his joy and amazement.

Chapter 14
Triad

20/2/700

Finally, Dragatu arrived at the hills, but for him it felt like no time had passed, his thoughts were consumed with the miraculous visit and a burning desire to use his gift. He went straight to the mouth of the canyon by the water source and found some sticks. His hands shook and he grinned with excitement as he gathered them together. With the pile made he sat staring at them, his face screwing up.

'How exactly do I do this?' "Focus on the object you wish to burn," he recalled.

He tried to concentrate on the sticks with his mind and wish them into flames, but nothing happened. He began sweating with the mental exertion. 'Burn. Burn. Burn,' he repeated, whilst staring intensely at the sticks, but still nothing happened.

Suddenly, as he was about to give up, he felt the same heat sensation he had had when the Messenger gave him the gift. It started in his heart again, flowed through his body like his blood and finally rushed up his neck and into his head. He felt his mind get hot, and tried to focus all his thoughts and the energy on the sticks. It was too much. He felt like his head would burst into consuming flames. Then, as he gave a last attempt to focus the heat on the sticks, he felt the heat leave as if through his eyes, and a small flame appeared on one of the sticks. Smoke began to rise as it burned and then the others caught fire. Dragatu no longer felt the heat in his mind, nor had the energy to conjure anymore, even if he wanted to. He felt dizzy and exhausted, sweat pouring down his face like a waterfall. He wanted the world to stop moving and he shut his eyes, lying down and almost falling sideways. As he lay there a small smile crept across his face. He had done it.

He lay still for a while, wishing he could create more fire, but he had no energy. He became frustrated at feeling weak and unable to use the gift until he recovered. He knew he had no choice, though the only way to improve was to sleep, eat, and drink as much as possible, then 'exercise' this gift like the Messenger had said. He let the exhaustion take him and fell asleep. Once he woke he ate and drank, then went for a quick hunt to prepare for his next attempt at the gift. The process then began again, and this went on for several days.

24/2/700

By the end of four days, it was ever so slightly easier to use the gift. Dragatu still had to eat and drink a lot and realised he must be eating the amount of food to nourish two people. The whole experience filled him with excitement, but he still found it very difficult, as he wanted to be able to set anything on fire like the dragon had. Yet it wasn't to be, and the process continued, testing his patience every time. When he wasn't asleep he just lay still for hours, often thinking about how people would respect his gift and were going to be shocked with his change in appearance. He wondered if he would ever get used to how exciting and bewildering it was. He was also filled with questions and hopes during the many hours he lay still. Like: 'How will Freta react? I will always use this gift to protect her. How will my brothers react?' And: 'I will help the people follow the Book of Law better and keep my promises to my father and the Creator.'

Dragatu stayed for another week, determined to be good at using the gift. He just wanted it to be easy and after much thought decided to keep the limitations a secret.

'People follow me because I'm strong and they can depend on me for my strength. Having this limitation will mean I look weak. I don't want this. I've always been strong and built up a reputation for this. It's what allows me to help people. I don't think I'll tell people the limitations. People need to be able to have faith in my ability to help them. This is the best way to do that and will help me be a leader. The Creator wants me to use the gift to be an example, and if they doubt me then they won't follow or trust my example. Yes, I'll only show them that I'm strong. It's the best way.'

6/3/700

Dragatu walked through the fields, absorbing the curious looks and expressions of amazement. He was excited to be back and able to tell people about the gift. Most of all he couldn't wait to show Freta, Honrus, the Hunora and his family.

Dragatu's path took him close to Unilus' favourite tree, the one that stood alone. There were two peculiar looking people by the tree. He decided to investigate. One had silver hair and the other's was white and long. As he got closer, walking through the white flowers, he saw who they were. It was Unilus and Phoenon, and from the changes in their appearance he knew what had happened. Part of him felt disappointment. He knew he shouldn't, but he had thought he was the only one to get a gift. Taking a deep breath, he tried to push the feelings down and forced a smile. But without realising it he gave himself away, his left hand flexing, curling into a ball, and flexing again.

Phoenon saw him, only caught the smile and smiled back, running up to him.

"Wow! You're huge," he said quickly, looking Dragatu up and down. The moment of impressed shock passed and Phoenon gave him a warm embrace, his head barely reaching Dragatu's chest. He released Dragatu and spoke very formally, his actions

160

contradicting the formality of his words as he bounced up and down on his feet with excitement.

"My title is now Phoenon."

As he said this, Dragatu got a better look at the changes and returned the welcome. "As you can guess, mine is Dragatu. I see you have a gift too? What's happened to your hair? It's silver. And look at your eyes. Your irises are orange."

Phoenon beamed. "Watch this." He shook his head and in the sunlight each hair burst into a vast spectrum of orange.

A faint memory of one of the many creatures appeared in Dragatu's mind. "In . . . credible . . ."

"It's wonderful, isn't it? We have so much to talk about. Come on . . ."

Phoenon grabbed Dragatu's arm with excitement, but was unable to move him until Dragatu followed to where Unilus sat under the tree.

As he walked Dragatu thought about Phoenon's orange eyes. They reminded him of how the Messenger's were four different colours. He wondered if his eyes were different and realised he hadn't checked his facial appearance. Dragatu thought about asking Phoenon if his own eyes were a different colour, but once they reached Unilus he decided to ask later, and asked a more pressing question instead.

"What gifts do you both have?"

Unilus had his back to Dragatu, facing the tree in a sitting position, but answered his question with an introduction.

"Hello, Dragatu."

There was a pause and Dragatu realised he needed to continue the formality.

"Hello, Unilus," he replied to his brother's back.

Unilus continued, not moving from his seated position.

"We have been greatly blessed to receive our gifts. It is best if we recount what has happened one at a time. The Messengers that came to Phoenon and I, and I'm assuming you . . ."

"Yes, a Messenger came to me," Dragatu replied, wondering what Unilus meant by 'Messengers.'

". . . told us we could speak of these things to each other, and I am happy this is the case. Phoenon and I know each other's story, but I suggest Phoenon tells you his encounter first as I think he'll explode with excitement if he does not."

Phoenon had continued bouncing on his toes as Unilus sat, still facing the tree as he spoke.

"Well, it happened, um, nineteen days ago."

With these words, Dragatu realised the people must have known about the Creator sending the Messenger and visiting them. He was disappointed again. He wanted to tell the people and another thought began to creep in, 'How am I to lead if my brothers have gifts too? Surely they couldn't lead as well?' He gave a half smirk at the last thought, but continued to listen curiously.

". . . I was out with some of the children and we were having such a fun time laughing and playing. We were playing between the houses and along the streets over there." He pointed across the many fields towards the improved, but still poorer part of the Nation. It could just be seen in the distance. "I heard the voice of a woman calling my name and I looked around. As I turned I saw a small girl with long black hair that covered her face, at the end of a row of houses. She was crying so I walked towards her to see if she was okay.

The children I told me I should stay with them, and have fun. But the girl was wearing sackcloth and was very muddy. She was crying and I said I wanted to see if she was okay. I left them and walked towards the young girl. She turned and started walking away, still crying. I followed her, and when I turned the corner I saw her running away. She was still sobbing, and I shouted after her asking if she was okay, and then she stopped. She turned to face me and looked up, her face was covered by her hair still so I couldn't see it, and again I asked what was upsetting her. She said nothing, turned towards another path and pointed as if I should follow her. She began to walk and I followed.

I followed her out of the streets to an open field of dry discoloured grass. She had climbed onto a rock and was sitting on it still crying. I walked to the rock and sat down next to her, asking what was wrong and if I could help her. She didn't answer and kept sobbing and crying. I noticed that despite her ragged appearance she had a bracelet that looked very valuable. It was made out of a dark yellow metal that glowed in the sun. On it were seven different coloured stones. They were blue, purple, yellow, white, red, green and orange.

I decide it would be best to try and cheer her up, so I asked if she had ever seen anyone juggle. She shook her head and looked at me with a few tears still running down her face. As she looked up her hair was brushed away by the wind. I gasped as I looked into her eyes, for they were a swirl of orange, red, green and blue. It took me by surprise and she looked back at the floor and began to sob.

As the shock faded, I decided to pick up three medium-sized stones from the ground and began to juggle. She looked at me again, a small smile appearing on her face. I kept juggling then dropped one. She let out a little giggle and I smiled back at her. Once again she looked down at the ground, looking very sad. I asked her what was wrong, but she stayed quiet. I told her I would try and help her if she would let me. She then looked at me, holding my gaze, almost as if she was doing more than just looking at me, as if trying to read my thoughts or something like that. I couldn't help but return her gaze and look at those unique eyes. Finally, she looked away.

After a moment of silence, I asked her if she knew any jokes. Again she shook her head and looked down, her hair covering her face again. I told her a joke and it got another little giggle, but she didn't look at me. I told her another one, this time she laughed out loud. I smiled softly when she looked up at me, and a smile crept across her face too. Then she finally spoke, but it wasn't the woman's voice I had heard before.

"Thank you," she said in a sweet little voice. "I am a Messenger from the Creator. Your kindness and patience are special Phoenon. They are qualities that could help you be a great leader and help the people. Sit beside me again, Phoenon," she had said and I did.

I told her I didn't want to be a leader, that you and Unilus were more suited to dealing with leadership. She said that it was one of the reasons I could be a leader, and humility was important. She told me I was to get a gift to help me lead and the gift I got would be my choice. She explained many things to me and told me I would see many of the creations made. Then I was to pick one that had the characteristics I felt would help the people the most. After this talk, she stood up and as I sat on the rock she put her hands on my eyes, one little hand over each eye.

When her hands touched my eyes there was a flash of light, bright like the sun and I was shown so many wonderful and beautiful things. I saw animals and creatures I could never have dreamed of, some looked fun, and some very scary. The one I chose was from a world with many mountains that reached high into the sky. The people were fighting over a creature that lived in the very tops of the mountains. This creature was like a bird. It had silver feathers when it was in the shade, but once it was in the sunlight the feathers burst into a hundred different shades of orange. Like my hair is now." He grinned at Dragatu. "The bird was so beautiful, with all the different kinds of orange shimmering in the sun. Do you remember it?"

Dragatu nodded, "A little bit . . . but a reminder would help."

"It sang lovely songs, like nothing I've ever heard. Anyone who was hurt could touch it and they would be healed. The people used the birds to heal diseases and physical infirmities. Some of the people wanted to capture the birds for their healing ability and this is why the people were fighting each other. They even used its strong metal like feathers as clothing when they fought and it protected them. I saw how special the bird was, as it could heal people. I thought it would be a wonderful way to help our people.

Once I had seen all the worlds I told the Messenger I had fallen in love with this creation. She said this creature was the phoenix. She told me I had the gift of the Breath of Life, and that when I touched people I could heal almost any disease, or wound. She said there was a consequence though, the healing

164

would give me the same relative pain the person was going through. She also said I would live a very long life. I would live many generations before I died. She told me that the family line of my first born would inherit this gift when I died, and it would be the first born of that line, and they would inherit it when they were eighteen. She then smiled sweetly at me and asked if I was sure this was the gift I wanted. I said yes.

She put her hands on the sides of my head and there was another flash of light, temporarily blinding my vision with whiteness. At that moment, I felt my lungs expand and they kept expanding as if they were about to burst. All of a sudden they deflated and my whole body felt light, as if it was full of air. The feeling rose to my head and gathered in it. I had to open my mouth and all the air I felt inside me rushed out in the longest exhale I had ever had. My vision returned and the Messenger stepped back from me. I felt different. I felt full of life, clearer in mind, and I felt like every breath I took could keep me alive forever. I also realised I took fewer breaths, about one every minute. I looked down at myself and I still looked the same, but I felt so different. She told me my name was now a title and this would be passed to the future child that inherited my gift. The Messenger's last words were, "Choose well." And in a flash of light she was gone.

It took me a while to gain my senses and to act. When I did, I went to the farms to look for Unilus, and to tell him what had happened. When I found him he looked different too, and I guessed he had been given a gift as well. When he heard me coming he put his hand up as if to say wait. I waited. After a while, he got up from the floor near the tree he was sitting at. He looked at me, and when he did I saw the changes he had gone through. He said I had changes too and took me to see my reflection in a bucket of water. I was overjoyed to see the changes and asked how Unilus had known he looked different. He said a friend in the forest had told him. I asked what he meant. He smiled and said it would all be clear in time."

Unilus interrupted, "I think I better take it from here Phoenon."

Phoenon smiled and nodded, clearly happy to have been able to tell his part of the story.

"No doubt you have many questions," Unilus said and Dragatu moved from where he had been standing to lean against the tree, facing Unilus. He had been curious to see if Unilus eyes were a different colour, but hadn't wanted to interrupt Phoenon's story. To his slight annoyance Unilus had his eyes closed as he continued talking.

"Many of your questions will have been answered, but once I've finished we can talk and try to answer any others. Although, I do feel some questions we won't be able to fully answer or understand."

Unilus suddenly opened his eyes and looked to Dragatu as he leant against the tree. Dragatu couldn't help but be captivated by the change. Staring up at him were emerald green eyes and he began to wonder about his own again.

"This is what happened to me when I received my gift," Unilus continued. "I was out on a long walk in the forests and found a peaceful, solitary area and sat to listen to the animals and my thoughts. I sat with my back against a tree and closed my eyes to meditate and listen.

After about an hour, I heard a woman's voice call my name and after looking around and not seeing anyone, I heard another sound. It was the neighing of a horse. It was peculiar to hear one of my favourite animals in the forest, for they usually stay in the open fields. I stood up and began to walk in the direction of the noise while trying to understand whose the woman's voice could have been. After ten minutes, I could hear the horse was close. I stepped from behind a tree and there it was. Though it was very different to a normal horse. It was the whitest horse I had ever seen, almost glowing as the sun hit it. It looked at me as I came out from behind the tree and it had the same coloured eyes as the girl Phoenon saw. It also had a tail that was dark yellow like the bracelet of the girl was, and the mane was also the same colours as the stones he described.

I raised my hands and in a calm voice I asked what it was doing out here. Through my calm tone, I hoped it would understand I wasn't a threat. It took a few steps back. I told it not to be afraid and that I would not hurt it. The perplexing thing was that it seemed to understand exactly what I said, and it let out a little neigh and trotted forwards. I also stepped forwards and put my hands out. It came up to me and I put my hand against its neck. It neighed again and I said hello, showing it I was a friend.

To my surprise I suddenly felt the horse's thoughts and feelings and I could understand them. It said it was a Messenger from the Creator. I dropped to my knees and I could still hear its thoughts. This Messenger told me it had a question for me. It asked me this riddle:

> *What can be harder than any substance?*
> *Or, like its lettering, as easy as three add three.*
> *There is always more than one, but it is only one word.*
> *It can separate the Beast from the Man.*
> *And it is required for the answer to this question.*

Still kneeling in the forest, I thought about it long and hard. I took the first line and thought about the wording. From the fact it said 'harder than any substance', I could tell it meant it wasn't a physical thing. I concluded it must be an emotion, or subject, or something similar to this.

I then asked for the second line to be repeated. It implied that the answer could either be easy, and as the first line said, hard. The phrase 'its lettering, as easy as three add three', was simple as it meant the answer had six letters.

The following line was confusing, and after trying to figure it out I moved on to the next: 'It can separate the Beast from the Man.' This implied that it can, and it cannot, separate the beast from the man. I tried to decide whether this meant animals from humans . . . or something different? I thought of how I have seen some humans act like animals at times. I thought this must be what it meant because of the wording, "the beast from the man", and not, "beast from man", or, "animal from man". The "the" implies a single entity, and not separate entities.

The last line was what gave me the answer. I thought long and hard about this line, and just as I was about to go back to line three I had the thought that I couldn't decide what the answer could be. I thought about the word 'decide' and how I couldn't decide. That's what gave it away. I had two answers I thought it could be.

The first answer I thought it could be was: 'riddle'. A riddle could be easy, or hard, and it had six letters. Knowing the answer could separate the Beast from the Man through intelligence, but the last line did not fit: 'it is required for the answer to this question.' If it had been worded: 'It is the answer to this question' I would have said riddle, but my other option worked so much better because the word 'required' implied an action that had to be made. This was all underlined by the fact I had two options, and I had to pick one, and this was the 'eureka' moment: I had to make a choice. I went through each line again, and my answer made sense. I told the Messenger the answer must be 'Choice'.

The horse like Messenger said my intelligence was impressive and such a quality could make me a great leader. It said I was going to be offered a gift and explained this to me.

After all the worlds had been shown to me I selected the unicorn. It was white, like the Messenger I saw, but it had a straight golden horn that came from the head, about two hands in length. I chose the unicorn because it could talk to any living creature, the way the Messenger spoke to me, and it had great intelligence. It talked to both animals and humans and passed wisdom and intelligence between both, allowing them to live in harmony. I want this for the people and the animals here. I believe animals can teach us a lot through their differences and knowing how we can work together to help each other would bring greater harmony and peace.

The Messenger explained I could talk to nature with my mind, when my eyes were closed and I was focused, but said I would still have to talk to humans to communicate with them. It also said I would have greater understanding, intelligence and knowledge of the world around me.

I was asked if this was still the gift I wanted. I said it was. It told me to stand and put its head against the side of mine, so we were cheek to cheek, and there was a flash of light. My head began to empty and I felt as if there was an infinite space in my mind. The feeling then changed, I felt as if something moved and grew inside my mind. It continued to grow and spread down the back of my neck, along my spine, and to my arms and legs. It stretched along the floor from my feet. I felt like part of me was growing and stretching along the earth. As this happened I could feel and hear all the creatures around me. I could hear the insects, the birds, and the plants. It was like I could sense all the life around me. Then as quickly as it had begun, it stopped. It all disappeared and it was just my own thoughts in my head. I regained my sight and the white horse still stood in front of me with its seven coloured mane and golden tail. The final thoughts and feelings translated into the words, "choose well", and in a flash the Messenger was gone.

I could only sit down on the ground and think about what had happened. After I had, I cleared my mind, closed my eyes and focused on just listening. At first there was nothing, but then I could hear, or rather sense, the insects in the grass around me. They didn't speak the way we do, it was like the Messenger, but theirs were fainter thoughts and feelings. It was very chaotic and I struggled to separate one creature from another. It's still very hard and even harder to describe what it's like.

After listening for a while, I both heard and felt something very powerful that overshadowed all the other noise and feelings. My internal sight focused on where this came from and it was coming from the tree nearest to me. I focused all my attention on it and words cannot describe the feelings of such a being. It was aware that I was trying to communicate and I felt surprise and curiosity come from it. It tried to push me out with negative feelings so I tried to give it positive feelings to show I wasn't a threat and this was very hard. After a few minutes it seemed to understand, sending positive feelings back. In these feelings, I felt wisdom of things past, and a transfer of knowledge took place. I understood more of how life functioned and how much life there was around me.

I decided to listen to more creatures around me, discovering that some had very little ability to communicate or feel, and others had greater abilities. Some were not even aware I was trying to communicate with them. A lot of time went by and I wanted to stay there forever, but I knew it was time to leave.

As I left, I saw a deer about ten metres ahead of me. I closed my eyes and reached out to it. When I connected with it I could hear very clear thoughts and emotions. It had seen me and was scared. I told it not to be frightened and that I was a friend. It was greatly intrigued. I told it again not to worry and that I wasn't going to hurt it. In its thoughts, it asked how this was possible. I told him a Messenger had come and given me a gift from the Creator. The deer then walked towards me. I stayed where I was and once again I told it not to worry and I put out my hand. It jumped up to me and I felt it lick my hand. I smiled and the deer told me the rest of his family wasn't going to believe this. I told him that I was the only one that could communicate with him and to still be wary of my kind. The deer understood. It said it knew I was different from the moment it saw me. I asked what it meant. It said my eyes and hair were like no other human. I was curious and it described what I looked like. I told him I had to go and I would be in the forest often and to keep a look out for me. I opened my eyes and it bounded off, looking very pleased with itself. I could tell it was excited by the news it was going to tell others of its kind. I smiled to myself and continued to walk in the direction of the Nation.

On the journey, my mind felt faster and I remembered things with ease, like I could reach into it and pull out anything I had seen before. I could see it clearly in my mind as if I was seeing it in front of me. I knew this would help when I wanted to learn more. I finally arrived here and went to a farm to see my own reflection and enjoyed seeing the changes. I then sat and practiced my gift with the tree. That is when Phoenon found me.

We talked about what had happened, trying to answer some of our questions, and wondered what might have happened to you. We finally decided to tell people the little we could. We also spent a long time waiting to see you, so we could see if you had received a gift from the Creator, too. We guessed that if we received one, you would be honoured one too. It is clear we guessed right. We were talking about this just before you arrived. It's good to have you back. There's a lot to discuss, isn't there?"

Dragatu had listened patiently and been thinking about the questions he had and wondered if these were the same as Unilus' questions. "Yes, there is a lot to talk about. Before we go any further, do I have different eyes?"

Unilus replied. "Yes you do. Phoenon let Dragatu see for himself."

Phoenon grabbed Dragatu's arm again, "We'll be back shortly," Phoenon called to Unilus, who shut his eyes again.

After a quick walk, they arrived at a farm. Dragatu looked into a barrel full of water and there staring back were two dark red eyes. Dragatu did a double take, staring with amazement at his whole face. He smiled with amusement. He loved the way he looked, with the three scar lines down his face and the red eyes. They made him look strong, and it certainly gave him a powerful presence. Dragatu finally pulled himself away from his reflection and walked back to the tree with Phoenon, leaning against it once more as Unilus continued.

"I'm glad we could answer that question for you. I think now would be a good time to hear about your encounter. Is that okay?"

Dragatu agreed. Unilus sat listening with his eyes closed and Phoenon joined him, but looked up at Dragatu expectantly. Once Phoenon was settled, Dragatu explained what had happened. As he did he explained the reasons for choosing the gift, but left out that he had to see to burn an object and that it took energy. Once he finished, Phoenon couldn't hold back his excitement any longer.

"Go on then. Let's see your gift in action," he said, and bounced to his feet, moving to break a branch off the tree.

"No!" Unilus shouted, eyes snapping open. He pointed to a dead branch that had already fallen off.

Phoenon apologised and brought the branch over to Dragatu and waited. Dragatu looked at it and let out a quick burst of fire. The branch ignited, and Phoenon laughed with amazement.

Dragatu smiled, thankful for the complement. Phoenon then sat down looking dismayed, chin in his hand.

"What's wrong?" Dragatu asked.

"I haven't used my gift yet. I'm too anxious," Phoenon replied.

Dragatu didn't say anything. In one quick motion, he drew a knife and cut the palm of his hand. Unilus looked at him with a combination of disapproval and agreement as if he wished Dragatu hadn't done it, but knew it was the best thing for Phoenon.

"It will be okay. Go ahead," Dragatu said, excited to see if Phoenon could actually heal him.

Phoenon stood up and took a deep breath out of habit, not because he needed the oxygen. Putting both hands around Dragatu's cut hand, he shut his eyes, his face screwing up with concentration. Suddenly he removed his hands, as if they had been burned, letting out a small yelp. Dragatu looked at his hand in bewilderment, holding it up and flexing it. It was whole once more, as if there had never been a cut there. He looked at Phoenon, and was about to laugh and tell him he was impressed, but saw a tear fall from Phoenon's eye.

"Are you all right?" Unilus asked, motioning to get up from the floor.

"I'm fine," Phoenon protested and Unilus let himself drop the small gap back to the floor. "I'm just not used to the pain," Phoenon said.

"It is a great gift, with equally great consequences," Unilus said.

Dragatu tried to console Phoenon. "It will get easier with time," he said. "Pain will always be pain, but it's something you can block out if you work hard at it."

"Thank you," Phoenon said affectionately.

Unilus then spoke.

"We have made a lot of progress already. This is good. There are still questions that need to be discussed though. I'll try to answer some other questions, if that's okay?"

Phoenon nodded and Dragatu said, "Why not? Go for it."

172

"Thank you," Unilus said. "A lot of this is for you, Dragatu, as Phoenon and I have had a chance to talk and discuss these questions already. It will be good to get your opinion.

Firstly, I think the changes in our eyes are linked to our gifts, like mine being green and my gift nature, Phoenon's being orange like the flying bird that could heal, and Dragatu's linking to his fire gift. The other changes also relate to our gifts. I think this is so we are separated from everyone else and can do as the Messenger said and lead and by so doing help the people. Do you agree Dragatu?"

"Yeah, it makes sense."

He was starting to accept the three of them had been given gifts to lead and not just him. But he was still slightly skeptical as neither of them were very confident. That was going to make things difficult for them.

"Good," Unilus affirmed. "It's probably best to go back to the start. The woman's voice we heard. I believe it was the Creator's . . ."

"That's what I thought," Dragatu interrupted.

". . . it's something only we can talk about and there's no way of knowing for sure so I haven't given it any more thought. Is there anything you wanted to say about it, Dragatu?"

"No. I think you're right. There's no way to know for sure."

"Okay. We'll move on. Each Messenger was different and Phoenon and I think this was because it's what we would be comfortable seeing. Again we cannot know, but it too makes sense, doesn't it?"

Dragatu nodded.

"Do you have any questions Dragatu?"

He had wanted to find out why it was okay to talk to his brothers, but he knew that now and skipped to his next question.

"What about the colours of the eyes and items the messenger had?" he asked, curious to know Unilus' thoughts.

"Honestly, I don't know," Unilus replied to Dragatu's disappointment. "Our eyes are each one of those colours, but I don't know what it means. Any ideas are just speculation and that's a dangerous path."

Dragatu had hoped for more than that, but kept quiet, keeping his own speculation to himself. He knew deep down that Unilus was right.

"Do you have any more questions?" Unilus asked him.

Dragatu shook his head.

"If ever you have any more questions in the future, we should talk about them, and try to understand our experiences and purpose better. Which brings me to the last two points I want to discuss: How are we going to fulfill our purpose? And what are we actually going to do to help the people?

As I have said, it is clear we have to lead together. We have to show the people how they can help each other, through us helping them. I know this is going to be difficult for the three of us, we are very different, but I think we were chosen for this reason. With the three of us together we'll be able to understand all the people and not just some.

I think we should spend time exploring our gifts and use them around people so they can come to terms with our changes. As we do this we can think of ways to help the people and meet again soon to discuss our ideas. Does that sound good?"

Dragatu and Phoenon nodded. Dragatu was glad he had met them before seeing anyone else, but was also glad to have some space to reflect and see the others he wanted to show his gift too.

"I'm going to go to the forest to do some more communing," Unilus said in conclusion. "Then I'm going to see Tursea and Mother."

Phoenon shared his plans as well, telling them he would go see Healana and some friends. Dragatu said he was also going home to see Healana. After that he would see Honrus, Reon, Linur and other friends, and then he would spend a few days with Freta and Jolonus.

With that, Dragatu and Phoenon said a warm goodbye to Unilus and walked home together. When Dragatu got home he shared his story and wrote what he could about his brothers and their gifts. Once all this was done he went to see Freta.

Chapter 15
Symbols

7/3/700

"Come in," the voice called weakly, before breaking into a rasping cough.

Dragatu entered the dome-house quickly.

"Who is it?" croaked Jolonus between coughs.

"It's me, Dragatu."

Jolonus squinted, trying to focus his aged and deteriorated eyes, all he could make out was a blurred figure. It sounded like Dragatu, but the silhouette was bigger. He pointed to a cup of water. Dragatu moved to the table as Jolonus sat up, the makeshift bed against the wall of the living room creaking as he did. Dragatu grabbed the cup, knelt beside the bed, and held the drink steady as the old man sipped.

"You seem different?" Jolonus asked as he handed the cup back, his voice still raspy, but the coughing fit under control.

"I'll explain everything soon," Dragatu replied, wanting to make sure the coughing fit had definitely passed. "First focus on your breathing and take some more water." He passed the cup back, keeping a caring eye on the old man.

Jolonus was the worst he had been, his once proud stature reduced to a bed-ridden old man in just a couple of months. It saddened Dragatu to see him like this.

"Is that better?" Dragatu asked.

"Yes. Thank you. Why do you look different? Is it to do with what happened to your brothers?"

Dragatu was happy to tell the story and told him everything he could. Jolonus lay listening intently, propped up with his back cushioned against the wall, eyes shut, nodding occasionally, his bushy eyebrows rising with fascination as tried to imagine the miraculous visitation with the little information Dragatu could give. When Dragatu finished there was a pause. Jolonus turned his head slowly and opened his eyes, breaking the brief silence.

"Who would have thought I would live to hear such things? Freta made the right choice when she went against me to keep you in her life. You've been good for her and I know she's been good for you. I have two requests of you Dragatu."

Dragatu leant forward, shuffling his knees closer to the bed. "What can I do?"

"Look after Freta. Keep her safe, and give her a better life than I did."

"I will, sir."

"Secondly lad, let's see that fire gift of yours. Well, as best as I can," he said, coughing a little and chuckling.

Dragatu smiled kindly and nodded. Taking the wooden cup, he put it on the floor and searched the room. Finding a metal sheet he placed the cup on it, inhaling deeply in preparation. He concentrated hard and set the cup on fire, it quickly burned to ashes.

"My! My!" Jolonus exclaimed with disbelief. "One more time for an old man?" he continued.

Dragatu hesitated, he had suddenly become very tired, but he couldn't refuse. He looked around again but couldn't see anything else. Jolonus noticed how Dragatu searched the room and pointed to an ornament that was on a small table. Dragatu went over to it and picked it up. Holding the deep yellow rock he wondered if he could set this on fire, it was rock and he was tired. Freta's father interrupted his struggle.

"Will that work?"

"I don't know. But I'll give it a try," Dragatu said, making up his mind. He placed the yellow rock on the floor, and drew a deep breath until his lungs were full. He focused all his energy on the stone, exhaling slowly as he did. Sweat broke out on his forehead and he began to shake. The flames seemed to be growing out of the rock, making a glowing yellow ball of fire. Dragatu's concentration waned and he felt dizzy. The rock began to glow brighter and he let out one giant burst of energy, lost control, fell sideways, and blacked out.

♠ ♨ ♠

"Dragatu? Dragatu! Please wake up!"

His head thumped, and every muscle ached as he stirred. He opened his eyes and saw Freta crouched over him. Smiling weakly, he cradled his head with one hand, trying to rub the soreness away. He looked up at her and saw confusion and grief written on her face, tears caressing her cheeks as they fell. Sitting up too quickly he went to ask what was wrong, but Freta threw herself around him, hugging him tightly. As she did he looked beyond her, seeing Jolonus on the bed, lying still, chest no longer struggling to rise and fall. Dragatu bowed his head, squeezing Freta a little. She sobbed in his arms and he looked up again, seeing a small smile on Jolonus' face. He let himself smile weakly in return, knowing he had given him an incredible show before he died.

A few moments passed, and Freta managed to control her sobbing. She pushed herself back and Dragatu dropped his arms. Turning she sat beside him and spoke, unable to contain the questions whirling in her mind.

"What happened to my father? What happened to you? You're so different. Is it like what's happened to your brothers?"

Dragatu repeated his story quickly, telling her how he had got a gift from the Creator too. He explained that Jolonus had asked to see it and that the gift took energy.

"Please keep this weakness a secret. I need to be seen as strong," he asked.

"I won't tell anyone," she said in return.

"Thank you. I must have passed out when trying to show Jolonus the gift. I'm so sorry that he has died Freta."

He hugged her again. As they embraced he glanced to the metal sheet. His eyes opened wide. The rock had liquidised and re-solidified. It was an even deeper yellow now and reminded him of the armour the Messenger had worn. He decided when he had the time, and more strength, he would burn some and see if he could make it shine like the strange apparel and weapon the Messenger had, now, however, was not the time.

"I didn't even get a chance to say goodbye," Freta sniffed.

"He was always proud of you," Dragatu replied. "You meant everything to him. I know you wish you could have said goodbye, but he knew you always loved him."

"I know," she said heavily, pulling herself away once again.

"I need some water and food," Dragatu said, beginning to feel dizzy again.

Freta looked at him. He was so pale and they both struggled to their feet, Dragtau's head nearly touching the ceiling. They stepped to her father and whispered a farewell. Freta kissed him on his forehead and pulled the blanket to cover him until he was buried. With this done they walked through to the back and into the small room to the right that served as a kitchen. They sat in silence while Dragatu ate a massive portion of food. When Dragatu finished he looked up and gave her a loving smile.

"I'll look after you now," he said. "If you want me to?"

"Of course I do," she said passionately. There was a moment of silence as they looked knowingly at each other, the emotions they felt saying all that was needed.

"Dragatu. Can I see your gift?" Freta asked after the silence.

He wanted to show her, but in a defeated tone replied, "I'm so tired. I need to sleep first then I'll show you."

"Okay," she nodded, hiding her slight disappointment.

They went to Freta's room, opposite the kitchen, and Dragatu lay on her bed taking up most of the room, but she squeezed in, snuggling beside him. It was mid-afternoon, but they slept, Dragatu fell asleep straight away, and Freta lay still for a while, thinking she wouldn't be able to, but in time her emotional exhaustion took her.

When Dragatu woke it was almost night, and Freta was gone. He guessed she had left to tell friends the sad news and to prepare Jolonus' body for burial. His muscles still ached and he rose slowly to get more food. Hearing noises, he took the food then found Freta sitting on the back step, watching a neighbour digging the grave. Dragatu sat next to her and she buried her head in his arm. A few minutes passed, and Dragatu stirred making Freta sit up. Without a word he stood and walked over to the man, took the shovel and began digging. The man nodded and left them out of respect. Seeing what Dragatu was doing, Freta walked to stand beside him.

"You don't have to do this if you're too tired," she said.

"I'm okay," he nodded. "It would be an honour."

She gave him a weak smile and turned, walking towards one of the torches that had been stuck into the ground, ready for when the light faded into night.

Dragatu noticed, walked over to her, put an arm on her shoulder and smiled softly.

"Watch," he whispered. He looked at the torch with those deep red eyes and it burst into flames. Freta gasped and let out a small laugh of amazement. Then sobered and said poignantly.

"I'm glad Father got to see it before he died."

Dragatu nodded and kissed her lightly on the forehead. He turned back to the grave and continued digging. Freta used the flaming torch to light more and sat on the steps, watching him. When the grave was finished it was late, and they went back to bed.

8/3/700

The sun had just shown its radiant face and filled the room with hazed light. Dragatu lay next to Freta, watching her sleep. Her beauty was captivating. As he watched, he hoped her sleep was free from thoughts of death. Half an hour went by and she woke, turning and smiling at him, then she remembered the tragedy of the previous day.

"I hoped it was only a nightmare," she said sadly as she closed her eyes again.

Dragatu stroked her hair softly with the back of his hand.

"Thank you," she whispered, her voice full of emotion.

Suddenly she took a controlled breath and sat up, swinging herself to perch on the side of the bed, holding the edge with both hands. After a pause, she stood up. Dragatu saw the effort and sadness in her movements. He got up too, following her to the kitchen and they made breakfast. The burial was that afternoon and the hours passed slowly. Neighbours and friends came to pay their respects and last of all Freta said her final goodbye. With the farewells spoken they buried Jolonus, reading several passages from the Book of Law as the grave was filled.

Once everyone had left, Freta and Dragatu went inside the house. Dragatu decided to update his journal while Freta slept. He wrote about how much he was going to miss Jolonus and how he had discovered the yellow rocks could be made into a precious metal.

11/3/700

The next few days were spent setting Jolonus' affairs in order. They agreed it would be good for Freta to stay with Dragatu, and she slept in a spare room on the top floor next to Healana's room. Dragatu was her strength in grief. He knew what it was like to lose a father. They distracted each other with talk of adventures and they planned trips to the forests and the hills. Dragatu decided to tell her about the yellow stones, but hadn't tried to change any yet. When he got the opportunity he knew he would.

During this time Phoenon had become braver with his gift and healed some people, but still struggled to cope with the pain. He became more popular because of this help and because people loved to see his hair burst into the array of orange shades in the sunlight.

Unilus also grew in popularity because he had gained some confidence. Tursea helped him with this, and he tried hard to improve because he wanted to be able to share the knowledge he gained with everyone. He also had some ideas for new projects to help the whole Nation. Dragatu, too, had come up with some ideas of his own, and after a short time the brothers met to discuss what they would do to help the people.

17/3/700

The brother's paths crossed in the house and they agreed to meet in the library to discuss their future plans. As they began, Unilus and Phoenon offered their condolences to Dragatu. He thanked them and sat as Unilus started the meeting. Dragatu's gaze lingered on his two brothers; the colour changes to their hair and eyes were going to take some getting used to.

"I'm glad we have met. I think we should meet often so we can work together to help the people as we promised we would. Does this sound like a good idea?"

Phoenon and Dragatu agreed.

"I propose every two weeks. Assuming I'm not away in the hills," Dragatu said, trying to make his presence felt.

Phoenon nodded in agreement, but Unilus shared his concerns.

"Two weeks is good, but I don't think you should go to the hills too much. You will be needed here a lot more now."

"I'll go if I want to go Unilus," Dragatu said flatly, not enjoying being told what to do. "But don't worry, when I'm here I'll attend our meetings and help as much as I can."

"Okay. If that's what you think is best," Unilus continued, not wanting to cause an argument. "Our first mission should be to make sure all the people know about our gifts, that the Creator sent a Messenger to give them to us and that our gifts were given to help all the people. We should continue as we have been and use our gifts when we can. This will allow the people to become familiar with them. It's important we don't come across as too different, or intimidating."

The last statement was subtly aimed at Dragatu, some of the people were already wary of him because of his strength and blunt way of doing things. Now that he was stronger and had great power they were even more cautious of him. Dragatu knew this and had seen it in some of the people, but ignored Unilus' statement. He didn't see the people's wariness as a problem. Their behaviour was a sign of respect and it made leading easier. It had worked for fighting the lions, for leading the Hunora, for getting his friends to help others and for achieving the goals he had made to honour his father. And now he had the gift their greater respect would help him lead even more effectively.

Dragatu simply matched Phoenon's nod, ignoring Unilus' caution. Phoenon then spoke up with an idea.

"We should have someway to tell everyone we'd use our gifts to help them. They should know they could come and talk to us if they need our help with anything. Then over time everyone will know they can always come to us."

Dragatu shuffled in his chair. "I don't like the idea of them always being allowed to approach us. I think that could hinder us," he said.

"It should be okay," Unilus said, casually dismissing the concerns.

Dragatu sat back and shook his head. 'How will we have time to listen to every person that comes up to us?' he thought. He didn't voice his concerns, feeling his brothers wouldn't listen.

A few more points were discussed and the meeting closed. The last point was to send out parchment declarations throughout the Nation so people knew about the gifts and their purposes. Unilus went to the scribers to get the declarations written up, but the scribers said it would be too much work to write up a declaration for every person and after some discussion they agreed on a better way. They decided the best way was to erect large wooden posts throughout the Nation and attach any declarations to them. Unilus left the mock declaration with the scribers to write up a couple of hundred copies and walked to the letter distributors and told them of the plans. The letter distributors agreed to help and once the scribers had written up the declarations the distributors would happily attach the declarations to each post on their rounds. It was a busy day for Unilus and after mapping out key points in the Nation he found some builders to organise the construction and erection of the posts.

1/4/700

Dragatu's concerns had been right and he pressed this fact at the next meeting, which took place in the library again.

"I told you, it's too much to have the people coming up to us with every little thing when we walk the streets. There must be more control and order."

"Okay," Unilus said in complete agreement. "We'll have to change how we do this. Phoenon and I have barely been able to move since we sent out the declaration."

Dragatu spoke, trying hard to take the lead. "I've been thinking about it. We should set aside two days a week where the people can visit us. That brings some structure to the chaos. We could do this in an unused field. There is nowhere else I can think of that will hold the volumes of people that might come. This means on the other days we can do what we want, or help the people."

Unilus and Phoenon saw the logic in what he said. They nodded their agreement as Dragatu continued to speak.

"What will also make this easier is some sort of symbol, or art work, that represents each of us. This can be put on a banner at the fields. The banner will show the people where we are and they can go to who they think will be the most help. This way we can deal individually with most of the problems. If it's a big problem we can bring it here to our meetings and discuss it."

"That's a good plan," Phoenon said.

"I agree. Good work Dragatu," Unilus complimented. "Shall we come up with some kind of symbol for the next meeting and tomorrow we can send out the newest declarations, telling the people that they should stop coming up to us unless it's an emergency. Also, it should tell them that in a few weeks, when we have our banners, that we will have days that they can come to the fields and see us."

Phoenon nodded and Dragatu smiled, giving a sideways nod.

The meeting adjourned and Dragatu was excited that his banner idea had worked. He had already come up with a few ideas. Unilus had inspired the idea for the banners, and for his own symbol. Unilus had always been interested in symbolism, especially in some of his drawings. Dragatu had remembered Unilus saying symbolism could get a lot of information across in a simple way, depending on what the symbol was, the context, and what meanings and ideas were attached to it. Dragatu wanted to use this to help them have more order and to stop people thinking he was nothing but physical strength.

Over the following two weeks, the brothers continued building the foundations to help people. As always Dragatu spent most of his time around the rich area, or amongst the ore pits, trying to help people. They would often shout for him to use his fire-gift, but he only did it on rare occasions. He wanted to retain a level of mystery, and because he didn't want them to see he had a weakness.

14/4/700

When it was time to show the symbols Dragatu took the lead. Surrounded by scrolls stacked on the library's shelves he held up a large piece of parchment and explained what he had drawn.

"I have chosen the triangle because it's the strongest structure," Dragatu said. Unilus had often declared this when building the supports for the channels of the water project, and Dragatu had used this. "The triangle is a symbol of strength and I wanted to use this to represent the strength I've been gifted with. The circle is a symbol of my leadership. Just like my leadership, my help, and my protection, it encircles the people. I have repeated the symbol inside itself because I wanted to represent the infinity of these ideals, showing they will continue to grow and last forever through the children I'll have one day.

184

As for the colours, I wanted them to be more things that represent me, so the black in the bottom right of the triangles is for my black hair, the red at the top represents my eyes, and the yellow on the left corner represents Freta's hair and how she is a part of my leadership. The flames around the symbol show my fire gift and the words at the bottom will be my motto." He had written the words, "Strength, Power and Control" below the symbol. "Oh, and I've kept the background white for ease," he concluded.

"Interesting," Unilus said a bit concerned with some of the explanations, but trying hard to be patient with Dragatu's way of doing things, "I see a lot of thought has gone into this. It's very impressive."

Dragatu smiled at the compliment and put the parchment on the floor next to his chair as he sat down.

"I will show you mine now," Unilus said as he held up his drawing. "The spiral you see coming from the centre has lines in it that start at the number one, and then you add that to the previous, which at the start would be zero. Then you have the number one again and add the two one's together, and have the number two. Then you add, two, to its previous number, and have three. The pattern is repeated and you get the following numbers: five, eight, thirteen, twenty-one, thirty-four . . . and this represents an important sequence of numbers found in nature. The spiral around the numbers symbolises progression, and the need for expansion of the self.

The spiral and the numbers have been placed in a circular symbol that represents balance, because life is full of opposites, like the black and white you can see. I have done this because life needs to balance. That if we try and balance negative and positives we will understand our own personalities more and, therefore, know how to use are strengths and improve our weaknesses, and therefore progress.

The green branches and flowers around the symbol represent nature, and also the theme that we need to progress and develop with nature. Like the branches, we also need to branch out in life to improve ourselves and to be able to help others more. All these things represent my gift and can apply to what I stand for. I also felt this symbol worked well because I have been gifted with the ability to commune with all life." A strange coincidence had occurred between his and Dragatu's symbol. "It is strange that both Dragatu and I have written our philosophies below our symbols and I have chosen the motto, "Chose, Choice, Choose" to represent the importance of freewill. The past tense: you 'chose' the present tense, you have a 'choice', and the future tense, you have to 'choose'; all represent these ideas of freewill and have symbolic representation of the self, and how things of the past, present and future add together to make up our personalities."

Dragatu and Phoenon couldn't help but be impressed with this symbol. When Unilus finished Dragatu ran his hand through his hair and stroked his short beard, confused by some of what Unilus had said and slightly frustrated that it looked so good. Phoenon, on the other hand, was feeling very inadequate. When Unilus had finished he quickly scribbled down three words as he hadn't thought of writing his philosophy, and looking up, realised it was his turn.

"This my symbol," he said as he tried to keep the parchment still, nerves getting the better of him, "The . . . the outline of the bird represents the phoenix gift that I have. And it's white to symbolise purity." Dragatu smirked in his mind, 'What was purity when compared with strength?' "The single eye in the chest is meant to represent that we should all look out for each other and care for each other with all our hearts, and this is also shown by the heart shaped pupil in the eye. It is also meant to symbolise being nice and nice character traits, like Compassion, Charity and Love, which are the words you can see I've put underneath, like you both did. The heart pupil is orange to represent my new eye colour and my hair colour when in the sun . . . and I guess that's about it," he said weakly and gave a nervous smile.

"That's very good Phoenon," Unilus said, trying to give him some encouragement. "I love the simplicity of it. It's exactly what symbolism should be. Simple and conveys your meaning well. I like it a lot."

Phoenon grinned putting the parchment on his lap face down. "Thank you," he said modestly. Dragatu gave a faint smile to Phoenon and reassuringly said, "It is very good." But he began to wonder: if Phoenon was this nervous about showing a simple symbol, how was he going to lead effectively?

"I like what we've done here," Unilus said. "The symbols are exactly what they need to be, and represent us well. The people will become familiar with them, and once they are on banners they will help them know who to go to when we have our allocated days to be visited.

Now that we have dealt with that I want to discuss a new project I think will be good for all our people." Dragatu shifted in his chair to relax, guessing Unilus was going to talk for a while. "I think we should improve the buildings and houses. We can use granite instead of bricks, and this would mean they needed repairing less and give better living to all the people. I want to do it to decrease the gap between rich and poor. I know there will most likely always be a class system, but I want to reduce that gap so there's a better level of equality. This way the people will be more likely to see each other as equals and treat each other with the same levels of kindness and respect."

Dragatu saw a flaw in the idea and interrupted.

"And how are we to afford such a massive project? It will take a lot of time and effort to do every single house. Plus, the only place to find granite is beyond the ore pits. This would take an incredible amount of labour and I don't know how we could make this work."

"I have thought about your concerns, and I believe there is a way," Unilus countered. "If we work together, as we have before, we can make this work. It will make the people a lot happier to have a new house and it is vital we improve the homes of the poorest people. Because some of the conditions they live in are unacceptable."

A debate ensued in which Dragatu's patience ran very thin. 'This would be so much easier if I were leading by myself,' he suddenly thought, drumming his figures on the arm of his chair while Unilus spoke about the importance of equality. 'Why is it so difficult to come to the obvious outcome? I know it's supposed to be good that we're different, but it's slowing down the ability to act.' A faint memory of his father's request to work with his brothers grazed his thoughts. He sighed to himself and noticed Unilus had finished. Taking a deep breath, he spoke up and made his points, trying to honour Branon's request at the same time.

After nearly an hour, a compromise was made. Through Dragatu's persuasion, and explanation that the workload was too much, it was decided only those with brick houses in the rich area, and some of the more affluent poorer people would get granite houses. Then the bricks taken from the old houses would be used to improve all the poorer houses. Unilus was concerned that the gap between rich and poor would still be too noticeable, but Dragatu convinced him it would be okay by saying, "The priority is to improve the houses first, complete equality can come later."

Satisfied with Dragatu's reasoning, they made a plan similar to the water project's construction. The work would be in stages and begin in the very centre of the Nation. This was shown on a map by an imaginary line where they felt the richer part finished and the poorer part started. Those in that area would have to live with other family, or friends. With the area clear the work force, led once more by Dragatu and the Hunora, would begin transporting granite and building the new houses. The granite would be built around the brick houses and the bricks would be taken down when the main structure was finished. The bricks would then be taken and used to build new houses for the poorer people.

"I have already communed with the animals at the farms, and in the forest, and they are willing to help," Unilus told them. "But only if they are treated with respect, and fed and watered well. We should send out two declarations: one explaining the plans we've constructed, asking the people if they feel it's a good idea, and the second to confirm the days we will see the people, telling them they should come to us with any concerns, worries or ways we can help them."

The meeting concluded. As they left, Unilus took the drawings for their banners to the loom workers and cloth makers.

23/4/700

Three big tents had been erected and each was crowned with a banner that flapped in the wind. It was the first day of officially meeting the people and hundreds had gathered, looking at the symbols with amazement, commending their beauty, and discussing what they thought they represented. It was a long day for the three brothers and as the sun set they told people to come back the next day. By the time everyone had left, night had fallen and the brothers sat outside Phoenon's tent, wrapped in warm furs to fight off the cooling air.

"They're very happy we've set apart days to see them," Phoenon said, beginning the debriefing optimistically.

"Yes, that seems to be something that everyone is happy with," Unilus agreed. He looked at Dragatu for confirmation on this topic and Dragatu nodded. "How did people take to the ideas for the new project?" Unilus continued.

"People seemed happy enough," Dragatu said, "They say it will be a lot of work, but a lot of those who came to see me said they wanted to help if I was going to lead them."

"Phoenon?" Unilus asked.

"A lot of people I spoke to loved the idea, but feel they will not be able to pay back such a gift."

"Well, they can help build them," Dragatu said.

"It's . . . not that simple," Phoenon replied hesitantly, "They have to work almost all day just to live and provide for themselves. To take time off without any support would leave them in a worse place than before."

"Well, the richer people can help provide the food and water the workers will need," Unilus said trying to mediate.

Once again Dragatu wasn't sure if that was a good idea. His brother's optimism and naivety about people's behaviour was frustrating. 'If the rich people will actually agree to do that?' he thought cynically. For Branon's sake, and for the sake of the promises, he kept his concerns to himself, but only just.

"It will work out even if we don't have more help from the richer people," Unilus continued, seeing the familiar concern on Dragatu's face. "However, there is something else, which isn't really a problem, but we hadn't thought about it. Some of the people who came to see me said they were happy with the houses they had, and didn't want to change them. I think we must make sure everyone knows they have a choice, and do not have to change. But from today's meeting with the people it's clear the majority of people want the improvement, and this means we should start the hard work soon." He paused, leaning back in his chair then continued.

"There was one final idea that someone brought to my attention. This was the opportunity to improve the system and infrastructure of water distribution. We have enough, but most of it goes to the reservoir here, and to the one at the ore pits. If we incorporate plans to channel the water to a few key points within the Nation, then people won't have to travel so far to get it. This would help a lot of people."

Dragatu smiled at this last idea, 'Finally, something practical and achievable.' It was nice to have something to agree on. Phoenon especially liked this idea and agreed it should be added into their plans.

🔥

Over the coming weeks, the fine details of the new project were made. As they did this, the brothers enjoyed watching the people come closer together thanks to their unified purpose. In turn it helped bring them closer together, once they had worked through their differences. Each day they clung to the knowledge they were honouring their father and the Creator. It brought them happiness and motivation in the face of the hard work that was ahead. From the water project and their many experiences, they had come to believe there were few things worth having that didn't require hard work.

With Honrus, Reon and Linur's help, Dragatu had recruited all the previous Hunora that still lived, and added some new ones to the list. However, despite appearing completely committed to this project Dragatu had been struggling with his own wishes. His inner debate finally coming to a conclusion as he sat alone thinking in the library, with his journal open deciding what to write.

'These responsibilities and this new project are taking up so much time. I really could do with a break at the hills. I also want to practice turning the yellow stones into the precious metal. But I don't have the time or the energy at the moment. I hate waiting. I have so much I want to do, but keep getting pulled away. I guess it'll happen eventually. I know the people must come first but it's just so difficult as I feel torn. I'll just have to use my fire gift as much as possible so if I do get some free time I can use it on the stones. But who knows when that'll be?'

Meanwhile, Unilus worked with Tursea to organise the animals and made sure they were ready for transporting granite from the canyons beyond the ore pits. They also recruited people who would look after the animals and make sure they were treated well.

Phoenon helped by healing any workers he could, and tried to recruit people from the poorer areas, but these were few. His concerns had been right, and they couldn't afford to give up their time without compensation of food and water. After knowing this for certain, Phoenon repeated Unilus' original request to Dragatu.

"They want to help, but can't. If you could just ask a few of the richer people to give up some of their excess, then we can have more workers and finish the project quicker."

"I can tell you now that most people won't just give away what's theirs," Dragatu replied. But that part of conscience, which was fueled by his promises, and recent feelings of unity stemming from the project persuaded him to go against his better judgment. "But I will try. Just don't get your hopes up."

"Okay. Thank you so much for trying. It's really important we get all the help we can." Phoenon smiled gleefully.

Dragatu did as he said he would. To his surprise a lot more of the richer people were willing to sacrifice what was theirs, but they did make sure it was only temporary sacrifice before they agreed.

21/5/700

A mass body of people and animals moved eastward, spreading between ore pits and houses like the roots of a tree. Dragatu led the Hunora with Freta at his side, Phoenon walked with the workers from the poorer areas, and Unilus and Tursea walked amongst the animals. Scattered around and in-between these three groups were more workers from many different trades, ready to do their part. The project had begun, and as the sun beat down on them they continued their first trip to quarry the granite.

Chapter 16
Unity

2/7/702

When the sun was at its brightest the white granite glowed like the edges of a cloud passing in front of the sun. Two years had gone by. Seeing the newly built houses shine this way made Unilus think of the majestic white horse that was the Messenger. The granite illuminated with a similar celestial splendor. It was a perfect day for his wedding.

It was to be a joint celebration, coinciding with the completion of the work that had taken over two years. He reflected on the project as he waited until it was time to leave to go to his wedding. He smiled to himself as he remembered the work moving forward at a good pace. Then his brow creased and he sighed, remembering how Dragatu and the Hunora had created a few teething problems. It hadn't taken long before people complained they were too strict and once more he, Dragatu and Phoenon had struggled to compromise, telling Dragatu he had to stop making them work so hard hadn't gone down so well.

"The work will be done as and when the people are able," Unilus remembered saying. "We are in no rush. It's more important to create unity than efficient and effective workers."

Dragatu hadn't agreed, but chose to accept what Unilus had said.

"It's just that the Hunora and I are doing most of the hard work, and everyone else should be trying to do the same. I think they should be working harder, but if you're not going to side with me then I guess I have to accept it. All I want to do is lead them the best way I can, but it seems like they don't want my leadership and help. There so ungrateful and idle sometimes . . ." The last statement had taken all three of them by surprise, and noticing his rare outburst Dragatu had quickly covered it up. "I'll make sure the people aren't pushed too much. Are we done here?" And with a nod from Unilus he had left.

It had taken a few weeks for the tension to fade, but focusing on the benefits of the project had helped. Six months of good work went by and the new skyline at the centre of the Nation was starting to take shape. Almost all the people were unified in helping the work continue now. Yet the time they could give wasn't much, as life had to go on, crops and livestock farms had to be maintained, ore had to be dug, hunting had to continue, and trades had to be practiced.

Unilus smiled again as he remembered that a new idea had been proposed in those first six months. The generosity of the people had touched him. The idea was for a large multi-purpose home, bigger than any other home or structure in the Nation, to be built in the very centre. He currently stood at the window of his room in that castle-like building, still watching the granite glow in the sun as he pondered.

It had been built for Phoenon, Dragatu, himself, and any family to live in, have their own meetings, and meet with the people. A declaration had been sent out to see if the extra work would be accepted. They had agreed to the extra work because they wanted to give something back to the three brothers. It had a large library and a welcoming hall on the ground floor, meeting rooms for each of the brothers on the first floor, and living areas on the top floor. There were also many spare rooms built on each floor for storage and at the back of the library there were three underground rooms. It was said that these were also for storage, which in part was true, but it was also where Unilus was going to keep the Book of Prophecy.

Healana still looked after it, but Unilus had wanted to be prepared in case she died, or for when he and Tursea took the step from engagement to marriage, with what was to occur that day his preparations had been wise. Once they had known the date of their marriage, the entrance from the library had been locked, and Unilus and Tursea had the only two keys. And today, after they were married, they would receive the Book of Prophecy from Healana and keep it hidden below the library. As a precautionary measure one other entrance did exist. This was from their room on the second floor, which descended to the third and final room below the library, where the Book of Prophecy would be kept.

The next year and a half had been spent building. It had been hard work, but Unilus thought about various special moments, as when the people cared for each other and the animals, Tursea lifting peoples spirits when they were low, Phoenon healing and telling jokes, and Dragatu's unbreakable commitment to working hard, and to the Hunora and Freta. He knew he owed each of these people a lot for who they were and what they did, but it was just hard to tell them this. He hung his head, 'Why can I understand so much, but no understand people or how to express myself well?' Quickly he shook it off, for it wasn't time for one of his intense reflecting sessions. He was getting married. Noticing the time he stepped away from the window and got ready. Finally, he left his room to marry the love of his life.

The sun still shone bright as he left the beautifully decorated castle, flowers covered the building on this special day. He had wanted to get married under the lone tree he liked, but Tursea had suggested it was better to get married at the front of the castle. It had become the heart of the Nation, and the people saw it as a symbol of their bright future. With this in mind he agreed, but suggested they met at the tree and walk through the Nation to the castle so people could share in the celebrations. Tursea had agreed this would be a lovely gesture.

The wedding ceremony was beautiful, and there were almost as many animals gathered in the streets as there were people, everyone having grown accustomed to Unilus' gift, blending them in a way that had never occurred before. The vows were read from the Book of Law and affirmed by the happy couple. Once it was over, Healana spoke to them alone and gave them the Book of Prophecy, and they made promises to read and protect its secrets. The married couple then took some belongings and set off to spend a few days in the forests. There wasn't much work planned over those days, except for what had to be done. It was time to celebrate, and people walked around the Nation to view the beautiful granite and brick houses, they had feasts, sang songs, and enjoyed the chance to share the fruits of their labours.

10/7/702

Unilus and Tursea returned and life continued as it always did. The people settled back into a routine of their own work, without much thought for anything else. It wasn't long before Dragatu could finally plan a trip to the hills and take a break from his responsibilities. He planned to take some of the yellow rocks with him and finally practice changing them. However, there was one thing he wanted to deal with before he left. He had noticed the lull in the effort people put into their work and helping each other. Watching this, he wondered why the people had become lax. 'What had changed?' He decided to keep an eye on their efforts, and formulated a few plans that might help and motivate the people to work the way they had on the housing project.

12/7/702

The heat in the blacksmith's forge was intense, but Dragatu didn't mind. Using his fire gift whenever he could he had grown accustomed to such temperatures.

"What do you think Honrus?" he said, explaining a plan to divide up the Hunora and send them to watch over different parts of the Nation. Their job would be to help and motivate the people to work harder and look out for one another.

"I like it. I think you're right. The people need to be encouraged and not be allowed to settle into a sluggish and idle lifestyle." Honrus paused. "You do know that people may object to this?" he continued hesitantly.

"Yeah, I know." Dragatu sighed, remembering the start of the housing project and Unilus' words. "But if we make sure people understand the Hunora are there to help them with their own work, or help them find people to work for, then it will be okay."

"What did your brothers say?"

"I haven't told them," Dragatu said casually. "I know it sounds bad, but I don't intend to. I really shouldn't need to run to them with every decision, it wastes time."

"I see," Honrus said, rubbing his face and wondering what their reaction would be when they found out, but didn't say anymore.

"Will you help tell the Hunora what I've told you?" Dragatu continued. "And tell them to meet me tomorrow so we can get this under way and organised."

"Of course."

"Tell them to meet me outside the castle at the third hour past high sun," Dragatu said, feeling the cooler air on his face as he left.

13/7/702

Dragatu told the Hunora and they agreed it was a great idea. He allocated them to the places he wanted them to oversee. Stressing heavily the points he had discussed with Honrus, Dragatu told them they were to help the people with their work and encourage them to work harder. Then while they were doing this, tell the people it was important as they would have more to trade with and more to give to others, and this in turn would give them all better lives.

19/7/702

The tension was like a solid entity that had been growing and pushing against them as the argument progressed in their meeting, and it was reaching its climax, ready to break, or break them. Dragatu was angry with both of his brothers. Many of the differences that had been apparent over the years were frustrating him, his patience was spent and as Unilus spoke he knew he couldn't hold his tongue any longer.

"Dragatu, what you have done is wrong," Unilus said, a rare tone of anger in his voice. "It is not in line with our responsibilities. We are to give people as much freedom as we can. You did not bring this idea to the meeting, instead you went ahead without any discussion and this shows you knew we would say it was wrong."

"I didn't tell you because you are too relaxed," Dragatu protested, leaning forward with both hands pressing down on the table they sat around. "Without the right motivation the people will go back to being idle and not working hard. The house building and the water project have shown us how hard they can work if they want to.

They need the Hunora and I to lead them. With our leadership, they would work hard and have better lives. I took the initiative. It's the best way for them to learn to help themselves. They just need a little push."

"No matter how much you justify this, it is still wrong," Unilus said flatly, also leaning forward, but cupping his hands together under the table, "You need to stop the Hunora. Some have been very strict on the poorer families, just because they are poor."

Dragatu's face dropped. Slowly the scar lines creased as his face began to tighten with confusion and frustration. He was fed up with having to justify his actions.

"It's probably because the poorer people were being lazy and not listening to the Hunora, and not taking the help offered." His voice rose as he spoke.

"You shouldn't be forcing them to do anything," Unilus said as calmly as he could, but a tone of command ebbed through.

"It's not forcing them. It's encouraging them!"

"The . . . the people have told me the Hunora . . . forced them to work at the ore pits," Phoenon said timidly, frightened by the growing tensions.

198

"That's an exaggeration, I'm sure," Dragatu said dismissively, trying to calm himself as he noticed Phoenon's slight fear, "I'll talk to the Hunora and reiterate that they are there only to motivate and offer support."

"No!" Unilus shouted, rising from his chair, finally losing his calm, "This must stop!"

After a moment of shock Phoenon nodded, affirming that he felt the same. The outburst from Unilus shocked Dragatu too and he withdrew his hands to the edges of the arms of his chair. He looked from one brother to the other. As the initial shock faded he felt like he was going to explode, shock turning to annoyance, then annoyance turning to hate. 'Why can't they understand what I'm trying to do? The people need this! Why won't they listen? If they want to do as the Creator wants, and help the people be better, then this is a good way.'

An awkward silence made the room feel empty as Dragatu struggled with his anger. Unilus stood looking at Dragatu waiting for a reply. A sudden 'CRACK!' broke the silence. Dragatu quickly let go of the arms of the chair, not realising he had been squeezing them so hard. The unexpected noise, and shock of seeing the broken wood diffused some of his anger and he put his arms on his lap apologetically.

"Fine. If that's what you both want then that's what will happen."

Unilus nodded, "Thank you." And he sat back in his chair, quickly changing the topic of conversation.

For the rest of the meeting, Dragatu sat in silence, knowing he should let this go, but feeling that his brother's weren't trying hard enough to help the people. He didn't understand how they could reject what was obviously a good idea. When they finished he said a strained farewell and left.

20/7/702

"We have to stop helping the people," Dragatu began, standing on the top step at the front of the castle.

There were shouts of complaint and the shaking of heads, but Dragatu continued.

"My brothers told me there have been complaints. They said some of you were too harsh on the poorer people. I think there has been a misunderstanding of our intentions. I know what we were trying to do was right, but we must stop, for now."

"Is there nothing we can do to continue helping?" Honrus shouted from the front of the crowd.

Dragatu smiled at his friend for his enthusiasm. "No, there is not, at least not for now. I'll find a way where we can help, but at this time I'm not sure what it is. I'll tell you when I have a plan. For now, we must stop, but I will contact you soon. Thank you for your willingness to help."

As the crowd dispersed he signaled to Honrus, Reon, Linur, and a few other close friends, turned and walked into the castle. Dragatu and those with him walked to his meeting room and discussed what could be done to help the people that wouldn't be rejected. Nothing conclusive was decided and Dragatu thanked them for trying, but dismissed them after half an hour.

It was late into the night, and Dragatu continued to sit alone in his meeting room contemplating his problems long after Freta had eaten with him and gone to bed. It was a painful process, but finally he made up his mind. Trying to achieve the two sides to his promises was a contradiction. He couldn't achieve his potential as a leader if he kept trying to work with his brothers.

'The problem is that my brothers can't make the difficult choices. I'm the strong leader, that's what the people need. I should be the only leader. It makes sense. I have been the one who has made the two great projects happen. My Hunora and I organised the people, led them in these things, and without me, and them, it would not have happened. I'm the one that helps them the most, but I could help them so much more.'

As he sat in the dim light of the glowing fire he hung his head in partial remorse.

'I'm sorry father. I've tried so hard to do as you asked, but it isn't working as well as it could. The people need someone who isn't afraid to tell them what they need to hear and not just what they want to hear. The Creator told us to lead the people and that's what I have to do. It's who I am. Of course, my brothers will help me and advise me, and deal with the people that follow them more. But the people need a strong leader to take control, someone who will have the last say on everything. I'm the best person to lead. There is so much evidence to prove this. There needs to be a change so I can help the people the way they need. This is the only way the chaos and struggles, created by the three of us trying to lead, will stop. I'm sorry. I can no longer 'try' and lead. I 'will' lead.'

21/7/702

The following morning he told Freta what he had decided. She listened intently as she brushed her golden hair. When he finished she shared some doubts.

"This might create a bigger divide, Dragatu. Are you sure this is the only option?"

"I have spent more hours than I care to say thinking and being torn about this. This is the only way everyone can be happy and do as the Creator would want. In time, they will see that having one leader will create unity."

Seeing his strong will and taking some time to think she agreed it was the best option for the people. Thanking her for her support, he left to speak to the Hunora. They were delighted with his plan, and said he had their complete backing. Dragatu was glad and thankful for the positive response. The hard part would come the following day. His brothers weren't going to accept this easily, but he had a plan.

22/7/702

"Yes you heard me right," Dragatu said as Unilus and Phoenon stared at him, sitting back in their chairs in bewilderment. "I want a declaration sent asking the people if they would have me as their only leader."

A few more moments of shocked silence went by and Unilus broke it, still trying to understand what Dragatu had proposed.

"You want to lead by yourself?"

"In a way, yes, but at the same time no. I'll have the last say in everything, but I'll have you both by my side. You will help and offer advice when it is needed. However, I will be in charge. You must see that it is for the best. It is the best way to help the people. The three of us leading just isn't working. It's too slow, too ineffective and creates too much division."

Unilus saw the determination in Dragatu's face, and in a pained tone repeated his question. "Is this really what you want?"

"Yes."

Unilus closed his eyes, hung his head and took a deep breath. As he exhaled he looked up, slowly glancing at Phoenon. Seeing the same hurt in his brother's face he reluctantly gave in, looking down at the table.

"Well, in that case, we must give the people a choice. But if they vote against you, this must be the last of these propositions," he said, raising his head heavily, forcing himself to look at Dragatu. "If you don't get your way you must accept the three of us should work together. If you do we will forget this hurtful desire not to be unified." He looked at Phoenon to see if he agreed. Phoenon nodded once but said nothing.

Dragatu thought for a second, 'If I explain this well to the people, I won't lose.' "Okay. I'll accept those terms," he replied.

Dragatu pulled a scroll of parchment from his pack and slid it across the table. Unilus and Phoenon read the mock declaration he had made and with heavy hearts they discussed it with him. With their acceptance he left, taking it to be distributed throughout the entire Nation. Excitement welled as he left the castle, the thought of leading without any constraints was liberating.

24/7/702

Dragatu's declaration brought people to the posts as quickly as fanned flames moving on a dry grass field in summer. The word of what was written on them whipped from one person to the next and everyone went to see the declaration the moment they could, and it was all anyone talked about. They were given a week to decide and people debated their own personal choices with one another.

The Hunora and those close to Dragatu, gathered support from the rich people, and tried to convince the poorer people and the farmers that it was in their best interest to make Dragatu their single leader. However, their reports to Dragatu showed there wasn't much support from these people. Those who lived at the ore pits hadn't forgotten Dragatu's generosity and help over the years, and with Freta having lived there, most of them backed him.

Unilus spent a day with some prominent thinkers and they invented a voting system. Over the course of two days each person would come to the castle, take some parchment, and write the outcome they wanted. They would put a one for Dragatu, or a three if they wanted it to keep the current leadership. The committee who came up with this method agreed it was only fair if the final decision was a majority of two thirds. If the margin was too narrow the vote would take place again the following week. If there was still no conclusive outcome it would take place a third time. If no decision could be made after three votes, the motion would be put on hold for a year. Then the vote would take place again until a conclusive decision was made. Phoenon and Dragatu agreed to this and vowed that when a final decision was made they would accept it and work their best, no matter what that decision.

1/8/702

It was a tense first day of voting. The brothers had recruited a group of people from all backgrounds to oversee the counting. The votes were to be split into two rooms and kept in piles of five hundred. By the end of the first day, it was difficult to tell who was in the lead. It looked like there was a bigger pile in favour of the three of them ruling, but there was still another day of voting.

Dragatu had noticed the seemingly bigger pile against him. His confidence began to wane, so he left the Nation, wanting solitude. It was late and dark, but he went for a walk in the forests.

2/8/702

Dragatu returned at first light. As he entered his room in the castle he saw Freta was lying on his bed, waking as he entered. She ran to him and hugged him tightly.

"Where have you been?"

"I needed to clear my head," Dragatu replied walking heavily towards the bed. "I'm sorry I didn't tell you where I had gone . . . my mind's a mess. I'm worried that I might not win after all."

"You'll be fine," she said smiling as he sat on the bed. "Whatever happens remember you already have a great impact on the people. You'll still be able to do the good you want, but just in a different way than maybe you'd prefer. But let's not think like that. You will be the leader Dragatu, and I'll always be by your side."

"Thank you Freta. I think I'll try and get some sleep," he said as he lay down. Freta joined him and they both fell asleep.

3/8/702

The votes were counted. Dragatu struggled to control his anger. He stormed out of the room when the verdict had been announced. He went straight to his room.

"Dragatu. Please listen," Freta pleaded as he paced, the fire almost visible in his eyes. He didn't reply.

"You must stay calm. You vowed to accept this if it was the outcome. I know it's not

what we want, but there's nothing we can do."

Dragatu stopped and looked at her. "I'm sorry. I can't," was all he said and he walked to a cupboard, opened it, took the journal and left her.

Journal Entry 3/8/702

What am I supposed to do? How am I supposed to help the people the way only I can, if they won't let me? We should have never had the vote. Unilus and Phoenon should have let me be the leader. How could the people not vote me to be their leader?

My stupid brothers have no idea what a mistake they have made. They have never trusted my choices. All that I have ever done has been to help the people. Why can they not see this? All the things I have done have been for nothing.

These people do not appreciate the things I've done. They are ungrateful, idle and weak. They do not deserve me to be their leader. They will remain in idleness forever, never learning to help each other enough to make the Creator happy. They will regret not voting me in. I will show them how good things could have been if they had chosen me.

I can't stand to be around my brothers any more. They don't understand me, and don't understand what I could have had, what good I would have done. It's their fault I'm so angry. I wouldn't be this angry if they had just made the right choice. I have to leave. I cannot stay here with them. If they don't want me, then they will not have me. I have to fulfill my potential, and they will not hold me back. I'll take those who want me as their leader and we will leave.

My brothers will learn it was a mistake not to let me lead. They will learn they were wrong. I know it will hurt a lot of people, but I must do this for myself, but most importantly for those who want to live a better way of life. We will follow the Book of Law closely and actively work to help one another and make sure everyone does the same. This is the only way I can help the people the way the Creator asked me to. I have to leave. I'll finally be able to achieve all my goals and not be held back as I have been, just like with the yellow rocks. I'll finally be able to try and make the precious golden metal.

The new day had calmed some of Dragatu's anger, but not his desire for change. He woke early and went to tell Freta about his plan, knocking on her door lightly. She opened it sleepily. Seeing him, the tiredness vanished and she opened the door wide to let him in. He walked into the room and paced a little, flexing his hands as he tried to decide how to start. Freta, leaning back against the closed door, saved him the trouble.

"We're leaving, aren't we?"

Dragatu stopped and stared at her. "How do you know?"

She gave him a little smile and then sobered. "I saw the anger and disappointment in your face when you left yesterday. I know you Dragatu. You are always so determined and I knew you had to follow this through to the end." She paused, pushed herself off the door and walked to him. Facing him, she smiled again and took his hand, walking him to her bed. They sat on the edge side by side, her hand still in his, and rested her head on his large arm. "Breaking the vow is wrong, but I understand Dragatu," she continued, "I've spent the night thinking about it. This was my home, but my place is with you, and I know you will always do your best. If leaving is what you think is best, then we shall leave together."

It took Dragatu a moment to reply, he had expected to justify his choice. "Thank you Freta," he said turning on the bed to face her, "I would be lost without you. I'm going to talk to the Hunora and tell them I'm leaving. I'm going to offer them a new start with us, away from my brothers and their misguided ways. I'll tell those who want to come to bring their families and tell all their friends that we're going to start our own Nation. I'll tell them that if they want a better life they should come with us."

"Where are we going?"

"The foot of the hills," Dragatu replied. "Next to the spring and reservoir. The land there has become good and it will sustain all those who want to come. There's also plenty of room to grow. We will have to take a lot of provisions, and we will have to plant crops and hunt, but I will build a Nation that is our own. I will lead in a more effective way than my brothers. In a way that helps the people be the best they can, so they are happy and we will live as the Creator wants us to."

"Are you definitely sure this is the choice you want to make?" she said hesitantly.

"Yes. I'm sure," he said with conviction. "It's the best thing for us and the people who want more than the life my brothers offer."

"A lot of people will be upset," she said squeezing his hand lovingly. "The Nation has always been one, like a family. It will be hard for the people to let us go."

"I know," Dragatu said, lightly nodding a few times and hanging his head. "But they have made their choice and I must make mine. They have to live with the consequences of their choices." Dragatu rubbed his thumb over the back of her hand and looked into her eyes.

"Okay," Freta said nodding once. "We will leave."

6/8/702

"If you do come you will need to bring all your provisions, as many animals as you can, all your tools, and as soon as we arrive we will start building a great Nation," Dragatu said as he stood on the steps of the castle once more with the Hunora gathered before him. "We will get materials from the woods in the hills, and make journeys to the ore pits and granite valley for strong materials.

It will be hard work, but we don't mind that." He laughed while others chuckled in agreement. "We will build spacious and beautiful houses for our families. If we bring red stones and all the jewels we have, we will array them on our homes and they will glimmer and shine in the sunlight. We will have large open spaces for children to play in, and water will always flow because we have the water source right next to us. Anyone who wants to come should meet at the water channels beyond the farms in a week."

He painted a paradise and they believed it was possible. Honrus, Reon, Linur and all the Hunora shouted they would come. They left excitedly and went to tell all their friends and family of the opportunity for change.

9/8/702

Dragatu hadn't spoken to his brothers since he stormed out of the meeting. They had decided to give him time to come to terms with the decision. When they heard about what he was planning, they were devastated.

"Please stay, Dragatu," Phoenon begged at a meeting he and Unilus had asked Dragatu to attend.

"Think of our family. Won't you stay for that?" Unilus asked.

"You have brought this on yourselves," Dragatu replied, trying to focus and push down the mixture of feelings that had unexpectedly crept in. "If you had just agreed and let me be the main leader then this wouldn't have had to happen."

"But you have a choice!" Unilus said loudly, his voice waving with rare emotion. "We did not make you do anything. The people voted and the majority of them want all of us to lead together. The Creator wants us to work together."

"That was never made clear," Dragatu said. "It's all choice, remember? We tried what we thought was best, but it just isn't working. If we want the people to be the best they can, and do the best we can, we need one ruler, and it should be me."

Unilus sighed, almost giving up, then spoke. "I disagree. If you had accepted the three of us leading, the greatest good would have been accomplished. The people would have chosen the right path in their own time, but your lack of understanding has created so many problems."

Dragatu was losing patience and buried the unexpected feelings of guilt and love for them. "What do the people know about choice?" he asked harshly. "They don't even know what they want. I was offering leadership, yet they follow you blindly, so I've given those who want a better life a choice."

208

Unilus went quiet again and Phoenon struggled to speak, the feeling of the pending separation becoming too much for him. Silent tears ran down his cheeks as he managed to make his plea to Dragatu.

"What about us? We are your family . . . we love you. We want you here. Remember when we wrote the letter for Freta? The three of us had fun working together. It can be like that again."

The words hurt Dragatu, brought back the guilt, and for a fraction of a second he doubted his choice, but it was only for a second. His mind was made up. He squeezed both his hands tightly, deciding to be completely honest.

"It's not enough. We were young then, and the responsibility we had was small. Things will never be that way again. I've tried, but I have to do what I believe is right."

There was a pause as the impact of what he said hit home. Still, Unilus tried again.

"Phoenon is right, Dragatu. Family is the most important thing. The loss of our father should have taught you that we needed to stick together. When we lose a family member it hurts."

"I can't apologise for my choice, and for doing what I feel is right. The people that are following me need my leadership. I will not let them down."

Unilus tried one last attempt. "My wife is pregnant, Dragatu."

Dragatu gave a weak smile. "I'm happy for you brother, but that will not change my mind."

Having done what he came to do, and because his deeply buried emotions still hurt, Dragatu stood up to leave. He gave them a last look and released some of that buried emotion. "Goodbye, my brothers," he said lovingly and walked out. As the door began to close he heard the fading sound of Unilus sighing heavily and Phoenon's silent tears transcending into sobs. He didn't look back.

Dragatu had packed all that he would need and went to make the hardest goodbye of them all. He knocked on the door and heard a voice calling through the sobs.

"Come in," Healana uttered hoarsely.

He entered and from a chair his mother looked up at him, tears running down her face. The sadness changed to a brief flash of anger and then back again to sadness.

"Why?" she said, her pain obvious.

Dragatu felt a pang of guilt and regret at her simple question. Then did his best to explain to her how he felt and why he had to leave.

"Will you come with me?" he asked when he had finished.

She looked at him for a few seconds, as if debating her answer.

"I cannot. This is my home. My time in this world is nearly over, and I want to spend my last days here. In the place that has always been my home."

Dragatu knew she was right and he realised this was probably the last time he would

see her. She knew it too and began to cry again, sobs shaking her frail frame. Dragatu wanted to say so much, but the only thing that came out was,

"I'm sorry for not keeping my promise to Father. I have failed to protect you, Unilus and Phoenon."

She stood up, and threw herself around him, hugging him tighter than he thought a woman of her age could.

"I love you," she said with a muffled voice. Turning her head to the side, she continued. "I'm proud of you. I wish you didn't have to go, but I do understand why you need to."

Dragatu could not have heard words more important to him, and whispered back, "I love you Mother. I will miss you."

She let him go. He turned quickly and walked out of the room, letting the tears he had been holding back tumble down his face.

He returned to his room and spent the last night with Freta, but he barely slept. By the time the sunlight crept through the windows he was already awake, and he began preparing himself for the journey ahead.

13/8/702

By the time he reached the meeting place, he had focused. No more was there any sadness or regret. Only excitement remained. He went over and over how he could now be the leader he was born to be. He had his gifts, his strength, and he had Freta by his side.

The sun reached its apex in the sky and Dragatu surveyed the people from the top of the cart. He gasped at the sea of heads that couldn't be counted. He took a guess, 'There must be about thirty or forty thousand people.' He had not expected so many would leave their homes. Most of them were from the rich people and ore pits, but this was good. 'These are the people most loyal to me,' he thought. They were now *his* people. The magnitude of the responsibility did not scare him. If anything it made him more determined to do the right thing by *his* people.

Before they all set off he climbed a tree to take one last look at the Nation where he had grown up. He saw people in the streets near the fields crying, begging people not to leave. Looking to the castle, he saw his banner being taken down and his brothers' banners still flapping in the wind. He felt anger and frustration at this, but controlled himself and let it go.

'I have to look to the future and forget this past. Leaving is the right choice for everyone. I must completely accept this new life, a life so much better for all these people, a life where I'm appreciated and respected, and a life where I can make the Creator happy by leading from the Book of Law.'

With these final thoughts, he climbed down, one last thought leaving his mind before his feet touched the ground and began their new path.

'If I never see you again, goodbye my brothers . . .'

Heat

Chapter 17
I Wish You Could See The World Through My Eyes: Part 1

Dragatu

2/9/702

They made it, just. The desert had been cruel and their supplies were nearly depleted. With wide eyes and dry mouths, they rushed to drink from the reservoir, the hills looming over them. Once refreshed Dragatu's people began pitching their tents and rejoicing. The punishing journey was over, and finally they had a plentiful supply of water. Amidst the rejoicing, many set out into the hills to find nuts, berries, roots, and to hunt there for fresh meat.

While crossing the great sea of sand Dragatu had gathered the Hunora and told them how the Nation would be structured. The plans were then spread by word of mouth amongst the people.

"I will pitch my tent at the very foot of the hills," Dragatu had said. "You Hunora and your families will do the same. I want you all close to me. The rest of the people will pitch in a semi-circle around us with the hills behind us. We will fan out to the east and west, and there will be order as we settle here. I want the majority of land to be allocated according to the size of family. If a family is small they will get a smaller portion of land than that of a big family. A lot of land to the west will be for crops and livestock as it's close to the reservoir and more fertile. Apart from a few exceptions the blacksmiths, glassmakers, potters, cloth weavers, parchment makers, and most of the other trades, will settle on the outskirts, closer to the desert. You will also construct some declaration posts while the people begin to settle. This way anything I need to tell them can be distributed easily."

9/9/702

The people settled well and despite the long journey they worked hard to make sure everyone had shelter, food, water and resources to establish their own trades. Dragatu decided they should have some time to celebrate before the real work of building houses and establishing an infrastructure began. There was one thing he wanted to do that would certainly give them cause for great celebrations and joy. He sat with Freta by the water source, ready to do what he had long put off. Watching the large wind catcher, he turned to her, taking her hands in his.

"Freta. I love you more than anything in this world. You have always stuck by me and there's no one else I would commit myself to. We have been through so much together, and now we have an opportunity to make life perfect. My perfect life would be to have you as my wife. Freta, will you marry me?"

There was a moment of silence. Dragatu struggled to read Freta's face and then a cheeky smile appeared.

"It's about time," she said.

Dragatu sighed with relief and smiled back.

"Of course I will be your wife," she continued. "You are my 'Someone' Dragatu. I want to grow old with you here in our new home." She leant forward, and half stood, kissing him. Continuing to sit by the water source, they discussed the wedding and planned a large celebration.

A massive mound of wood had been gathered to begin the celebrations. The people had gathered in anticipation and Dragatu used his gift to start it. It burst into flames and roared as the people cheered and clapped. After beholding the spectacle they broke into groups and played music, told stories, had contests of strength, and danced. The celebrations lifted the people and they felt renewed after the hardship of the journey.

Two days into the celebrations the fire still roared. Fresh wood was regularly added and its light held the darkness of the night back. Freta walked through the open path between the people, her dress a deep red and covered with finely stitched majestic black patterns. Her blonde hair, normally tied back, tumbled down her back beautifully and looked like sunbeams in the illumination of the stars and fire. Dragatu stood close to the fire watching her approach, Honrus at his side holding the Book of Law, ready to read the marriage vows and rites.

Dragatu couldn't help but grin from ear to ear as Freta took the last few steps to stand on the other side of Honrus. She returned the grin and gave him a loving wink. Honrus took a step back to face them and the crowd, and faintly felt the heat of the fire on his back. He gave them a quick smile of approval and pride. They smiled back warmly and Honrus began.

"Tonight we have the joy of witnessing the marriage of two of the greatest people any of us have ever known, or ever will know. Their generosity and accomplishments are more than most dream of. On my right, we have our leader and friend, Dragatu, the chosen and gifted. He has used his strength to help us any way he can and guided us here to have the life we wanted. On my left is Freta, who slew the wolf with Dragatu, who has been a friend to all, and whose strengths go far beyond our own. She is kind and loving, but always the speaker of truth and willing to correct us when we could do better. In many ways, she has been like a mother to us. Never have there been two people more suited for each other and I am humbled to have the privilege of reading the vows."

Honrus looked down at the Book of Law and began to read.

'I, Honrus, have been asked to bind, Dragatu, and Freta, in marriage, here in the witness of all those who can hear my voice, all those who cannot, all those below, all those above, all those in front, and all those behind.

In the presence of the Creator, we ask a blessing upon, Dragatu and Freta as they make their vows and promises and as they live their lives as husband and wife.

Do you, Dragatu, and you Freta, promise to live by the Book of Law and by so doing obey the marriage promises within? To provide for your family first and foremost, and then work together to help all those you can from this day forward?'

Honrus looked up to Freta, who smiled and looking at Dragatu replied, "I do." Honrus turned to look at Dragatu, who returned Freta's loving gaze, "I do."

'The vows are confirmed,' Honrus continued. 'I now pronounce you husband and wife.'

Dragatu and Freta kissed. Those who could see cheered and clapped and it rippled through the crowd and spread amongst almost all those who had gathered. The sound echoed like thunder and everyone stood shocked by the immensity of sound, laughing as it faded.

"Your people honour you," Honrus said.

"And we will honour them as we have promised," Dragatu replied, Freta nodded in agreement.

The following day a declaration was sent out and posted on the few declaration posts that had been erected. On the declaration Dragatu had written his promises to the people and what he expected from them. He told them that riches would flow, that he would expect them to work hard, that they should help each other whenever they could, and lastly that his Hunora were to have a new name. They would be known as the Coriol Hunora, Strongest Watchers/Overseers, and they would be there to help the people and be spoken to if they had any concerns they wanted Dragatu to know about.

***

Dragatu's Journal Entries

Journal Entry 14/9/702

I'm in my tent. It has been a busy week and I'm starting to miss the comforts of the castle. But I must not think about it and forget the past. Despite wanting the comforts of a house, words cannot describe how happy I am. Freta and I are married and the building of our great Nation is about to start. One day I will have a great house and we shall all live lives that are full of hard work, happiness and luxury.

J.E 17/9/702

I have met with Honrus and my followers. We've decided to look for granite so we don't have to go back across the desert. We've drawn up detailed plans for where the buildings will go and we've added areas for games, fighting and practicing hunting skills. We will be a strong people and have many ways to show our strengths to each other and the Creator.

J.E 22/9/702

The Coriol Hunora have reported that there's granite to the northeast in the hills. I will take a look myself and organise a workforce to quarry and transport it.

J.E 28/9/702

I've come back from the granite and it appears to be perfect for what we need, although we will not be able to tell for sure until the quarrying gets under way.

J.E 5/10/702

The foundations of the houses have been started and I'm happy with how hard the people are working. I'm doing my best to help and I'm getting regular reports telling me the people are working to the standard I desire. The plans for my house are the most extensive and I plan to work on this while helping others with theirs too.

J.E 2/1/703

It has been a couple of months since my last entry. All is going well with the buildings and the people are working hard and seem very happy. I have great news and that's why I wanted to write an update. Freta is pregnant. I cannot wait to be a father and I will prepare our child for the legacy I'm creating.

J.E 15/8/703

We have been here nearly a year and I have a baby son. He was born on the thirtieth day of the fifth month. He has my thick black hair and I'll protect him with my life. Freta is so happy to be a mother. We have named our son Pyros.

I know I have not kept this record as frequently as perhaps I should, or once did, but life is exactly how I want it. There isn't much I need to write. The majority of my time is spent with the Coriol Hunora, helping the people, and working with them. Any spare time I spend with Freta and Pyros, so writing isn't my priority.

J.E 23/8/704

It has been another year since my last entry. I felt I should still keep this record from time to time, as those who come after me deserve to know about all that happens here.

A lot of the houses owned by my Coriol Hunora are nearly finished. Mine is about half finished and the rest of the Nation is at a similar stage. Unfortunately, the people have slowed down in their efforts and I can tell they're losing motivation.

Since being here, I have been keeping a lot of the yellow stones in the hills and have experimented on them when I can. My gift has increased in strength and I can melt the stones into the precious metal without feeling tired at all. I call it unnum metal, gifted metal, because I saw it when I got my gift. I have also decided to try and make a weapon like the Messenger had. I will call it an unnatu, but have not quite mastered making one yet.

To help motivate the people, I have turned some of the unnum into little pieces like pebbles. I will distribute it amongst them and it should encourage them to work hard.

J.E 20/9/704

The unnum was welcomed with amazement and the people keep asking me where it came from. I tell them it's a secret and that they should use it as they wish, whether for trading, or to keep for themselves. They have thanked me for the gift and I have told them there will be more unnum if they continue to work hard. They have said they would.

J.E 15/6/707

Time just slips by without any sign of letting us catch our breath. Pyros is growing up so fast. It seems like yesterday that he was born and now he is four years old. He loves to wrestle and he is so strong already. I think he is going to be a great hunter and fighter.

He loves to watch the fighting competitions we hold. We have these half-yearly. People come and show their strength, or watch and see the strength of others. A lot of people enter the competition and the Nation has been divided into sections. The five best fighters from each area fight in the finals to gain honour and respect.

Both men and women fight and there are categories for men and women to fight separately, or against each other. It's very different to how it was with my brothers. There it was very rare for women to even hunt, but I believe my people should be free to do as they will, and if women want to fight with men they should have the opportunity. They often beat the men because they are faster and somewhat more agile. It makes the competition so much more exciting. It allows for the use of both strength and speed to be shown, not just brute strength because there's more to fighting than this.

We hold the finals in the center of the Nation and people gather on rooftops to watch it. Pyros loves it and says he'll win the competition one day. He often asks why I don't fight. I tell him it would be unfair for me to join in with my gift. However, I always give the people a show by fighting the most ferocious beast they can find from the hills, or entertain them with a display of my fire gift.

J.E 28/8/707

We have been here nearly five years now and everyone is so happy. All the buildings have been finished and they are so beautiful. We have inlaid unnum into some of the faces of the houses and it looks incredible when the sun sparkles off it. I have distributed more unnum, and there is also a prize of unnum for the winner of the fighting competition.

The people continue to work hard with farming and raising animals. We have everything we ever need: we have our families and friends, we can do what we want in the way we want, and my leadership is doing so much good for the people. I continue to hold meetings with my Coriol Hunora and we discuss how the people are doing and what we can do to better their lives.

Recently we've noticed that people don't follow the Book of Law as well as perhaps they could and have made sure every family has a copy. When this was done some people said they didn't want one. They said they didn't believe the Creator existed. It seems outrageous that they still don't believe, even when my gift is clear evidence there's a Creator.

It brought back a faint memory of Corich, who was killed by a lion when we were young. I remembered how Corich and I debated this, and spent some time thinking about that day when the lions attacked and he died. I wish he could have been here with me and seen all that has happened. I'm going to read over my early entries and see what I wrote about that day and try to remember Corich more. He died helping protect the farms and I should have done more to remember and honour him.

As for the people, I told them they needed to have a Book of Law and would be happier if they followed its teachings. I told them the Coriol Hunora would visit them to offer help and read the book with them from time to time, and that they should use the Book of Law as a guide to know how to help others. They seemed to accept this.

J.E 5/9/707

I have looked back over my journal and have read things I should never have forgotten. I'm so angry with myself, but I'm determined to correct my mistakes.

I enjoyed reading the things I've done in my life, like how much stronger I've become and the things that have happened to help me be the great leader I am. Unfortunately, I came to a few entries that made me disappointed in myself. I read how Corich and I debated about the Creator and how his father didn't believe. It wasn't long after the wolf killed my own father and I wanted to read a secret book he told me about, called the Book of Prophecy. I read something from it. What I read didn't make any sense at the time, so I ignored it.

How I wish I had taken it seriously. Yet I was young and had no idea what the prophecy meant. How could I have? I now know the Book of Prophecy has prophecies that come true. I know this because I re-read the one I had recorded in here. It said . . .

> *'When the three are divided and two remain, the third will be the bringer of misery and pain.'*

I thought long and hard about this when I re-read it. I tried to think of things that involved the number three. Then, out of nowhere, I realised the truth. It meant my brothers and I. There were three of us, and when I had left them, they remained, which is two. Then it said the third, which must mean I, 'Will be the bringer of misery and pain.'

I tried to think how this could relate to me because I have brought joy to those who followed me. Then I remembered the faces of the people as we left. They were sad and miserable because we were leaving. I didn't think the wording was very accurate, because they brought the misery and pain on themselves, but I could see that if people didn't know any better it looked like it was my fault. But I know it wasn't. I was trying my hardest, but working with my brothers wasn't bringing unity. I will not feel sorry for my choices. My people are happy because we chose to change and not stay in the non-progressive life my brothers had created.

From re-reading my journal, I remembered that my father told me the Book of Prophecy was from the Creator. I am still confused that I should be accused of bringing misery and pain, as all I have ever done is what the Creator would want me to. It must mean at that specific time. I will do better though, and try to think of more ways to help my people be happy, and obey the Book of Law . . . .

6/9/707

I've thought about how I can do this and have decided to hold meetings once a week where the people will come together in small groups. At these meetings their progress on obeying the Book of Law can be monitored by the Coriol Hunora. They can encourage each other and special help will be given to those who might be struggling. I will discuss this with the Coriol Hunora and get their opinions and ideas on the subject.

As for now, I cannot stop thinking about the Book of Prophecy. Why hadn't I seen the truth sooner? I could have taken the Book of Prophecy to guard it and keep it safe. I could have read it and learned of its secrets. Imagine knowing the future? That would make me even stronger. People would marvel at my knowledge of the future. I would be able to know what to do before something happened. I would be loved by all the people. Everyone would come to me for my knowledge. I could even unite the people as one again. We may be divided now, but they would change their minds and follow me if I had the book. People would leave my brothers and have me as their true leader. The way it should have been. I must find a way to get this book.

I once vowed to my father that I would protect this book. I know that with its secrets, I could unite the people again and I would teach them these secrets. The secrets must be good and meant for us otherwise the Creator would not have given it. I will please the Creator by using whatever knowledge is in it to help the people. I will continue thinking on this and how I can get the book from Unilus, who is probably keeping all the secrets to himself.

J.E 13/9/707

I'm finding it hard not to think about the Book of Prophecy. I want it. I have talked to Freta about it. She suggested that I send some people to my brothers and ask for it, to tell my brothers it will be safer in my hands. I think this is the best option.

I have also met with the Coriol Hunora and they've agreed with my idea to have one day a week set apart so people can meet in small groups. On this day, they will discuss what they are doing to better the lives of others and what they are doing to keep the laws. We have decided the same areas we use to separate the Nation for the competitions will be used. The day will be called Confession and Progression day.

On this day, the Coriol Hunora will gather together those they are assigned to, and each person will stand before the group to tell the others what laws they are keeping well, and what laws they are struggling with. They will also be expected to ask for help and people will be expected to help one another. They will also be told to report to the assigned Coriol Hunora if they see anyone from the group not obeying the laws. The Coriol Hunora will report to me and I'll have an overall picture on how well the people are keeping the laws and if we are pleasing the Creator.

J.E 20/9/707

The declaration with ideas from my last entry has been sent out. The majority of people have accepted it as a good idea. However, there always seem to be doubters and rebels. They said that this declaration was invading their private lives and they didn't want to give information out to people about what choices they decided to make. They said it broke the law in the Book of Law that said not to judge.

I spoke with these people. I said it was not judging. Explaining to them it was just giving everyone the opportunity to improve, see their weaknesses, and help them change to become stronger. I told them it would be better for everyone as we would become closer. That no one should have anything to hide so it shouldn't be a problem. I told them it was going ahead and that they would be expected to participate like everyone else. They said they would, but I could tell they still didn't fully see the good that could come of this. I know in time they will see how it will help them.

J.E 23/9/707

I have gathered some of my closest Coriol Hunora together and told them I wanted them to cross the desert and get the Book of Prophecy from Unilus. I didn't tell them of its importance or its title. I told them it was just a book my father had given to me, which I had left behind, and that it was very precious to me and I wanted it for Pyros and my family. I said Honrus would lead them and he would know the details of the book I wanted.

After talking to them, I asked Honrus to stay behind. I asked him to do all he could to get the book and make sure no one read it. I told him it was called the Book of Prophecy and very important to me. It was hard to trust anyone with this. I was even worried about trusting him, but he promised to do all he could to get it, and make sure no one read it.

I would have gone myself, but I don't want to see my brothers. I'll send Honrus and the others in a couple of days. I hope they bring it back to me. I really want to know the secrets of the future.

J.E 26/9/707

Honrus and the others have left to get the Book of Prophecy and we have had our first day of Confession and Progression. The reports seem to be very positive, but there's still room for improvement if we're to please the Creator and live happily. I've told the Coriol Hunora to visit those who needed their help the most and continue reporting back to me.

Reon has suggested there be something to separate the Coriol Hunora from the people. I've spoken with all the Coriol Hunora and we've decided to make long dark-red robes for all of us. These will have a hood for prominence and my symbol will be on the back. These robes will give them a symbol of authority that the people will respect and honour.

J.E 30/9/707

I've decided to go to the place I keep all my unnum. There's still plenty left, even after giving much of it to the people. My efforts to make my unnatu are improving. I'm going to make one that I'll wear as a symbol of my power. I'll put the largest precious red stone that I found at the ore pits in the pommel of the hilt of the unnatu. This will make it look spectacular.

J.E 4/10/707

I have spent many hours making my unnatu and it has finally turned out how I wanted it to. I used my gift to heat the rocks to make the unnum and melt it so I could mold it in the way I wanted. I have melted the hilt at the end, and used a mould so the red stone could fuse with the liquid unnum as it solidified. After polishing the unnatu and stone, I held it up to the light. It is so beautiful. I cannot wait for people to see it.

J.E 8/10/707

I've returned wearing my unnatu around my waist instead of my knives. I attached it to my belt like the Messenger had his. The people haven't been as welcoming of it as I thought they would. A lot of people have seen me wearing it, and they have either looked at it confused, walking away scared, or have whispered and pointed with their friends as I walked by.

I asked Reon why the people didn't admire the unnatu and want to see it. He said it was because the people weren't sure of its purpose. Most could only come to the conclusion that it was for killing other humans. He told me they were afraid of my reason for having it. I was shocked and confused by this. How could they misjudge me so badly after all I've done? I told Reon that I would never use it for the intent of killing someone. I got the Coriol Hunora together and reminded them that no person in our history had ever killed another and I certainly wouldn't do such a thing.

I decided to send out a declaration to the people saying the unnatu would be a symbol of my leadership and was meant to be a symbol of our strength, and that it would never be used to harm people. I told them it was ornamental, and that it would be passed down to Pyros when he became their leader.

J.E 11/10/707

Since the declaration people have seemed to accept the unnatu as the symbol for which it was intended for, and not a weapon for killing. However, its edges are sharp and could do a lot of damage to someone if it were necessary, but their fears are illogical. I don't need to use it if I ever had to defend myself. I have my fire gift and strength.

J.E 3/12/707

I haven't been sleeping well and have been very distracted. I don't spend as much time with Pyros, or Freta as I used to. I have been going into the hills alone a lot. Freta has noticed and expressed her concerns. She came to see me last night as I sat in my meeting room thinking about the Book of Prophecy.

"Dragatu," she said in a hesitant tone.

I looked up from the table where I was sitting.

"What?" I snapped regrettably, her interruption disturbing my thoughts.

Her face dropped, and I saw pain in her eyes. Ashamed of my unnecessary tone, I apologised. "Sorry, my love. I was just deep in thought and was startled by the interruption."

She looked at me with concern, then walked to the chair next to mine and sat down. Taking a deep breath she spoke.

"I'm worried about you Dragatu. You've been so distracted lately and so focused on what the Book of Prophecy might contain. You mutter under your breath about what you will do if you don't get it. I see it's always on your mind. You've not been as focused as you usually are. You disappear for days at a time. I have to tell the people who ask to see you that you are away hunting, or checking the water supply, when in reality, I have no idea what you are doing." She had started to raise her voice at this point. "Maybe it would be best if you let this obsession go. You're neglecting your responsibility as leader, but more importantly as father to our son, and as my husband. You're not yourself and I want the man I fell in love with back. I want the man I could joke and laugh with. I want the man who would help people in the street if they were carrying something too heavy, the man whose thoughts were always to improve the lives of others."

I couldn't help but be frustrated. Out of all people, she should have understood.

"Can't you see it? That is what I'm doing. I've organised the people into groups that allow them to help themselves. They meet once a week to help each other so that I don't have to baby them the way my brothers did. You say I've not been focused on helping them . . ." she went to interrupt, but I had more to say, ". . . but my thoughts are always on the people. That is why I'm so distracted lately. The Book of Prophecy could make life so much better for our people. Imagine if I knew the future. I could prepare them for things to come. I could use this knowledge to unite *all* the people again under my leadership. They would finally recognise I'm trying to help them the way I always have.

I've also been distracted by thoughts of what else the book might contain. The Book of Law's purpose is to help us keep laws that will prepare us to return to the Creator. I can't figure out the Book of Prophecies purpose, though. It must have something to do with this, but there are so many questions surrounding it. Will it tell us the time when we will be ready to return to the Creator? Or if there is more we need to know about life, or what comes after death?

Father told me these things would come forward when the time is right. I feel in my heart that it is time. We have a right to know what's in both books. I believe the Creator wants a true leader to have this information, that way it will help the people the best, and I must be that person. That is why I am so distracted. I want to know what's in the book so I can use it to help everyone. Anyway, it's too late, you know Honrus and the others have gone to go get it."

"But what happens if they don't bring it back? What will you do then?"

"Whatever it takes," I replied. "Why can't you see how important this is? Everything that has happened since I can remember has lead to this point: the loss of my father, the promises I made to protect the book, the Creator giving me my gift, moving here, and me reading the prophecy again. It's all a sequence of events that has lead to this choice. If I do not get the Book of Prophecy, I fail. If I do not help the people to the best of my ability, I fail. I have the strength, I have the gift to lead, and with the Book of Prophecy, I can always succeed. I need you to understand what I'm trying to do. I cannot do this without you. You have always been by my side. Without you, I am alone. I don't want to be alone again."

She was quiet for a few seconds, thinking hard.

"I'll always stand by your side Dragatu, always," she said. "But I need you to understand that I had to make sure this is the path we are to take. What we do from here could have bigger consequences than maybe you realise. I fear you may do something you will regret in trying to get the book.

Nevertheless, I can see that we are on this road together and I'm here to help you be the best person you can be. If you want it I'll advise you as best I can, but you have to listen to me. I'll support you, but sometimes you get carried away, and you focus your mind on something and don't listen to those around you. Please promise me that you will listen to me? Will you promise to spend more time with Pyros and with the people? Your leadership and fatherhood is not just sending out orders. You need to go spend time with them. They'll respect and love you even more if you do this."

There was a pause as I thought about what she said and looking into her beautiful face I realised she was right. It was difficult to accept, but there were things I had been neglecting.

"I promise you that I will do my best to listen to your advice," I said taking her hand. "I will spend time with Pyros and the people. Thank you for understanding me my love and reminding me of my responsibilities." I then dropped my head, ashamed of not being the man I should have been.

She raised her free hand and caressed the side of my cheek, lifting my head and looking me in the eye. "I will do my best to support you in getting this book and together we will learn its secrets, and then help the people. In return, you will let me advise you when I feel you need it, and you will take time to be with Pyros and the people?"

I nodded and she let her hand drop and I leant forward and kissed her.

I'm so thankful for the strength she has. I know I'm stubborn and many people think I'm too strict. I know because of this they often don't object to what I say and I've grown accustomed to this, but Freta doesn't see me that way. It's refreshing not to always have to be the one who makes the choices without anyone else contributing. She knows that my forceful nature is just so things get done, and so people listen to me. I love her more because she understands me and is trying to help.

J.E 27/12/707

I've kept my promise to Freta and have sent a declaration to the people. I said that on Confession and Progression day I would visit different groups each week and told them I would do my best to support them in any way I could. The declaration seems to have been met with a good response.

J.E 2/1/708

I've visited my first group of people and it has opened my eyes. Many wouldn't even look at me as I sat listening to them talk about their struggles, and how they are trying to help one another. Many people said it was hard to find time to help others as they had to earn a living first, that this took up all their time. They said they either had to farm, or do their work all day to have a sufficient amount of goods to trade with. They said they had hoped when they moved here it wouldn't have been such a struggle. They always seemed very apologetic when they said this. Always finishing by saying something like, "we are happy though", or, "we are grateful for your leadership".

I told them I would make it a priority of mine to find ways to make life better for them. I told them I would get more people to farm land and hunt beasts so that there was more food for everyone and their basic needs would be met. I reassured them they would see a change very quickly.

After the meeting, I went straight to the head farmers and asked them why there wasn't enough wheat made to make bread and other food for the people. They said that the land required a lot more water than they had anticipated and sometimes crops failed because of this. I asked them why they hadn't told me. They apologised, and said they didn't want to disturb me as they knew I was busy. I told them if this happens again they need to tell me and that was the only way I would be able to solve the problem.

I decided this would be a great opportunity to spend some time with Pyros as I had to go check the water source in the hills. Once I have done this I'll create a team from amongst the people whose job it will be to improve the channels and make them bigger so we get more water. I'm looking forward to spending time with Pyros and I'll tell him about how the channels were built and take him hunting.

Having done this my mind is less preoccupied with the Book of Prophecy, although I am still anxious for Honrus to return. I told Freta about taking Pyros to the water source and she says it's a wonderful idea. She seems a lot happier since we spoke. I think it's because I've helped her see how important the Book of Prophecy is, and now she understands. Together we'll do incredible things. I need to make sure I spend time with the people and Pyros. But soon I'll have the Book of Prophecy and be able to do more to help everyone.

Chapter 18
Making It Right

We've packed and Pyros is very excited. He hasn't stopped talking about our little adventure since I told him we were going.

"Are we really going to see the water source?" he keeps asking.

"Yes Son," I tell him.

He smiles every time. He's very inquisitive and asks a lot questions like: what it's like? And what he should take? And how big is it? I try to answer, but sometimes I do get weary of his questioning and tell him to wait, and he'll find out when we get there. I'm going to try and be more patient with him. I want to be, but it's just difficult sometimes.

J.E 12/1/708

We're at the water source. I showed Pyros all the channels as we walked. He's still very young, but I've shown him how it all works. I want him to know as much as he can so he's prepared for the time when he becomes the leader of the people. He loves it up here with all the water, and was so quiet when he saw all the channels and mechanisms. He keeps asking me the same question.

"Did you really build this Father?"

"Well, not just me." I laugh. "I led the Hunora and the people," I replied.

One time when he asked I accidentally mentioned my brothers. He asked why we didn't see Unilus and the other people. The question brought up some of the feelings I knew I shouldn't feel and it was because of them I had to leave. Regrettably, it made me speak harshly to Pyros, I told him not to ask such questions again. However, after a few moments I realised it was time he heard the truth from me and I said I was sorry. It was time to tell him he would inherit my powers. Freta and I had always agreed he was too young to understand, and kept putting it off, but I felt strongly that this was the right time. I also felt it was time to tell him he had a cousin and all the things that had happened to make us leave them and live here.

I started telling by him about the visit from the Messenger and how my brothers and I had been given gifts from the Creator. I also tried to explain about how I had done my best to lead the people, but it hadn't worked out and they had not wanted me as their leader.

"Why wouldn't they want you as their leader?" he asked. "You're strong and brave, and always busy trying to help people."

This last statement gave me a pang of guilt as I felt he wished some of that time had been given to him. I knew if this was the case he was right, and I'm trying to make up for it.

"I can't understand either," I replied. "But leaving was the best option," I reassured him.

"Do you miss them?"

The mature question took me by surprise. I considered it for a second.

"No," I answered honestly. "They never truly understood me and I'm happier here than I ever could have been there. I will let you into a secret though."

His ears pricked up at this.

"I have a plan to unite the people again under my leadership. Everyone deserves to be happy. And if my plan works I'll be able to show the people I can be the leader they deserve and help them be happier. It'll mean that one day you'll be the leader of all the people without any division."

He looked at me when I said this, but didn't say anything. He seemed to be thinking very hard about what he should say. I saw doubt and fear in his eyes and tried to comfort him.

"One day you'll take my place as leader and you will do great things. Right now I'm making hard decisions so it'll be easier for you. But you are my son and will be a great leader. You'll have to make hard decisions that people won't understand too, but I'll teach you how, and one day you'll have my gifts so there's nothing to worry about."

Learning that he would inherit my gift didn't seem to make a difference. He was still quiet and looked at the ground. So I took my unnatu and gave it to him.

"One day this will be yours Pyros," I said. He looked up at me and gave a little nod. "It will be a symbol that you rule over the people. You will inherit it like you will inherit my gifts. You will be ready and have no need to fear. But I need you to know that my brothers, Unilus and Phoenon, have gifts too, and Unilus has a son. He'll be just older than you are. He'll inherit the gifts of Unilus and it will be the same if Phoenon has children. I'm telling you all this so you are prepared. I'm not going to let it happen, but if my plans don't work you need to know the truth. Then you can try and unite the people so they can be happy again. As you get older I will explain this more if I need to. I know it's a lot, as you're so young, but you're my son and I know you can handle it. Do you think you can?"

There was a pause as he looked at me and in a very quiet voice he answered,

"I can Father. With you helping me, I'll be ready."

He smiled and I smiled back so proud of him.

"Son, you know I love you?"

"I know. I love you too," he replied.

We hugged and I asked if he would like to join me in some hunting. He nodded enthusiastically and we went hunting.

We're now home. The time I've spent with Pyros was what we both needed. I've been failing him, but no more. I've always been busy with the people and I haven't focused on him enough. Being with him has brought back memories of losing my father. I don't want Pyros to feel similar hurt and pain because I've not been around. If my father had been around he would have helped me in so many ways. I could have been more prepared and an even greater help for the people. I just want to help Pyros so he's ready and doesn't have to feel alone. I've given him a great foundation, and my people have achieved so much in a short time. The houses are incredible, the water is flowing better so more crops will grow, and the weekly meetings are perfect to help solve any struggles they have. When the Book of Prophecy arrives I'll be able to do even more to build the foundation for him and I'll help the people more than ever before.

I'll return to the people at the Old Nation. With the Book of Prophecy and its secrets, I'll be able to convince them to come here and have me as their leader. I'll forgive that they didn't want me to be their leader at first. After all, it was my brothers' fault, not theirs. My brothers should have seen my leadership would help the people be more active in doing what the Book of Law says. I wish Father could have seen what good I've done and I'm going to do. I'm going to re-unite the people so there are no divisions. Pyros won't have to suffer what I have and when I see him next I'll tell him I'm going to spend a lot more time with him.

J.E 24/1/708

Honrus and the Coriol Hunora have returned. They have failed me. They didn't return with the Book of Prophecy. I told them to do everything to get the book, and yet they didn't return with it. I'm so angry. I know I should have more patience, as ultimately it's not their fault, but I expected to have the Book of Prophecy by now. Once again my brothers have created problems because of their ignorance.

I was in the large meeting hall of my house, thinking about the book, when a messenger came and said Honrus and the others had just entered the Nation. I stood up from my chair and was about to go and meet them when Freta entered. She looked at me, knowing I was going to rush to them, and she spoke.

"Wait for them to return here. They've had a long journey and will need food and water. They'll come here and bring you the book. Be patient my love."

I wanted to ignore her and leave, but I remembered my promise to listen to her and gave in, sitting back into my chair.

"Of course. I will wait."

She came and sat beside me, taking my hand as we waited. The whole time I felt like I was going to explode with anticipation. As they entered the hall they looked at the floor and wouldn't look at me. Seeing the failure in their body language, I lost my temper.

"Where is it?"

Honrus stepped forward. "They wouldn't let us have it."

There was silence for a few seconds, but I couldn't control my temper as my blood boiled. I'm not proud of what I did next. Smoke began to rise from the carpet near the Coriol Hunora. I just stared at it. I couldn't control myself. The flames began to move towards them and they took several spaces back. I felt Freta's hand squeeze mine.

"That's enough Dragatu," she said firmly. "They tried their best."

I looked up at them. They had such fear in their eyes and I continued to look at them for a few seconds. At that moment, I felt such control. They would do anything for me because I was so strong. I had such strength, control and power. I quickly put this thought from my mind though, and casually told them to put out the flames. Water was brought and the flames were extinguished.

"I'm greatly disappointed," I said. "You may all leave. Go see your families and recover from the journey."

They left quickly, but Honrus stayed. He stood there in front of me but didn't say anything.

"Speak," I said flatly, when I saw he hadn't left.

"May I speak openly?" he asked.

"You may my friend."

"Do not be so hard on them," he pleaded. "We tried extremely hard to convince Unilus, but he would not listen. It's him that you should punish, not us."

I thought about this and realised my anger was misplaced.

"You're right. I'm sorry. You may take some unnum and trade it for food and drink for those who went. Send them my thanks for their efforts, but before you do I would like to talk with you."

"Of course," he said.

"Walk with me as we talk," I said as I let go of Freta's hand and smiled to her to reassure her everything was okay.

I was still angry though but buried these thoughts. Honrus was right, my anger should be towards my brothers. I tried to think clearly of what to do next. A new plan would have to be made to get the Book of Prophecy. As we walked out the room and down the corridors of my house, I continued the conversation.

"We've been close friends for many years now, have we not?"

"We have."

"Do you still remember our first encounter?"

"Of course I do. You left bruises on me I could never forget."

We laughed with a mutual understanding.

"Things have certainly changed since then, haven't they?" I asked.

"They certainly have. If I may speak openly once more?" he requested.

I nodded.

"I knew from that moment that you would do great things. I was greatly impressed with your physical strength, but also your inner strength. I was greatly impressed that you weren't afraid to do what was needed to correct my mistakes, even if it did hurt me a lot. It was the kind of leadership I needed. I was frustrated with the lack of leadership amongst our people and that's why I felt it okay to take the water. I didn't think anyone would stop me, but part of me wished someone would, and you did. Since then I've always followed you."

I nodded again as a sign of my acknowledgment of his friendship.

"This is not the way your brothers live," he continued. "They still haven't learned how to lead like you. When I arrived at the Nation, and went to your brothers, I felt what we were trying to do would fail. I felt that your strength and gift would have been more convincing to get them to hand over this book.

Having seen them following so blindly without order, I knew something had to be done to give them the life we've created here. A life with rules and consequence to their actions is needed, but more importantly, a life with leadership that follows the Creator's laws to the letter. When I saw them I realised this is what they need and that I had to tell you how I felt. If the Book of Prophecy is so important I think more drastic measures are going to be needed. I think we have to return to show them our ways and stop your brothers. That way you'll get the Book of Prophecy too."

He paused for a few moments, waiting to see what I'd say to such an idea.

"As you have said, I too had guessed," I replied as we reached the back entrance and stepped out into the open grass there. "They need our way of life to better themselves, but they're so blinded by the ease of their lives that they don't realise the better path. The easy way to solve this would have been if my brothers had handed over the book. I could have convinced the people to follow me because of the knowledge in it. This is still my plan, but as you say more drastic measures are going to be needed. As we've walked my thoughts have turned to things I've seen, things I cannot tell you about, but they can solve this problem."

I unsheathed my unnatu and offered it to him. He hesitated, but I insisted. He took it reluctantly, proceeding to swing it through the air.

"Feels good, doesn't it? Like it's actually a part of you," I said.

He nodded. His eyes fixed on the unnatu before him.

"I think I know what to do. If I make enough of these, and give them to those who'll follow me, we can rescue the people from my brothers' stagnant way of life. Then I can have the book, as you said, and I can show them a better way to live."

I looked at Honrus. He had stopped swinging the unnatu and stared at me.

"What would we do with the unnatu? Would we attack people?" he asked.

"No, we wouldn't," I said quickly. "The goal would be to go to the house of my brothers and retrieve the book. Having the unnatu will show them we are not playing games. It will be a bluff, but it will work. They wouldn't risk being hurt."

He nodded his understanding and I continued.

"Once the book is mine I can learn of the knowledge within. I will tell all the people and we'd all return here. They can live to the east and west of us, and our Nation will grow along the hill-foots. My brothers would then realise their mistakes. There is a very small chance they'll try and stop us, but we have to be committed. Do you understand fully, the path we may have to take? The unnatu are a bluff, but there is a very slim chance we may have to hurt some people if they try and stop us, not seriously, but enough to achieve our goals. I don't want to hurt anyone, but this is so important for the overall happiness of the people. The Book of Prophecy is that important."

There was silence from us both. Then he spoke.

"I do understand Dragatu. But is it really worth hurting people for, even if the chances are slim? There might be another way to help free the people."

"We can try and think of another way," I said. "But this is the best I can think of. It's direct and will guarantee our success. There will be no more room for failure. If all we do is get the Book of Prophecy it will have been worth it. If the people still don't listen after showing them its secrets we can leave. Our lives will be even greater and happier with the Book of Prophecy's knowledge. But they will follow, so don't worry."

"Okay. Sorry for questioning you," Honrus replied. "I just had to be sure. It does seem like the best way. I've always followed and trusted you Dragatu, and it's always been for the best. I will do so now. I won't let you down again."

"Thank you." I placed my hand on his shoulder. "You are a loyal friend." With this settled, I asked him some questions that had been growing in my mind. "What's the Nation like? Are we likely to get much resistance if we go there? Any news from my mother?"

He replied hesitantly, "I hate to bring you bad news, but your mother is dead. Unilus told me she died peacefully in her sleep. I'm sorry Dragatu."

"It's okay Honrus. I had prepared myself for this. Please continue."

"When we arrived, we were met with great apprehension. The farmers and workers left their fields and ran to their houses. As we walked through the Nation we saw people going about their daily business, but no one would speak to us. They seemed very surprised and scared of us. There's a chance we'll meet some resistance when we return again, but it'll just be vocal protests. They have become a very passive people. They don't seem to pay attention to the Book of Law as we do, either. I did see copies in some people's possession, but I didn't see many. If we can help them with this it will be of great benefit to them. We need to help them remember that obeying the law is the most important thing if they want to be happy and please the Creator.

We arrived at the castle and requested to see Unilus. After a little wait he arrived with Tursea and your nephew, Branon."

This was a surprise. Hearing my father's name again stirred feelings of him and my old family, but I focused on what Honrus was saying.

"Unilus seems to have changed a lot," Honrus continued. "He was more confident than I remember. As we met he welcomed us and offered us food and water. After we were refreshed he asked how you were. I told him you were leading the people well and that our people were strong and obeying the laws with exactness. He didn't say anything to this. I told him you had a son and that everything was perfect for us. I said that we had come to retrieve something that was rightly yours. He seemed intrigued by this and told us to speak openly. I told him we were there to get a book called the Book of Prophecy. That it belonged to you as your father had asked you to protect it, but couldn't do that with it in their possession.

Unilus asked why you wanted it now and what you wanted it for? I told him that it was none of his concern and that if he would hand over the book we would leave, but we wouldn't leave easily if he refused.

He said he could not give us the book and it was a pointless endeavour, and that we should return and tell you to forget about the book as it was not meant for you. I told him it would be easier for everyone if he gave us the book and he should consider the consequences of not giving it to us.

He thought for a short time and repeated that he would not give it to us. He said we were welcome to stay for a while and rest, but would appreciate if we left, and didn't return unless with a more peaceful objective. I told him that we would stay for a while and give him time to reconsider. We left and went to the rooms we were given.

After a few days he still refused to give the book up. I debated on ways to convince him. I even considered violence, but this would be wrong, and I didn't even know where the book was to get it for you. There was nothing I could do, and eventually, I became tired of not getting anywhere and decided to return home. You must understand that I tried. Forgive me for failing you."

"You did your best and that's what I asked," I said. "Thank you again for your loyalty. There's much to do. We need to convince our people that returning with unnatu is the best way of freeing the people across the desert. We need to tell them that my brothers have failed those there and given them a life without proper law and consequence. Our people need to believe we can free them and give them the better way of life that we have. We need to promise those who help us that they'll be given rewards for the good they do and will be Hunora to my brothers' people. They'll be given power to help and teach them the correct way of following the Book of Law.

The only problem is finding people that will be completely committed and not give up if any difficulties arise. The question is how do we find these people? I know you and the Coriol Hunora will do this, but we need a lot of men and women to be with us to guarantee success."

"What about the competition fights?" Honrus suggested. "Those that enter are strong and we can judge who'll be worth having with us from the fighters. We can offer them the rewards and they'll follow us to free the people. You could also announce to everyone here that you want to set the people free and tell them your plan. This way people who want to help can sign up at the weekly meetings. We can arm them and take them to free the people?"

"That's perfect," I replied. "Your ideas show your commitment so thank you. We're much alike, my friend, your counsel is important to me."

"Thank you," he said, bowing his head.

I could tell he was very grateful for this compliment and I started to wrap up the conversation.

"As for now, you must go to those who went with you and give them the unnum for a reward. Then get all the Coriol Hunora together and tell them of the plans. Tell them at the next set of competitions that they're to approach fighters from their areas, offer them the rewards, tell them they'll be Hunora of my brothers' people, and that we must set the other people free. Then we'll watch the competitions to find those who show greatness and strength. I'll announce my plans at the end of the final and see what happens. Then we'll begin preparations to return to pay my brothers a visit."

Honrus agreed and we walked back inside to get the unnum. We said goodbye and I told Freta what we decided and wrote this update. I'm still frustrated at not having the Book of Prophecy, but this new plan won't fail.

Chapter 19
Still Blood Brothers

J.E 30/1/708

I've spent some time in the hills worrying and making plans. There isn't much unnum left. I need more to make my plans work. I've decided to take some Coriol Hunora and wagons to the ore pits of the Old Nation. We'll take the raw unnum rocks we find and I'll be able to make unnatus. We'll also be able to maintain the wealth we have.

I've spoken to Freta and she's asked if I have to use unnum to make the unnatus. She knows going back will be difficult and suggested using another metal. I told her using unnum was the best way and I could work with the blacksmiths to make them. She's accepted this and is coming so she can visit Jolonus' grave. We've decided to take Pyros too, but first the competitions are going to be held.

J.E 2/2/708

The competitions are well under way. I've spent a lot of time with Pyros and we've travelled all over the Nation and watched a lot of the beginning stages of the competition. He still asks me to fight and I've told him I can't, but a part of me really wants to. I think I'm going to challenge the top six of the competition.

The people would enjoy the spectacle, and it will be good for me to have a challenge.

J.E 4/2/708

I've decided I will fight at the end of the competition. All the fights have been enjoyable to watch and there are a few obvious contenders for the finals. One fight was over in five seconds. The fighter dodged once, then an uppercut punch and that was it, it was incredible. I want to describe our competitions so if one day they no longer exist people can read about them.

The fights are held within a triangle that's ten metres on every side. The goal is either: to get the opponent out of the triangle, to pin them into submission, or to beat your opponent so severely that it's clear who has won. The judge of the fight is also the Coriol Hunora, who leads the Confession and Progression day in that area. This person will decide if any of the three ways of winning have been achieved. The prizes of unnum and donated gifts, such as elaborate sculptures, decorated drinking horns, skillfully crafted hunting bows and knives, are widely sought after. But more importantly it's a show of strength, and the honour of winning is just as important as the prizes.

J.E 12/2/708

It's the day of the final. The competition's three categories have eight remaining contestants in each. There are five men and three women in the combined male and female category. Then there are the eight best fighters in the male and female only category. The great thing about the competition is people can enter both categories. This has meant we've ended up with nineteen finalists in total: five of those from the male/female category being in the individual male and female categories too.

I also sent a declaration out on the day after my last entry, telling everyone I had decided to fight and will fight the top six fighters at the final. These will be the two last fighters from each category, or the last six if someone is in finals for both the single and combined categories.

I'm about to go and take my place to watch the top eight from each group fight. I can hear the noise of the crowd already and I'm excited to watch, and to take part.

J.E 14/2/708

The competition is over. What a spectacle of strength it was. How incredible my people have become. When I arrived, I was welcomed with cheers and shouts from the thousands of people who had come to watch. People had built towers, platforms and scaffolding around the houses and these allowed more people to see the competition. It was amazing to see how industrial my people can be. I took my usual place outside a house we used every competition final, close to the fighting area, and there was a procession of those who would be fighting. After the procession, the category for women was fought first. They were divided randomly into four sets of two, and each winner would go through to the next round until only two fighters were left. There were also fights between those who lost, so the full hierarchy could be established and each person ranked. The fights were very exciting. I'm so proud of those that fought.

The next category was the men. Honrus was in the last eight. He's an old man, but still has incredible strength. I knew he would do well. He made it all the way to the final and beat his opponent by a dramatic submission. When he won there were cheers from the entire crowd and I realised the people had a lot of love and respect for him. When he came forward to be announced winner and victor I gave him his prize, which I had prepared for him. It was an unnatu in a decorated scabbard. It was not as elaborate as mine but was strong and sharp. As I brought it out, there was a gasp from the crowd, which was followed by silence. Honrus looked at me, kneeling on one knee. I spoke to the crowd.

"As a symbol of commitment and loyalty to us, for his dedication to obeying the laws and being a strong and great fighter, I, Dragatu, give Honrus this unnatu. It was made using the gift the Creator gave me. He should use it to do all the Creator would have him do, and especially to help all our people."

I told him to rise and take the unnatu. As he rose the silence broke and the people cheered, clapped and shouted their agreement at my gift. He thanked me and I told him he could get cleaned up.

Once the people were quiet, I announced the start of the last category. None of those who had entered both categories got past the first round, but there were cheers for their efforts. The fights were a great spectacle of agility, tactics, endurance, strength, bravery and power. After the fights of this category was over the best two fighters from each of the three categories were dismissed to get ready for the final fight of the day, the fight against me.

I then went inside the house we'd sat in front of to get ready. I was actually a bit nervous. As I got ready I looked at myself in the mirror and I realised how much I had changed since I was a boy. There I stood, over two metres tall, with my short, thick black hair, the three scars down my face, and various other scars on my body. On top of this were my deep red eyes staring back at me. They always reminded me of my responsibilities and my gift.

When alone and feeling reflective I often take a simple object and use my gift on it as it calms me. I took a cup out of a cupboard and placed it on the floor in front of the mirror. I looked at it and let it burn slowly. It always helps me focus my thoughts. The cup turned to ash and I continued to burn that until nothing was left. I remembered how hard it had been when I first got my gift, and how it was so easy now.

I thought about how many things had changed, how I had always done what I needed to do to make changes in my life, and in the lives of those around me, and how there were still a lot of changes ahead. I realised my thoughts were becoming unfocused so took out another cup and watched it vanish in a ball of flames. I looked in the mirror again and could hear the cheers from the crowds as the six finalists returned. Freta entered.

"You don't have to do this, you know," she said. "You don't need to prove yourself all the time."

"I know." I sighed. "But I need to prove to myself I'm still the fighter I've always been. I need to prepare myself for what is to come. Plus, the people will enjoy the entertainment." I smiled. "They'll be reminded of my strength and why they chose me as their leader. I've no doubt I'll win, but I hope those I'm going to fight will do the best they can."

"Just be careful, okay?" she said hugging me.

I squeezed her lightly and we walked out together. As I came out the crowd erupted with cheers. I raised my hands to acknowledge them and I spoke to them, raising my voice as loudly as I could.

"What a competition it has been. What great people we are to have such strong and committed fighters. It's now time for the last event of the day. The top six will fight me." When I said this there were more cheers and claps. Once they faded I continued, "Awards will be given for those who are the bravest and don't hold back. I'll fight the best I can and whatever the outcome this will be a day you remember for the rest of your lives!"

I stepped forward into the triangle. My six opponents did the same, a few looking nervous. As I looked around I saw Honrus, and he just winked at me. I smirked back. I think he was looking forward to the odds being more in his favour for once, unlike when we practiced fighting together one-on-one.

The people were silent as I walked to the centre of the triangle, my competition in twos at each point. Several people had been assigned to judge this unique fight and the chief judge asked if we were ready. We all nodded.

"Let it begin," he called loudly.

I looked around at each corner, waiting to see who would attack first. I numbered the corners one, two and three. Two of the fighters came at me and they seemed to be fueled by my promise of gifts. One came from corner one, the other from three. The female from corner one reached me first, throwing a very powerful but uncontrolled punch. I dodged it, moving backwards. Her back was slightly exposed. I shoved her off balance, knocking her to the floor, but she rolled quickly and was on her feet in seconds. The male fighter from corner three was on me now, wrapping both arms around my chest, trying to throw me to the floor. He was reasonably tall, but I pushed out with my arms, knocking him back and I spun round. He was close to the edge of the triangle so I rushed forward, throwing several punches. He dodged a couple, but the third caught him on the side of the face. Spinning with the force, he was knocked backwards to the floor, over the line of the triangle. As he started to look up I nodded my approval for his bravery.

Hearing footsteps behind me, I turned quickly, feeling a kick to my chest. I locked my legs as quickly as I could. The impact pushed me back a step and I felt my chest heave as the wind was knocked out of me. Recovering quickly, I looked down to see the woman crouched in front of me. She growled with disappointment, having hoped to catch me off guard and knock me over the line. She had suddenly sprung with an uppercut, catching me on the chin. The punch wasn't too strong, but I bit my tongue and spat out blood as if it were rew berry juice. At that moment, I quickly circled to the right to get away from the edge of the triangle. The woman had taken a couple of steps back and was trying to shake off the pain in her hand. I glanced to all three corners, no one else had moved. I guessed they were letting this fight finish before making their attempts.

I looked back at the woman. She was walking backwards towards the far edge of the triangle. I charged, taking a few swings. She dodged them. On my last punch, she moved under my arm, pulling herself onto my back. Suddenly she locked her arms around my neck. I tried to grab her, but she moved too quickly. Her arms were tightening and I tried to breath, but couldn't. Realising I might lose, I dropped to one knee and leant forward. Putting both my hands over my back I managed to grab her, throwing her over my shoulder to the floor. I took the same approach, locking my arms around her neck from behind and applied pressure. She struggled and jolted, trying to get free. After struggling some more, she stopped, tapping the ground to submit.

I let her go and the crowd cheered and shouted. I looked up and all the people were standing and applauding. We both stood up, panting to catch our breath. I looked at the woman, bowing my head and clapping. I raised my arm towards the people, gesturing for her to enjoy the moment. She turned and bowed to the crowd and smiled at the appreciation she was getting. She walked out of the fighting triangle, sitting with the other finalist while the healers made sure she wasn't seriously hurt.

I turned my attention back to the fight, and took a deep breath as the chokehold had taken a lot out of me, and signed for it to continue. I looked at the corners, noticing that number one and three only had one man and point two had Honrus and another woman. He was standing behind her with his arms crossed. I gave him a puzzled look, but he just grinned at me. I glanced at the other fighters, who looked at each other and nodded as one. They all took a step forward, keeping an equal distance from me. It was going to be three on one. Honrus still stood there smiling and I realised he wanted to be the last to fight me. Whether this was his tactic, hoping I would be tired, or if he knew it would be a great fight, and was saving it to the end for dramatic effect, I didn't know. I didn't have any more time to think about this as my opponents attacked.

They approached with incredible force, which I admired. They began to swing a barrage of punches. I managed to dodge the first few swings, but with the attack coming from all sides I struggled, losing my concentration. Their punches hit me as I tried to block and dodge. I had to tuck my head down, with my arms blocking my face and I began to feel the heat rising inside me. I wasn't used to this and could feel the anger pulsing through me. I wasn't angry with them, but with myself for having to defend so much. I should have been attacking.

With this thought, I picked my first victim, launching a fast powerful jab towards his chest. I saw all the air rush out of him and he staggered backward. I followed, throwing a punch at his face. He attempted to block, but my first punch had already done its job, weakening him. My punch caught him on the side of the face and he dropped to the floor. The other two opponents stopped their attacks, stepping back in shock. We all paused to see if he was going to continue. He took a few seconds to move and with a dazed look stared up at me, spitting a lot of blood from a split lip. Staggering to his feet he got up, stuttering that he was fine, but he lost his balance and staggered to the left, nearly falling over. I caught him before he fell and told him he fought with honour and commitment, but it was time to accept defeat. He hung his head and was helped out of the triangle. I spoke to one of the men, telling them to make sure he was well looked after.

I turned back to the fighters and nodded to continue. They looked at each other and began their attack again. It was fierce. The man's blows were powerful and I had to defend again. The woman was using less power, but she was fast, and more attacks hit me. I had to be quick to avoid any serious damage. I started to feel myself being pushed back towards the line of the triangle. Tiredness was creeping in and I struggled to think what I should do. As I backed toward the line, the man put his leg behind mine and pushed against my chest with all his strength. The women saw her chance, jump kicking me in the chest. As she did, I managed to move to the side a little, trapping her leg between my arm and my chest. I grabbed it and swung her to the opposite side of me as I lost my balance and fell over the man's leg. As I fell, I let go of her. The momentum carried her through the air and she landed outside the line, being stopped from re-entering by one of the judges. She was angry that she had been overconfident, but I didn't get a chance to see anymore as the man jumped on me.

I lay close to the line and he took the opportunity to try and win. He started punching viciously at my face while he knelt over me. A blow got through now and then and my vision began to double. I focused quickly and as his punches came down I grabbed both his wrists, one in each hand. I squeezed them hard. I saw him wince and he tried to kick me. I moved my legs into a position so I could stand. As I got to my feet, I re-adjusted my hands, holding his arms near the shoulders so they were locked. I lifted him until he was face to face with me. The crowd was silent as I held him, his legs flailing above the ground. He tried to headbutt me, but I held him at arm's length. I snarled, took a few steps forward, and half placed, half threw him over the line. He landed heavily, stumbling backwards to the ground. The crowd stayed silent with shock. They hadn't known the full extent of my strength.

I realised then that I had been holding back at times because I wasn't entirely sure how much damage I would do if I didn't. I hadn't held back to beat him.

The silence began to break and I heard a few people whispering. I called the two fighters forward, telling them they would be greatly rewarded for their efforts. They thanked me and went to the side to get cleaned up. At this, the crowd broke their silence, cheering loudly. The fighters stopped, bowed to the audience, and then to me. I bowed back. When the crowds calmed, I turned and looked at Honrus. He was still standing, smiling smugly and clapping slowly. I took a few steps towards him but was still a bit dizzy. I could feel bruises all over my body like I had been meat tenderised for cooking. I pushed aside the pain and some tiredness. He walked forward as I did and giving a half jest called to me.

"Do you want a rest first?"

"That won't be necessary." I smirked, but thought it wouldn't have been a bad idea. "My next opponent shouldn't be too much of a challenge."

He chuckled deeply. As we got closer everything went still and quiet again and everyone watched expectantly. We came within a couple of paces of each other and stopped, Honrus spoke again.

"By the look of you, we certainly have great fighters. If anything goes wrong when we get the unnum and the book, we're in good hands." I agreed and he continued. "Your people know what great strength you have. Your display today has re-confirmed why they chose you as their leader. It has been entertaining, and an honour to see you in all your strength and glory. Shall we entertain them for one last time?"

I laughed, spread my hands and nodded for him to go ahead. He took a couple of steps forward and started the fight, jabbing up at my face. As well as being strong he's a great tactical fighter, knowing how to use his strength efficiently. I blocked and dodged the advances. He managed to get a few hits, but nothing critical. I ducked low and went for a powerful uppercut. He saw it and threw his head back fast. My uppercut missed by a hair's width. I couldn't help but grin as he took a few steps backwards. He raised his eyebrows and tilted his head to show he knew the blow was close. I winked and continued my attack, deciding to follow his tactic by throwing a few jabs at him. He blocked well, but I swung a right hook and it got through. It caught him on the nose and blood poured into his mouth. He spat, taking a few more steps back.

"Time to get serious," Honrus breathed.

"What are you waiting for?" I asked.

He smirked and began to sidestep left. I followed. Getting closer, he began swaying from side to side. Moving forward, he faked a few punches. I tried to block, thinking they were real and he kept doing this. Every now and then he added a real punch and it caught me off guard several times. My face was sore and I felt like I had bruises upon bruises. His tactic made me nervy and I knew I had to be quick. He was tiring me out. I let my guard down and he thought this was a mistake and threw harder punches. I felt them heavy on my face but managed to grab his left wrist, pulling him violently forward and throwing him off balance. I turned and let him go past me. His arm was behind him, still locked in my tight grip. I whipped him back towards me as hard as I could. He winced from the sudden jerk and I sidestepped, throwing out my arm and locking it as his neck contacted. I heard the crowd gasp as his feet came off the ground and he fell backwards to the floor. I followed him down as he went. I went to pin him, but as I did he raised a leg fast and it got me right under the chin. I fell backwards into a sitting position, holding my face. It took me several seconds to recall where I was, by which time he had got to his feet and pounced. I went to block. I was too slow and he hit me perfectly on the side of the face and I fell to the side. As I lay there I saw out the corner of my eye the whole crowd staring, absorbed in every movement. Suddenly Honrus was on top of me pushing my face into the ground, taking one of my hands and putting it behind my back, trying to pin me. I was not going to let it happen. I pulled myself round onto my back. He still held my hand and I put my free one behind his head, bringing it sharply forward and headbutted him violently. I let go of his hand and he let go of mine as he staggered backwards. I lay there in the dirt as he continued staggering and fell backwards into a sitting position, holding his head. When his hands came down, I saw his face. It was bruised, battered and covered in blood from his nose and dirt from the ground. I guessed I didn't look much better. I started to get up, my body hurting all over. I was barely able to focus and watched the partly blurred Honrus slowly get to his feet too. We must have been a sight to behold. The crowd was silent again, waiting for the first person to continue the fight. I stammered the words.

"How you doing over there?"

"Never better." He grinned with a bloody mouth. "You?"

"Been worse," I said breathing heavily.

He laughed. "The funny thing is you probably have. I'm not as young as I used to be. I'm nearly spent. Shall we have one last crack at this? All out?"

"I was going all out." I laughed. "Let's end this so we can go relax."

"You never relax, but it'll be good to be able to breathe through my nose again."

"Sorry about that," I said.

"It's fine. How's your chin?"

"Let's just say chewing food may never be the same. Shall we end this?"

"I was just giving you time to recover," he said taking a deep breath.

I laughed again, shaking my head as I straightened myself. I shook my arms and held them up ready, stepping forward cautiously.

As we moved towards each other, the crowds broke their silence and cheered, not one of them sitting. With the eruption of cheers we threw away caution and in those few metres between us we sprinted at each other. We kept eye contact, trying to read what the other was going to do. Honrus lowered his stronger hand as if to uppercut, and kept his other hand by his face. I fell for his trap, thinking he was bluffing again. However, he did uppercut. At the last second, I realised and jumped to the side. The momentum of his jumping uppercut took him forward a metre. I spun around to face him and as he turned I stepped forward, punching him in the chest. He flew back from the combination of being off balance and the power in the punch. He tumbled backwards, going over himself several times. When he stopped he was in a crouching position facing me, but swaying slightly. I could see he was struggling to breathe and keep his focus. As he looked at me I just grinned and winked. Confusion spread across his face. I looked down towards his feet. He followed my gaze and looked down. There in front of him was the line, and he was on the wrong side. He sighed as he looked at it. The crowd gasped as they realised what had happened. I saw every muscle relax in his body and he started to fall forwards. I ran forward and crouching quickly caught him. I lifted him to his feet and the crowd erupted once more. A few people came over to us and helped me steady him. I let them support him and looked at him, concerned for my friend. He slowly looked up and smiled a bloody smile.

"Y-you got lucky," he stammered.

"No, just gifted," I replied seriously.

He understood and nodded his gratitude. He needed cleaning up and was taken away. The crowds were still roaring. Freta came over, helping me to where she had been seated. She got a cloth and cleaned me up as best she could. The crowds were still on their feet cheering and I decided to speak to them. I gently raised my hand to stop Freta then got to my feet. I raised my hand higher and the crowd went silent. I spoke to them, but it took a lot of effort as my jaw throbbed.

"Your applause is appreciated. Thank you for coming today to see one of the many reasons we are so great. The fighters have been incredible. They'll be rewarded for their strength and to help them to a speedy recovery. I'm proud of every fighter that took part in all the stages of the competition. They have achieved greatness in combat that'll never be forgotten. However, I wish to speak of another type of greatness. This is the greatness of all those people here in our Nation. Since we moved here, we have grown and have incredible wealth and commitment to the laws. These laws are what set us free. We are free because we are a people guided by the laws from our Creator and we keep them well. This is what makes everyone here great. You, my people are great."

At this, the crowd cheered. I raised my hand again to silence them.

"Some of you may know I sent messengers to our old home. You may wonder why I did this. I did this because we have a wonderful life, and I want those we left behind to have the happiness and greatness we enjoy. I wanted to see what the Old Nation was like and if we could help them. The messengers have reported that the people are still being led poorly by my brothers. They still pay little attention to the laws we follow so obediently and I want to help them.

I feel strongly that it's our duty and responsibility to help remind them of what they've forgotten. Then they can have the opportunity to become great as we are, and we can show them the ways that we've become committed to the laws. We can be their guides to enlighten them and they'll please the Creator the way we have. I'm going to send a declaration when I've recovered and it will tell you what I have planned. I hope when you read it you will be willing to help. As for now, please enjoy the rest of your day. May we welcome back the fighters and I'll reward them with their prizes."

The fighters returned and I gave them the prizes they were due, and parted with the unnum, that is now all gone. Once the celebrations ended, Freta, Pyros and I returned home with many of the Coriol Hunora. They were all talking about their favourite fights. It was a great day and my plans to get the Book of Prophecy are in full motion.

J.E 16/2/708

The declaration has been sent. It explains everything they need to know: that I want them to come with me to free those in the Old Nation in a few months, to help me remind them of the importance of the Book of Law and obeying it, that the unnatus were a necessary bluff, that they would be Hunora over the people from the Old Nation, that I have to go back first to get more unnum for the unnatus, and to tell the Coriol Hunora at the next few Confession and Progression days if they're willing to help me free the people.

I haven't mentioned the Book of Prophecy yet. I know it'll be a great help to all the people, but I'm not sure what it will contain. I need to study it first before I reveal its existence to all the people.

J.E 20/2/708

I've met with the hundred Coriol Hunora who are coming to get the unnum and we're leaving tomorrow with wagons and tools. We'll follow the water source and head east to where Freta lived. Thanks to the Coriol Hunora's early recruitment we have five hundred of the strongest fighters already committed to freeing the people. It's a good start and they'll be added to the Coriol Hunora to watch over all the people when we go to free the Old Nation.

J.E 4/3/708

We arrived at the ore pits without too much difficulty. As we arrived, people ran from us to their houses. I guess we must have looked intimidating to them, or maybe they had not expected us to return and didn't know how to respond so fled out of fear. We ignored this and got to work straight away and began mining the raw unnum rocks. As we did, I realised we were taking a lot, and there wouldn't be much left once we were finished. If we ever need more, we'll need to find another source.

It wasn't long before some people did come and ask us to leave. I told them we would be leaving when we'd finished. They didn't argue and left us alone. I've practiced making unnatu to pass the time and my friends enjoyed watching as I melted the unnum, using my tools to fold the metal and make it stronger. Freta spent a lot of time with Pyros, telling him about his granddad and how I had proved myself by working in the ore pits. He enjoyed seeing all the places she showed him. However, it's time to leave. I've told the Coriol Hunora that the unnum will be stored in my house and thanked them for all they do. I said they would get their fair share of it and I would always reward them greatly for their help.

♠ ♨ ♠

As Dragatu took the unnum some of the local people saw him making unnatus and heard what he called them. They knew who he was and without delay went to tell Unilus and Phoenon. The brothers were very worried when they heard this. They remembered some of the worlds they had seen and how unnatus had been used to hurt and kill. As they speculated about Dragatu's intentions, an intense fear came over them. Running quickly, they left the castle to talk to him and find out what he was doing. However, they were too late. By the time they arrived, Dragatu and his people were gone.

They returned to the castle dismayed: the messengers Dragatu had sent earlier gave away his intention. After a short debate, Unilus and Phoenon decided he was going to use force to take the Book of Prophecy. Phoenon wanted to hand the Book of Prophecy over to avoid any conflict, but after asking for a lot of trust, Unilus convinced him Dragatu couldn't have it. They decided the only way to prepare was to have unnatus as well, and they came up with a design for protective shields. It hurt them both to do this, and they knew the people would find it difficult, but it was the only way they could protect themselves and the Book of Prophecy. With heavy hearts, they sent out a declaration explaining Dragatu had been seen making unnatu, and would likely return and try to be their leader again. Their oaths meant they had to keep the Book of Prophecy a secret, but remembering the reasons why Dragatu had left, they suspected his desire to lead contributed to his actions.

To give themselves even more of an advantage they began making a wall around the northern area of the Nation, using wood with earth behind it. It was a turbulent time for everyone and some objected to taking up unnatus and building the wall. They had never been subjected to such things and couldn't imagine someone hurting them this way. Yet with a lot of effort Unilus and Phoenon managed to convince most of the people it was necessary.

By the time they were prepared, arming fifty thousand people with unnatus and shields, Dragatu had been home, made his unnatus, and was half way back across the desert. He had gathered twenty thousand of his men and women: all motivated by promises of riches, responsibilities, and freedom. All armed with unnum unnatus and experienced hunters and fighters, and all lead by Dragatu and his own obsessive desire for the Book of Prophecy.

Chapter 20
Preparations

J.E 27/3/708

Everything is going to plan. We've recruited more people than I imagined and with hard work we've made unnatus for them all. Their desire to help the people is humbling. I've spoken to Freta and we've decided to go to the Old Nation together. At first I asked her to stay, but she wouldn't listen. It took some convincing, but I realised it would be nice to have her with me when I get the Book of Prophecy and free the people. We're going to leave Pyros in the loving care of Reon's wife, Liapus, and I'm going to spend as much time with him before we leave.

J.E 28/3/708

I've just got back from being with Pyros. I decided to let him see the unnum that was left after making the unnatu. After this, I took him for a walk and we sat at the reservoir by the farms.

"Son, I've something I want to show you, something that one day you will be in charge of," I said when I found him playing in his room this morning.

"What is it?"

"Wait until I show you. You'll like it."

We went to the room where the unnum is being kept. I opened the door with the key I had and he gasped as he saw the piles of unnum.

"There's so much," he said.

"One day it'll all be yours," I replied, "and when you lead the people, as a strong leader, the way I'll teach you, you'll have all this unnum to use as you think best."

"All of this will be mine?" he said with wide eyes.

I smiled, "Yes Son. As well as my gifts, and leading the people, you'll have all this wealth. I know you're young, but you'll continue my legacy. When I've done what I need to, you'll rule over a far greater number of people than I do now."

He looked at the floor when I said this.

"What's wrong?" I asked.

"How will I know what to do? You lead so well. Can't you always lead them?"

I smiled at the innocence of his question.

"No. I'm afraid I can't always lead. One day I will die, and then you'll have to be strong and lead with power. Do not worry though. I'm here now and will show you how to lead. You should always ask me if you aren't sure about something or have questions. Watch how I lead and learn from me. Then you'll be the best leader you can be."

He looked up and smiled at me. "Thank you Father. It'll be good to spend more time with you."

"I promise that I'll spend a lot more time with you, but first your mother and I have to go to the Old Nation again but only for a little while."

"Do you have to go?" he said, looking at me with begging eyes.

"Yes, Son," I said. "This is one of those choices that's for the good of everyone. You must be strong while we're away, but we'll return soon. I promise."

"Okay. I'll be strong, but I'll miss you and Mother."

"We'll miss you too, but let us enjoy the time we have now while I'm still here. Shall we go on a trip to the reservoir?"

"Can we run there?" he asked in an excited voice.

"Of course we can," I said.

I bent down and he jumped on my back. In an instant, we were off running down the corridors. We must have looked ridiculous, but it was refreshing to hear him laugh, shouting to go faster. For the first time in a long time, I felt carefree and not burdened by my responsibilities. It was nice to be able to have some fun.

I envy Pyros. Even though he knows he's destined for greatness and to rule, he doesn't feel the weight of this and could just have fun. I know one day this will change for him and I really hope he'll get a lot of these fun moments before then.

After I was a lion, and then a horse, thanks to Pyros' good imagination, we arrived at the reservoir. I took him off my back and placed him on the ground. He looked at me and smiled.

"Thank you. That was fun."

I smiled back and we sat under a tree.

"Tell me the story of how you got your necklace, and when you met Mother?" he asked.

As we sat there I told him what had happened and he would exclaim, "Wow!" and, "Really?" He would get frightened at the wolf fight, and then would cheer at the end. He makes me smile. He's heard the story many times, but still gets so excited by it, acting like it's the first time. When I finished, I took off the necklace and showed it to him. It was big in his hands.

"How about you look after it?" I said.

"Really?" he asked.

"Of course. When your mother and I return you can run up to me, give me a big hug, and put it around my neck. Then you can tell me how well you looked after it. Does that sound like a good idea?"

"I would like that a lot."

He hugged me and I put it around his neck. It was far too big, so I wrapped it around several times. I asked him if he would like to climb the tree. He looked at me, and in a matter-of-fact way said, "I know I'm tall for my age, but this tree is far too big for me to climb."

I laughed, bent down and pointed to my back. He smiled and jumped on. I made sure he was holding on tightly, and then up we went. It had been a long time since I climbed a tree. I think the last time was when we left the Nation six years ago. I had this thought in the tree, and did what I had done all those years ago, and looked back to the Old Nation many miles across the desert. I realised this time I was looking forward, forward to an even better future than I had created. I sat there thinking about this on a branch, with Pyros leaning against me. This had to be one of life's perfect moments.

As the sun began to set, I broke the silence and told him we must get home or Freta would worry. He smiled and said he'd enjoyed the day and looked forward to the time we would spend together. I told him I would make sure I spent more time with him when I returned. He smiled at this. When we were on the ground I picked him up like a hug, and he put his head on my shoulder. As I walked, he fell asleep.

J.E 30/3/708

Freta and I have said a difficult goodbye to Pyros. We're at the channels with wagons loaded with supplies and unnatus. I've written out a plan of action and given copies to the Coriol Hunora to distribute. We will camp half a day's journey from the Old Nation, where no one will be able to see us. Then at first light we will leave and enter the Nation by high sun. We will go straight to the castle, where my brothers stay, and surround it. I'll go in with the best fighters and the most loyal Coriol Hunora. I'll tell my brothers we're there to teach the people of our better way of life and get the Book of Prophecy from Unilus. Depending on what happens I'll instruct my Coriol Hunora as I need to. All the people have gathered and it is time to leave.

We've been walking for a few hours now and when we left I stood on a wagon and raised my unnatu in the air. I pointed it in the direction of the Old Nation to signal it was time to leave. The sunlight shone off the beautiful unnum and red stone, and all the people went quiet as my unnatu shone and glimmered. I got down and we began the journey across the desert.

J.E 13/4/708

We're half a day from the Nation, but we're running low on water: there are too many of us to get a surplus from the channels each day. We've decided to send some people to the reservoir at night and fill as many water holders as possible. This will be to help the most thirsty and fatigued. Unfortunately, when we all advance we'll have to divert to the reservoir so that everyone can regain the water they need.

J.E 18/4/708

I'm about to leave the main group of people with Freta and a small group of Coriol Hunora and fighters. I've returned to my tent to update what has happened before I leave. The reason I'm taking this small group is because something terrible has happened. Once again my brothers have managed to hinder my plans, but I will not stop until I achieve my goals.

After we'd replenished our water, we journeyed to the fields where we would gather to enter the Nation. Regrettably, I've underestimated my brothers and I'm trying to stay calm and not be angry. They've managed to be prepared in a way I could never have expected. I'm not sure how they knew we were coming, but they did. I'm still in shock and angry, but I must stay focused.

As we approached the fields under the bright sun, we saw tens of thousands of people. They were standing at the edge of the Nation and behind them was a crude wall, just taller than I am. The people were armed with unnatu and a cowardly device on one arm that protects them. The shields and the wall are typical of Unilus. He always used his intelligence for cowardly reasons.

When we first saw this, I was furious. I wanted to burn all the crops and the land between us and them. But I knew I must control myself, losing my temper wasn't going to solve this. My people were also bewildered. Many of them began to complain, saying they weren't going to fight and wanted to return home.

I quickly told the Coriol Hunora to go amongst the people and tell them we were not going to fight, that they should trust me and have courage in the fact I would solve this problem. They did as I said. The reports back all seemed to confirm that everyone had stopped complaining, and were awaiting orders.

I called together the Coriol Hunora and fighters, Freta insisted on coming too. As I arrived to speak to them, everyone looked to me expectantly. There had been a debate going on before I arrived. One side said we should go and fight them because they were weak, and would be no match for us, that we didn't need to hurt them too much, but show them our strength. Once they knew our strength we could talk with them and show them that our way of life was better and remind them how important the Book of Law was. The others were saying that we shouldn't fight, that we should besiege the water supply. Then, in time, my brothers wouldn't have enough water, and they would give up. Then we could go in and show them that we were just there to give them a better way of life.

I considered these two arguments, but neither was good enough. I couldn't wait any longer. I was going to have the Book of Prophecy as soon as possible and this would solve all the division and uncertainty. Once I had it, I would be able to study it and use its knowledge to pacify and unite all the people. It was time to reveal the rest of my plan.

"There's so much we don't know about our existence," I began, "The Book of Law teaches us that we are to obey the laws so we can be happy and one day live with the Creator. We have done this well, but we want to do more to please the Creator. That is why we're here. We want to help all the people understand this.

However, because of what's happened it's time I told you a secret: there's another book that the Creator gave that will help us. Unilus has it. It is called the Book of Prophecy. The Creator gave it to my family and we were to keep it a secret and one day its secrets would be revealed. I believe it is time to reveal those secrets. It will help all the people be happy. It will teach us about the future and hopefully more about what we can do to honour the Creator. I've returned here to get this book.

As a young boy, I read a prophecy from this book, and I've seen the prophecy come true. That is why we must have this book. The knowledge in it can help all the people. I also believe there's a lot in this book that will give us knowledge of the Creator, and ourselves, but I cannot be sure until I read it. The biggest problem is my brothers. Unilus inherited the Book of Prophecy, and he has read it and knows of its secrets. Unfortunately, he is weak, and he is not using this knowledge to help the people. That is why we must get this book.

I need a small group of you to come with me to get the book. We will go west, through the forests, then south, and then east into the Nation without being seen. We'll come up from behind and enter the castle. The Book of Prophecy will be kept in Unilus' room. We'll take it, walk right up to my brother's people from behind, and tell them we're not going to hurt them, but going to set them free, that we have the Book of Prophecy, which my brothers have kept a secret from them. They'll let us pass and wonder what the Book of Prophecy is and why my brothers kept it a secret.

Then, when the seeds of doubt have been planted, we'll tell the people to go to their houses, and that we are there to show them a better way of living. I'll send out a declaration telling them about how the Book of Law has helped us be happy and our way of life is what the Creator would want. I'll explain about Confession and Progression day and what the Coriol Hunora can do to help them. But most importantly I'll tell them what the Book of Prophecy is and that I'm reading it to reveal its secrets to everyone."

When I finished speaking, there was a lot of whisperings. I went amongst them and selected fifty to come with me. Once I had done this Honrus came up to me, disappointed that I hadn't chosen him.

"And what of me? Should I not be with you on this adventure?"

"I have an important task for you my friend," I replied. "I need you to lead the people while I'm gone."

I lifted my hand and called to everyone there.

"Many of you are wondering why you're not coming. I assure you your company would be greatly appreciated, but I have another task for you. When the rest of us are gone you need to keep the people in order. You need to prepare them for any outcome. I'm leaving Honrus in charge while I'm away. You'll report to him, and listen to him as if it was I who spoke.

In two days, at high sun, I need you to march with the people and decrease the gap between you and my brother's people by half. There will be two outcomes to this, either they'll stand their ground, or they'll march forward and expect to meet you in a fight. This second outcome must not happen. If they begin to march forward, you must stop with enough distance to let them stop. They'll not fight you if you stop. They seem to think we're here to attack them, but they'll not attack us unless we do first. I know there has been much I've overlooked, but I can guarantee this. When you're marching forward, we'll be heading towards the castle. What your doing will distract them so we can enter without being discovered. I fear my brothers will try and protect the house, but with all our people marching forward we'll draw those guards away. If it doesn't we'll overpower them, but not hurt any of them seriously. We're skilled fighters so we'll disarm them with ease, or at the worst slash their sword arms so they can't fight. Every possible outcome has been accounted for in this plan. Does everyone understand the plan and what their responsibilities are?"

They all bowed their heads and said they did.

"Good," I replied. "Then those of you who are staying, may the Creator watch over you. By the end of the second day, I'll see you again and I'll have the Book of Prophecy. You may leave."

As they left Honrus turned to me. "Thank you for this great honour," he said.

"Remember . . . strength, power and control," I replied.

He nodded and left. I addressed all those that remained, Reon and Linur standing beside me.

"I've chosen you because I trust you. I've chosen you because you are the strongest and best fighters. You've proved this at our competitions. I need you to prove this here and now. The task ahead should be straight forward, but if there are still people guarding the house I need to know you are all committed. Anyone who doesn't feel up to the task needs to leave now."

They all looked around, but no one left.

"Good. We need to set off as soon as we can. We'll meet back here as soon as you get provisions. We'll be leaving straight away. You're dismissed."

They left in a hurry, many of them excited for the adventure and the chance to prove themselves. I turned to Freta and smiled at her. She smiled back.

"This plan is good. In just over two days I will have the Book of Prophecy," I said.

"Yes you shall, and we can unite the people and return home to Pyros. I miss him so much."

"I do too, but what we're doing will make his life so much better. As he grows older, he won't have to worry about the things I've had to. He'll be able to lead with ease when the time comes and not have to do what we have done. The time away now will mean better times in the future, I promise."

"I know. I just wish it could have been safe to bring him."

I walked over to her. "We'll return as soon as we can. If all goes well, we should be able to organise all the people in a week or two. Then we can return home."

"Okay. I'll focus on helping you so we can return sooner."

"Thank you."

"I'm coming with you to get the Book of Prophecy," she said in a tone of defiance, as if she expected me to say no.

"Yes. That would be good," I replied. She looked surprised. "We've been through so much together," I continued, "and you know I love you. I would prefer you to be at my side when I get the book. It's not just my victory, but yours too. It'll change both our lives for the better."

As I said this, people had already started to return and I kissed her on the cheek, and then turned to welcome them back.

She quickly whispered in my ear, "I will go get some provisions ready."

As she left I spoke to those who had already returned.

"I must leave for a short time, but will return as quickly as I can."

I left to get my journal and write this update. It's incredible to think that in just over two days I'll be able to return and write the secrets of the Book of Prophecy.

Combustion

Chapter 21
I Wish You Could See The World
Through My Eyes: Part 2

Freta

J.E 9/5/708

I must keep this record, at least for now. I am Freta.

I returned to the tent with provisions and waited for Dragatu. He arrived and was quieter than usual. I was worried for him. I could tell he was nervous about what was going to happen. Everyone else thinks he's focused when he's like this, but I know it was nerves. He was going over and over the plans, making sure he hadn't missed any possible outcome.

I stayed close to him as he checked to make sure all those who were coming had returned. Once everyone was accounted for we left the tent. I followed close behind him, and the others followed behind me. The evening was still and the sun was setting. We left at this time to use the darkness as a shield and shroud against being seen, and we took no torches.

We took a path going northwest. The sun had set and the stars of night could be seen as we left the fire and torches of our large camp. Once away from the camp we changed our direction to southwest, our eyes adjusting to the limited light. Eventually, we arrived at the edge of the forest. It was dark and very still as we entered. Despite the stillness, I felt like we were being watched the whole time. I'm used to night hunts, but it was eerily quiet.

The only time we saw anything was when a stag darted across our path. Dragatu looked at me and smiled, wanting me to shoot it with my bow. I drew an arrow, but it had already run off into the thick of the forest. We continued our journey through the forest, setting up camp when it was very late. At first light, we continued walking south. I was glad for the light that crept through the canopy of the trees, as it dispelled some of the disquiet, but not all.

After walking the whole day, we finally travelled south enough to go east. We waited until nightfall before entering the Old Nation. Under the dark sky, we crept through the streets to Dragatu's first house. Everyone must have been at the fields as we didn't see anyone, and we hoped we weren't seen. After a brief pause of reverie, Dragatu entered the house and we followed. It hadn't been lived in for a long time and was very dusty. There was no furniture, but it gave us the cover and shelter we needed. Dragatu told everyone to find a room, to rest, and that tomorrow would be the most important day of their lives. He said we would leave early in the morning and work our way north to the castle, where the Book of Prophecy would be.

Once everyone had dispersed, I followed Dragatu to the top floor where we entered the room I had once stayed in. We took off the thick night coats and laid one of them on the floor. We sat down on it and he wrapped his large coat around us.

"How are you feeling?" I asked.

"Everything is fine," he replied. "Tomorrow is going to be a special day for everyone."

I could still see past his mask and that he was nervous.

"It will be a special day, but how do you truly feel, my love? I know you better than to believe 'fine' is all you feel."

He smiled at me. "I can't hide from you, can I?"

"Nope. But that's a good thing."

"I know. I'm lucky to have you. Only you get to see this side of me. I trust only you to see all of me. The truth is . . . I'm very distracted. I'm sorry for being so quiet. I'm trying to keep all my thoughts under control. I cannot give the Coriol Hunora any reason to doubt what we're doing, or my leadership. I've covered every possible outcome so the plan won't fail, but I keep going over and over it to make sure I haven't missed anything."

"It's okay to feel this way," I said comfortingly. "You take all this responsibility on yourself and it's bound to be a burden. If you need to talk about it, then I'm here to lighten that burden."

"Thank you. I don't know what I would do without you," he said. "It feels like everything that has happened in my life has led me and prepared me to do what we'll do tomorrow. Everything will get better once I have the Book of Prophecy. I feel the Creator watching over me. I was meant to have the Book of Prophecy and help all the people. Nothing can stop me now"

"You are doing great Dragatu. I'm so happy to be here with you."

I then hesitated, as I had a question, but was afraid to ask in case he thought I doubted him. I had to ask it, though, if only to reaffirm my own commitment.

"Is this really the best path, Dragatu?" He looked at me confused, but I continued. "I will always follow you because I love and trust you, but is this definitely what the Creator would want? Are we not just following a series of choices that has led us to this outcome?"

He was frowning. I could see he was hurt and a bit angry.

"Since re-reading the prophecy I've never doubted that this is my destiny. I was meant to be here at this point. I was meant to keep the Book of Prophecy safe. I promised my father and I'll keep that promise. I've been given my gifts to lead and that's what I'm doing. It's what the Creator wanted. The prophecy said the three would be divided, and it came true. Everything since then couldn't have been coincidence. Why do you doubt this? You're the one person who's always believed in me. Your belief gives me strength to do what I need to. I need you to believe."

"I do. I do," I replied quickly, taking his hand, "I just want to hear your commitment so that mine is strengthened. I'm not as strong as you, but I do believe in you. After tomorrow everything will change, and I'm a bit scared. I do believe in you, Dragatu, please don't doubt that. I just needed some reassurance."

He smiled softly at me then, his hurt disappearing. "I understand. I'm thankful that you question me. It helps me reassure myself as well. Do not be afraid. Together we'll get the Book of Prophecy, and everything will be wonderful. The secrets will bring us all closer together and take away many of our doubts. We will know more about the future and the Creator. We'll all be happier."

"I know we will," I said, now as certain of our path as he was.

It was late, and with nothing more to say we fell asleep in each other's arms.

I had my head resting against his shoulder as I woke the following morning. He was looking down at me, smiling. I smiled back and he re-moved his arm that had been around me as I slept. He stood up and looked out of the window. I got up and stood by his side. He was quiet for a little while then spoke.

"Thank you, Freta. Thank you for last night. Thank you for listening to me. Thank you for questioning me, but more importantly for believing in me. From a young age I always felt no one believed in me, or understood me. The only other person I felt would have was my father, but he is dead. I was close to my mother, but she always favoured Phoenon and my brothers never understood me. Even with my friends I never felt I could be my whole self. I had to struggle to be the best I could be without the support I needed. Then I met you and things changed. You saw me for all the good that I am and believed that I could make a difference. I always believed it, but never felt like anyone else truly did, until you. You were always by my side when I needed you, as you are now. Thank you for this, I couldn't have gotten this far without you believing in me."

"Don't doubt that I will always be by your side," I replied firmly.

He turned to me. I looked up into those deep red eyes that conveyed how special he was. He was special because he believed in doing good. I know that sometimes his ways seemed extreme, but he did everything he could to help people. A lot of people never understood this. As I looked in those eyes, I could see his greatness. The same greatness I saw the day we met and killed the wolf together. The same greatness I fell in love with.

As I looked at him, he stepped forward and took me in his arms.

"Today will be a busy day for us all," he said. "I want you to know that I love you and cannot wait to share the secrets of the Book of Prophecy with you. However, there is still much work to be done. Can you go make sure all the people are awake, and tell them we will be leaving soon?"

I withdrew from his embrace and did as he asked. I walked down the empty stairs, entering rooms and making sure everyone knew we would be leaving shortly. I knew Dragatu was upstairs pacing back and forth, looking out of the window towards where the Book of Prophecy would be. I wished I could be with him, but I knew it was best to let him prepare the way he needed to.

As people gathered in the hall, kitchen, and rooms on the ground floor, he walked confidently down the stairs. A few steps from the bottom, he stopped and thanked them for their commitment. He reminded them that this was going to be a glorious day for them all. He then came over to me and stood beside me. He was silent and expressionless, having focused himself, he was ready to achieve his goal. I envied his level of focus.

Dragatu stepped out into the light first and he didn't say anything more. Everyone knew the plan and no more words were needed, it was time for action. We walked in silence through the streets that were so familiar, and yet so different. We passed house after house and most were empty. Every so often we heard movement, but saw no one. We arrived, as planned, at high sun. In the distance, we could hear the echoing shouts and footsteps of thousands of people. It was like a deafening storm in the empty silence of the seemingly deserted Nation. We knew Honrus was marching them forward bravely, giving the distraction we needed.

We approached the castle slowly and saw twenty men gathered at the front entrance. They all stared towards the magnificent sounds, shock and fear painted on their faces. I could tell they wanted to leave and help their people, but they stayed. Dragatu turned to us and moved to the centre so all the Coriol Hunora could hear him.

"This is it. This is the moment that history will remember you for. This is where we make a difference. Our people are out there." He pointed in the direction of the noise. "Not only those who came with us from our great Nation, but those who live here. They are our people. It's time to reunite them all. The guards you see are scared. They are afraid. They will back down if we all go at once. Then you will stay with them while Freta and I enter the house and retrieve the Book of Prophecy. Does everyone understand?"

Some nodded while others said yes. He turned and we followed as we revealed ourselves to the men who stood guarding the entrance to the castle. When the first person saw us, he shouted, and all the others turned in surprise. Dragatu began to speak boldly.

"Friends, we mean you no harm. We've come to collect something that is rightfully mine. As you can see, there are far more of us here than you. We are trained fighters and hunters, and you are no match for us. Put down your unnatus and you'll not be harmed. But if you try to resist we'll be forced to stop you. I don't want this to happen. Put down your unnatus."

They began to look at each other, as if they didn't know what to do. They stupidly decided to stand their ground, giving looks of defiance. Dragatu then responded.

"You're certainly braver than I expected, but just as stupid."

He signaled for the Coriol Hunora to surround them in a semi-circle, backing them onto the steps of the castle. He then told us to stand our ground. He walked forward by himself. It took the Coriol Hunora and me by surprise and we protested, but he raised a hand to silence our fears and walked up to the men. One came forward with his unnatu and shield, ready to fight. Dragatu smiled as the man ran forward. He swung his weapon at Dragatu, who easily defended himself with his own unnatu and struck it down on the man's shield, splitting it in two. The man screamed as the blow vibrated up his arm. He withdrew back into the group, dropping his unnatu and cradling his arm.

"As you can see, your resistance is pointless," Dragatu declared. "Please don't make me hurt any more of you."

They looked at one another, admitted defeat and dropped their unnatus and shields to the floor. Dragatu signaled to a few Coriol Hunora to collect the unnatu and shields. Standing on top of the steps, he told the Coriol Hunora to watch the guards, and not let anyone in, or out, of the building. They all nodded that they understood. He looked at me and smiled.

"Better leave your bow here," he said. "It'll only slow us down inside."

I nodded and told one of the Coriol Hunora to look after it. Dragatu looked deep into my eyes.

"Time to change the world," he said warmly.

I smiled back, and we entered the castle together.

Chapter 22
Pardon Me For The Hurricane

It was very quiet as we entered. Our footsteps echoed loudly as we made our way to Unilus' room. We entered and stopped in surprise as we saw Tursea standing by the door at the back of the room. At the same time, we heard a noise to our left and felt the air from an open window. Turning to look we saw two swallows on the window ledge, they had a key gripped between them. Dragatu stepped forward and they flew away. We were confused but turned our attention back to Tursea. She had her back to the door and with a look of fear dropped a piece of parchment.

"What's that?" Dragatu said angrily.

When she didn't reply, he stepped forward and picked it up, reading it aloud.

'Dragatu is coming. Could be there any second. Put the book in the underground room and lock the door. Phoenon and I are on our way. We'll be there soon.'

"You cannot have the book. It's not meant for you," Tursea said, her fear turning to defiance.

"Get out of the way!" Dragatu shouted. "You're not going to stop me after I've come so far!"

"It's locked, and the swallows have the key. You'll not get through this door."

Dragatu laughed. "My gift will burn that door. Now get out of my way!"

Smoke rose from the edge of her skirt. Fear returned as she wiped some of her golden hair from her face. She shouted at us.

"I'm not moving! You'll have to kill me!"

Dragatu said nothing. She began to wince and pant from the heat and pain.

"Dragatu stop!" I shouted.

I ran forward and grabbed his arm. With my touch, he seemed to come out of a trance and looked at me. There was an anger in his face I had never seen before.

"Enough," I said gently. "We can go through the library."

"But we are so close!"

"Doing it this way will not get the people on your side."

He thought for a second. "You're right. Let's go to the library."

He was disappointed, but we left. As we did, I looked back and saw Tursea putting out the flames with some sheets. As she winced in pain, she gave me a look of gratitude and concern. I ignored it and turned to follow Dragatu. He spoke as we ran down the stairs.

"How could they know we are here? We did everything we could to make sure they didn't know. The parchment said they'll be here soon. I guess it doesn't matter. Our people will stop them. Let's hurry to the library."

I was very worried. That look of anger, and what he had done to Tursea, shocked me a little, but there was no time to lose focus. I followed him to the library and we ran to the back. He looked at the wooden door and the metal bars strengthening it, and smirked. The lock began to glow red and melted and the door swung open. We went down the stairs to the rooms below. It was dark, but there were torches, and as we rushed by them Dragatu lit them with a glance. We walked through several rooms and came to the last. It had a long staircase at the back, leading to where we had come from. Dragatu turned on the spot, lighting all the torches in the room, and there in the center, on a column of granite, sat the Book of Prophecy.

With the torches lit, Dragatu stood staring at it. He drew his unnatu and placed it next to the column, the hilt resting against the column with the point on the ground. He put his hand forward slowly and ran it lightly over the front cover of the book. He opened the first page and began to read, suddenly turning to another part of the book and continued reading. I interrupted him.

"We should take it and get out of here," I said uncertainly.

He looked back and smiled. "Do not fear. No one will disturb us. The Coriol Hunora will not let anyone enter. I want to take a look at a few things first. It will answer some of the questions I have. Then we can leave . . . I promise."

As he read, we heard noises from the door above us. It opened suddenly and Unilus and Phoenon ran down the stairs. Dragatu looked up at them. I saw his initial confusion turn to rage. Neither of us could understand how they got past our people. I stared at them as they came down the stairs. Unilus looked older. Not only with age, but as if stress had aged him. His hair was longer, and it was still white as snow. He wore white robes that were not that different from the robes of the Coriol Hunora, except his were tighter and there was no hood. His symbol was also on the back of his. For a split second, I thought this was an interesting coincidence. He looked down at us as he ran, taking a few steps at a time. I saw his emerald green eyes in the torchlight and was stunned with the reminder of how majestic they were.

I then glanced up beyond him and looked at Phoenon. His hair was still silver and his eyes orange, like the sun and sky can look at twilight. He was still the same youthful man he was when we left. I say man, but his features were still that of a boy, even though he was the age of a man. His round face didn't show any sign of aging like Unilus' had, and he didn't wear robes, but wore common clothes.

As they came to the bottom of the stairs, they looked out of breath. They reached the bottom and Dragatu's rage flowed out of him.

"How did you get in here?" Dragatu demanded. "How did you get passed my guards? Why can't you just accept that the Book of Prophecy is mine? How did you know we were here?"

Unilus stepped forward.

"Dragatu, you need to calm down."

"I will not calm down! Answer my questions! How did you know we were here? How did you get passed my guards?"

"As always you underestimate the things around you. You think you are superior, that you are stronger than everyone and everything. You need to understand that there are other types of strength. You underestimated nature and my gift. When you were in the forest, did you see a stag?

Dragatu struggled to speak and I was about to nod that we had.

"I can see by the expression on your face that you did," Unilus continued. "Well, he was an old friend of mine. He was the one who I first met after I got my gift. He saw you and knew who you were. He left and came and told me that you were heading south through the forests. At this point, we thought you were with your people in the fields. My friend arrived just after your people began to march forward.

I had to think quickly. I wrote a note to Tursea, telling her to put the book where you see it now, and to lock the entrance from our room. I debated what to do and told my people to hold their ground and let your people come to us before we defended ourselves. Just after I said this, your people stopped. I decided to take the risk and take a hundred men armed with unnatus and shields. I was sure you had told your people to march forward as a distraction, and you were trying to get the book. It appears my guess was right. With the hundred men we ran here as quickly as we could, and found your people guarding the entrance. I tried to reason with them, but they wouldn't listen. Regrettably, we had to fight them.

My hundred men fought knowing they were defending their families from the control you wished to impose on them. They fought well, but it was a close fight. Your people are well trained, but we managed to overpower them. Both sides suffered many wounds from the unnatus, but no one was seriously injured. When your people realised they were beaten, they gave up their weapons and Phoenon quickly began healing everyone's wounds. We left our hundred men to watch your people and went straight to my room. We arrived to see Tursea sitting on the floor, her back to the door, suffering from the burns on her legs. It wasn't wise to hurt her Dragatu, and lucky for you that Phoenon healed her. If she'd been permanently hurt, you would have regretted it!"

Dragatu smirked at him. "What exactly do you expect to achieve by such idle threats? You've never had the strength to stand up for yourself. Your words are admirable, but you never could follow through by yourself. You always needed me."

"A lot has changed brother, but obviously you haven't. You're still obsessed with control and power. Can you not see what you're doing is wrong?" Unilus asked.

The rage still held Dragatu and it shocked me, but I understood his frustration as Unilus was so obstinate and patronizing. I couldn't understand why they didn't see all the good Dragatu had tried to achieve. In his rage, Dragatu spat his next words.

"Wrong? You've done nothing . . . you have done *nothing* to help these people become better. What have you done to help the people keep the laws to a high standard? There's no leadership and accountability here. We're here to change this and to help the people do what is right. This is far from wrong . . ."

Unilus interrupted, "Whatever you believe, this is not the right way to help the people. They do need guidance, I agree with you on this point, but they also need choice. If they do not wish to do something, we should not force them to do so. It's important that over time they come to the right conclusions themselves. We need to trust them and hope they'll achieve their potential themselves."

Dragatu went to cut him off, but Unilus held up a hand.

"Let me finish, brother!" he said loudly.

Dragatu struggled, but held his words back as Unilus continued.

"If we had led them together, using the three gifts and strengths we've been given, this would have happened in time, but you couldn't see this. Your desire for power and control, and your lack of patience with the people has meant we cannot succeed the way we could have. The consequences of your actions have created more problems than you realise. And now you're trying to steal the Book of Prophecy. You've no idea what troubles could come if the secrets were to be given to the people before they were ready."

Dragatu had had enough. "What makes you think they aren't ready now? Who gave you the power to judge when the people are ready?"

"That is none of your business. You've lost the right to know such things by your blatant rebellion. All you need to know is that now is not the right time."

"I disagree," Dragatu cut in. "The people should be given the chance to decide for themselves, this is *their* right and *their* choice. I've just read some of the secrets and the people need to know them. With this knowledge, they would choose better, but they would need someone to guide them and that's why I'm here. Let me have the book and you'll save yourself a lot of trouble."

"I cannot allow you to have it. You must leave now and take all your people with you. You must let go of this obsession for power, and for this book. The secrets will come forward when the people are ready."

"They'll come forward now, and I will reveal them!"

Dragatu stepped forward and placed his hand on the book.

"Take your hand off the book brother," Unilus said sternly.

"Don't tell me what to do Unilus, unless you're willing to do something about it."

Unilus stepped forward drawing an unnatu he had around his waist.

"Wow! You have changed!" Dragatu smirked. "But your threats are pointless. This ends here. You will no longer threaten me, or have disbelief in my ability to lead. You always treated me with disrespect, but no more. I'll finish this here and now. It's time to free the people from your false leadership and weakness."

Everything that happened next happened very fast. Orange and red flames ignited on the hem of Unilus' white robes and spread quickly. Phoenon, who had kept quiet, looked from Unilus to Dragatu in horror, but suddenly rushed forward, picked up Dragatu's unnatu in both hands, and pointed it at Dragatu's chest.

"Stop it! Or I will stop you," he said, his voice and the unnatu shaking.

"Wow! Look who's decided to be the hero. Put down my weapon, Phoenon. Don't pretend to know what it would take to stop me."

Dragatu kept looking at Unilus and the flames rose up his robes. As they began to burn him he fell to the floor, rolling around and screaming in agony.

"Stop it now!" Phoenon screamed, looking from Unilus to Dragatu.

"You cannot stop me," Dragatu replied, his eyes still on Unilus.

I heard Phoenon whisper words that turned my blood cold.

"Sorry, brother."

I knew what he was going to do, but I didn't have time to react. He stepped forward and thrust the unnatu into Dragatu's lower chest. I watched in horror as the tip appeared through Dragatu's back and then vanished as Phoenon pulled it out. He turned quickly and I heard the unnatu clatter on stone as he ran to Unilus, who was writhing and thrashing on the floor, engulfed in a ball of flames

My initial shock vanished and I darted forward, slowing Dragatu's sideways fall as best I could, but he still hit the floor with a heavy thud. I crouched over him, barely able to breathe. I didn't know what to do. He looked up at me, coughing up some blood as he tried to speak. He spoke as quickly as his gasping breaths would allow.

"Tell Pyros I'm sorry . . . I failed him . . . tell him I loved him . . . . I love you Freta." He coughed again. I held his hand

and knelt over him, my eyes locked on his face as he continued. "Write in my journal what's happened. Most importantly write this. The Book of Prophecy contains so much more than Prophecies."

He groaned, coughed again and winced with pain as he tried to reveal what he had read. He continued, but he was turning pale and I could see his life fading. All I could do was listen.

"It tells us more about the three gifts . . . how one person can have more . . . and that the gifts are the key to return to the Creator. Take the book if you can . . . but don't risk yourself . . . teach our son its secrets . . . or find a way to get it. Promise me you will . . ." He coughed violently and with a whisper uttered his final word. "Promise . . ."

"I promise." I managed to utter. Then he was silent and still.

As he died, there was a bright white flash of light in the corner of my eye. I looked to where it came from and saw Phoenon engulfed in white flames, lying next to Unilus. Unilus was stirring and there was no sign he had been on fire. He got up and looked around. The white flames that covered Phoenon suddenly disappeared and Phoenon got up too. He looked up at Unilus, and gave a brief look of relief, then looked at Dragatu. I'm not sure exactly what happened, but Phoenon must have healed Unilus. Phoenon stared at Dragatu's lifeless body and began to cry. He looked like he was about to step forward, but stumbled backwards until his back met the far wall. He continued to cry, but his gaze dropped as he looked at the burned flesh on his hands.

I was overwhelmed by so many emotions and didn't know what to do, but the strongest emotion was rage. I wanted to punish Unilus and Phoenon for what had happened. I wanted to grab Dragatu's unnatu and kill them both, but Dragatu's words were still fresh in my mind. I looked at the tear-blurred image of the Book of Prophecy and stood, stepping towards the pillar of stone.

Chapter 23
Broken Promises

Unilus walked forward quickly, picking up his unnatu, half raising it towards me. Taking another step forward he spoke as he picked up Dragatu's much heavier unnatu by the hilt, the point remaining on the floor, blood dripping down the blade and creating a small pool.

"Don't be irrational, Freta," he said flatly. "Learn from your husband's mistakes. Leave now. Return to your people and don't come back. We'll leave you alone if you do this."

I didn't know what to do, the pain of losing Dragatu, and the anger I felt made it impossible to think clearly, then thoughts of Pyros appeared. They won over my desire for immediate revenge and I went to turn and leave. Stopping abruptly, I took a last look at Dragatu's body, a stab of pain cutting into my soul. I was torn between staying with him and fleeing to somehow get back to my son. I knew what Dragatu would want me to do: Pyros mattered most.

I ran through the rooms, up the stairs and out of the library. Halfway down the corridor I stopped, everything seemed to be spinning. I'm not sure how long I stood, propped against a wall, but the sudden sound of footsteps pushed me forward. I continued to half run, half stagger, through the halls and out of the front doors. The bright sunlight hurt my eyes, dazzling me. Once everything came into focus I saw Unilus' men. A few of them ran towards me, their unnatus pointing. As they approached, I heard Unilus call from behind me.

"It's okay. Let her go. She has suffered enough for today. We will escort them all back to the fields. They can rejoin their people there."

I continued to walk in a trance, supported by a couple of our people. We were marched north towards the fields and Reon spoke to me.

"Where's Dragatu? What happened?"

All I could manage was, "He's dead. Phoenon killed him."

Reon was speechless for a few moments before he spoke again.

"Phoenon? Phoenon killed Dragatu? But how?"

I didn't know how to answer and simply said, "Yes, Phoenon killed him."

He could see I was devastated and consumed by my emotions so didn't question me any further. Those around us had heard and the news spread amongst them. There were many questions going back and forth as to what they should do. I heard someone say, "Should we try fighting the guards and get the book?"

I managed to focus enough to object to this idea. I told those closest to me it would only end in our deaths. They tried to argue, but their voices and faces blurred as the reality of what happened began to hit me. I stopped and was violently sick. Reon took my arm to steady me. When I managed to compose myself we continued walking, but this time in silence, those who had wanted to fight realised it was best to return without incident. As we arrived, Unilus' people made a path and we walked through it. We arrived at the far end and in front of us, about five hundred metres away, were our people. Honrus was standing at the front, watching us appear from the opposite host. Unilus came up to me and spoke.

"It is tragic that you lost your husband today, but remember we lost a brother. He brought this on himself with his stubbornness and lack of clear vision. Do not repeat his mistakes. Return home and live in peace. If one day you truly want peace with us, you should return and we can talk, but until then don't return. You will only meet more pain and misery if you come looking for revenge. These people are free and will stay free. Now leave and remember my words. You may only return for the right reasons, but don't come back until then."

He signalled to his men to let us go and we walked towards our people. Though we were defeated and broken, our people cheered thinking we had achieved our goal. After a few seconds, however, they realised Dragatu wasn't amongst us, as he stands above most men. There was suddenly a confused silence and Honrus ran straight to me.

"What happened? Where's Dragatu?"

I could still only stammer the words, "He . . . he's dead."

The more I said it, the more it became real. Suddenly, it was too much. I broke. I fell to my knees, clutching my aching heart, crying uncontrollably. Honrus looked across the field at Unilus and Phoenon's people. There was horror on his face, followed by anger, and then violence. He drew his unnatu, but as he did I managed to summon the words,

"No . . . don't cause more pain."

He looked down at me, his expression tense as he struggled to control his anger and shock. He lifted me to my feet.

"Come on. Let's get you somewhere safe and you can explain what's happened when you're ready."

I don't really remember much of what happened next. I remember getting Dragatu's body back and being in my tent, but time seemed to vanish. I remember giving a brief account of the events to Honrus, and telling him we had to leave and return home, but apart from that I don't remember the journey back. The overwhelming emptiness and ache of what I had lost was too much. I became a numb shell.

When we did get home, and when I was finally more able, I asked Honrus what had happened.

"We stayed for one more night," he said. "We had debated and discussed what to do, and whether to fight, but decided to do what you had said, and return to our people. We packed that afternoon and sent messengers to Unilus, telling him we would be leaving in the morning, and to return Dragatu's body.

In the morning, we received Dragatu's embalmed and fragranced body. I spoke with Unilus, as he was there when we got the body, and I demanded the unnatu of Dragatu back. He refused and said it was a symbol of all this pain and misery. He said it would stay with them as a symbol of what is bad in this world. He said it would serve to remind his people of this time, and how close they were to losing everything. I argued with him for some time, but he would not give in, so we took the body. I must admit I was tempted to take his life as revenge, giving no thought to my own, but the thought of getting you home stopped me. It's also against the Creator's ways and Dragatu wouldn't have wanted me to do it. We then finished packing and began the journey home.

You slept little, but when awake you weren't really there, and would mutter a lot under your breath. Usually it consisted of Dragatu's name, of revenge, of Pyros and something about a promise. I stayed with you most of the time to make sure you were okay. You didn't really come back to us until we returned and you saw Pyros."

This is when I have clearer memories. Amongst all the chaos crashing and pounding in my mind, there came a voice of peace and stillness. A voice I recognised straight away. It seemed like the sun had appeared in the night sky and all the blackness dispersed into nothingness. My mind became clear instantly and I began to feel again. The numbness that had engulfed me since I broke down in front of Honrus was gone. All I felt at that moment, when my numbness was gone was an overwhelming tiredness. I was so exhausted. I felt drained of all energy and life, and then I heard that voice call me again.

"Mother?"

I looked down, and there in front of me was Pyros. He looked at me with such confusion and worry. I put forward my hand and touched his cheek, half expecting it to be a dream. I felt like I had lost everything, but as I touched his cheek love returned. I fell to my knees pulling him towards me in a tight embrace. I began to cry again and was both glad and disappointed that I could feel. I glanced around and saw that we had just left the desert and where on the edge of our Nation. I pulled him away from me and looked him in the eyes. He was so confused and bewildered. He kept looking around and down at his hand. I looked down and saw the wolf tooth necklace.

"Where's Father?" he asked. "I kept this safe for him. I kept my promise. I looked after it until he returned."

I stared at him. I felt the pain of what I must tell him, how much it would break his heart, and how confused he was going to be.

"Son," I started. "I'm sorry. Your father is dead. This is going to be hard to understand, but his brother killed him. You're going to have to be strong. It's what he would have wanted. Can you be strong?"

He didn't seem to understand. He kept looking around, hoping to see his father. As he couldn't see him he started to begin to accept this horrible truth, and his voice began to quiver.

"Where is he?"

There was a brief pause, and then he screamed at me.

"Where is he? He promised he would return! Where is he? He always kept his promises! Where is he?"

I looked at him and tried to be calm, even though I was shocked by his outburst. I should have expected it, but I wasn't thinking clearly. I debated what to do. His fit of anger wasn't stopping. He just kept shouting.

"Where is he? Where's my father? He's not dead! You're lying! He's strong! He's not dead!"

The people walking by just looked at us, and hung their heads with looks of understanding and sympathy. I continued to debate what I should do. He was so young, so fragile in my eyes, but he was his father's son. He had to be strong if he was going to live up to his responsibilities. I made up my mind.

"Take my hand. I will show you where he is."

He glared at me and took my hand. We began walking back to our house and Pyros was silent as we made our way through the streets. Honrus had taken Dragatu's body there to be cleansed properly and embalmed once more so it was ready for burial. As we entered the room I tried to be strong for Pyros, it was one of the hardest things I have ever had to do. I just wanted to throw myself on Dragatu, never leave and forget that he was gone, but I couldn't. He was gone. I had to come to terms with this and help Pyros come to terms with it as well. When he saw Dragatu he just walked up to the body and spoke, "Wake up. Please wake up. I have your necklace. I did well . . . I looked after it. You can have it back now."

He began to cry. He hung his tiny head against Dragatu's large arm and sobbed deeply, understanding his father was gone. A few tears fell from my eyes. I wanted to protect him from the pain, but this was the best way for him to understand his father was gone. As I looked at him, I heard a light cough behind me, and it was Honrus. I wiped my tears and he gave me a weak smile of approval, it was the right choice to bring Pyros here. I walked to Honrus and thanked him for all he had done.

"I am always glad to serve you, your family and the people," he said. "If it's not too soon I have a suggestion for the burial. I think Dragatu would've wanted his remains dealt with in a different way than the usual manner."

"What do you mean?" I asked.

"I think he would've wanted his body burned. I know it's never been done before, but I feel it would be fitting with who he was and how special he was. He lived his life by the flame and it would be fitting if the flame took his body. I think we could do it as a ceremony to honour all he did and tried to do for us. What do you think?"

I was quiet for a few seconds.

"That is beautiful Honrus. You are indeed a great friend. I agree. This is what he would have wanted. It will be the best way to give him a proper goodbye. Can you make the arrangements for tomorrow evening?"

"It will be difficult to organise, but I'll get all the Coriol Hunora to help, and we'll be ready to have a ceremony at the edge of the Nation." He scratched his beard and added, "If that's what you think is best?"

"That is a good idea. That way people can come and say goodbye to one of the greatest men they ever knew. Thank you again, Honrus."

With this, he left and I turned back to Pyros. He was still sobbing hysterically. I wanted to hug his grief away. Between his sobs, I could make out a few phrases.

"You promised. Necklace. Why? I need you."

It was tearing my heart apart watching him. He had always been his father's son. Even though Dragatu was busy a lot of the time, and didn't spend much time with him until recently, Pyros had always idolised his father. He only ever wanted to make him happy and be like him. Recently I had seen a new bond form between them, and I thought they would be inseparable. I was wrong. Death has played its destructive card.

I stepped forward, putting my hand on his back and rubbing it softly. He looked round with tears in his eyes and flung himself at me, hugging me tightly.

"We should get cleaned up. We can say a proper goodbye tomorrow night. We're going to have a funeral ceremony to honour him."

I kept my hand lightly pressed against his back and guided him away from Dragatu's body. He took a look back and then looked into his hands.

"That's now yours," I said. "It's one of the many things you will inherit from your father. You will be strong like he was, and great like he was."

In a quiet whisper he said, "I will be great, Mother."

We walked to his room and I washed his face, telling him he could go play if he wanted.

"I would rather stay here," he replied.

"Are you sure?" I asked, worried for him.

"Yes," he said firmly.

Reluctantly I left him as he lay on his bed, solemn and quiet, still looking at the necklace. I left and tried to busy myself with unpacking. I also walked through the house, tidying where I could, trying to distract myself. It was hard. I kept seeing

Dragatu's face, so still and expressionless. It sent chills up my spine every time.

In the end, I realised it was late and went to see if Pyros was okay. As I put my head around the door I saw him lying on his bed, he was asleep. I went in and pulled a blanket out, putting it over him. He stirred a little but stayed asleep. For now, he was at peace, but when he awoke all that would change, sleep would not be a permanent solution to his pain, but for the present it offered a small consolation. I got another blanket and sat in a chair by his side and watched him as he slept. I kept telling myself I would protect him and love him twice as much to make up for the loss of Dragatu. And then I thought about this journal. He wanted me to keep a record, so I got up, went to his belongings, and found his journal to read, and write this account.

It has been one of the hardest things I've done. I read Dragatu's last entry and cried for a long time. Finally, I knew I had to write. At first I only wrote what happened. I knew if I wrote too much of my emotions I might stop. I had to honour Dragatu's wish and to make sure Pyros and the people had a written record of Dragatu's last moments. As I wrote, it became easier. I've expressed my pain and surprisingly it has helped to write about it. However, words cannot match my pain.

I've also realised there's a lot of confusion in me too. I have this knowledge about the Book of Prophecy: it contains more information about the gifts that they are the key to returning to the Creator, and it holds prophecies of the future too. Yet, what do I do with this information? I know I will tell the people, but what purpose does it serve if we don't have the book? When I think about this, I spiral into thoughts of getting the Book of Prophecy and getting justice and reparation for what I've lost. And then I remember what Phoenon did to Dragatu, but also what Dragatu had done to Tursea, and how he had tried to kill Unilus. I didn't believe Dragatu capable of killing a person, but I saw him try, and I'm confused. I guess he believed in the Book of Prophecy that much, but it goes against what the Book of Law says. I just don't understand it all. It's too much. I'm so exhausted and should try to sleep. Maybe in time I'll understand. All I know for sure is I want justice.

Chapter 24
Watch Me Burn

It has been a day since my last entry. I am still so tired. Though I do feel a tiny sense of recovery and focus. I have had some time to think and have a better understanding of things. I think a good sleep has helped. The pain and loss is still immense, but in time it will ease. Yet, a part of me doesn't want it to. It reminds me of Dragatu and I never want to forget the man who made me so happy. I'm torn between wanting the pain to stop, and the desire to never forget. If the pain eases I might forget how much I loved him, but this pain is such a heavy price to pay. How can I live with it? If it wasn't for Pyros, I would be completely lost. This morning I woke to him patting my arm.

"Mother?" he said. I woke and looked at his face. "So it wasn't a nightmare?"

"No. It was not," I said sympathetically.

He hung his head, climbed onto my lap and rested his head on my shoulder, hugging me. I was thankful for this, it gave me a reason to exist, to carry on. His little voice asked the question I was too afraid to ask myself.

"What are we going to do now?"

"I don't really know, but we're going to take one day at a time," I said breathing deeply. I also thought about my desire for justice, but he was too young to understand such things, so I tried to comfort him. "In time we can begin rebuilding our lives, and one day you will get your father's powers. You will lead the people the way he would've wanted, but for now we'll concentrate on today. There's a ceremony tonight to say goodbye to your father. Let's focus on that, and tomorrow we'll decide about tomorrow."

"Okay," he whispered, snuggling into me.

My own words comforted me. It felt nice to only think about today, but it didn't last long. As we sat there cuddling, all the desires for justice, the confusion, and the concerns about the future, crept into my mind. After some time thinking, I realised two key points. Firstly, Unilus and Phoenon deserve any pains they suffer. Phoenon showed his true colours by killing Dragatu and perhaps Dragatu understood this better than I did. That's why he tried to kill Unilus, I think he was just anticipating them. He had given them plenty of opportunities to trust him and let him achieve the goodness the Book of Law teaches. They had always hindered him, and he must have felt using such force was his only option. Secondly, although Dragatu was great and brilliant, he had been impatient at times. I know he had been waiting a long time for the Book of Prophecy, but if he had waited a little longer he would still be alive. It was not his fault though, it was his brothers', but with a bit of patience our goals could have been achieved. This has made me realise my desire for justice needs to be controlled. Unilus said if we return we will be not be welcomed unless for peace. Knowing what they're capable of we cannot go rushing in. We will have to make a plan. With enough thought and careful planning I know I'll have my justice.

It was a strain to dwell on what happened, but it was good to gain some understanding and perspective. Eventually, I had to disturb Pyros and said we should get breakfast. He climbed off my lap and we went to the kitchen to eat. After this, I took him to stay with Reon's family and told them I would return later in the afternoon. I left and went to meet Honrus at his house.

"Everything is going to plan," he said as we sat in his lounge. "I've sent a declaration out that tells everyone what happened in the old Nation. It also tells them that tonight there will be a ceremony to say goodbye to Dragatu. Is there anything else you would like me to do, Freta?"

"I would like to give a speech in his honour, but I don't feel I could compose myself to do it justice. I would like you to give a speech on my behalf."

"It would be an honour."

"Thank you Honrus. I really don't know what I would do without you."

"It's the least I can do . . ." he said and hesitated. I told him to continue and he did. "I know now isn't a good time to ask such questions, but I feel strongly that it needs to be discussed, or we could have issues from people aspiring when they shouldn't. What will become of the people, Freta? They need a new leader. You should take up Dragatu's position until Pyros is of age."

"Not me," I replied.

"But I thought you'd want to lead and get justice, and reparations for what happened to Dragatu. Unilus and Phoenon must be punished for their crimes against the Book of Law and the Creator."

"I will have justice, but this morning I realised we shouldn't rush into anything but take our time. Once we have burned Dragatu, and returned to some normality, we can get the Coriol Hunora together and plan what we are to do. I will not lead, though. I want to focus on Pyros and prepare him for his unique destiny. I would also ask for your help in this. He would benefit greatly from your teaching and guidance. You've always been like the grandfather he never had. Would you continue to take up this role?"

"I will continue to help any way I can. He is a wonderful child, and I will teach him as if he were my own son," he replied. "But what are we to do about our Nation? Who's going to lead the people?"

I smiled at him. Like Dragatu, he always thought of the people. "It's less complex than you think," I said. "You were always Dragatu's most trusted friend, and the people love you. They will look to you for leadership now. I will send a declaration of my own, telling the people that you should lead us. I'm sure they already believe it to be the case. They will accept you with open arms."

"Are you sure?" he said sitting back in his chair.

"Yes I'm sure."

"It is too great an honour, Freta. Are you sure this is the way you want things to be?"

"Yes. Things are best this way."

"Then I humbly accept," he said, leaning forward with conviction. "I will do my best to lead and to help prepare Pyros for what he will inherit. I vow to fulfill this promise with the utmost commitment."

"I keep saying it, but I do mean it, thank you Honrus. I will see you tonight at the ceremony."

With that I wrote my declaration to the people, and readied myself for the ceremony. I realised at that point it would be the last time I saw Dragatu's body. This thought inflamed the aching inside me, but I knew I had to be strong for Pyros. I returned home and prepared for twilight, when we would say our last goodbye.

When twilight approached, I went to get Pyros. As we walked to the ceremony, we saw many people carrying torches that were unlit. I didn't really take much notice of it at the time. We arrived at the edge of the Nation, where a huge pile of wood had been shaped into Dragatu's symbol: a triangle, then circle in the middle, with lots of triangles and circles in it, exactly the same as the flag. It was spectacular. Next to it stood Honrus.

Pyros and I joined him. Honrus wore the dark red robes the Coriol Hunora wore on Confession and Progression day. The people had already started to gather, and formed a circle around where we stood. The first few rows consisted of Dragatu's Coriol Hunora and those that knew him best. They wore their robes too, and all carried unlit torches. I assumed they were for the darkness that was upon us, but I was wrong.

Pyros and I stood beside Honrus and he pointed towards the crowd. It parted. Dragatu's body was being carried on a stretcher, elevated on the shoulders of eight robed Coriol Hunora. Everyone was very quiet. They placed his body in the center of the wooden symbol, and then joined the circle of people. There was a slight breeze, which caught robes and made flapping sounds, but apart from that everyone was still and silent as Honrus spoke.

"My friends. Thank you for coming to witness the goodbye ceremony of our great leader. Thank you for your dedication over the years, and thank you for all that you've done to make this Nation great. However, we are not here to thank ourselves. We are here to thank the man who led us to be great, whose vision and dedication made us greater than we ever thought we could be. He sacrificed much for us: his time, his efforts, and finally his life, all in the hope that we could have a better one, but not only a better life for us, but for all people.

Sadly, those who didn't share his vision and dedication have cut his life short. They have taken from us the greatest man we ever knew. The greatest leader we will ever have. We must not forget what he did for us, and what he could have done for us if he were still alive. We must continue to live as he would have wanted, to live in a way that helps us be better, and observe the laws to the best of our ability while improving our lives with wealth and sustenance.

I recall to your memory that it was he who led many of us to build the great water project that improved the lives of all the people. I ask you to remember who it was who fought wild beasts to protect us, who beat the wolf with Freta to avenge his father. He gave us unnum, allowing us to have great wealth. He helped us organise ourselves to be better than we are. This man who lies still before us did all this. May he never be forgotten. Honour him by being the best you can be, do not let his life be for naught. Join me now in saying farewell to this great man. Join me in saying goodbye to Dragatu."

He bent down and took out two flint stones, lighting a small fire in front of him. He took a torch off the floor and lit it, sticking it into the ground. He looked at me and gestured to the body. I took Pyros' hand and we walked over to Dragatu. I looked longingly into his face as he lay still and kissed him once on the forehead.

"Goodbye, my Someone. I will keep my promises," is all I could utter.

I let go of Pyros' hand and he placed it in his father's, squeezing tightly. He then let go and, without saying anything, turned to me, taking my hand again. We returned to Honrus' side. He leant down and gave us an unlit torch each. He picked up the one he had lit and walked towards the symbol, setting the corners ablaze. The flames rushed around the wood and set the symbol on fire. Honrus extinguished his torch and waited. Once the body began to burn he stepped forward and re-lit his torch from the flames close to Dragatu. As he did so he shouted with a loud voice, "His gift was fire. He used his gift to light our lives with his actions. Those who promise to live as he did, and light the lives of those around them with their own actions, come partake of his flame, that it may burn forever in your hearts."

He looked at me, gesturing to the torch. Pyros and I stepped forward and he lit our torches with his. Then a few Coriol Hunora came forward and lit theirs from ours. Once theirs burned brightly they walked away and lit more torches. The fire spread from one person to another until the thousands of torches burned as one. The fires burned bright in the darkness. I began to cry, I was so thankful for the beautiful ceremony, and that I had been able to say a final goodbye. We all stood in reverence. Tears blurred my vision, but those of us close enough to see watched as the symbol burned and his body was finally consumed by the fire, and with that he was gone.

Not long after that I noticed people returning to their homes in silence. I stayed with Pyros, and so did Honrus, and the Coriol Hunora, all dressed in their dark red robes. We watched until the flames died away. As the firelight faded, the darkness began to encroach on us. Our torches only provided sufficient light to see the immediate area. I turned to those that were there, and thanked them for their loyalty to Dragatu over the years. I then said, "On his eighteenth birthday, Pyros will inherit Dragatu's gift. I hope you will be as loyal to him as you were to Dragatu. Until then, we will continue to live as he wanted, and with Honrus as our new leader. Thank you again for a beautiful ceremony."

It was time to leave and I walked through the crowd, Honrus on one side, and Pyros on the other, the people bowing their heads as we passed. I knew they were acknowledging their respect for Honrus, as their new leader, and for Pyros, and all that he would inherit from his father. As we returned through the Nation, there were a lot of people going to and from houses with belongings. I thought it must have been because of the ceremony and because people were still trying to get their lives in order after returning from the Old Nation.

When we got home, I said good night to Honrus, and once again thanked him for all he had done in preparing such a wonderful ceremony. I took Pyros inside and we went to his room. I tucked him in and dug deep to find the strength to talk without crying.

"You have been very strong. Your father would have been so proud, and know that I am very proud of you Pyros. Today has been very hard on you and I'm sorry you had to experience this loss at such a young age. I promise that in time it will become easier to cope with the pain and emptiness you feel."

I stroked his black hair away from his eyes, struggling with my emotions as I looked at his tear stained face.

"What happens if I forget him?" he whispered. "What happens if I'm not all I should be? What happens if I'm not strong like he was?"

My heart nearly broke as I saw the fears we shared for the future. Dragatu's death seems to have awoken a lot of fear in us all.

"Oh, my son, do not fear your destiny. You will be as strong as he was if you want to be. You will grow up to be what you want to be, and if you want to be as strong as he was, or even stronger, you must put in the effort that is required to do so. I will help you, love you, protect you, and you will be what you want to be. Your father spoke to me just before he died, and I made him a promise. He told me to tell you that he loved you. He told me to tell you about the Book of Prophecy. It is a book he tried to retrieve from his brothers. He wants you to have this book and succeed where he failed. Together we will achieve this goal and do it in his name to honour him. I promised him that I would protect you. I will keep my promises. We'll find a way to get the Book of Prophecy.

Your father also kept a journal. You can read it whenever you want. I will also continue to write in it like he did. When you're ready you can write in it yourself, but for now, do not worry about this. In time, you will grow to be strong. You will be prepared to be your father's son. All these things will mean we never forget him. I won't let it happen, I promise."

When I finished I saw something different in his eyes, a determination that I hadn't seen before.

"Thank you Mother," he said. "I will not fear. I will not let you, or Father, down."

He smiled as best he could and I returned it.

"I know you won't," I said, using my sleeve to wipe tears from my face. "Try and get some rest. Tomorrow we'll have a fresh start and decide what we want to do for the day. Does that sound good?"

"Yes," he replied.

He turned on his side, facing away from me. As I left the room, I heard him mutter softly.

"I will make you proud Father."

Then he was quiet.

I returned to Dragatu's and my room. It all seemed so empty without him. I took a blanket, picked up his journal, and returned to Pyros' room. It was becoming a comforting habit. He was breathing heavily and already deep in sleep as I entered. The day's events had clearly exhausted him. I sat in the chair by his bed once more and wrote all that had happened.

And now Dragatu is gone, but his journal remains and it will remind us of whom he was. I will protect it and cherish it with all my heart. I'm so proud of Pyros for his bravery and his strength.

He may fear because he's still young, but I can already see he has the determination of his father. We will keep our promises and achieve our goals. Plans will be made when we have the time, and one day justice will be ours. I can feel this desire growing as the numbness subsides slightly. I think in turn it helps focus my mind, distracting me from my emptiness and grief.

Chapter 25
Got A Match?

J.E 11/5/708

Events have taken an unexpected turn. They have caused me more grief, but they have also been a catalyst to bring about the justice the traitors of the Book of Law deserve.

I woke this morning to a frantic knocking at the door. It was Honrus.

"Sorry to interrupt your morning," he began, as I gestured at him to enter the house. We walked to the meeting room and sat at a table. "There's something I you need to tell you. It's not good news," he said hesitating.

"What's wrong, Honrus?" I prompted.

He cleared his throat. "When I went outside to get some water this morning I saw lots of people with all their belongings. They had their animals and wagons, and were heading south towards the desert. I quickly ran back inside, got my coat and followed them.

I followed them to the edge of the Nation. What I saw broke my heart, Freta. Half of our people had gathered, thousands of them, all packed and walking south. My hurt turned to anger. They're oath breakers, Freta, and have left us in our time of need. I can't understand why, but they've gone back to Unilus and Phoenon.

In my anger, I ran to a man and asked why he and the others were betraying us. He said they no longer felt they had a future here, and that they had only stayed because they feared Dragatu and the Coriol Hunora. He said they were no longer afraid and wanted fewer restrictions and control over their lives. He told me they wanted their old lives back.

As you can imagine, I really struggled to control my temper. I wanted to beat some sense into him. I tried to explain why it was so important to live our lives the way we did instead. He wouldn't listen. I'm so sorry, Freta. There was nothing I could do by myself. After hearing what the man said I rushed here. If you want, I can gather the Coriol Hunora and try to talk some sense into those who haven't left yet?"

My heart sank for a moment and I paused to think. It wasn't long before I realised the truth of what had happened.

"No, Honrus, this is for the best. I don't understand why they would go back, but we are better off without them. If their allegiance is changed so easily then I don't want them. We need commitment and loyalty, now more than ever. They obviously have neither."

I paused again, this time to let Honrus think. He sat back in his chair, stroking his grey beard as he collected his thoughts.

"You are right," he said finally. "This will be a struggle, but you're right, we are better off without them. It will be easier if we move all the people into the houses closest to the foot of the hills and figure out what trades we've lost, etcetera. Then we can make sure we have enough farmers and traders providing what we need to live. Once again we find ourselves with work to do, but I guess it'll only continue to make us stronger, the way the Creator and Dragatu would want. The first thing I'm going to do is meet with the Coriol Hunora and discuss what's happened. We'll make plans to number the people who remain and send out declarations explaining the betrayal. I will need you there, Freta, to offer your advice in this meeting. Is that okay?"

"Yes, I'll help any way I can," I said. "We can also tell the people you're the new leader."

"Okay," Honrus replied. "Shall we meet at high sun by the reservoir?"

"Yes, that works for me."

"I'll go speak to some of the Coriol Hunora then. They'll spread the word about the meeting."

With that said he rose, his chair scraping across the floor. Ignoring the brash sound, we said a brief farewell.

Once he was gone, I went to check on Pyros. He was still asleep. I sat in my usual chair and began to think. I tried to understand why the people had left, but I couldn't. All I could think about was how they were liars and traitors. They had come all the way across the desert to have a better life, and now that they've got a better life they want to throw it all away! Why? What I said is right, we are better off without them. It still hurts, though. As I sat there, feeling the pain of their betrayal, I thought about justice. All the past pain and the new fueled my desires, and I formed a plan to protect us, a plan that would bring about the beginning of our reparations and justice.

With the plan formed I woke Pyros and we got some breakfast. After the late breakfast, Pyros tidied the kitchen and I wrote down my plans to show the Coriol Hunora. Once we were finished, we changed into day clothes, packed some food and toys for Pyros to play with, and then I took Pyros to stay with Liapus. Once he was in her care, and after a brief chat with Liapus, I went to the reservoir.

The sun beat down on us as I joined those Coriol Hunora already gathered at the water's edge. The heat felt like a manifestation of my anger towards those who had left, and I could sense the same anger coming from many of the Coriol Hunora too. They were debating and arguing in groups when I arrived. Honrus addressed them all as I walked towards him and they went quiet. He welcomed them and asked if they would accept him as their new leader. I told them he had my blessing. They cheered and were happy for him to lead as Dragatu had. Once the noise died down I spoke to them to find out their thoughts on those who had left and what we should do now. A few people took turns to speak and I learned a few things from this.

Firstly, they seemed happy to make the Nation smaller and move all the people closer to the hills. Secondly, some wanted to use the materials from abandoned houses to build a wall around the Nation in case Unilus came back to attack us. Their fears were similar to some of my own, and although I thought the idea of a wall wasn't as good as my plan, I was glad they understood we needed protection. Although some disagreed and said Unilus' people wouldn't return. That was when I explained my plan.

"We cannot know what they'll do," I said as I took out the parchment with my plans on it and used it as a guide. "They killed Dragatu. How can we trust them to leave us alone? How do we know they won't change their minds and try to kill us all? They hate our way of life, and, in time, they might try and stop us from living the way we know is right. Our way of life needs to be protected. There is only one way to ensure we are safe . . . we need to leave." There was a lot of muttering and whispering. "I know this is our home and we have worked so hard to make it a paradise. However, our numbers are so few that if Unilus wants us gone he could come here and end us with ease. Yes, we would put up a good fight, but the sheer volume of numbers he can bring would overwhelm us. This is why we must leave. We do not have to travel far. If we go into the hills, and build a new, smaller Nation, next to the water supply, we will have all the water we need. We will have plenty of food from the animals, the berries, and fruits from trees. This will keep us alive until the seeds we plant on the valley floor grow and provide the crops we need. We will be hidden from anyone who comes looking for us. We can have scouts to watch from the hilltops and if they saw anyone coming they could kill them, so they cannot return and report of our existence, or if their numbers are too great, we can retreat north, hiding in the valleys until they leave."

At the mention of 'kill' there were gasps and more mutters.

"I wish we didn't have to resort to this," I said, interrupting them, "but I have thought about it long and hard about this.

They have rejected the Book of Law's teachings by killing Dragatu and living in idleness. We follow the Book of Law exactly, but we must also defend its teachings. It says not to kill but if we're attacked, we must be willing to protect the Book of Law and our way of life. I hope this never happens, but we must be prepared for the worst. It's better to kill to protect the truth, than to be killed and lose all we have worked so hard to achieve." After I said this a lot of people nodded and agreed. "Good," I replied seeing their positive replies. "Moving to live near the water source and being prepared is how we'll survive and continue to live as the Creator wants us too. I'm grateful for your understanding.

There is also a second part to my plan. It will be the start of the justice and reparations they owe for what they have done." I paused as I felt the impact of what I was about to say. "We need to destroy the water project."

A deep silence came over the Coriol Hunora as they understood the consequences of this action and Honrus spoke up.

"Coriol Hunora! Do not let false ideas of compassion cloud your judgment! Have we been shown any compassion by them? They killed Dragatu! What Freta has suggested is right. It's time to do what needs to be done to protect and continue our way of life."

It was enough to dispel their doubts and some smiled at the thoughts of justice. I shared their sentiments but remained expressionless. Honrus continued.

"Leaving our homes to live by the water source and destroying the water project is the best plan we have. I believe it is what must be done. All those in favour of this raise your hand."

The vote was unanimous. I was very happy. I have a deep respect for these great people. They are willing to make the difficult choices to defend what is right. It is why Dragatu always tried to help them. I expressed my respect and love for them.

"Thank you for being open minded and seeing that this is the right choice. Your loyalty and commitment are overwhelming. Thank you for being who you are. In a time of such loss, it helps

310

to know I have friends who stay true to doing what's right even though it's difficult."

I stopped and smiled at Honrus, allowing him have the last word as their leader.

"It is settled," he said. "I will begin by sending out a declaration to the people explaining that we will be leaving and why. We will aim to leave in a week from today. This should give us enough time to prepare our belongings and get all the essentials we'll need. We will move to the hills and begin building a new home by the water source. We will burn the channels that lead from it so that we will be the only ones to enjoy the abundance it gives.

"As Freta said, we will set up a watch on the tops of the hills. If a small group of people return, we will wait to see what they do. If they are wise, they will see that we have gone and leave us alone, but if they venture into the hills, they will not be welcome. They will get the message quickly and they will think twice before coming again.

"If they return in large numbers, and come into the hills we will be ready to fight, or hide to the north. Eventually, they will give up and leave us alone. As for now, I suggest you go and begin preparing to move. Tell all the people you meet that I will lead them as Dragatu did. That we've been abandoned by cowards and traitors and that we're moving to the hills and why. Tell them to expect the declaration explaining everything in detail. Thank you for your loyalty, Coriol Hunora."

With that they began to leave in groups of three and four, discussing the changes that were about to take place. I turned to Honrus and spoke my thoughts.

"Having to leave again is going to be a strain on the people."

"They are strong and will adapt," he replied. "Your plan is the best option to protect our people. We have an opportunity to grow and build our Nation the way it should have from the beginning, with only those who are completely committed to Dragatu's vision. In a way the people leaving has been beneficial for filtering out the weak. In time, we will grow stronger and Pyros will lead. I know he will want justice and reparations for what he has lost. I probably won't be around to see it, but I know you can find ways to achieve it. Have you had any thoughts on this? Or on how we can get the Book of Prophecy?"

"It has been on my mind," I said, "yet I don't know what we can do to achieve any more justice and get the Book of Prophecy. It's too much at the moment. So much has changed and is still changing. Let's focus on getting life back to normal, and then try to make plans. If we can find a way to get the Book of Prophecy, then we should, but I cannot see how. It's going to be difficult and we're going to have to be very patient. We need to think long term and not put ourselves in a position where Unilus and Phoenon can hurt us again."

"You're right," Honrus admitted. "We must focus on what's happening right here and now, and what you have proposed will mean we survive. Whatever happens in the future will happen, and we will be prepared. Return to your home, begin packing, and we can discuss more plans in the future."

"Thanks Honrus. Will I see you soon?" I asked.

"I'll bring the declaration to you to make sure it has all the information it needs."

"Thank you," I said, and he departed. I decided to sit by the water and think, watching the sun glimmer and sparkle on the reflection of the hills and sky.

Later, once I had returned home with Pyros, Honrus came by the house and we had dinner and discussed the declaration. We finished it and he left to make sure copies were made and that they were posted. I spent some time with Pyros then took him to bed. Once he was asleep, I began writing this entry, telling of the disappointing, but ultimately cleansing, events of today. When we've settled and moved everything, I'm going to suggest we burn this Nation to the ground. The destruction will be a warning and deterrent to anyone who comes looking for us.

J.E 20/5/708

It has been over a week since my last entry. The declaration was received well and no one spoke out against moving. Everyone packed and prepared to move into the hills, it was a busy week for everyone. We tried to help each other and made sure we had all the possessions we needed. We left on the assigned day. It was a dark day for everyone, but I wasn't as sad as I thought I would be. I don't think anything could be as painful as what I've already experienced. Any other pain feels dulled.

We arrived at our new home and set up tents. Honrus and some Coriol Hunora went to stop the water source from flowing. Once it had, they destroyed the channels using controlled fires. I wish I could see the faces of the people when they realise it has been stopped. They'll start to realise it was a mistake to leave us, and neglect doing what the Creator would want. They'll have to go back to the way things were, back to not having the same luxuries they have now. It'll be a struggle and their true nature will shine through. I imagine they'll have people fighting for water, and keeping it for themselves. The division amongst them will grow. It will teach them the lessons they could have learned without as much struggle.

Once the water source was stopped, we started to cut trees and prepare wood for the houses we will build here. They won't be as elaborate as the ones we've left behind, but these basic houses are only temporary. Then, if we can protect our way of life, without having to leave, we will build another splendid Nation like we had at the foot of the hills.

I've suggested to Honrus to burn our Old Nation, once we've taken everything we need, and he has agreed it's the best idea. He's said we should wait another week so that people can settle into the new way of living. I agreed. In a week, we'll burn our Old Nation.

I've been with Pyros, teaching him more about hunting and letting him have a look at my bow. I'll continue to teach him all I can, and especially all the things he needs to know to be a great leader like his father. Honrus has said he'll train him to fight, wrestle, and make sure he's strong and prepared for the future too.

We're going to continue the Confession and Progression day, and plan to do the competitions to make sure we are strong. We'll maintain the lifestyle Dragatu gave us and continue to better ourselves, and we'll keep the laws the way he and the Creator would want. If we can find a way to get the Book of Prophecy we will, but we will be patient.

Epilogue
I Wish You Could See The World
Through My Eyes: Part 3

Pyros' Legacy

Six weeks went by and a small group arrived from the First Nation. Unilus had sent them to find out why the water no longer flowed in the channels. He told them to be cautious and to take special care if they had to make contact with Dragatu's people. When the group approached the foot of the hills they saw the desolation of the Nation, the ashes, and the destruction of the water channels. It was a clear message that Dragatu's people didn't want to be found and had destroyed the channels to hurt Unilus and Phoenon's people. With this knowledge those who had been sent didn't dare venture further to look at the water source, and followed Unilus' counsel, returning home to report what they had seen. Unilus and Phoenon discussed this knowledge when the group returned and agreed that they should leave Freta's people alone, another water source would have to be found.

Years then went by and Freta's people were thankful to be left alone. They began to build their New Nation, and used the little granite they had salvaged and quarried more from the northeast, as before. There was less space around the canyon entrance to the water source so the buildings were smaller and built very close together. They melted down a lot of their unnum, the majority coming from all the unused unnatus left behind, and they used it to decorate houses, themselves, and for trade. As the years passed they became intoxicated by their desire for justice. However, for fear of what would happen, Freta and the Coriol Hunora kept theirs and everyone's desire to act at bay. They came up with plans, but none were good enough to guarantee success, so they made sure Pyros, and his generation knew they had to continue this legacy. One day they hoped he, or his descendants, would have the numbers, or a good plan, to bring about total justice on Unilus and Phoenon, or their descendants. The desire for justice was intertwined with getting the Book of Prophecy and Dragatu's Journal, and all it revealed to Pyros and Freta, and those they shared it with. The Coriol Hunora continued to teach from the Book of Law and continued to make sure the laws were kept with exactness. They were so strict in this that it wasn't long before they punished people with public beatings if a law was known to be broken. Everyone accepted it, as only those most loyal had remained after Dragatu's death, and to them the harsh consequences were only just. Honrus died five years after they moved and Freta decided it was okay to lead. She felt it was best to teach Pyros by example, but she counted the days until his eighteenth birthday when he would receive his gift and take up the mantle of his father.

🔥

J.E 30/5/721

My name is no longer Pyros. I am Dragatu. At last I have inherited my birthright. So many years I've waited, so much I've had to wait for, but now it's all mine. I can finally lead the way I should've always been able to. Finally, my father's legacy will continue through me.

Last night I lay on my bed, thinking about what today would bring. What would happen? Would I feel different? I had so many questions and so much anticipation. It wasn't until the early hours of the morning that I fell asleep. I had dreams of my father, dreams of fire and creatures I had never seen before. When I woke, I knew these creatures were dragons. The images were so clear they burned themselves into my mind. The last thing I remember was what my father described in his journal when he got his gift. I felt heat in my heart, and then it spread to my whole body. Suddenly I woke and sat up very fast. I was covered in sweat, and touched my face to make sure I was awake and not still dreaming. I wasn't. I rolled my legs out of my bed and sat on the edge.

Once I had got over the shock, I smiled. I could feel and see a change. I was by no means small originally, but when I looked down, I knew I was taller, and my muscles were much larger and stronger. Still smiling, I almost laughed, but when I thought about my gift to control fire my smile faded. I've studied my father's journal and know what I must do, but I have a few doubts, which prevent me from using it. I'm not sure what will happen. So many times over the years I've wondered about this. Now I can finally find out I'm too scared to try. What will happen? Will I be as my father was when he first got his gift, and be tired and have to train myself? Or will it be as I want it to be? Will I be at the same stage he was, having full power over my gift and be able to use it without it making me tired and exhausted?

Mother is going to be angry that I have these doubts, but I'll speak to her and will try the gift for the first time with her. Actually, I'll tell her I wanted to wait to show her and not share my fears. This way I'll have her there to give me courage, but she won't be angry with me.

When I had decided what to do I quickly wrote this, my first update as Dragatu.

🔥 🔥 🔥

I'm back from speaking with my mother. On the way, I saw myself in the mirror in the hall. I look incredible, I'm large and powerful, and in a strange way majestic. The first thing I noticed was my eyes. I had almost forgotten these would change as well. I stood there, staring into my own eyes. The dark red irises were hypnotizing. I had a few faint memories of my father's eyes, and mine were identical. I smiled at this sentiment. I wondered if I looked like him. In my mind, I did, as the memory of my father was very similar to what I saw before me in the mirror, but I couldn't be certain if my memory was true. So I left the mirror and found Mother. As I entered the kitchen, she had her back to me. When she heard me, she spun around and in an excited voice said, "Well?"

As she saw me, her face went blank. She walked towards me with her hand outstretched. I wasn't sure what to do, so let her touch my face. She seemed to be in a dream, as if she wasn't sure where she was. All of a sudden she smiled.

"Forgive me Pyros, I mean Dragatu. You look so much like your father. I mean you always did, but now you look even more like he did."

I smiled. I'm glad I look like my father.

"Your face is different," she continued, "but your stature and eyes remind me of him. How do you feel?"

"Very good," I said, continuing to smile. "I've waited so long for this, and now I have what I always wanted."

"Have you used your fire gift yet?" she asked.

"Not yet. I wanted to be with you when I tried it for the first time."

"Thank you," she said.

My lie worked. Having her there gave me courage to try. She took a wooden bowl and placed it on the floor between us.

I looked at it for a few seconds hesitating.

"What's wrong?" she asked.

"Nothing," I lied. I found some courage and concentrated the way my father had. I imagined it burning and as I did, I felt the heat in my heart. The heat then did as it had done with my father, and finally escaped through my eyes. Straight away the bowl began to smoke, but as quickly as it had I felt exhausted, dizzy and lost my balance. I fell forward onto my knees, then onto my face.

The next memory I had was of mother pouring water into my mouth. As I opened my eyes, I shut them again. I knew what had happened and felt so disappointed and angry. I have to start from the beginning again. I'm still so angry. I just wanted it to be easy.

After I recovered I drank and ate a lot more than I usually do. Mother knew my frustrations and said with hard work using the gift would become easy, but I didn't want to talk about it and left her. I came here to write what had happened. I really wish I could've written a better outcome. It should've been easier, but I will dedicate myself to using the gift as much as possible, so I can increase in power. Then I will show the people my power and Mother will no longer lead them, I will. They will respect me fully, and I can find a way to finally have my justice. I will find a way to return, and get the Book of Prophecy, to learn the secrets of how one person can get the other gifts, what all the prophecies are, and hopefully discover why they are the key to returning to the Creator. I can also get my father's unnatu back. I will use it to kill those who took my father away from me. I've missed out on so much because of what they did. I recently read over his last entries. We had just begun to build a relationship and he was going to spend more time helping me be prepared for this moment. How much more prepared would I have been if he were around? I wouldn't have feared, or doubted if he were here.

Mother has tried to be there for me, but there was always something missing. Honrus did his best to help too, and I miss him, but I would be so much greater if my father had been around. Everyday I'm reminded of what I could've had. I see children in our Nation with their fathers and I envy them.

I will inflict pain upon my uncles. They'll regret not giving him the Book of Prophecy and killing him when he was only trying to help everyone. Mother says I have to be patient, as we're not strong enough. I find this very hard to believe. I'll progress in my gift as quickly as I can. I'll be powerful and we'll return to the First Nation. Mother says I should wait as our numbers are too few and justice may not be achieved in our lifetime.

I struggle to believe this. They cannot be stronger than us. I've seen our people fight on the competition days, and we are strong. I know she is wise, but I think she underestimates our people. She says the First Nation has many tens of thousands of people, and they would overpower us. Surely they can't have that many.

I think I'll return alone and see the First Nation for myself. I'll return and watch from the forests that Mother says are in the west. Then I'll know the truth and decide what to do, but for now I must strengthen my gift.

J.E 1/6/721

I've told Mother I'm going to the First Nation. She begged me not to and said it will serve no purpose, except to put me in danger. She asked me to trust her, but I told her I had to do this. I said I had to see it for myself before I could believe her. I told her the destruction of the water project might mean they are weaker, and their population smaller. After arguing a lot she accepted my choice and I'm going to leave in two weeks.

Before I go I'm going on a long hunt. This'll let me practice my gift away from everyone's expectations to see it. Hopefully, I'll be able to start a small fire with ease before I get back. Being able cook food with my gift will make my journey to the First Nation easier.

J.E 17/6/721

I've returned from my hunting trip and increased in strength. My gift is easier to use, but I still have a long way to go before it's effortless. I've packed for my long journey and Mother has drawn a rough map. She told me the path she's drawn out is where the old channels were and that I should see some of the wood from time to time. I'm to follow it until I see fields in the distance, then to head southwest. She kept telling me I should stay as far away from the First Nation as I could, and eventually I would reach the forests. She said I should go in far enough to get cover, and turn south, walking a day's journey. Then head east and I would see the First Nation. She told me to be aware of the animals as Unilus' gift means he can commune with them and they might tell him I was there. I told her I would be careful. I'm taking as little as possible so I asked her to keep the journal until I returned. She said she would.

J.E 15/7/721

I was wrong. I hate having to write this. How could there be so many people? When I emerged from the treeline to see the First Nation I saw so many buildings, it took my breath away. All I could see were endless rows of houses and people going about their business. I was so angry and frustrated. They looked healthy, and there was no clear sign the loss of the water project had affected them. I didn't know what to do.

I decided to go to where Mother said the original reservoir had been so I could see if it was full or not. I took cover in the forest and went north, staying close to the edge. As I saw more of the people, I began to despair.

How are we ever going to keep the promise we made to my father? There were just so many people, and even though we are strong, I now understand why Mother has tried to teach me patience. Even after the weeks that've passed I still struggle to accept this, but I must. I've spent all my life thinking my gift would allow me to get justice and the Book of Prophecy. Now I have to try and accept it may not be possible for me. It's just not fair.

Seeing the reservoir in the distance, I waited until night and crept out. It wasn't empty, but neither was it full. I hoped it meant they only have enough water to sustain themselves, and thought that maybe in time they would suffer. However, I wanted it to be worse now, and seeing they had enough added to my growing despair and it peaked while I was at the reservoir. I realised all hope for justice was gone. I couldn't bear the anger and frustration, so I left, making sure I had enough food and water for the journey home.

It's hard to admit I was wrong, but I've promised Mother, and I'll continue to make sure I always remember the promises. I'll teach the next generation the way she has taught me. They'll be prepared to do what needs to be done to keep the promises made to the first Dragatu, to my father. I'll always try and think of a way to do this myself, but I don't see how. I'll teach the children I have patience. They'll have the journal and they'll know when the time is right. They'll remember the wrongs done to us and one day we'll have justice and the Book of Prophecy, even if I'm long dead. The Creator will be happy that we showed patience.

I will continue to update this journal, and new ones will be made for every Dragatu, and the people will read them and know the truth. I make a promise by every vow ever uttered, or possible, that I will continue to plant seeds of remembrance and one day they'll grow, and these good people will reap justice for the pain, loss and suffering we've experienced. They'll have the Book of Prophecy, learn of its secrets and how to get the other gifts for themselves, and obtain power untold. With this power, they'll unite the people the way my father would've wanted. They'll live in a way that helps them keep the laws with exactness. All these things I promise will come to pass. I will keep my promise Father. I will keep my promise Creator.

Appendix A: What Happened To Phoenon When He Healed Unilus

Unilus was engulfed in flames when Dragatu had tried to kill him. Phoenon had stabbed Dragatu and rushed to Unilus, who was only seconds from death. Phoenon ignored the fire and put his hands on Unilus' arms, holding him as best he could. It was almost impossible to heal him. However, Phoenon gave it everything he could and felt unimaginable pain from the effort. There was so much pain that it should have killed him because no person should have endured that much pain. The phoenix gift, however, accommodated for the pain, and stopped him from dying. He burst into white flames and in a way he was born again, like the phoenix when they died of old age. From that day forward, he never felt pain when healing people. This was because he had experienced such a level of pain that it was as if he had conquered death itself, and the consequences of pain were voided by a higher law of equivalency.

As Phoenon cradled his burned hands, Unilus made a difficult choice, telling Phoenon he would return as quickly as he could. He let Dragatu's unnatu fall to the floor and left to chase after Freta. Phoenon was alone and sat tormented by the fact he had been the first person to take the life of another human being. He was terrified of what people would think of him. He had always been the nice, cheerful, compassionate person, but now he had done something vile and awful. He felt that the people would reject him and see him as a monster. He began to doubt his ability to be the man he had been before. Everything had changed for him, and he couldn't understand it all. He had thoughts of running away and living in exile as a punishment for his crime. He wished the very earth would open up and engulf him so he no longer existed.

As he sat there, he found it so hard to look up from the ground. In front of him, not fifteen metres away, lay the body of his dead brother and the weapon that had killed him. In his mind, he could still see the image of Dragatu's face as he drove the unnatu into his chest. It had happened so fast and he had turned to heal Unilus without thinking about it, but the brief image of Dragatu's face as the unnatu went in would haunt Phoenon all his life. Time seemed to stand still as he sat there with all these thoughts going through his head.

Eventually, Unilus returned with some men. He knelt down in front of Phoenon and put both his hands gently on his brother's cheeks, lifting his head up. He looked him right in the eyes, speaking the best words of comfort he could find.

"Thank you, Brother. I am in your debt and owe you my life. Because of you I will see my wife and son again. Because of you I can still look you in the eye and speak to you. I know you're hurting. However, you mustn't focus on the melancholy of what has happened. Rather focus on the fact you saved a brother, and saved all the people. Your actions today means I am still alive, it means Dragatu didn't get the Book of Prophecy, and this is very important. He would only have used it for control, and put the people you love under a burden too heavy to bear. I don't like seeing you so upset. You're the light and joy for so many here, remember the good you did today, not the bad.

You must realise that by doing something that we've always seen as wrong, you've done what was right. You've saved that which needed to be saved. I hope this consolation will outweigh the pain that you feel now. I don't say this enough brother, as you know I find it hard to express my emotions, but I love you. I loved Dragatu, but he was so far gone in his path for control that there was no hope for him. Maybe in death he will find some peace.

As for here and now, I must make sure his people leave. Don't worry about this, I will organise it, but you must apply what I've said and realise the truth of it. This was the only choice you had that was right. The pain and loss you would've felt if Dragatu had lived would have been far greater. Please, find some strength from this fact."

Unilus broke his eye contact and looked down at the floor. Phoenon then spoke in a quiet, tired voice, that was almost a whisper, and he took deep breaths in between sobs and sniffs.

"Thank you . . . I just feel overwhelmed by darkness. I just killed our brother. What should I do? I feel like I can never be happy again . . . like there's no goodness in me. What if the people never want to speak to me again because of what I've done?"

"Don't worry about the people. I'll write a declaration of events explaining what happened, and they will understand. They know your character and that you are all things good. You've shown this over the years, and they will not easily forget this. Now you must do as you always have, but this time for yourself: heal, brother. Learn to heal yourself. You always went to help others when they were hurt. Don't forget this. This is your strength. You help people. You change the lives of so many, just by being you, and if this is what you need to do now, then go see those who you help. Go see the children who love to play and have fun with you. It will remind you of the good that you have inside you. Then you will remember the reasons why we had to protect the people. Then you will begin to heal and the darkness will be replaced by the good that it has temporarily overpowered."

As he focused on going to see those he loved and cared for, Phoenon smiled weakly. At that moment, he felt a glimpse of light and hope began the long journey back into his heart. He hugged Unilus and they both turned to Dragatu, and mourned the loss of their brother, saying their farewells for the last time.

Finally, Unilus spoke to the men who had been standing reverently and quietly, waiting for his instructions. He told one man to take Dragatu's unnatu to his meeting room, and the other men were told to put Dragatu's body on a stretcher and carry him to be embalmed. Unilus followed the body and Phoenon went to a healer to have his hands taken care of. When his hands were cleaned and bandaged, he went to find those he could feel some happiness with. Only then could he begin to heal from this burden of being the first person to kill another human.

Appendix B: A Few Worlds the Brothers Saw

World: A

This world was covered in the greenest of grass, and there were trees with leaves of yellow, brown, purple and red. It also had many hills and mountains, and in the forests were animals the brothers recognised, but they were all much bigger than on their world. The biggest change in size was that of the spiders, for they were the size of cattle and moved incredibly fast, spinning giant webs in the forest to capture other animals to eat. There were also giant birds of every kind that ate the spiders. There were no humans on this world.

World: B

This world had many humans and the environment varied. Some areas were dry and desert-like, some had plentiful lakes and hills, and other areas were open fields of grass that stretched for miles. There were humans scattered everywhere, either living in great big white stone buildings, with huge towers, or living in wooden houses in small villages. They also had many tall buildings with telescopes on them for looking at the night sky, and many other buildings for staying in to write, read and talk.

This world also had many recognisable animals, but their horses were very different. They were pure white and had a long gold horn on their heads that shone in the sun like the unnum. This creature could communicate with all the other animals, and was the Unicorn that Unilus chose.

Trees were able to move, and the people seemed happier, dancing and singing with joy.

World: C

This world was very strange, for it was just a world filled with water the likes of which the brothers had never seen. In the water were common fish like on their world, but there were also giant fish-like creatures the size of many houses.

World: D

This was a simple world with strange glowing balls that looked as though they were made of light. There was nothing more than a ground of dry dirt and the glowing balls simply floated around, bumping into one another. Once they connected, they would either stay the same and not move, or split into two smaller balls so there would be four, rarely, they would fuse together to make one bigger ball.

World: E

This was a world of many mountains that reached high into the sky. There were humans, but they constantly fought each other over the creature Phoenon chose: the phoenix. This creature was like a bird with dazzling silver feathers in the shade and feathers of a hundred different shade of orange in the sunlight. The healing power it possessed was sought after, and the killing of the birds for its strong feathers endangered the majestic bird. If left to die naturally, the phoenix would live for seven hundred years before being reborn within a ball of flames.

Appendix C: Reference List of Names and Words

Names:

Benue: ben-way = Dragatu's Friend

Branon: brar-non = Dragatu's Father

Branon 2nd: Unilus' Son = Named after his grandfather

Corich: cor-reck = Dragatu's Friend

Dragatu: dra-gar-too = Main Character

Farmer Heth and Old Shire Horse Gynopa: jin-o-pa

Freta: fret-a = Dagatu's Wife

Healana: heal-arn-ar = Dragatu's Mum

Honrus: hon-russ = Dragatu's Friend

Jolonus: jol-on-us = Freta's Father

Liapus: liar-pus = Reon's Wife

Linur: lin-ur = Dragatu's Friend

Phoenon: fee-non = Dragatu's Brother

Pyros: pie-ross = Dragatu's Son

Reon: ree-on = Dragatu's Friend

Tero: teh-ro = Dragatu's Friend

Ternon: ter-non = Dragatu's Friend

Tursea: tur- see- ar = Unilus' Wife

Unilus: u-nigh-lus = Dragatu's Brother

Yelhen: yell-en = Dragatu's Friend

Other Words:

Coriol Hunora- Co-ree-o-l Hun-or-ra = Strong Watchers/Overseers

Delda Plant: Dell-dar = Leaves that add flavor to food/like herbs

Gealor Herbs: gee-lor = Green herbs that when crushed make a thick paste and when applied to wounds can help fight infection

Huetire (Blue) Gems: hoo-tie-r

Hunora: hun-or-ra = Watchers/Overseers

Illona Sap: ill-o-na = Makes wood more water-resistant/stops rotting

Inuade (Green) Gems: in-way-d

Joben Nuts: jo-ben = Food

Onta (Purple-Black) Berries: on-ta = Used for dye, but rare

Red (Stones) Gems (no name given)

Rew (Red) Berries: roo = Common berry

Unnatu: un-ar-too = Sword/Weapon the Messenger had

Unnum Metal: Un-num = Dark yellow rocks/Gifted Metal

Acknowledgements

Firstly, a special thank you to my dear friends and beloved family. The patience, encouragement, belief and love that you have shown me has helped more than you will ever know. Thank you all so much for being the incredible and wonderful people that you are.

There are a few people that must be thanked by name for how they have helped me with *The Book of Prophecy*. Editing: Andy McDonald, Cheryl White, Sammy HK Smith, Meaghan Searle and Caro. Front Cover: Fred Smith and Ken Dawson. Thank you to the three friends who read one of the first drafts at the birth of this project four years ago: George Stewart, Garret Prather and Eoina Rodgers. Many thanks to those who brought the original self-published version titled *The Journal of Fire*.

Thank you to my friend Richard Wills. You lived with me when I began writing stories and saw the obsession I have with writing when it was at its most intense. We laugh about it now, but thank you for putting up with those unique times.

Thank you to my High School English teacher Mrs Burns. If it wasn't for your teaching and the study of Hamlet I don't think I would have understood the personal impact a character can have on an individual. Thank you for introducing me to the word catharsis.

Thank you if you are reading this and have brought the Book of Prophecy. I hope you enjoyed the adventure.

Lastly, a massive thank you must go to those at Kristell Ink. Thank you, Ken Dawson, for using your talents to create a wonderful cover. Thank you, Caro, for your final edits. Thank you, Zoë Harris for the typesetting and all the hours that went in to getting *The Book of Prophecy* ready for publication. However, the biggest thanks must go to Sammy HK Smith. Your talents and skills are matched by few. Thank you for your belief in me and my story. Thank you for working with me to make *The Book of Prophecy* the best it could be. The time, money, and friendship you have invested will never be forgotten and always cherished.

About the Author

Steven J. Guscott lives in Scotland, and at the beginning of 2010 discovered an unhealthy obsession with writing; creating fantasy/sci-fi stories is the second-most rewarding thing in his life, the first being spending time with family and friends.

His hobbies include drawing, reading, watching films, rock-climbing, and playing the board game *Risk* with friends. He also loves most types of music, and is always searching for books and films that make him feel like he's experienced something of value, or come to understand himself, or life, better through the medium of catharsis.

Steven is delighted to be able to share *The Book of Prophecy* with you, the first story in a series of six called *The Chronicles of Elementary*. To keep up to date with other writing projects he's working on, visit www.stevenjguscott.com

Other Titles from Kristell Ink

Strange Tales from the Scriptorian Vaults

A Collection of Steampunk Stories edited by Sammy HK Smith

All profits go to the charity First Story.

October 2012

Healer's Touch by Deb E. Howell

A girl who has not only the power to heal through taking life fights for her freedom.

Llew has a gift. Her body heals itself, even from death, but at the cost of those nearby. In a country fearful of magic, freeing yourself from the hangman's noose by wielding forbidden power brings its own dangers. After dying and coming back to life, Llew drops from the gallows into the hands of Jonas: the man carrying a knife with the power to kill her.

February 2013

Darkspire Reaches by C.N. Lesley

The wyvern has hunted for the young outcast all her life; a day will come when she must at last face him.

Abandoned as a sacrifice to the wyvern, a young girl is raised to fear the beast her adoptive clan believes meant to kill her. When the Emperor outlaws all magic, Raven is forced to flee from her home with her foster mother, for both are judged as witches. Now an outcast, she lives at the mercy of others, forever pursued by the wyvern as she searches for her rightful place in the world. Soon her life will change forever as she discovers the truth about herself.

A unique and unsettling romantic adventure about rejection and belonging.

March 2013

Shadow Over Avalon by C.N. Lesley

Fortune twists in the strongest hands. This is no repeat; this is what happens next.

A man, once a legend who bound his soul to his sword as he lay dying, is now all but a boy nearing the end of his acolyte training. Stifled by life in the undersea city of Avalon, Arthur wants to fight side by side with the air-breathing Terrans, not spend his life as servant to the incorporeal sentient known as the Archive. Despite the restrictions put on him by Sanctuary, he is determined to help the surface-dwellers defeat the predators whose sole purpose is to ensure their own survival no matter the cost.

October 2013

The Sea-Stone Sword by Joel Cornah

"Heroes are more than just stories, they're people. And people are complicated, people are strange. Nobody is a hero through and through, there's always something in them that'll turn sour. You'll learn it one day. There are no heroes, only villains who win."

Rob Sardan is going to be a legend, but the road to heroism is paved with temptation and deceit. Exiled to a distant and violent country, Rob is forced to fight his closest friends for survival, only to discover his mother's nemesis is still alive, and is determined to wipe out her family and all her allies. The only way the Pirate Lord, Mothar, can be stopped is with the Sea-Stone Sword – yet even the sword itself seems fickle, twisting Rob's quest in poisonous directions, blurring the line between hero and villain. Nobody is who they seem, and Rob can no longer trust even his own instincts.

Driven by dreams of glory, Rob sees only his future as a hero, not the dark path upon which he draws ever closer to infamy.

June 2014

Atlantis and the Game of Time by Katie Alford

A tale of two great powers and a battle across the breadth of time as Atlantis, a peaceful culture of academics intent on conserving the flow of time, struggles against a new rising power determined to reform it.

After decades of quiet time watching, the Atlanteans are caught off guard by a sudden wave of destruction, travelling up the timeline from the distant past, threatening to destroy all known civilisations and even, finally, that of Atlantis itself.

All that remains behind the time change is a single culture, one world and one history. Can the peaceful culture of Atlantis find the power to battle this new war ready culture and return history to its former glory or is the history they have protected for centuries doomed to be lost forever?

August 2014

Non-Compliance: Equilibrium by Paige Daniels

The alliance with the Magistrate is now in shreds, and the sector is descending into chaos as sickness and starvation spread. The crew must figure out how to solve the detrimental supply shortage, and the dangerous secrets hidden in the vaccine, before the whole Non-Compliance Sector revolts. Shea faces heart wrenching personal news that forces her to weigh her family's welfare against her belief for truth and justice. In this conclusion to the Non-Compliance series, the crew will face life-altering decisions while revealing the plots that have twisted all of their lives.

October 2014

kristell-ink.com